SHADOWS OF
SHERLOCK HOLMES

SHADOWS OF SHERLOCK HOLMES

Selected and introduced by
David Stuart Davies

WORDSWORTH CLASSICS

This edition published 1998 by
Wordsworth Editions Limited
Cumberland House, Crib Street
Ware, Hertfordshire SG12 9ET

ISBN 1 85326 744 9

Typeset by Antony Gray
Printed and bound in Great Britain by
Mackays of Chatham plc, Chatham, Kent

CONTENTS

INTRODUCTION

The Hub and its Spokes

There has been murder done, and the murderer was a man. He was more than six feet high, was in the prime of life, had small feet for his height, wore coarse, square-toed boots and smoked a Trichinopoly cigar. He came here with his victim in a four-wheeled cab, which was drawn by a horse with three old shoes and one new one on his off foreleg. In all probability the murderer had a florid face, and the fingernails of his right hand were remarkably long. These are only a few indications, but they may assist you.

The words are those of Sherlock Holmes making a series of startling deductions in what has become his very imitable way. Later in the scene, set in a derelict house on the Brixton Road complete with a corpse and strange writing in blood on the wall, Holmes justifies all his descriptions regarding the circumstances of the murder and his assessment of the killer. To him, it is all elementary.

The story was *A Study in Scarlet*, the novella, first published in *Beeton's Christmas Annual* for 1887, which introduced this now famous character and detective icon to the reading public. Sherlock Holmes was created by an impoverished doctor by the name of Arthur Ignatius Conan Doyle (1859–1930), who was living in Portsmouth when he hit upon the idea of creating a scientific detective. In the longueurs between the infrequent patients, he played around with the idea that his detective would reach the solution to a mystery by deduction and rationality, not by accident or through the carelessness of the criminal. Later in life, he explained his thoughts on the genesis of the most famous sleuth of all time:

> I was educated in a very severe and critical school of medical thought, especially coming under the influence of Dr Bell of Edinburgh who had the most remarkable powers of observation. He prided himself that when he looked at a patient he could tell not only their disease, but very often their occupation and place of residence. Reading some detective stories I was struck by the fact that their results were obtained in nearly every case by chance. I thought I would try my hand at writing a story in which the hero would treat crime as Dr Bell treated disease and where science would take the place of chance.

Conan Doyle's hero, originally christened Sherringford and then changed to Sherlock, demonstrated this facility within the opening pages of *A Study in Scarlet* when, on meeting Dr Watson for the first time, he observed: 'You have have been in Afghanistan, I perceive.' Holmes goes on to explain how he reached this conclusion very much in the manner of Dr Bell:

> The train of reasoning ran: 'Here is a gentleman of a medical type, but with the air of a military man. Clearly an army doctor, then. He has just come from the tropics, for his face is dark, and that is not the natural tint of his skin, for his wrists are fair. He has undergone hardship and sickness, as his haggard face says clearly. His left arm has been injured. He holds it in a stiff and unnatural manner. Where in the tropics could an English army doctor have seen such hardship and got his arm wounded? Clearly in Afghanistan.' The whole train of thought did not occupy a second.

If we compare that *tour de force* with a description of Bell's own methods with a patient, as described by Conan Doyle in his autobiography *Memories and Adventures*, we can see how closely the author followed Bell's approach to analysis:

> In one of [Bell's] best cases he said to a civilian patient: 'Well, my man, you've served in the army.'
> 'Aye sir.'
> 'Not long discharged?'
> 'No, sir.'
> 'A Highland regiment?'
> 'Aye, sir.'
> 'A non-com. officer?'
> 'Aye, sir.'

'Stationed at Barbados?'

'Aye, sir.'

'You see, gentlemen,' he would explain, 'the man was a respectful man but did not remove his hat. They do not in the army, but he would have learned civilian ways had he been long discharged. He has an air of authority and he is obviously Scottish. As to Barbados, his complaint is elephantiasis, which is West Indian and not British.'

To his audience of Watsons it all seemed miraculous until it was explained, and then it became simple enough. It is no wonder that after the study of such a character I used and amplified his methods when in later life I tried to build up a scientific detective who solved cases on his own merits and not through the folly of the criminal.

Thus, using Bell as his basic template, Arthur Conan Doyle created Sherlock Holmes. But the author knew that if Holmes were to appeal to the Victorian reader, he had to be more than a mere scientific cipher, a mechanical detecting machine. He had to be a fascinating character in his own right. To the schizophrenic society of the time – one which allowed prostitution and poverty to flourish in London's East End and yet, for the sake of decorum, covered up the legs of the piano – there was nothing more fascinating than the bohemian, the independent, the flamboyant fellow who disregarded the social conventions of the period. Conan Doyle imbued his detective creation with a fascinating array of idiosyncracies. Before Sherlock Holmes makes his very first appearance in *A Study in Scarlet* we are told that he has a habit of 'beating the subjects in the dissecting rooms with a stick . . . to verify how far bruises may be produced after death'. He is also a misogynist: 'I am not a whole-souled admirer of womankind. Women are never to be entirely trusted – not the best of them.' On one level, he was unemotional. We are told: 'All emotions . . . were abhorrent to his cold, precise, but admirably balanced mind.' And yet he was a man of passion: 'My mind rebels at stagnation. Give me problems, give me work, give me the most abstruse cryptogram or the most intricate analysis, and I am in my proper atmosphere.' The paradoxical and contradictory nature of the man enhanced his fascination for the public.

The reader is afforded a glimpse into the quirky domestic scene at Baker Street in the story 'The Musgrave Ritual', which begins with a catalogue of the detective's *outré* habits:

. . . when I find a man who keeps his cigars in the coal-scuttle, his tobacco in the toe end of a Persian slipper, and his unanswered correspondence transfixed by a jack-knife into the very centre of his wooden mantelpiece, then I begin to give myself virtuous airs. I have always held, too, that pistol practice should distinctly be an open-air pastime: and when Holmes in one of his queer humours would sit in an armchair, with his hair-trigger and a hundred Boxer cartridges, and proceed to adorn the opposite wall with a patriotic V.R. done in bullet-pocks, I felt strongly that neither the atmosphere nor the appearance of our room was improved by it.

Here Conan Doyle is reinforcing Sherlock Holmes's oddness. He knew the character's appeal lay in his total difference from the man in the street, the reader: an important point that other detective story writers were to pick up – and, in fact, still do. One need only think of Colin Dexter's Inspector Morse with his miserly ways, fondness for real ale and his passions for crosswords and opera to realise that he is following the tradition initiated by Conan Doyle.

And then of course there was Holmes's drug-taking: a seven-percent solution of cocaine. This habit, first mentioned in the second novel *The Sign of the Four*, was a further extension of Holmes's bohemian character. Conan Doyle had been commissioned to write this novel by the editor of *Lippincott's Magazine* during a lunch engagement at the Langham Hotel. Also present on this occasion was Oscar Wilde, whose extravagant behaviour Conan Doyle found fascinating. Indeed, there are echoes of Wilde in the character of Thaddeus Sholto in the novel, but Conan Doyle's meeting with Wilde prompted him to add a more outrageous element to his detective hero and drug-taking was his choice. So by the time Sherlock Holmes appeared in the *Strand Magazine*, in a series of short stories from 1891, his character was fully formed in a most imaginative and engaging way. Here was a detective unlike any other and, while the two novels had enjoyed only moderate success, his stories in this new monthly magazine very soon captured the reading public's imagination. Within less than six months, the main selling point of the *Strand* was the new adventure of Sherlock Holmes within its pages.

The lean, ascetic sleuth of Baker Street has maintained a hypnotic hold on the public ever since. Conan Doyle's Holmes tales have never been out of print and they are found in most languages of the world. One can even obtain braille and shorthand editions. And, of course, Sherlock Holmes is the most filmed of all fictional characters.

One other aspect of these stories which makes them so marvellous is the use of the narrator, Dr Watson. All events are presented to us as Watson sees them, interpreted through his commonsense but limited understanding of things. This allows the reader to feel somewhat superior to Watson, while at the same time realising that Sherlock Holmes is streets ahead of everyone at all times. That is part of the genius of these tales. While Watson may not be particularly astute as a detective, he is a wonderful word painter and his descriptions add the richness to the text which graces both the plot and the characters with such vivid qualities.

Notwithstanding all this, Conan Doyle did not invent the detective or the detective story. Actually the history of detective fiction is far from straightforward and elements of it can be found in ancient and classical writings. A case has been made that Sophocles' play *Oedipus the King* (*circa* 430 BC) approaches the genre in that it deals with an attempt to discover the identity of a murderer which is raised as a central problem at the beginning of the drama and solved in a most dramatic fashion at the end. Oedipus, charged with the task of discovering who killed his wife's first husband, spends a great deal of the play in this inquiry and a final interrogation of a shepherd reveals the horrible truth: Oedipus himself is the murderer. Dramatic events are further heightened by the fact that unknown to him the murdered man was his father and therefore he has unwittingly married his mother.

Similarly Herodotus, often called the 'father of history', provided a tale in Book II of his *Histories* which Conan Doyle would no doubt have called 'The Adventure of the Headless Thief'. The incident deals with an Egyptian monarch, King Rhampsinitus, who had a vast chamber of stone built to house his great wealth. The builder was greedy and had designs on these treasures for himself and so contrived to insert a loose stone in the wall of the treasure house which could easily be removed to allow access. For some time he availed himself of small portions of the king's riches. Time passed and he fell fatally ill. On his deathbed he revealed his secret to his two sons who, before their father's corpse was cold, began raiding the treasure house. They were not as cautious or as prudent as their father and helped themselves to large quantities of gold and trinkets. It was not long before Rhampsinitus noticed the deficit in his store of riches. Puzzled as to how anyone could gain access to the chamber when all the seals were perfect and the fastenings of the room were secure, the king, acting now as detective, determined to solve this mystery and set a series of traps in the room. That very night one of the brothers, more eager than the other, rushed into the treasure chamber and was caught in a vicious trap. There was no escape. He begged his brother to cut off his head so that when his body was found it wouldn't be recognised, thus it would not implicate his brother and sully their dead father's reputation. Reluctantly the other thief agreed and decapitated his brother, taking his head away with him. The next day the king entered the chamber and was shocked to discover a headless corpse. It was in essence a locked-room murder mystery.

The king ordered the corpse to be exhibited on the walls of the city and set two of his men to guard it. Rhampsinitus reasoned that someone would mourn the death of this headless man – a wife, a mother or sister – and they would not be able to resist visiting the place of his exhibition to mourn. Anyone doing so would be seized and brought to him. His reasoning was sound, for the dead thief's mother ordered the surviving brother to devise some scheme to retrieve the corpse in order for it to have a proper burial. If he did not, she would expose his crime. With the aid of a some skins of wine, the thief disabled the guards. While they slumbered in an alcoholic daze, he removed the body and took it home for his mother, but not before shaving half the beards of the two sleeping guards for devilment.

The king was both perplexed and annoyed to receive the news of the thief's audacious actions. He contrived another ploy to trap him. It was an equally audacious scheme. He sent his daughter out into the town, into the lowest dives, to beg men to tell her what was the cleverest and most wicked thing they had ever done. If anyone told her the story of how he robbed the king, she was to lay hold of him and not allow him to escape. Now the thief heard of this and was well aware of the king's motive. He decided to accept the challenge. He procured a fresh corpse and cut off one of the arms at the shoulder and secreted it under his tunic. He went off into the town and found the king's daughter. He told her the most wicked thing he had ever done was cutting off the head of his brother when he was caught in a trap in the king's treasury, and the cleverest was making the guards drunk so that he could carry off his body. As he confessed these things, the princess caught hold of his arm – or what she thought was his arm. It was in fact the arm of the corpse. With ease, the thief slipped away and made his escape.

When the king heard what had happened he was amazed at the nerve and ingenuity of this man and he sent messengers out to proclaim a free pardon for the thief and the promise of a rich reward if he came to the palace and made himself known. The thief, believing the proclamation, duly appeared before him. The king kept his word. Admiring the wisdom of the thief, he gave him his daughter in marriage, saying: 'The Egyptians excel all the rest of the world in wisdom, and this man excels all other Egyptians.'

This story contains many of the elements found in the Holmes stories and those of his rivals: the apparently inexplicable crime, the use of a central character as bait, the brilliant criminal and the determined sleuth and the surprise ending in which the 'detective' pronounces his own judgement on the matter rather than that of the law.

Since words were written there have been instances of mysteries presented and then solved in an ingenious manner and I could fill a substantial volume with examples, but, for the purposes of this introduction, let me refer to just one more. And for this I go to the great Aesop, in his fable of the fox and the lion. 'Why do you not come to pay your respects to me?' asks the lion of the fox. 'I beg your majesty's pardon,' replies the fox, 'but I notice the track of many animals that have already come to you; and, while I see many hoof and paw marks going in, I see none coming out. Till the animals that have entered your cave come out again, I prefer to remain in the open air.' One might add, 'Elementary, my dear Leo.' Certainly, Sherlock Holmes could not have reasoned more lucidly from these observations.

So while there were elements of detective fiction found in many diverse sources and guises, it was not until the nineteenth century dawned that all these elements became focused and gradually formalised into the detective story as we know it. For this we must thank Edgar Allan Poe, for it is this strange American writer who is considered to be the father of the modern detective story. In five stories published in the first half of the nineteenth century, 'The Murders in the Rue Morgue', 'The Purloined Letter', 'The Mystery of Marie Roget', 'Thou Art the Man' and 'The Gold Bug', he laid out and clarified most of the ground rules. The first three stories feature C. Auguste Dupin, a brilliant private detective residing in Paris. His activities are recorded by an unnamed chronicler, an admiring and somewhat slow-witted fellow – the Watson figure. Dupin is not only brilliant and disdainful of the official police, he is also eccentric. Shunning daylight, he lives behind closed shutters, his room illuminated only by 'a couple of tapers which, strongly perfumed, threw out only the ghastliest and feeblest of rays'. Like a sleuthing vampire, he takes to the streets at night to enjoy the 'infinity of mental excitement'. He is also given to astounding his companion by reading his thought processes. Conan Doyle thought Poe 'the master of all'. In his book *Through the Magic Door*, Conan Doyle was generous and admiring enough to confess:

> To him must be ascribed the monstrous progeny of writers on the detection of crime . . . But not only is Poe the originator of the detective story; all treasure-hunting, cryptogram-solving yarns trace back to his 'Gold Bug' . . .

Perhaps the most famous and certainly the grisliest of the Dupin tales is 'The Murders in the Rue Morgue'. An old woman and her daughter are found murdered in a locked room with no apparent means of entry or exit. The police are baffled. Dupin deduces and solves the mystery. This is a seminal story in crime fiction. Dorothy L. Sayers in her introduction to *The Omnibus of Crime* presented a brilliant analysis of this tale:

> [The story features] a combination of three typical motifs: the wrongly suspected man, to whom all the superficial evidence (motive, access, etc.) points; the hermetically sealed death chamber (still a favourite theme); finally the *solution by unexpected means*. In addition we have Dupin drawing deductions, which the police have overlooked, from evidence of witnesses (superiority in inference), and discovering clues which the police had not thought of looking for owing to obsession by an *idée fixe* (superiority in observation based on inference). In this story also are enunciated for the first time those two great aphorisms of detective science: first, that when you have eliminated all the possibilities, then whatever remains, *however improbable*, must be the truth; and secondly that the more *outré* a case may appear, the easier it is to solve. Indeed, take it all round, 'The Murders in the Rue Morgue' constitutes in itself almost a complete manual of detective theory and practice.

A complete manual it may have been but it was not fully utilised until Conan Doyle created Sherlock Holmes and this initiated an explosion of Sherlockian copycats and wannabees. In the interim there had been some interesting experiments: Inspector Bucket in Charles Dickens's *Bleak House* (1853) and Sergeant Cuff in Wilkie Collins's *The Moonstone* (1868), perhaps the first detective novel.

And then there was Eugène François Vidocq (1775–1857). He was a real-life criminal who became the first chief of the French Sûreté. His ghosted autobiography not only had a great influence

on authors of mystery fiction in his own lifetime, but also on
detective writers after his death. In his *Mémoires* Vidocq records
many instances of adopting a disguise to carry out his policework.
He seems to relish changing his appearance in a most spectacular
manner. He writes of staining his face with walnut liquor, creating
false wrinkles and garnishing his features with coffee beans plastered on with gum arabic to create various effects. In his old age
Vidocq visited London and told *The Times* that 'by some strange
process connected with my physical formation, I have the faculty of
contracting my height by several inches'. Of course Sherlock
Holmes was also an expert at disguise and, in 'The Empty House',
Conan Doyle actually has him state: 'I am glad to stretch myself,
Watson. It is no joke when a tall man has to take a foot off his
stature for several hours on end.' The link is obvious.

Staying with the French for the moment, mention must also be
made of Émile Gaboriau (1835–73), who created the detective
Monsieur Lecoq in *L'Affaire Lerouge* (1866). This and subsequent
novels focused attention on Lecoq's gathering and interpreting of
evidence in the detection of crime. We know for a fact that Conan
Doyle had read Gaboriau's works for, rather tongue in cheek, he
has Sherlock Holmes comment on one in *A Study in Scarlet*:

> 'Lecoq was a miserable bungler,' [Holmes] said in an angry
> voice; 'he had only one thing to recommend him, and that was
> his energy. That book made me positively ill. The question was
> how to identify an unknown prisoner. I could have done it in
> twenty-four hours. Lecoq took six months or so. It might be
> made a text book for detectives to teach them what to avoid.'

In the same sequence, Conan Doyle also has his detective blasting
Poe's Dupin;

> 'Now in my opinion, Dupin was a very inferior fellow. That
> trick of his of breaking in on his friends' thoughts with an
> apropos remark after a quarter of an hour's silence is really very
> showy and superficial.'

Showy and superficial it may be, but it was a trick perpetrated by
Holmes on Watson several times.

So Arthur Conan Doyle, like all writers beachcombing along the
shores of literature, was not only influenced by what had gone
before, but he adopted and adapted elements of what had gone
before, too. He also drew on his personal experiences. The real
genius was to blend these disparate parts with his own ingredients

into one of the most potent and remarkable fictional characters of all time.

Once the success of Holmes was established, other authors were inspired either to copy or experiment with the ingredients found in the stories. Conan Doyle had fashioned the hub of this magical wheel, and then others created their own spokes which radiated outwards. From that time onwards the reading public has been swamped with brilliant, idiosyncratic crime-solvers. At first there was a trend for writers to give their detective one very peculiar trait, a novelty element which made the character unique in some way, like the blind Max Carrados who could make the most incredible deductions through the senses of smell, touch and hearing. Or the 'crime doctor', who treated crime as a disease and approached it from a psychological angle. There were female detectives, too, like Loveday Brooke. And purely scientific ones such as Professor van Dusen who became known as The Thinking Machine. And there were those characters who worked on the other side of the law, like A.J. Raffles, Colonel Clay and Simon Carne, the Prince of Swindlers, all, in various ways, echoing Conan Doyle's criminal mastermind, Professor Moriarty, Sherlock Holmes's arch enemy.

Sadly many of the rivals of Sherlock Holmes are out of print today because one assumes that they are considered insignificant beside the colossus of Baker Street. It is true that very few literary characters can compare, but that is no reason to neglect these wonderful creations with their tantalising mysteries, surprising denouements and odd little ways. They are still splendid.

In this edition I have collected a cross section of stories featuring those noble and not so noble men and women who, like Sherlock Holmes, were involved in the world of puzzles, mysteries and crime. We start pre-Holmes with Poe and sample a tale of mystery from Wilkie Collins, before we move to that golden time when Sherlock was ensconced in Baker Street and, if our friendly scribes are to be believed, London was a place where amateur and professional detectives, all eager to unravel the mystery and point an accurate finger at the villain, were rife. The stories are presented in an approximate order of publication, but I have not kept strictly to this rule in order to maintain a level of variety for the reader.

It is time to open that magic door and step into that strange and exciting world peopled with the shadows of Sherlock Holmes.

THE AUTHORS AND THEIR DETECTIVES

EDGAR ALLAN POE (1809–49)

Often regarded as the father of the detective novel, Poe, an American, is more widely known for his tales of terror such as 'The Fall of the House of Usher' and 'The Pit and the Pendulum'. Poe created the detective Auguste Dupin to perform feats of ratiocination – a word he coined himself – in the solving of a crime. He set the template for fictional detectives which other writers have used and adapted for themselves ever since.

WILKIE COLLINS (1824–89)

English novelist and friend of Charles Dickens, Collins wrote one of the best Victorian mystery stories, *The Moonstone*, which T. S. Eliot regarded as 'the first, longest and best' classical detective story. In 'The Biter Bit', the story featured in this collection, we meet the arrogant and incompetent Matthew Sharpin and the exasperated Chief Inspector Theakstone.

BRETT HARTE (1836–1902)

An American writer who lived in London for a time after serving as US consul in Glasgow, Francis Brett Hart made few forays into detective fiction, but his story 'The Stolen Cigar-Case' was described by Ellery Queen as 'probably the best parody of Sherlock Holmes ever written'. It features the remarkable sleuth Hemlock Jones.

C. L. PIRKIS (1840–1910)

Probably C. L. Pirkis's greatest claim to fame was that, with her husband, she founded the National Canine Defence League in

1894. However, before then she penned several undistinguished novels as well as a lively series of stories featuring Loveday Brooke, Lady Detective. Brooke is one of the earliest female investigators and appeared only a few years after the original Sherlock Holmes stories were published.

ROBERT BARR (1850–1912)

A journalist and editor as well as author, Robert Barr created the French detective Eugène Valmont, who acts as his own storyteller. There are some remarkable similarities between Valmont and that Belgian detective Hercule Poirot, although Barr's creation predates Agatha Christie's by about twenty years.

ANTON CHEKHOV (1860–1904)

A Russian writer, better known as a dramatist of note with plays such as *The Cherry Orchard*, *The Seagull* and *Uncle Vanya*, Chekhov was also a prolific short-story writer. He often provided a surprise ending to his narrative, as he does in *The Swedish Match*, which features a humorous detective duo, Tchubikov and his over-enthusiastic assistant Dyukovsky.

DICK DONOVAN (1843–1924)

(Pseudonym of Joyce Emmerson Preston Muddock.) Donovan wrote what seemed to be an endless stream of short stories which appeared in the *Strand Magazine*. These featured Donovan himself as the detective hero recounting his various adventures with sinister secret societies, supervillains and incredible crimes. What the stories lack in finesse, they make up in pace and panache.

GRANT ALLEN (1848–99)

British author, philosopher and scientist whose two most notable works were literary breakthroughs. The first, *The Woman Who Did* (1895), created a sensation on its publication because of its frank discussion of sexual matters. The second, *An African Millionaire* (1897), contained a series of tales featuring Colonel Clay, the first important rogue in short crime fiction who is the hero, and not a subsidiary character or villain or anti-hero. He preceded Raffles, the gentleman crook, by two years. Allen's friend Arthur Conan Doyle completed his last novel *Hilda Wade*, using the author's notes, when Allen fell ill and died before he was able to finish it.

GUY CLIFFORD

I could find little information about Guy Clifford. It would seem that he was a jobbing writer who turned his hand to various forms of fiction. His detective, Robert Graceman, whose exploits were described by his 'friend and partner' Halton, was featured in the *Ludgate Monthly*. 'A Clever Capture' appeared in 1895.

E.W. HORNUNG (1866–1921)

Ernest William Hornung, author of crime and mystery fiction, became Arthur Conan Doyle's brother-in-law and fell under his literary influence. It must have been with a sly smile that he created Raffles, the gentleman crook, who is almost a dark reflection of Sherlock Holmes. It was said that Conan Doyle did not approve of an 'amateur cracksman' being presented as a hero. Hornung's other character, Dr John Dollar, the crime doctor, was firmly on the side of law and order. He was one of the first detectives to solve crimes using psychological means.

CLARENCE ROOK (? –1915)

An American writer who lived in London in the latter years of the nineteenth century. Rook's sleuth was a American female investigator, operating in the British capital. Female detectives were quite rare when the story 'The Stir outside the Café Royal' was published in the *Harmsworth Magazine* in 1898, but it was rarer for a male writer to use one as his central character.

GUY BOOTHBY (1867–1905)

Australian novelist who moved to Britain in 1894. His most masterful creation was the devilish Dr Nikola, a Moriarty-like character who appeared in five novels: *A Bid for Fortune or Dr Nikola's Vendetta* (1895), *Doctor Nikola* (1896), *The Lust of Hate* (1898), *Dr Nikola's Experiment* (1899) and *Farewell, Nikola* (1901). Boothby also created Simon Carne, whose exploits were featured in a series called 'A Prince of Swindlers', published in *Pearson's Magazine*. Carne was another of the gentlemen crooks, in company with the aforementioned Raffles and Colonel Clay.

JACQUES FUTRELLE (1875–1912)

An American journalist who created one of the most unusual investigators of all time, Professor Augustus S. F. X. van Dusen – The Thinking Machine. He is one of the greatest scientific detectives, a master logician who solves cases brought to him by a reporter, Hutchinson Hatch, who also acts as his assistant. The story featured in this collection also contains a preface which explains how this strange little man became known as The Thinking Machine.

HESKETH PRICHARD (1876–1922)

A great traveller and hunter, Prichard included many of his own exploits in his stories. He used his outdoor experiences as background for his series of stories featuring November Joe, 'the Detective of the Woods'. Possibly the most unusual detective in this collection, November Joe uses his native skills for detective purposes in the wilds of Canada.

HERBERT JENKINS (1876–1923)

Jenkins was a prolific writer and he created the Sherlock Holmes would-be clone, Malcolm Sage, who runs his own detective bureau with his secretary Gladys Norman, his assistant James Thompson, and William Johnson, the office junior who has ambitions to become a Great Detective. The tales were lightweight, but the puzzles still remain intriguing.

ERNEST BRAMAH (1868–1942)

(Pseudonym of Ernest Bramah Smith.) Bramah created the fantastic Kai Lung, the Chinese storyteller, and Max Carrados, the blind detective, one of the greatest detectives of all time. Carrados, a charismatic character, is able to sleuth so amazingly well because Bramah enhanced his other senses to a remarkable degree to compensate for his blindness. He is, for instance, able to read the newspaper by running his sensitive fingers over the newsprint. Carrados is assisted in his investigations by his butler Parkinson.

SEXTON BLAKE

Sexton Blake was known as the office boy's Sherlock Holmes probably because there was an air of comic-book heroics about many of the stories. He was created by Harry Blyth (1852–98) and made his first appearance in the boy's weekly paper the *Halfpenny Marvel* in 1893, in the story 'The Missing Millionaire'. Since then over a hundred known authors (mostly British and many of them well known outside the genre), as well as countless anonymous ones, have created exploits for Sexton Blake. 'The Time-Killer', which was originally published in the *Union Jack, Sexton Blake's Own Paper* in 1924, has no author credit but it is a stirring tale told with broad strokes and is typical of its kind. Apart from Blake, we meet Tinker, Blake's young assistant, Mrs Bardell, the detective's 'worthy house-keeper' who has a tendency to exclaim 'Lawks amercy' at moments of concern, and a range of richly colourful characters.

BARONESS ORCZY (1865–1947)

Baroness Emmuska Orczy is best known as the creator of the Scarlet Pimpernel, the espionage agent active in the days of the French Revolution. However, she also wrote many detective stories, including a series featuring 'The Old Man in the Corner', one of the greatest of all armchair detectives, several volumes recording the exploits of Lady Molly Robertson-Kirk of Scotland Yard and a number of tales involving the detective featured in this collection, Patrick Mulligan, whose nickname is Skin o' My Teeth. Mulligan is an Irish lawyer who resorts to detective work to help win his cases. He is somewhat unscrupulous and is one of the least physically attractive of fictional sleuths.

The Purloined Letter

EDGAR ALLAN POE

Nil sapientiae odiosius acumine nimio.

SENECA

At Paris, just after dark one gusty evening in the autumn of 18—, I was enjoying the twofold luxury of meditation and a meerschaum, in company with my friend, C. Auguste Dupin, in his little back library, or book-closet, *au troisième*, No. 33 Rue Dunôt, Faubourg St Germain. For one hour at least we had maintained a profound silence; while each, to any casual observer, might have seemed intently and exclusively occupied with the curling eddies of smoke that oppressed the atmosphere of the chamber. For myself, however, I was mentally discussing certain topics which had formed matter for conversation between us at an earlier period of the evening; I mean the affair of the Rue Morgue, and the mystery attending the murder of Marie Rogêt. I looked upon it, therefore, as something of a coincidence when the door of our apartment was thrown open and admitted our old acquaintance, Monsieur G—, the prefect of the Parisian police.

We gave him a hearty welcome; for there was nearly half as much of the entertaining as of the contemptible about the man, and we had not seen him for several years. We had been sitting in the dark, and Dupin now arose for the purpose of lighting a lamp, but sat down again, without doing so, upon G—'s saying that he had called to consult us, or rather to ask the opinion of my friend, about some official business which had occasioned a great deal of trouble.

'If it is any point requiring reflection,' observed Dupin, as he forbore to enkindle the wick, 'we shall examine it to better purpose in the dark.'

'That is another of your odd notions,' said the prefect, who had the fashion of calling everything odd that was beyond his comprehension, and thus lived amid an absolute legion of oddities.

'Very true,' said Dupin, as he supplied his visitor with a pipe, and rolled towards him a comfortable chair.

'And what is the difficulty now?' I asked. 'Nothing more in the assassination way, I hope?'

'Oh no; nothing of that nature. The fact is, the business is *very* simple indeed, and I make no doubt that we can manage it sufficiently well ourselves; but then I thought Dupin would like to hear the details of it, because it is so excessively *odd.*'

'Simple and odd,' said Dupin.

'Why, yes; and not exactly that either. The fact is, we have all been a good deal puzzled because the affair is so simple, and yet baffles us altogether.'

'Perhaps it is the very simplicity of the thing which puts you at fault,' said my friend.

'What nonsense you *do* talk!' replied the prefect laughing heartily.

'Perhaps the mystery is a little *too* plain,' said Dupin.

'Oh, good heavens! who ever heard of such an idea?'

'A little *too* self-evident.'

'Ha! ha! ha! – ha! ha! ha! – ho! ho! ho!' roared our visitor, profoundly amused, 'oh, Dupin, you will be the death of me yet!'

'And what, after all, *is* the matter on hand?' I asked.

'Why, I will tell you,' replied the prefect, as he gave a long, steady, and contemplative puff, and settled himself in his chair. 'I will tell you in a few words; but, before I begin, let me caution you that this is an affair demanding the greatest secrecy, and that I should most probably lose the position I now hold were it known that I confided it to anyone.'

'Proceed,' said I.

'Or not,' said Dupin.

'Well, then; I have received personal information, from a very high quarter, that a certain document of the last importance has been purloined from the royal apartments. The individual who purloined it is known; this beyond a doubt; he was seen to take it. It is known, also, that it still remains in his possession.'

'How is this known?' asked Dupin.

'It is clearly inferred,' replied the prefect, 'from the nature of the document, and from the non-appearance of certain results which would at once arise from its passing out of the robber's possession; that is to say, from his employing it as he must design in the end to employ it.'

'Be a little more explicit,' I said.

'Well, I may venture so far as to say that the paper gives its holder a certain power in a certain quarter where such power is immensely valuable.' The prefect was fond of the cant of diplomacy.

'Still I do not quite understand,' said Dupin.

'No? Well; the disclosure of the document to a third person, who shall be nameless, would bring in question the honour of a personage of most exalted station; and this fact gives the holder of the document an ascendancy over the illustrious personage whose honour and peace are so jeopardised.'

'But this ascendancy,' I interposed, 'would depend upon the robber's knowledge of the loser's knowledge of the robber. Who would dare – '

'This thief,' said G—, 'is Minister D—, who dares all things, those unbecoming as well as those becoming a man. The method of the theft was not less ingenious than bold. The document in question – a letter, to be frank – had been received by the personage robbed while alone in the royal boudoir. During its perusal she was suddenly interrupted by the entrance of the other exalted personage from whom especially it was her wish to conceal it. After a hurried and vain endeavour to thrust it in a drawer, she was forced to place it, open as it was, upon a table. The address, however, was uppermost, and, the contents thus unexposed, the letter escaped notice. At this juncture enters Minister D—. His lynx eye immediately perceives the paper, recognises the handwriting of the address, observes the confusion of the personage addressed, and fathoms her secret. After some business transactions, hurried through in his ordinary manner, he produces a letter somewhat similar to the one in question, opens it, pretends to read it, and then places it in close juxtaposition to the other. Again he converses, for some fifteen minutes, upon the public affairs. At length, in taking leave, he takes also from the table the letter to which he had no claim. Its rightful owner saw, but, of course, dared not call attention to the act in the presence of the third personage, who stood at her elbow. The minister decamped, leaving his own letter – one of no importance – upon the table.'

'Here, then,' said Dupin to me, 'you have precisely what you demand to make the ascendancy complete – the robber's knowledge of the loser's knowledge of the robber.'

'Yes,' replied the prefect; 'and the power thus attained has, for some months past, been wielded, for political purposes, to a very dangerous extent. The personage robbed is more thoroughly convinced, every day, of the necessity of reclaiming her letter. But this, of course, cannot be done openly. In fine, driven to despair, she has committed the matter to me.'

'Than whom,' said Dupin, amid a perfect whirlwind of smoke,

'no more sagacious agent could, I suppose, be desired, or even imagined.'

'You flatter me,' replied the prefect; 'but it is possible that some such opinion may have been entertained.'

'It is clear,' said I, 'as you observe, that the letter is still in the possession of the minister; since it is this possession, and not any employment of the letter, which bestows the power. With the employment the power departs.'

'True,' said G—; 'and upon this conviction I proceeded. My first care was to make thorough search of the minister's *hôtel*; and here my chief embarrassment lay in the necessity of searching without his knowledge. Beyond all things, I have been warned of the danger which would result from giving him reason to suspect our design.'

'But,' said I, 'you are quite *au fait* in these investigations. The Parisian police have done this thing often before.'

'Oh, yes; and for this reason I did not despair. The habits of the minister gave me, too, a great advantage. He is frequently absent from home all night. His servants are by no means numerous. They sleep at a distance from their master's apartment, and, being chiefly Neapolitans, are readily made drunk. I have keys, as you know, with which I can open any chamber or cabinet in Paris. For three months a night has not passed during the greater part of which I have not been engaged, personally, in ransacking the D— *hôtel*. My honour is interested, and, to mention a great secret, the reward is enormous. So I did not abandon the search until I had become fully satisfied that the thief is a more astute man than myself. I fancy that I have investigated every nook and corner of the premises in which it is possible that the paper can be concealed.'

'But is it not possible,' I suggested, 'that although the letter may be in the possession of the minister, as it unquestionably is, he may have concealed it elsewhere than upon his own premises?'

'This is barely possible,' said Dupin. 'The present peculiar condition of affairs at court, and especially of those intrigues in which D— is known to be involved, would render the instant availability of the document – its susceptibility of being produced at a moment's notice – a point of nearly equal importance with its possession.'

'Its susceptibility of being produced?' said I.

'That is to say, of being *destroyed*,' said Dupin.

'True,' I observed; 'the paper is clearly then upon the premises. As for its being upon the person of the minister, we may consider that as out of the question?'

'Entirely,' said the prefect. 'He has been twice waylaid, as if by footpads, and his person rigorously searched under my own inspection.'

'You might have spared yourself this trouble,' said Dupin. 'D—, I presume, is not altogether a fool, and, if not, must have anticipated these waylayings, as a matter of course.'

'Not *altogether* a fool,' said G—, 'but then he is a poet, which I take to be only one remove from a fool.'

'True,' said Dupin, after a long and thoughtful whiff from his meerschaum, 'although I have been guilty of certain doggerel myself.'

'Suppose you detail,' said I, 'the particulars of your search.'

'Why, the fact is, we took our time, and we searched *everywhere*. I have had long experience in these affairs. I took the entire building, room by room, devoting the nights of a whole week to each. We examined, first, the furniture of each apartment. We opened every possible drawer; and I presume you know that, to a properly trained police agent, such a thing as a "secret" drawer is impossible. Any man is a dolt who permits a "secret" drawer to escape him in a search of this kind. The thing is *so* plain. There is a certain amount of bulk – of space – to be accounted for in every cabinet. Then we have accurate rules. The fiftieth part of a line could not escape us. After the cabinets we took the chairs. The cushions we probed with the fine long needles you have seen me employ. From the tables we removed the tops.'

'Why so?'

'Sometimes the top of a table, or other similarly arranged piece of furniture, is removed by the person wishing to conceal an article; then the leg is excavated, the article deposited within the cavity, and the top replaced. The bottoms and tops of bedposts are employed in the same way.'

'But could not the cavity be detected by sounding?' I asked.

'By no means, if, when the article is deposited, a sufficient wadding of cotton be placed around it. Besides, in our case, we were obliged to proceed without noise.'

'But you could not have removed – you could not have taken to pieces *all* articles of furniture in which it would have been possible to make a deposit in the manner you mention. A letter may be compressed into a thin spiral roll, not differing much in shape or bulk from a large knitting-needle, and in this form it might be inserted into the rung of a chair, for example. You did not take to pieces all the chairs?'

'Certainly not; but we did better – we examined the rungs of every chair in the *hôtel*, and, indeed, the jointings of every description of furniture, by the aid of a most powerful microscope. Had there been any traces of recent disturbance we should not have failed to detect it instantly. A single grain of gimlet-dust, for example, would have been as obvious as an apple. Any disorder in the gluing – any unusual gaping in the joints – would have sufficed to ensure detection.'

'I presume you looked to the mirrors, between the boards and the plates, and you probed the beds and the bedclothes, as well as the curtains and carpets.'

'Yes, of course; and when we had scrupulously examined the contents in this way, then we examined the house itself. We divided its entire surface into compartments, which we numbered, so that none might be missed; then we scrutinised each individual square inch throughout the premises, including the two houses immediately adjoining, with the microscope, as before.'

'The two houses adjoining!' I exclaimed; 'you must have had a great deal of trouble.'

'We had; but the reward offered is prodigious.'

'You include the *grounds* about the houses?'

'All the grounds are paved with brick. They gave us comparatively little trouble. We examined the moss between the bricks, and found it undisturbed.'

'You looked among D—'s papers, of course, and into the books of the library?'

'Certainly; we opened every package and parcel; we not only opened every book, but we turned over every leaf in each volume, not contenting ourselves with a mere shake, according to the fashion of some of our police officers. We also measured the thickness of every book-*cover*, with the most accurate admeasurement, and applied to each the most jealous scrutiny of the microscope. Had any of the bindings been recently meddled with, it would have been utterly impossible that the fact should have escaped observation. Some five or six volumes, just from the hands of the binder, we carefully probed, longitudinally, with the needles.'

'You explored the floors beneath the carpets?'

'Beyond doubt. We removed every carpet, and examined the boards with the microscope.'

'And the paper on the walls?'

'Yes.'

'You looked into the cellars?'

'We did.'

'Then,' I said, 'you have been making a miscalculation and the letter is *not* upon the premises, as you suppose.'

'I fear you are right there,' said the prefect. 'And now, Dupin, what would you advise me to do?'

'To make a thorough re-search of the premises.'

'That is absolutely needless,' replied G—. 'I am not more sure that I breathe than I am that the letter is not at the *hôtel*.'

'I have no better advice to give you,' said Dupin. 'You have, of course, an accurate description of the letter?'

'Oh, yes!' And here the prefect, producing a memorandum-book, proceeded to read aloud a minute account of the internal, and especially of the external appearance of the missing document. Soon after finishing the perusal of this description, he took his departure, more entirely depressed in spirits than I had ever known the good gentleman before.

In about a month afterward he paid us another visit, and found us occupied very nearly as before. He took a pipe and a chair and entered into some ordinary conversation.

At length I said: 'Well, but G—, what of the purloined letter? I presume you have at last made up your mind that there is no such thing as overreaching the minister?'

'Confound him, say I – yes; I made the re-examination, however, as Dupin suggested – but it was all labour lost, as I knew it would be.'

'How much was the reward offered, did you say?' asked Dupin.

'Why, a very great deal – a *very* liberal reward – I don't like to say how much, precisely; but one thing I *will* say, that I wouldn't mind giving my individual cheque for fifty thousand francs to anyone who could obtain me that letter. The fact is, it is becoming of more and more importance every day; and the reward has been lately doubled. If it were trebled, however, I could do no more than I have done.'

'Why, yes,' said Dupin, drawlingly between the whiffs of his meerschaum. 'I really – think, G—, you have not exerted yourself – to the utmost in this matter. You might – do a little more, I think, eh?'

'How – in what way?'

'Why – puff, puff – you might – puff, puff – employ counsel in the matter, eh? – puff, puff, puff. Do you remember the story they tell of Abernethy?'

'No; hang Abernethy!'

'To be sure! hang him and welcome. But, once upon a time, a

certain rich miser conceived the design of sponging upon this Abernethy for a medical opinion. Getting up, for this purpose, an ordinary conversation in private company, he insinuated his case to the physician as that of an imaginary individual.

' "We will suppose," said the miser, "that his symptoms are such and such; now, doctor, what would *you* have directed him to take?"

' "Take!" said Abernethy, "why, take *advice*, to be sure." '

'*But*,' said the prefect, a little discomposed, '*I* am *perfectly* willing to take advice, and to pay for it. I would *really* give fifty thousand francs to anyone who would aid me in the matter.'

'In that case,' replied Dupin, opening a drawer, and producing a cheque-book, 'you may as well fill me up a cheque for the amount mentioned. When you have signed it, I will hand you the letter.'

I was astounded. The prefect appeared absolutely thunder-stricken. For some minutes he remained speechless and motionless, looking incredulously at my friend with open mouth, and eyes that seemed starting from their sockets; then, apparently recovering himself in some measure, he seized a pen, and after several pauses and vacant stares, finally filled up and signed a cheque for fifty-thousand francs, and handed it across the table to Dupin. The latter examined it carefully and deposited it in his pocketbook; then, unlocking an *escritoire*, took thence a letter and gave it to the prefect. This functionary grasped it in a perfect agony of joy, opened it with a trembling hand, cast a rapid glance at its contents, and then scrambling and struggling to the door, rushed at length unceremoniously from the room, and from the house, without having uttered a syllable since Dupin had requested him to fill up the cheque.

When he had gone, my friend entered into some explanations.

'The Parisian police,' he said, 'are exceedingly able in their way. They are persevering, ingenious, cunning and thoroughly versed in the knowledge which their duties seem chiefly to demand. Thus, when G— detailed to us his mode of searching the premises at the Hôtel D—, I felt entire confidence in his having made a satisfactory investigation – so far as his labours extended.'

'So far as his labours extended?' said I.

'Yes,' said Dupin. 'The measures adopted were not only the best of their kind, but carried out to absolute perfection. Had the letter been deposited within the range of their search, these fellows would, beyond question, have found it.'

I merely laughed – but he seemed quite serious in all that he said.

'The measures then,' he continued, 'were good of their kind, and well executed; their defect lay in their being inapplicable to the case and to the man. A certain set of highly ingenious resources are, with the prefect, a sort of Procrustean bed, to which he forcibly adapts his designs. But he perpetually errs by being too deep or too shallow for the matter in hand; and many a schoolboy is a better reasoner than he. I know one about eight years of age, whose success at guessing in the game of "even and odd" attracted universal admiration. This game is simple, and is played with marbles. One player holds in his hand a number of these toys, and demands of another whether that number is even or odd. If the guess is right, the guesser wins one; if wrong, he loses one. The boy to whom I allude won all the marbles of the school. Of course he had some principle of guessing; and this lay in mere observation and admeasurement of the astuteness of his opponents. For example, an arrant simpleton is his opponent, and, holding up his closed hand, asks, "Are they even or odd?" Our schoolboy replies, "Odd," and loses; but upon the second trial he wins, for he then says to himself: "The simpleton had them even upon the first trial, and his amount of cunning is just sufficient to make him have them odd upon the second; I will therefore guess odd;" – he guesses odd, and wins. Now, with a simpleton a degree above the first, he would have reasoned thus: "This fellow finds that in the first instance I guessed odd, and, in the second, he will propose to himself, upon the first impulse, a simple variation from even to odd, as did the first simpleton; but then a second thought will suggest that this is too simple a variation, and finally he will decide upon putting it even as before. I will therefore guess even;" he guesses even, and wins. Now this mode of reasoning in the schoolboy, whom his fellows termed "lucky" – what, in its last analysis, is it?'

'It is merely,' I said, 'an identification of the reasoner's intellect with that of his opponent.'

'It is,' said Dupin, 'and, upon enquiring of the boy by what means he effected the *thorough* identification in which his success consisted, I received answer as follows: "When I wish to find out how wise, or how stupid, or how good, or how wicked is anyone, or what are his thoughts at the moment, I fashion the expression of my face, as accurately as possible, in accordance with the expression of his, and then wait to see what thoughts or sentiments arise in my mind or heart, as if to match or correspond with the expression." This response of the schoolboy lies at the bottom of all the spurious profundity which has been attributed to Rochefoucauld, to La Bougive, to Machiavelli and to Campanella.'

'And the identification,' I said, 'of the reasoner's intellect with that of his opponent depends, if I understand you aright, upon the accuracy with which the opponent's intellect is admeasured.'

'For its practical value it depends upon this,' replied Dupin; 'and the prefect and his cohort fail so frequently, first by default of his identification, and, secondly, by ill-admeasurement, or rather through non-admeasurement, of the intellect with which they are engaged. They consider only their *own* ideas of ingenuity; and, in searching for anything hidden, advert only to the modes in which *they* would have hidden it. They are right in this much – that their own ingenuity is a faithful representative of that of *the mass*; but when the cunning of the individual felon is diverse in character from their own, the felon foils them, of course. This always happens when it is above their own, and very usually when it is below. They have no variation of principle in their investigations at best, when urged by some unusual emergency – by some extraordinary reward – they extend or exaggerate their old modes of *practice*, without touching their principles. What, for example, in this case of D—, has been done to vary the principle of action? What is all this boring, and probing, and sounding, and scrutinising with the microscope, and dividing the surface of the building into registered square inches – what is it all but an exaggeration *of the application* of the one principle or set of principles of search, which are based upon the one set of notions regarding human ingenuity, to which the prefect, in the long routine of his duty, has been accustomed? Do you not see he has taken it for granted that *all* men proceed to conceal a letter, not exactly in a gimlet-hole bored in a chair-leg, but, at least, in some out-of-the-way hole or corner suggested by the same tenor of thought which would urge a man to secrete a letter in a gimlet-hole bored in a chair-leg? And do you not see also that such *recherchés* nooks for concealment are adapted only for ordinary occasions, and would be adopted only by ordinary intellects; for, in all cases of concealment, a disposal of the article concealed – a disposal of it in this *recherché* manner – is, in the very first instance, presumable and presumed; and thus its discovery depends, not at all upon the acumen, but altogether upon the mere care, patience and determination of the seekers; and where the case is of importance – or, what amounts to the same thing in political eyes, when the reward is of magnitude – the qualities in question have *never* been known to fail. You will now understand what I meant in suggesting that, had the purloined letter been hidden anywhere within the limits of the prefect's examination – in other words, had the principle of its concealment been comprehended within the principles of the prefect – its discovery would have been a matter altogether beyond question. This functionary, however, has been thoroughly mystified; and the remote source of his defeat lies in the supposition that the minister is a fool, because he has acquired renown as a poet. All fools are poets; this the prefect *feels*; and he is merely guilty of a *non distributio medii* in thence inferring that all poets are fools.'

'But is this really the poet?' I asked. 'There are two brothers, I know; and both have attained reputation in letters. The minister I believe has written learnedly on the differential calculus. He is a mathematician, and no poet.'

'You are mistaken, I know him well; he is both. As poet *and* mathematician, he would reason well; as mere mathematician, he could not have reasoned at all, and thus would have been at the mercy of the prefect.'

'You surprise me,' I said, 'by these opinions, which have been contradicted by the voice of the world. You do not mean to set at naught the well-digested idea of centuries. The mathematical reason has long been regarded as *the* reason *par excellence.*'

' "*Il y a à parièr*," ' replied Dupin, quoting from Chamfort, ' "*que toute idée publique, toute convention reçue, est une sottise, car elle a convenue au plus grand nombre.*" The mathematicians, I grant you, have done their best to promulgate the popular error to which you allude, and which is none the less an error for its promulgation as truth. With an art worthy a better cause, for example, they have insinuated the term "analysis" into application to algebra. The French are the originators of this particular deception; but if a term is of any importance – if words derive any value from applicability – then "analysis" conveys "algebra" about as much as, in Latin, "*ambitus*" implies "ambition", "*religio*" "religion" or "*homines honesti*" a set of *honourable* men.'

'You have a quarrel on hand, I see,' said I, 'with some of the algebraists of Paris; but proceed.'

'I dispute the availability, and thus the value, of that reason which is cultivated in any especial form other than the abstractly logical. I dispute, in particular, the reason educed by mathematical study. The mathematics are the science of form and quantity; mathematical reasoning is merely logic applied to observation upon form and quantity. The great error lies in supposing that even the truths of what is called *pure* algebra are abstract or general truths. And this error is so egregious that I am confounded at the universality with which it has been received. Mathematical axioms are *not* axioms of general truth. What is true of *relation* – of form and quantity – is

often grossly false in regard to morals, for example. In this latter
science it is very usually untrue that the aggregated parts are equal
to the whole. In chemistry also the axiom fails. In the consideration
of motive it fails; for two motives, each of a given value, have not
necessarily a value, when united, equal to the sum of their values
apart. There are numerous other mathematical truths which are
only truths within the limits of *relation*. But the mathematician
argues from his *finite truths*, through habit, as if they were of an
absolutely general applicability – as the world indeed imagines them
to be. Bryant, in his very learned *Mythology*, mentions an analogous
source of error when he says that "although the pagan fables are not
believed, yet we forget ourselves continually, and make inferences
from them as existing realities". With the algebraists, however, who
are pagans themselves, the "pagan fables" *are* believed, and the
inferences are made, not so much through lapse of memory as
through an unaccountable addling of the brains. In short, I never
yet encountered the mere mathematician who could be trusted out
of equal roots, or one who did not clandestinely hold it as a point of
his faith that $x^2 + px$ was absolutely and unconditionally equal to q.
Say to one of these gentlemen, by way of experiment, if you please,
that you believe occasions may occur where $x^2 + px$ is not altogether
equal to q, and, having made him understand what you mean, get
out of his reach as speedily as convenient, for, beyond doubt, he will
endeavour to knock you down.

'I mean to say,' continued Dupin, while I merely laughed at his last
observations, 'that if the minister had been no more than a mathematician, the prefect would have been under no necessity of giving me
this cheque. I knew him, however, as both mathematician and poet,
and my measures were adapted to his capacity, with reference to the
circumstances by which he was surrounded. I knew him as a courtier,
too, and as a bold *intriguant*. Such a man, I considered, could not fail
to be aware of the ordinary political modes of action. He could not
have failed to anticipate – and events have proved that he did not fail
to anticipate – the waylayings to which he was subjected. He must
have foreseen, I reflected, the secret investigations of his premises.
His frequent absences from home at night, which were hailed by the
prefect as certain aids to his success, I regarded only as ruses, to
afford opportunity for thorough search to the police, and thus the
sooner to impress them with the conviction at which G—, in fact, did
finally arrive – the conviction that the letter was not upon the
premises. I felt, also, that the whole train of thought, which I was at
some pains in detailing to you just now, concerning the invariable

principle of political action in searches for articles concealed – I felt
that this whole train of thought would necessarily pass through the
mind of the minister. It would imperatively lead him to despise all
the ordinary *nooks* of concealment. *He* could not, I reflected, be so
weak as not to see that the most intricate and remote recess of his
hôtel would be as open as his commonest closets to the eyes, to the
probes, to the gimlets and to the microscopes of the prefect. I saw, in
fine, that he would be driven, as a matter of course, to *simplicity*, if
not deliberately induced to it as a matter of choice. You will
remember, perhaps, how desperately the prefect laughed when I
suggested, upon our first interview, that it was just possible this
mystery troubled him so much on account of its being so very self-
evident.'

'Yes,' said I, 'I remember his merriment well. I really thought he
would have fallen into convulsions.'

'The material world,' continued Dupin, 'abounds with very strict
analogies to the immaterial; and thus some colour of truth has been
given to the rhetorical dogma that metaphor, or simile, may be made
to strengthen an argument as well as to embellish a description. The
principle of the *vis inertiae*, for example, seems to be identical in
physics and metaphysics. It is not more true in the former, that a
large body is with more difficulty set in motion than a smaller one,
and that its subsequent momentum is commensurate with this
difficulty, than it is in the latter, that intellects of the vaster capacity,
while more forcible, more constant, and more eventful in their
movements than those of inferior grade, are yet the less readily
moved, and more embarrassed, and full of hesitation in the first few
steps of their progress. Again, have you ever noticed which of the
street signs over the shop doors are the most attractive of attention?'

'I have never given the matter a thought,' I said.

'There is a game of puzzles,' he resumed, 'which is played upon a
map. One party playing requires another to find a given word – the
name of town, river, state or empire – any word, in short, upon the
motley and perplexed surface of the chart. A novice in the game
generally seeks to embarrass his opponents by giving them the most
minutely lettered names; but the adept selects such words as stretch,
in large characters, from one end of the chart to the other. These,
like the overlargely lettered signs and placards of the street, escape
observation by dint of being excessively obvious; and here the
physical oversight is precisely analogous with the moral
inapprehension by which the intellect suffers to pass unnoticed
those considerations which are too obtrusively and too palpably

self-evident. But this is a point, it appears, somewhat above or beneath the understanding of the prefect. He never once thought it probable, or possible, that the minister had deposited the letter immediately beneath the nose of the whole world by way of best preventing any portion of that world from perceiving it.

'But the more I reflected upon the daring, dashing and discriminating ingenuity of D—; upon the fact that the document must always have been *at hand*, if he intended to use it to good purpose; and upon the decisive evidence, obtained by the prefect, that it was not hidden within the limits of that dignitary's ordinary search – the more satisfied I became that, to conceal this letter, the minister had resorted to the comprehensive and sagacious expedient of not attempting to conceal it at all.

'Full of these ideas, I prepared myself with a pair of green spectacles, and called one fine morning, quite by accident, at the ministerial *hôtel*. I found D— at home, yawning, lounging and dawdling, as usual, and pretending to be in the last extremity of *ennui*. He is, perhaps, the most really energetic human being now alive – but that is only when nobody sees him.

'To be even with him, I complained of my weak eyes, and lamented the necessity of the spectacles, under cover of which I cautiously and thoroughly surveyed the whole apartment, while seemingly intent only upon the conversation of my host.

'I paid especial attention to a large writing-table near which he sat, and upon which lay, confusedly, some miscellaneous letters and other papers, with one or two musical instruments and a few books. Here, however, after a long and very deliberate scrutiny, I saw nothing to excite particular suspicion.

'At length my eyes, in going the circuit of the room, fell upon a trumpery filigree card-rack of pasteboard that hung, dangling by a dirty blue ribbon, from a little brass knob just beneath the middle of the mantelpiece. In this rack, which had three or four compartments, were five or six visiting cards and a solitary letter. This last was much soiled and crumpled. It was torn nearly in two across the middle – as if a design, in the first instance, to tear it entirely up as worthless, had been altered, or stayed, in the second. It had a large black seal, bearing the D— cipher *very* conspicuously, and was addressed, in a diminutive female hand, to D—, the minister, himself. It was thrust carelessly, and even, as it seemed, contemptuously, into one of the uppermost divisions of the rack.

'No sooner had I glanced at this letter than I concluded it to be that of which I was in search. To be sure, it was, to all appearance, radically different from the one of which the prefect had read us so minute a description. Here the seal was large and black, with the D— cipher; there it was small and red, with the ducal arms of the S— family. Here, the address, to the minister, was diminutive and feminine; there the superscription, to a certain royal personage, was markedly bold and decided; the size alone formed a point of correspondence. But, then, the *radicalness* of these differences, which was excessive; the dirt; the soiled and torn condition of the paper, so inconsistent with the *true* methodical habits of D— and so suggestive of a design to delude the beholder into an idea of the worthlessness of the document; these things, together with the hyper-obtrusive situation of this document, full in the view of every visitor, and thus exactly in accordance with the conclusions to which I had previously arrived; these things, I say, were strongly corroborative of suspicion in one who came with the intention to suspect.

'I protracted my visit as long as possible, and, while I maintained a most animated discussion with the minister, upon a topic which I knew well had never failed to interest and excite him, I kept my attention really riveted upon the letter. In this examination, I committed to memory its external appearance and arrangement in the rack; and also fell, at length, upon a discovery which set at rest whatever trivial doubt I might have entertained. In scrutinising the edges of the paper, I observed them to be more *chafed* than seemed necessary. They presented the *broken* appearance which is manifested when a stiff paper, having been once folded and pressed with a folder, is refolded in a reversed direction, in the same creases or edges which had formed the original fold. This discovery was sufficient. It was clear to me that the letter had been turned as a glove, inside out, re-directed and re-sealed. I bade the minister good morning, and took my departure at once, leaving a gold snuff-box upon the table.

'The next morning I called for the snuff-box, when we resumed, quite eagerly, the conversation of the preceding day. While thus engaged, however, a loud report, as if of a pistol, was heard immediately beneath the windows of the *hôtel*, and was succeeded by a series of fearful screams, and the shoutings of a terrified mob. D— rushed to a casement, threw it open, and looked out. In the meantime I stepped to the card-rack, took the letter, put it in my pocket, and replaced it with a facsimile (so far as regards externals) which I had carefully prepared at my lodgings – imitating the D— cipher, very readily, by means of a seal formed of bread.

'The disturbance in the street had been occasioned by the frantic behaviour of a man with a musket. He had fired it among a crowd of women and children. It proved, however, to have been without ball, and the fellow was suffered to go his way as a lunatic or a drunkard. When he had gone, D— came from the window, whither I had followed him immediately upon securing the object in view. Soon afterwards I bade him farewell. The pretended lunatic was a man in my own pay.'

'But what purpose had you,' I asked, 'in replacing the letter by a facsimile? Would it not have been better, at the first visit, to have seized it openly and departed?'

'D—,' replied Dupin, 'is a desperate man, and a man of nerve. His *hôtel*, too, is not without attendants devoted to his interests. Had I made the wild attempt you suggest, I might never have left the ministerial presence alive. The good people of Paris might have heard of me no more. But I had an object apart from these considerations. You know my political prepossessions. In this matter, I act as a partisan of the lady concerned. For eighteen months the minister has had her in his power. She has now him in hers – since, unaware that the letter is not in his possession, he will proceed with his exactions as if it was. Thus will he inevitably commit himself, at once, to his political destruction. His downfall, too, will not be more precipitate than awkward. It is very well to talk about the *facilis descensus Averni*; but in all kinds of climbing, as Catalani said of singing, it is far more easy to get up than to come down. In the present instance I have no sympathy – at least, no pity – for him who descends. He is that *monstrum horrendum*, an unprincipled man of genius. I confess, however, that I should like very well to know the precise character of his thoughts when, being defied by her whom the prefect terms "a certain personage", he is reduced to opening the letter which I left for him in the card-rack.'

'How? did you put anything particular in it?'

'Why – it did not seem altogether right to leave the interior blank – that would have been insulting. D—, at Vienna once, did me an evil turn, which I told him, quite good-humouredly, that I should remember. So, as I knew he would feel some curiosity in regard to the identity of the person who had outwitted him, I thought it a pity not to give him a clue. He is well acquainted with my manuscript, and I just copied into the middle of the blank sheet the words –

> *Un dessein si funeste,*
> *S'il n'este digne d' Atrée, est digne de Theyste.*

They are to be found in Crébillon's *Atrée.*'

The Biter Bit

WILKIE COLLINS

From Chief Inspector Theakstone, of the Detective
Police, to Sergeant Bulmer of the same force

London, 4th July 18—

SERGEANT BULMER – This is to inform you that you are wanted to
assist in looking up a case of importance, which will require all the
attention of an experienced member of the force. The matter of the
robbery on which you are now engaged, you will please to shift over
to the young man who brings you this letter. You will tell him all
the circumstances of the case, just as they stand; you will put him up
to the progress you have made (if any) towards detecting the person
or persons by whom the money has been stolen; and you will leave
him to make the best he can of the matter now in your hands. He is
to have the whole responsibility of the case, and the whole credit of
his success, if he brings it to a proper issue.

So much for the orders that I am desired to communicate to you.

A word in your ear, next, about this new man who is to take your
place. His name is Matthew Sharpin; and he is to have the chance
given him of dashing into our office at a jump – supposing he turns
out strong enough to take it. You will naturally ask me how he
comes by this privilege. I can only tell you that he has some
uncommonly strong interest to back him in certain high quarters
which you and I had better not mention except under our breaths.
He has been a lawyer's clerk; and he is wonderfully conceited in his
opinion of himself, as well as mean and underhand to look at.
According to his own account, he leaves his old trade, and joins ours
of his own free will and preference. You will no more believe that
than I do. My notion is that he has managed to ferret out some
private information in connection with the affairs of one of his
master's clients, which makes him rather an awkward customer to
keep in the office for the future, and which, at the same time, gives
him hold enough over his employer to make it dangerous to drive
him into a corner by turning him away. I think the giving him this
unheard-of chance among us, is, in plain words, pretty much like

giving him hush-money to keep him quiet. However that may be, Mr Matthew Sharpin is to have the case now in your hands; and if he succeeds with it, he pokes his ugly nose into our office, as sure as fate. I put you up to this, sergeant, so that you may not stand in your own light by giving the new man any cause to complain of you at headquarters, and remain yours,

FRANCIS THEAKSTONE

From Mr Matthew Sharpin to Chief Inspector Theakstone

London, July 5th 18—

DEAR SIR – Having now been favoured with the necessary instructions from Sergeant Bulmer, I beg to remind you of certain directions which I have received, relating to the report of my future proceedings which I am to prepare for examination at headquarters.

The object of my writing, and of your examining what I have written, before you send it in to the higher authorities, is, I am informed, to give me, as an untried hand, the benefit of your advice, in case I want it (which I venture to think I shall not) at any stage of my proceedings. As the extraordinary circumstances of the case on which I am now engaged make it impossible for me to absent myself from the place where the robbery was committed until I have made some progress towards discovering the thief, I am necessarily precluded from consulting you personally. Hence the necessity of my writing down the various details, which might, perhaps, be better communicated by word of mouth. This, if I am not mistaken, is the position in which we are now placed. I state my own impressions on the subject, in writing, in order that we may clearly understand each other at the outset; and have the honour to remain, your obedient servant,

MATTHEW SHARPIN

From Chief Inspector Theakstone to Mr Matthew Sharpin

London, 5th July 18—

SIR – You have begun by wasting time, ink and paper. We both of us perfectly well knew the position we stood in towards each other when I sent you with my letter to Sergeant Bulmer. There was not the least need to repeat it in writing. Be so good as to employ your pen, in future, on the business actually in hand.

You have now three separate matters on which to write to me. First, you have to draw up a statement of your instructions received from Sergeant Bulmer, in order to show us that nothing has escaped your memory, and that you are thoroughly acquainted with all the circumstances of the case which has been entrusted to you. Secondly, you are to inform me what it is you propose to do. Thirdly, you are to report every inch of your progress (if you make any) from day to day, and, if need be, from hour to hour as well. This is *your* duty. As to what *my* duty may be, when I want you to remind me of it, I will write and tell you so. In the meantime, I remain, yours,

FRANCIS THEAKSTONE

From Mr Matthew Sharpin to Chief Inspector Theakstone

London, 6th July 18—

SIR – You are rather an elderly person, and, as such, naturally inclined to be a little jealous of men like me, who are in the prime of their lives and their faculties. Under these circumstances, it is my duty to be considerate towards you, and not to bear too hardly on your small failings. I decline, therefore, altogether, to take offence at the tone of your letter; I give you the full benefit of the natural generosity of my nature; I sponge the very existence of your surly communication out of my memory – in short, Chief Inspector Theakstone, I forgive you, and proceed to business.

My first duty is to draw up a full statement of the instructions I have received from Sergeant Bulmer. Here they are at your service, according to my version of them.

At number 13, Rutherford Street, Soho, there is a stationer's shop. It is kept by one Mr Yatman. He is a married man, but has no family. Besides Mr and Mrs Yatman, the other inmates in the house are a young single man named Jay, who lodges in the front room on the second floor; a shopman, who sleeps in one of the attics; and a servant-of-all-work, whose bed is in the back-kitchen. Once a week a charwoman comes for a few hours in the morning only, to help this servant. These are all the persons who, on ordinary occasions, have means of access to the interior of the house placed, as a matter of course, at their disposal.

Mr Yatman has been in business for many years, carrying on his affairs prosperously enough to realise a handsome independence for a person in his position. Unfortunately for himself he endeavoured to increase the amount of his property by speculating. He ventured boldly in his investments, luck went against him, and rather less than two years ago he found himself a poor man again. All that was saved out of the wreck of his property was the sum of two hundred pounds.

Although Mr Yatman did his best to meet his altered

circumstances, by giving up many of the luxuries and comforts to which he and his wife had been accustomed, he found it impossible to retrench so far as to allow of putting by any money from the income produced by the shop. The business has been declining of late years – the cheap advertising stationers having done it injury with the public. Consequently, up to last week the only surplus property possessed by Mr Yatman consisted of the two hundred pounds which had been recovered from the wreck of his fortune. This sum was placed as a deposit in a joint-stock bank of the highest possible character.

Eight days ago, Mr Yatman and his lodger, Mr Jay, held a conversation on the subject of the commercial difficulties which are hampering trade in all directions at the present time. Mr Jay (who lives by supplying the newspapers with short paragraphs relating to incidents, offences, and brief records of remarkable occurrences in general – who is, in short, what they call a penny-a-liner) told his landlord that he had been in the city that day, and had heard unfavourable rumours on the subject of the joint-stock banks. The rumours to which he alluded had already reached the ears of Mr Yatman from other quarters; and the confirmation of them by his lodger had such an effect on his mind – predisposed as it was to alarm by the experience of his former losses – that he resolved to go at once to the bank and withdraw his deposit.

It was then getting on towards the end of the afternoon; and he arrived just in time to receive his money before the bank closed.

He received the deposit in bank-notes of the following amounts: one fifty-pound note, three twenty-pound notes, six ten-pound notes, and six five-pound notes. His object in drawing the money in this form was to have it ready to lay out immediately in trifling loans, on good security, among the small tradespeople of his district, some of whom are sorely pressed for the very means of existence at the present time. Investments of this kind seemed to Mr Yatman to be the most safe and the most profitable on which he could now venture.

He brought the money back in an envelope placed in his breast-pocket; and asked his shopman, on getting home, to look for a small flat tin cashbox, which had not been used for years, and which, as Mr Yatman remembered it, was exactly the right size to hold the bank-notes. For some time the cashbox was searched for in vain. Mr Yatman called to his wife to know if she had any idea where it was. The question was overheard by the servant-of-all-work, who was taking up the tea-tray at the time, and by Mr Jay, who was coming downstairs on his way out to the theatre. Ultimately the cashbox was found by the shopman. Mr Yatman placed the bank-notes in it, secured them by a padlock, and put the box in his coat-pocket. It stuck out of the coat-pocket a very little, but enough to be seen. Mr Yatman remained at home, upstairs, all the evening. No visitors called. At eleven o'clock he went to bed, and put the cashbox along with his clothes, on a chair by the bedside.

When he and his wife woke the next morning, the box was gone. Payment of the notes was immediately stopped at the bank of England; but no news of the money has been heard of since that time.

So far, the circumstances of the case are perfectly clear. They point unmistakably to the conclusion that the robbery must have been committed by some person living in the house. Suspicion falls, therefore, upon the servant-of-all-work, upon the shopman, and upon Mr Jay. The two first knew that the cashbox was being enquired for by their master, but did not know what it was he wanted to put into it. They would assume, of course, that it was money. They both had opportunities (the servant, when she took away the tea – and the shopman, when he came, after shutting up, to give the keys of the till to his master) of seeing the cashbox in Mr Yatman's pocket, and of inferring naturally, from its position there, that he intended to take it into his bedroom with him at night.

Mr Jay, on the other hand, had been told, during the afternoon's conversation on the subject of joint-stock banks, that his landlord had a deposit of two hundred pounds in one of them. He also knew that Mr Yatman left him with the intention of drawing that money out; and he heard the enquiry for the cashbox, afterwards, when he was coming downstairs. He must, therefore, have inferred that the money was in the house, and that the cashbox was the receptacle intended to contain it. That he could have had any idea, however, of the place in which Mr Yatman intended to keep it for the night, is impossible, seeing that he went out before the box was found, and did not return till his landlord was in bed. Consequently, if he committed the robbery, he must have gone into the bedroom purely on speculation.

Speaking of the bedroom reminds me of the necessity of noticing the situation of it in the house, and the means that exist of gaining easy access to it at any hour of the night.

The room in question is the back-room on the first-floor. In consequence of Mrs Yatman's constitutional nervousness on the subject of fire (which makes her apprehend being burnt alive in her room, in case of accident, by the hampering of the lock if the key is turned in it) her husband has never been accustomed to lock the bedroom door. Both he and his wife are, by their own admission, heavy sleepers. Consequently, the risk to be run by any evil-disposed persons wishing to plunder the bedroom was of the most trifling kind. They could enter the room by merely turning the handle of the door, and if they moved with ordinary caution, there was no fear of their waking the sleepers inside. This fact is of importance. It strengthens our conviction that the money must have been taken by one of the inmates of the house, because it tends to show that the robbery, in this case, might have been committed by persons not possessed of the superior vigilance and cunning of the experienced thief.

Such are the circumstances, as they were related to Sergeant Bulmer when he was first called in to discover the guilty parties, and, if possible, to recover the lost bank-notes. The strictest enquiry which he could institute failed of producing the smallest fragment of evidence against any of the persons on whom suspicion naturally fell. Their language and behaviour, on being informed of the robbery, was perfectly consistent with the language and behaviour of innocent people. Sergeant Bulmer felt from the first that this was a case for private enquiry and secret observation. He began by recommending Mr and Mrs Yatman to affect a feeling of perfect confidence in the innocence of the persons living under their roof; and he then opened the campaign by employing himself in following the goings and comings, and in discovering the friends, the habits, and the secrets of the maid-of-all-work.

Three days and nights of exertions on his own part, and on that of others who were competent to assist his investigations, were enough to satisfy him that there was no sound cause for suspicion against the girl.

He next practised the same precaution in relation to the shopman. There was more difficulty and uncertainty in privately clearing up this person's character without his knowledge, but the obstacles were at last smoothed away with tolerable success; and though there is not the same amount of certainty, in this case, which there was in that of the girl, there is still fair reason for supposing that the shopman has had nothing to do with the robbery of the cashbox.

As a necessary consequence of these proceedings, the range of suspicion now becomes limited to the lodger, Mr Jay.

When I presented your letter of introduction to Sergeant Bulmer, he had already made some enquiries on the subject of this young man. The result, so far, has not been at all favourable. Mr Jay's habits are irregular; he frequents public-houses, and seems to be familiarly acquainted with a great many dissolute characters; he is in debt to most of the tradespeople whom he employs; he has not paid his rent to Mr Yatman for the last month; yesterday evening he came home excited by liquor, and last week he was seen talking to a prize-fighter. In short, though Mr Jay does call himself a journalist, in virtue of his penny-a-line contributions to the newspapers, he is a young man of low tastes, vulgar manners and bad habits. Nothing has yet been discovered in relation to him which redounds to his credit in the smallest degree.

I have now reported, down to the very last details, all the particulars communicated to me by Sergeant Bulmer. I believe you will not find an omission anywhere, and I think you will admit, though you are prejudiced against me, that a clearer statement of facts was never laid before you than the statement I have now made. My next duty is to tell you what I propose to do, now that the case is confided to my hands.

In the first place, it is clearly my business to take up the case at the point where Sergeant Bulmer has left it. On his authority, I am justified in assuming that I have no need to trouble myself about the maid-of-all-work and the shopman. Their characters are now to be considered as cleared up. What remains to be privately investigated is the question of the guilt or innocence of Mr Jay. Before we give up the notes for lost, we must make sure, if we can, that he knows nothing about them.

This is the plan that I have adopted, with the full approval of Mr and Mrs Yatman, for discovering whether Mr Jay is or is not the person who has stolen the cashbox:

I propose, today, to present myself at the house in the character of a young man who is looking for lodgings. The back-room on the second-floor will be shown to me as the room to let; and I shall establish myself there tonight, as a person from the country who has come to London to look for a situation in a respectable shop or office.

By this means I shall be living next to the room occupied by Mr Jay. The partition between us is mere lath and plaster. I shall make a small hole in it, near the cornice, through which I can see what Mr Jay does in his room, and hear every word that is said when any friend happens to call on him. Whenever he is at home, I shall be at my post of observation. Whenever he goes out, I shall be after him. By employing these means of watching him, I believe I may look forward to the discovery of his secret – if he knows anything about the lost bank-notes – as to a dead certainty.

What you may think of my plan of observation I cannot undertake to say. It appears to me to unite the invaluable merits of boldness and simplicity. Fortified by this conviction, I close the present communication with feelings of the most sanguine description in regard to the future, and remain your obedient servant,

MATTHEW SHARPIN

From the same to the same

7th July

SIR – As you have not honoured me with any answer to my last communication, I assume that, in spite of your prejudices against me, it has produced the favourable impression on your mind which I ventured to anticipate. Gratified beyond measure by the token of approval which your eloquent silence conveys to me, I proceed to report the progress that has been made in the course of the last twenty-four hours.

I am now comfortably established next door to Mr Jay; and I am delighted to say that I have two holes in the partition, instead of one. My natural sense of humour has led me into the pardonable extravagance of giving them appropriate names. One I call my peep-hole, and the other my pipe-hole. The name of the first explains itself; the name of the second refers to a small tin pipe, or tube, inserted in the hole, and twisted so that the mouth of it comes close to my ear, while I am standing at my post of observation. Thus, while I am looking at Mr Jay through my peep-hole, I can hear every word that may be spoken in his room through my pipe-hole.

Perfect candour – a virtue which I have possessed from my childhood – compels me to acknowledge, before I go any further, that the ingenious notion of adding a pipe-hole to my proposed peep-hole originated with Mrs Yatman. This lady – a most intelligent and accomplished person, simple, and yet distinguished, in her manners – has entered into all my little plans with an enthusiasm and intelligence which I cannot too highly praise. Mr Yatman is so cast down by his loss, that he is quite incapable of affording me any assistance. Mrs Yatman, who is evidently most tenderly attached to him, feels her husband's sad condition of mind even more acutely than she feels the loss of the money; and is mainly stimulated to exertion by her desire to assist in raising him from the miserable state of prostration into which he has now fallen.

'The money, Mr Sharpin,' she said to me yesterday evening, with tears in her eyes, 'the money may be regained by rigid economy and strict attention to business. It is my husband's wretched state of mind that makes me so anxious for the discovery of the thief. I may be wrong, but I felt hopeful of success as soon as you entered the house; and I believe, if the wretch who has robbed us is to be found, you are the man to discover him.' I accepted this gratifying compliment in the spirit in which it was offered – firmly believing that I shall be found, sooner or later, to have thoroughly deserved it.

Let me now return to business; that is to say, to my peep-hole and my pipe-hole. I have enjoyed some hours of calm observation of Mr Jay. Though rarely at home, as I understand from Mrs Yatman, on ordinary occasions, he has been indoors the whole of this day. That is suspicious, to begin with. I have to report, further that he rose at a late hour this morning (always a bad sign in a young man), and that he lost a great deal of time, after he was up, in yawning and complaining to himself of headache. Like other debauched characters, he ate little or nothing for breakfast. His next proceeding was to smoke a pipe – a dirty clay pipe, which a gentleman would have been ashamed to put between his lips. When he had done smoking, he took out pen, ink and paper, and sat down to write with a groan – whether of remorse for having taken the bank-notes, or of disgust at the task before him, I am unable to say. After writing a few lines (too far away from my peep-hole to give me a chance of reading over his shoulder), he leaned back in his chair, and amused himself by humming the tunes of certain popular songs. Whether these do, or do not, represent secret signals by which he communicates with his accomplices remains to be seen. After he had amused himself for some time by humming, he got up and began to walk about the room, occasionally stopping to add a sentence to the paper on his desk. Before long, he went to a locked cupboard and opened it. I strained my eyes eagerly, in expectation of making a discovery. I saw him take something carefully out of the cupboard – he turned round – and it was only a pint bottle of brandy! Having drunk some of the liquor, this extremely indolent reprobate lay down on his bed again, and in five minutes was fast asleep.

After hearing him snoring for a least two hours, I was recalled to my peep-hole by a knock at his door. He jumped up and opened it with suspicious activity.

A very small boy, with a very dirty face, walked in, said, 'Please, sir, they're waiting for you,' sat down on a chair, with his legs a long way from the ground, and instantly fell asleep! Mr Jay swore an oath, tied a wet towel round his head, and going back to his paper, began to cover it with writing as fast as his fingers could move the pen. Occasionally getting up to dip the towel in water and tie it on again, he continued at this employment for nearly three hours; then folded up the leaves of writing, woke the boy, and gave them to him, with this remarkable expression: – ' Now, then, young sleepy-head, quick-march! If you see the governor tell him to have the money ready when I call for it.' The boy grinned, and disappeared. I was sorely tempted to follow 'sleepy-head', but, on reflection, considered it safest still to keep my eye on the proceedings of Mr Jay.

In half an hour's time, he put on his hat and walked out. Of course, I put on my hat and walked out also. As I went downstairs, I passed Mrs Yatman going up. The lady has been kind enough to undertake, by previous arrangement between us, to search Mr Jay's room while he is out of the way, and while I am necessarily engaged in the pleasing duty of following him wherever he goes. On the occasion to which I now refer, he walked straight to the nearest tavern, and ordered a couple of mutton chops for his dinner. I placed myself in the next box to him, and ordered a couple of mutton chops for my dinner. Before I had been in the room a minute, a young man of highly suspicious manners and appearance, sitting at a table opposite, took his glass of porter in his hand and joined Mr Jay. I pretended to be reading the newspaper, and listened, as in duty bound, with all my might.

'Jack has been here enquiring after you,' says the young man.

'Did he leave any message?' asks Mr Jay.

'Yes,' says the other. 'He told me, if I met with you, to say that he wished very particularly to see you tonight; and that he would give you a look in, at Rutherford Street, at seven o'clock.'

'All right,' says Mr Jay. 'I'll get back in time to see him.'

Upon this, the suspicious-looking young man finished his porter, and saying that he was rather in a hurry, took leave of his friend (perhaps I should not be wrong if I said his accomplice) and left the room.

At twenty-five minutes and a half past six – in these serious cases it is important to be particular about time – Mr Jay finished his chops and paid his bill. At twenty-six minutes and three-quarters, I finished my chops and paid mine. In ten minutes more I was inside the house in Rutherford Street and was received by Mrs Yatman in the passage. That charming woman's face exhibited an expression of melancholy and disappointment which it quite grieved me to see.

'I am afraid, ma'am,' says I, 'that you have not hit on any little criminating discovery in the lodger's room?'

She shook her head and sighed. It was a soft, languid, fluttering sigh – and, upon my life, it quite upset me. For the moment I forgot business, and burned with envy of Mr Yatman.

'Don't despair, ma'am,' I said, with an insinuating mildness which seemed to touch her. 'I have heard a mysterious conversation – I know of a guilty appointment – and I expect great things from my peep-hole and my pipe-hole tonight. Pray, don't be alarmed, but I think we are on the brink of a discovery.'

Here my enthusiastic devotion to business got the better of my tender feelings. I looked – winked – nodded – left her.

When I got back to my observatory, I found Mr Jay digesting his mutton chops in an armchair, with his pipe in his mouth. On his table were two tumblers, a jug of water, and the pint bottle of brandy. It was then close upon seven o'clock. As the hour struck, the person described as 'Jack' walked in.

He looked agitated – I am happy to say he looked violently agitated. The cheerful glow of anticipated success diffused itself (to use a strong expression) all over me, from head to foot. With breathless interest I looked through my peep-hole, and saw the visitor – the 'Jack' of this delightful case – sit down, facing me, at the opposite side of the table to Mr Jay. Making allowance for the difference in expression which their countenances just now happened to exhibit, these two abandoned villains were so much alike in other respects as to lead at once to the conclusion that they were brothers. Jack was the cleaner man and the better dressed of the two. I admit that, at the outset. It is, perhaps, one of my failings to push justice and impartiality to their utmost limits. I am no Pharisee; and where vice has its redeeming point, I say, let vice have its due – yes, yes, by all manner of means, let vice have its due.

'What's the matter now, Jack?' says Mr Jay.

'Can't you see it in my face?' says Jack. 'My dear fellow, delays are dangerous. Let us have done with suspense, and risk it the day after tomorrow.'

'So soon as that?' cried Mr Jay, looking very much astonished. 'Well, I'm ready, if you are. But, I say, Jack, is Somebody Else ready too? Are you quite sure of that?'

He smiled as he spoke – a frightful smile – and laid a very strong emphasis on those two words, 'Somebody Else'. There is evidently a third ruffian, a nameless desperado, concerned in the business.

'Meet us tomorrow,' says Jack, 'and judge for yourself. Be in the Regent's Park at eleven in the morning, and look out for us at the turning that leads to the Avenue Road.'

'I'll be there,' says Mr Jay. 'Have a drop of brandy and water? What are you getting up for? You're not going already?'

'Yes, I am,' says Jack. 'The fact is, I'm so excited and agitated that I can't sit still anywhere for five minutes together. Ridiculous as it may appear to you, I'm in a perpetual state of nervous flutter. I can't, for the life of me, help fearing that we shall be found out. I fancy that every man who looks twice at me in the street is a spy – '

At those words, I thought my legs would have given way under me. Nothing but strength of mind kept me at my peep-hole – nothing else, I give you my word of honour.

'Stuff and nonsense!' cried Mr Jay, with all the effrontery of a veteran in crime. 'We have kept the secret up to this time, and we will manage cleverly to the end. Have a drop of brandy and water, and you will feel as certain about it as I do.'

Jack steadily refused the brandy and water, and steadily persisted in taking his leave.

'I must try if I can't walk it off,' he said. 'Remember tomorrow morning – eleven o'clock, Avenue Road side of the Regent's Park.'

With those words he went out. His hardened relative laughed desperately, and resumed the dirty clay pipe.

I sat down on the side of my bed, actually quivering with excitement.

It is clear to me that no attempt has yet been made to change the stolen bank-notes; and I may add that Sergeant Bulmer was of that opinion also, when he left the case in my hands. What is the natural conclusion to draw from the conversation which I have just set down? Evidently, that the confederates meet tomorrow to take their respective shares in the stolen money, and to decide on the safest means of getting the notes changed the day after. Mr Jay is, beyond a doubt, the leading criminal in this business, and he will probably run the chief risk – that of changing the fifty-pound note. I shall, therefore, still make it my business to follow him – attending at the Regent's Park tomorrow, and doing my best to hear what is said there. If another appointment is made the day after, I shall, of course, go to it. In the meantime, I shall want the immediate assistance of two competent persons (supposing the rascals separate after their meeting) to follow the two minor criminals. It is only fair to add that if the rogues all retire together, I shall probably keep my subordinates in reserve. Being naturally ambitious, I desire, if possible, to have the whole credit of discovering this robbery to myself.

I have to acknowledge, with thanks, the speedy arrival of my two subordinates – men of very average abilities, I am afraid; but, fortunately, I shall always be on the spot to direct them.

My first business this morning was, necessarily, to prevent mistakes by accounting to Mr and Mrs Yatman for the presence of two strangers on the scene. Mr Yatman (between ourselves, a poor feeble man) only shook his head and groaned. Mrs Yatman (that superior woman) favoured me with a charming look of intelligence.

'Oh, Mr Sharpin!' she said, 'I am so sorry to see those two men! Your sending for their assistance looks as if you were beginning to be doubtful of success.'

I privately winked at her (she is very good in allowing me to do so without taking offence), and told her, in my facetious way, that she laboured under a slight mistake.

'It is because I am sure of success, ma'am, that I sent for them. I am determined to recover the money, not for my own sake only, but for Mr Yatman's sake – and for yours.'

I laid a considerable amount of stress on those last three words. She said, 'Oh, Mr Sharpin!' again – and blushed of a heavenly red – and looked down at her work. I could go to the world's end with that woman, if Mr Yatman would only die.

I sent off the two subordinates to wait, until I wanted them, at the Avenue Road gate of the Regent's Park. Half an hour afterwards I was following in the same direction myself, at the heels of Mr Jay.

The two confederates were punctual to the appointed time. I blush to record it, but it is nevertheless necessary to state, that the third rogue – the nameless desperado of my report, or if you prefer it, the mysterious 'Somebody Else' of the conversation between the two brothers – is a woman! and, what is worse, a young woman! and what is more lamentable still, a nice-looking woman! I have long resisted a growing conviction that wherever there is mischief in this world, an individual of the fair sex is inevitably certain to be mixed up in it. After the experience of this morning, I can struggle against that sad conclusion no longer. I give up the sex – excepting Mrs Yatman, I give up the sex.

The man named 'Jack' offered the woman his arm. Mr Jay placed himself on the other side of her. The three then walked away slowly among the trees. I followed them at a respectful distance. My two subordinates, at a respectful distance also, followed me.

It was, I deeply regret to say, impossible to get near enough to them to overhear their conversation, without running too great a risk of being discovered. I could only infer from their gestures and actions that they were all three talking with extraordinary earnestness on some subject which deeply interested them. After having been engaged in this way a full quarter of an hour, they suddenly turned round to retrace their steps. My presence of mind did not forsake me in this emergency. I signed to the two subordinates to walk on carelessly and pass them, while I myself slipped dexterously behind a tree. As they came by me, I heard 'Jack' address these words to Mr Jay: 'Let us say half-past ten tomorrow morning. And mind you come in a cab. We had better not risk taking one in this neighbourhood.'

Mr Jay made some brief reply, which I could not overhear. They walked back to the place at which they had met, shaking hands there with an audacious cordiality which it quite sickened me to see. They then separated. I followed Mr Jay. My subordinates paid the same delicate attention to the other two.

Instead of taking me back to Rutherford Street, Mr Jay led me to the Strand. He stopped at a dingy, disreputable-looking house, which, according to the inscription over the door, was a newspaper office, but which, in my judgement, had all the external appearance of a place devoted to the reception of stolen goods.

After remaining inside for a few minutes, he came out, whistling, with his finger and thumb in his waistcoat pocket. A less discreet man than myself would have arrested him on the spot. I remembered the necessity of catching the two confederates, and the importance of not interfering with the appointment that had been made for the next morning. Such coolness as this, under trying circumstances, is rarely to be found, I should imagine, in a young beginner, whose reputation as a detective policeman is still to make.

From the house of suspicious appearance, Mr Jay betook himself to a cigar-divan, and read the magazines over a cheroot. I sat at a table near him, and read the magazines likewise over a cheroot. From the divan he strolled to the tavern and had his chops. I strolled to the tavern and had my chops. When he had done, he went back to his lodging. When I had done, I went back to mine. He was overcome with drowsiness early in the evening, and went to bed. As soon as I heard him snoring, I was overcome with drowsiness, and went to bed also.

Early in the morning my two subordinates came to make their report.

They had seen the man named 'Jack' leave the woman near the gate of an apparently respectable villa-residence, not far from the

Regent's Park. Left to himself, he took a turning to the right, which led to a sort of suburban street, principally inhabited by shopkeepers. He stopped at the private door of one of the houses, and let himself in with his own key – looking about him as he opened the door, and staring suspiciously at my men as they lounged along on the opposite side of the way. These were all the particulars which the subordinates had to communicate. I kept them in my room to attend on me, if needful, and mounted to my peep-hole to have a look at Mr Jay.

He was occupied in dressing himself, and was taking extraordinary pains to destroy all traces of the natural slovenliness of his appearance. This was precisely what I expected. A vagabond like Mr Jay knows the importance of giving himself a respectable look when he is going to run the risk of changing a stolen bank-note. At five minutes past ten o'clock, he had given the last brush to his shabby hat and the last scouring with bread-crumb to his dirty gloves. At ten minutes past ten he was in the street, on his way to the nearest cab-stand, and I and my subordinates were close on his heels.

He took a cab, and we took a cab. I had not overheard them appoint a place of meeting, when following them in the park on the previous day; but I soon found that we were proceeding in the old direction of the Avenue Road gate.

The cab in which Mr Jay was riding turned into the park slowly. We stopped outside, to avoid exciting suspicion. I got out to follow the cab on foot. Just as I did so, I saw it stop, and detected the two confederates approaching it from among the trees. They got in, and the cab was turned about directly. I ran back to my own cab, and told the driver to let them pass him, and then to follow as before.

The man obeyed my directions, but so clumsily as to excite their suspicions. We had been driving after them about three minutes (returning along the road by which we had advanced) when I looked out of the window to see how far they might be ahead of us. As I did this, I saw two hats popped out of the windows of their cab, and two faces looking back at me. I sank into my place in a cold sweat; the expression is coarse, but no other form of words can describe my condition at that trying moment.

'We are found out!' I said faintly to my two subordinates. They stared at me in astonishment. My feelings changed instantly from the depth of despair to the height of indignation.

'It is the cabman's fault. Get out, one of you,' I said, with dignity – 'get out and punch his head.'

Instead of following my directions (I should wish this act of disobedience to be reported at headquarters) they both looked out of the window. Before I could pull them back, they both sat down again. Before I could express my just indignation, they both grinned, and said to me, 'Please to look out, sir!'

I did look out. The thieves' cab had stopped.

Where?

At a church door!!!

What effect this discovery might have had upon the ordinary run of men, I don't know. Being of a strong religious turn myself, it filled me with horror. I have often read of the unprincipled cunning of criminal persons; but I never before heard of three thieves attempting to double on their pursuers by entering a church! The sacrilegious audacity of that proceeding is, I should think, unparalleled in the annals of crime.

I checked my grinning subordinates by a frown. It was easy to see what was passing in their superficial minds. If I had not been able to look below the surface, I might, on observing two nicely-dressed men and one nicely-dressed woman enter a church before eleven in the morning on a weekday, have come to the same hasty conclusion at which my inferiors had evidently arrived. As it was, appearances had no power to impose on *me*. I got out, and, followed by one of my men, entered the church. The other man I sent round to watch the vestry door. You may catch a weasel asleep – but not your humble servant, Matthew Sharpin!

We stole up the gallery stairs, diverged to the organ loft and peered through the curtains in front. There they were all three, sitting in a pew below – yes, incredible as it may appear, sitting in a pew below!

Before I could determine what to do, a clergyman made his appearance in full canonicals, from the vestry door, followed by a clerk. My brain whirled, and my eyesight grew dim. Dark remembrances of robberies committed in vestries floated through my mind. I trembled for the excellent man in full canonicals – I even trembled for the clerk.

The clergyman placed himself inside the altar rails. The three desperadoes approached him. He opened his book, and began to read. What? – you will ask.

I answer, without the slightest hesitation, the first lines of the Marriage Service.

My subordinate had the audacity to look at me, and then to stuff his pocket-handkerchief into his mouth. I scorned to pay any attention to him. After I had discovered that the man 'Jack' was the bridegroom, and that the man Jay acted the part of father, and gave away the bride, I left the church, followed by my man, and joined the other subordinate outside the vestry door. Some people in my position would now have felt rather crestfallen, and would have begun to think that they had made a very foolish mistake. Not the faintest misgiving of any kind troubled me. I did not feel in the slightest degree depreciated in my own estimation. And even now, after a lapse of three hours, my mind remains I am happy to say, in the same calm and hopeful condition.

As soon as I and my subordinates were assembled together outside the church, I intimated my intention of still following the other cab, in spite of what had occurred. My reason for deciding on this course will appear presently. The two subordinates were astonished at my resolution. One of them had the impertinence to say to me; 'If you please, sir, who is it that we are after? A man who has stolen money, or a man who has stolen a wife?'

The other low person encouraged him by laughing. Both have deserved an official reprimand; and both, I sincerely trust, will be sure to get it.

When the marriage ceremony was over, the three got into their cab; and once more our vehicle (neatly hidden round the corner of the church, so that they could not suspect it to be near them) started to follow theirs.

We traced them to the terminus of the South-Western Railway. The newly-married couple took tickets for Richmond – paying their fare with a half-sovereign, and so depriving me of the pleasure of arresting them, which I should certainly have done, if they had offered a bank-note. They parted from Mr Jay, saying, 'Remember the address – 14 Babylon Terrace. You dine with us tomorrow week.' Mr Jay accepted the invitation, and added, jocosely, that he was going home at once to get off his clean clothes, and to be comfortable and dirty again for the rest of the day. I have to report that I saw him home safely, and that he is comfortable and dirty again (to use his own disgraceful language) at the present moment.

Here the affair rests, having by this time reached what I may call its first stage.

I know very well what persons of hasty judgement will be inclined to say of my proceedings thus far. They will assert that I have been deceiving myself all through, in the most absurd way; they will declare that the suspicious conversations which I have reported, referred solely to the difficulties and dangers of successfully carrying out a runaway match; and they will appeal to the scene in the church as offering undeniable proof of the correctness of their assertions. So let it be. I dispute nothing up to this point. But I ask a question, out of the depths of my own sagacity as a man of the world, which the bitterest of my enemies will not, I think, find it particularly easy to answer.

Granted the fact of the marriage, what proof does it afford me of the innocence of the three persons concerned in that clandestine transaction? It gives me none. On the contrary, it strengthens my suspicions against Mr Jay and his confederates, because it suggests a distinct motive for their stealing the money. A gentleman who is going to spend his honeymoon at Richmond wants money; and a gentleman who is in debt to all his tradespeople wants money. Is this an unjustifiable imputation of bad motives? In the name of outraged morality, I deny it. These men have combined together, and have stolen a woman. Why should they not combine together, and steal a cashbox? I take my stand on the logic of rigid virtue; and I defy all the sophistry of vice to move me an inch out of my position.

Speaking of virtue, I may add that I have put this view of the case to Mr and Mrs Yatman. That accomplished and charming woman found it difficult, at first, to follow the close chain of my reasoning. I am free to confess that she shook her head, and shed tears, and joined her husband in premature lamentation over the loss of the two hundred pounds. But a little careful explanation on my part, and a little attentive listening on hers, ultimately changed her opinion. She now agrees with me, that there is nothing in this unexpected circumstance of the clandestine marriage which absolutely tends to divert suspicion from Mr Jay, or Mr 'Jack', or the runaway lady. 'Audacious hussy' was the term my fair friend used in speaking of her, but let that pass. It is more to the purpose to record that Mrs Yatman has not lost confidence in me and that Mr Yatman promises to follow her example, and do his best to look hopefully for future results.

I have now, in the new turn that circumstances have taken, to await advice from your office. I pause for fresh orders with all the composure of a man who has got two strings to his bow. When I traced the three confederates from the church door to the railway terminus, I had two motives for doing so. First, I followed them as a matter of official business, believing them still to have been guilty of the robbery. Secondly, I followed them as a matter of private speculation, with a view to discovering the place of refuge to which

the runaway couple intended to retreat, and of making my information a marketable commodity to offer to the young lady's family and
friends. Thus, whatever happens, I may congratulate myself beforehand on not having wasted my time. If the office approves of my
conduct, I have my plan ready for further proceedings. If the office
blames me, I shall take myself off, with my marketable information,
to the genteel villa-residence in the neighbourhood of the Regent's
Park. Anyway, the affair puts money into my pocket, and does credit
to my penetration as an uncommonly sharp man.

I have only one word more to add, and it is this: If any individual
ventures to assert that Mr Jay and his confederates are innocent of
all share in the stealing of the cashbox, I, in return, defy that
individual – though he may even be Chief Inspector Theakstone
himself – to tell me who has committed the robbery at Rutherford
Street, Soho.

I have the honour to be,

Your very obedient servant,

MATTHEW SHARPIN

From Chief Inspector Theakstone to Sergeant Bulmer

Birmingham, July 9th

SERGEANT BULMER – That empty-headed puppy, Mr Matthew
Sharpin, has made a mess of the case at Rutherford Street, exactly as
I expected he would. Business keeps me in this town; so I write to
you to set the matter straight. I enclose, with this, the pages of
feeble scribble-scrabble which the creature, Sharpin, calls a report.
Look them over; and when you have made your way through all the
gabble, I think you will agree with me that the conceited booby has
looked for the thief in every direction but the right one. You can lay
your hand on the guilty person in five minutes, now. Settle the case
at once; forward your report to me at this place; and tell Mr Sharpin
that he is suspended till further notice.

Yours,

FRANCIS THEAKSTONE

From Sergeant Bulmer to Chief Inspector Theakstone

London, July 10th

INSPECTOR THEAKSTONE – Your letter and enclosure came safe to
hand. Wise men, they say, may always learn something, even from a
fool. By the time I had got through Sharpin's maundering report of
his own folly, I saw my way clear enough to the end of the

Rutherford Street case, just as you thought I should. In half an hour's time I was at the house. The first person I saw there was Mr Sharpin himself.

'Have you come to help me?' says he.

'Not exactly,' says I. 'I've come to tell you that you are suspended till further notice.'

'Very good,' says he, not taken down, by so much as a single peg, in his own estimation. 'I thought you would be jealous of me. It's very natural; and I don't blame you. Walk in, pray, and make yourself at home. I'm off to do a little detective business on my own account, in the neighbourhood of the Regent's Park. Ta-ta, sergeant, ta-ta!'

With those words he took himself out of the way – which was exactly what I wanted him to do.

As soon as the maidservant had shut the door, I told her to inform her master that I wanted to say a word to him in private. She showed me into the parlour behind the shop; and there was Mr Yatman, all alone, reading the newspaper.

'About this matter of the robbery, sir,' says I.

He cut me short, peevishly enough – being naturally a poor, weak, womanish sort of man. 'Yes, yes, I know,' says he. 'You have come to tell me that your wonderfully clever man, who has bored holes in my second-floor partition, has made a mistake, and is off the scent of the scoundrel who has stolen my money

'Yes, sir,' says I. 'That is one of the things I came to tell you. But I have got something else to say, besides that.'

'Can you tell me who the thief is?' says he, more pettish than ever.

'Yes, sir,' says I, 'I think I can.'

He put down the newspaper, and began to look rather anxious and frightened.

'Not my shopman?' says he. 'I hope, for the man's own sake, it's not my shopman.'

'Guess again, sir,' says I.

'That idle slut, the maid?' says he.

'She is idle, sir,' says I, 'and she is also a slut; my first enquiries about her proved as much as that. But she's not the thief.'

'Then in the name of heaven, who is?' says he.

'Will you please to prepare yourself for a very disagreeable surprise, sir?' says I. 'And in case you lose your temper, will you excuse my remarking that I am the stronger man of the two, and that if you allow yourself to lay hands on me, I may unintentionally hurt you, in pure self-defence?'

He turned as pale as ashes, and pushed his chair two or three feet away from me.

'You have asked me to tell you, sir, who has taken your money,' I went on. 'If you insist on my giving you an answer –'

'I do insist,' he said, faintly. 'Who has taken it?'

'Your wife has taken it,' I said very quietly, and very positively at the same time.

He jumped out of the chair as if I had put a knife into him, and struck his fist on the table, so heavily that the wood cracked again.

'Steady, sir,' says I. 'Flying into a passion won't help you to the truth.'

'It's a lie!' says he, with another smack of his fist on the table – 'a base, vile, infamous lie! How dare you – '

He stopped, and fell back into the chair again, looked about him in a bewildered way, and ended by bursting out crying.

'When your better sense comes back to you, sir,' says I, 'I am sure you will be gentleman enough to make an apology for the language you have just used. In the meantime, please to listen, if you can, to a word of explanation. Mr Sharpin has sent in a report to our inspector, of the most irregular and ridiculous kind; setting down, not only all his own foolish doings and sayings, but the doings and sayings of Mrs Yatman as well. In most cases, such a document would have been fit for the wastepaper basket; but, in this particular case, it so happens that Mr Sharpin's budget of nonsense leads to a certain conclusion, which the simpleton of a writer has been quite innocent of suspecting from the beginning to the end. Of that conclusion I am so sure, that I will forfeit my place if it does not turn out that Mrs Yatman has been practising upon the folly and conceit of this young man, and that she has tried to shield herself from discovery by purposely encouraging him to suspect the wrong persons. I tell you that confidently; and I will even go further. I will undertake to give a decided opinion as to why Mrs Yatman took the money, and what she has done with it, or with a part of it. Nobody can look at that lady, sir, without being struck by the great taste and beauty of her dress – '

As I said those last words, the poor man seemed to find his powers of speech again. He cut me short directly, as haughtily as if he had been a duke instead of a stationer.

'Try some other means of justifying your vile calumny against my wife,' says he. 'Her milliner's bill for the past year is on my file of receipted accounts at this moment.'

'Excuse me, sir,' says I, 'but that proves nothing. Milliners, I must tell you, have a certain rascally custom which comes within the daily experience of our office. A married lady who wishes it, can keep two accounts at her dressmaker's; one is the account which her husband sees and pays; the other is the private account, which contains all the extravagant items, and which the wife pays secretly, by instalments, whenever she can. According to our usual experience, these instalments are mostly squeezed out of the housekeeping money. In your case, I suspect no instalments have been paid; proceedings have been threatened; Mrs Yatman, knowing your altered circumstances, has felt herself driven into a corner; and she has paid her private account out of your cashbox.'

'I won't believe it,' says he. 'Every word you speak is an abominable insult to me and to my wife.'

'Are you man enough, sir,' says I, taking him up short, in order to save time and words, 'to get that receipted bill you spoke of just now off the file, and come with me at once to the milliner's shop where Mrs Yatman deals?'

He turned red in the face at that, got the bill directly, and put on his hat. I took out of my pocketbook the list containing the numbers of the lost notes, and we left the house together immediately.

Arrived at the milliner's (one of the expensive West-end houses, as I expected), I asked for a private interview, on important business, with the mistress of the concern. It was not the first time that she and I had met over the same delicate investigation. The moment she set eyes on me, she sent for her husband. I mentioned who Mr Yatman was, and what we wanted.

'This is strictly private?' enquires her husband. I nodded my head.

'And confidential?' says the wife. I nodded again.

'Do you see any objection, dear, to obliging the sergeant with a sight of the books?' says the husband.

'None in the world, love, if you approve of it,' says the wife.

All this while poor Mr Yatman sat looking the picture of astonishment and distress, quite out of place at our polite conference. The books were brought – and one minute's look at the pages in which Mrs Yatman's name figured was enough, and more than enough, to prove the truth of every word I had spoken.

There, in one book, was the husband's account, which Mr Yatman had settled. And there, in the other, was the private account, crossed off also; the date of settlement being the very day after the loss of the cashbox. This said private account amounted to the sum of a hundred and seventy-five pounds, odd shillings; and it extended over a period of three years. Not a single instalment had been paid on it. Under the last line was an entry to this effect: 'Written to for the third time, June 23rd.' I pointed to it, and asked the milliner if that meant 'last June'. Yes, it did mean last June; and she now deeply regretted to say that it had been accompanied by a threat of legal proceedings.

'I thought you gave good customers more than three years credit?' says I.

The milliner looks at Mr Yatman, and whispers to me – 'Not when a lady's husband gets into difficulties.'

She pointed to the account as she spoke. The entries after the time when Mr Yatman's circumstances became involved were just as extravagant, for a person in his wife's situation, as the entries for the year before that period. If the lady had economised in other things, she had certainly not economised in the matter of dress.

There was nothing left now but to examine the cash-book, for form's sake. The money had been paid in notes, the amounts and numbers of which exactly tallied with the figures set down in my list.

After that, I thought it best to get Mr Yatman out of the house immediately. He was in such a pitiable condition, that I called a cab and accompanied him home in it. At first he cried and raved like a child: but I soon quieted him – and I must add, to his credit, that he made me a most handsome apology for his language, as the cab drew up at his house door. In return, I tried to give him some advice about how to set matters right, for the future, with his wife. He paid very little attention to me, and went upstairs muttering to himself about a separation. Whether Mrs Yatman will come cleverly out of the scrape or not, seems doubtful. I should say, myself, that she will go into screeching hysterics, and so frighten the poor man into forgiving her. But this is no business of ours. So far as we are concerned, the case is now at an end; and the present report may come to a conclusion along with it.

I remain, accordingly, yours to command,

THOMAS BULMER

P.S. I have to add, that, on leaving Rutherford Street, I met Mr Matthew Sharpin coming to pack up his things.

'Only think!' says he, rubbing his hands in great spirits, 'I've been to the genteel villa-residence; and the moment I mentioned my business, they kicked me out directly. There were two witnesses of the assault; and it's worth a hundred pounds to me, if it's worth a farthing.'

'I wish you joy of your luck,' says I.

'Thank you,' says he. 'When may I pay you the same compliment on finding the thief?'

'Whenever you like,' says I, 'for the thief is found.'

'Just what I expected,' says he. 'I've done all the work and now you cut in, and claim all the credit – Mr Jay of course?'

'No,' says I.

'Who is it then?' says he.

'Ask Mrs Yatman,' says I. 'She's waiting to tell you.'

'All right! I'd much rather hear it from that charming woman than from you,' says he, and goes into the house in a mighty hurry.

What do you think of that, Inspector Theakstone? Would you like to stand in Mr Sharpin's shoes? I shouldn't, I can promise you!

From Chief Inspector Theakstone to Mr Matthew Sharpin

July 12th

SIR – Sergeant Bulmer has already told you to consider yourself suspended until further notice. I have now authority to add that your services as a member of the Detective Police are positively declined. You will please to take this letter as notifying officially your dismissal from the force.

I may inform you, privately, that your rejection is not intended to cast any reflection on your character. It merely implies that you are not quite sharp enough for our purpose. If we *are* to have a new recruit among us, we should infinitely prefer Mrs Yatman.

Your obedient servant,

FRANCIS THEAKSTONE

Note on the preceding correspondence, added by Mr Theakstone: The Inspector is not in a position to append any explanations of importance to the last of the letters. It has been discovered that Mr Matthew Sharpin left the house in Rutherford Street five minutes after his interview outside of it with Sergeant Bulmer – his manner expressing the liveliest emotions of terror and astonishment, and his left cheek displaying a bright patch of red, which might have been the result of a slap on the face from a female hand. He was also heard, by the shopman at Rutherford Street, to use a very shocking expression in reference to Mrs Yatman; and was seen to clench his fist vindictively, as he ran round the corner of the street. Nothing more has been heard of him; and it is conjectured that he has left London with the intention of offering his valuable services to the provincial police.

On the interesting domestic subject of Mr and Mrs Yatman still less is known. It has, however, been positively ascertained that the medical attendant of the family was sent for in a great hurry, on the day when Mr Yatman returned from the milliner's shop. The neighbouring chemist received, soon afterwards, a prescription of a soothing nature to make up for Mrs Yatman. The day after, Mr Yatman purchased some smelling-salts at the shop, and afterwards appeared at the circulating library to ask for a novel, descriptive of high life, that would amuse an invalid lady. It has been inferred from these circumstances, that he has not thought it desirable to carry out his threat of separating himself from his wife – at least in the present (presumed) condition of that lady's sensitive nervous system.

The Stolen Cigar-Case

BRETT HARTE

I found Hemlock Jones in the old Brook Street lodgings, musing before the fire. With the freedom of an old friend I at once threw myself in my old familiar attitude at his feet, and gently caressed his boot. I was induced to do this for two reasons: one that it enabled me to get a good look at his bent, concentrated face, and the other that it seemed to indicate my reverence for his superhuman insight. So absorbed was he, even then, in tracking some mysterious clue, that he did not seem to notice me. But therein I was wrong – as I always was in my attempt to understand that powerful intellect.

'It is raining,' he said, without lifting his head.

'You have been out then?' I said quickly.

'No. But I see that your umbrella is wet, and that your overcoat, which you threw off on entering, has drops of water on it.'

I sat aghast at his penetration. After a pause he said carelessly, as if dismissing the subject, 'Besides, I hear the rain on the window. Listen.'

I listened. I could scarcely credit my ears, but there was the soft pattering of drops on the pane. It was evident, there was no deceiving this man!

'Have you been busy lately?' I asked, changing the subject. 'What new problem – given up by Scotland Yard as inscrutable – has occupied that gigantic intellect?'

He drew back his foot slightly, and seemed to hesitate ere he returned it to its original position. Then he answered wearily: 'Mere trifles – nothing to speak of. The Prince Kopoli has been here to get my advice regarding the disappearance of certain rubies from the Kremlin; the Rajah of Pootibad, after vainly beheading his entire bodyguard, has been obliged to seek my assistance to recover a jewelled sword. The Grand Duchess of Pretzel-Brauntswig is desirous of discovering where her husband was on the night of the 14th of February, and last night' – he lowered his voice slightly – 'a lodger in this very house, meeting me on the stairs, wanted to know why they don't answer his bell.'

I could not help smiling – until I saw a frown gathering on his inscrutable forehead.

'Pray to remember,' he said coldly, 'that it was through such an apparently trivial question that I found out why Paul Ferroll killed his wife and what happened to Jones!'

I became dumb at once. He paused for a moment, and then suddenly changing back to his usual pitiless, analytical style, he said: 'When I say these are trifles – they are so in comparison to an affair that is now before me. A crime has been committed, and, singularly enough, against myself. You start,' he said; 'you wonder who would have dared to attempt it! So did I; nevertheless, it has been done. *I* have been *robbed!*'

'*You* robbed – you, Hemlock Jones, the Terror of Peculators!' I gasped in amazement, rising and gripping the table as I faced him.

'Yes; listen. I would confess it to no other. But you who have followed my career; who know my methods; yea, for whom I have partly lifted the veil that conceals my plans from ordinary humanity; you, who have for years rapturously accepted my confidences, passionately admired my inductions and inferences, placed yourself at my beck and call, become my slave, grovelled at my feet, given up your practice except those few unremunerative and rapidly-decreasing patients to whom, in moments of abstraction over my problems, you have administered strychnine for quinine and arsenic for Epsom salts; you, who have sacrificed everything and everybody to me – *you* I make my confidant!'

I rose and embraced him warmly, yet he was already so engrossed in thought that at the same moment he mechanically placed his hand upon his watch chain as if to consult the time. 'Sit down,' he said; 'have a cigar?'

'I have given up cigar smoking,' I said.

'Why?' he asked.

I hesitated, and perhaps coloured. I had really given it up because, with my diminished practice, it was too expensive. I could only afford a pipe. 'I prefer a pipe,' I said laughingly. 'But tell me of this robbery. What have you lost?'

He rose, and, planting himself before the fire with his hands under his coat tails, looked down upon me reflectively for a moment. 'Do you remember the cigar-case presented to me by the Turkish ambassador for discovering the missing favourite of the Grand Vizier in the fifth chorus girl at the Hilarity Theatre? It was that one. It was encrusted with diamonds. I mean the cigar-case.'

'And the largest one had been supplanted by paste,' I said.

'Ah,' he said with a reflective smile, 'you know that.'

'You told me yourself. I remember considering it a proof of your extraordinary perception. But, by Jove, you don't mean to say you have lost it.'

He was silent for a moment. 'No; it has been stolen, it is true, but I shall still find it. And by myself alone! In your profession, my dear fellow, when a member is severely ill he does not prescribe for himself, but calls in a brother doctor. Therein we differ. I shall take this matter in my own hands.'

'And where could you find better?' I said enthusiastically. 'I should say the cigar-case is as good as recovered already.'

'I shall remind you of that again,' he said lightly. 'And now, to show you my confidence in your judgement, in spite of my determination to pursue this alone, I am willing to listen to any suggestions from you.'

He drew a memorandum book from his pocket, and, with a grave smile, took up his pencil.

I could scarcely believe my reason. He, the great Hemlock Jones! accepting suggestions from a humble individual like myself! I kissed his hand reverently and began in a joyous tone:

'First I should advertise offering a reward; I should give the same intimation in handbills, distributed at the pubs and the pastry-cooks. I should next visit the different pawnbrokers; I should give notice at the police station. I should examine the servants. I should thoroughly search the house and my own pockets. I speak rela-tively,' I added with a laugh, 'of course, I mean *your* own.'

He gravely made an entry of these details.

'Perhaps,' I added, 'you have already done this?'

'Perhaps,' he returned enigmatically. 'Now, my dear friend,' he continued, putting the notebook in his pocket, and rising – 'would you excuse me for a few moments? Make yourself perfectly at home until I return; there may be some things,' he added with a sweep of his hand towards his heterogeneously filled shelves, 'that may interest you and while away the time. There are pipes and tobacco in that corner and whisky on the table.' And nodding to me with the same inscrutable face, he left the room. I was too well accustomed to his methods to think much of his unceremonious withdrawal, and made no doubt he was off to investigate some clue which had suddenly occurred to his active intelligence.

Left to myself, I cast a cursory glance over his shelves. There were a number of small glass jars, containing earthy substances, labelled 'Pavement and road sweepings', from the principal thoroughfares and suburbs of London, with the sub-directions 'For identifying foot tracks'. There were several other jars, labelled 'Fluff from omnibus and road-car seats', 'Coconut fibre and rope strands from mattings in public places', 'Cigarette stumps and match ends from floor of Palace Theatre. Row A, 1 to 50'. Everywhere were evidences of this wonderful man's system and perspicacity.

I was thus engaged when I heard the slight creaking of a door, and I looked up as a stranger entered. He was a rough-looking man, with a shabby overcoat, a still more disreputable muffler round his throat, and a cap on his head. Considerably annoyed at his intrusion I turned upon him rather sharply, when, with a mumbled, growling apology for mistaking the room, he shuffled out again and closed the door. I followed him quickly to the landing and saw that he disappeared down the stairs.

With my mind full of the robbery, the incident made a singular impression on me. I knew my friend's habits of hasty absences from his room in his moments of deep inspiration; it was only too probable that with his powerful intellect and magnificent perceptive genius concentrated on one subject, he should be careless of his own belongings, and, no doubt, even forget to take the ordinary precaution of locking up his drawers. I tried one or two and found that I was right – although for some reason I was unable to open one to its fullest extent. The handles were sticky, as if someone had opened them with dirty fingers. Knowing Hemlock's fastidious cleanliness, I resolved to inform him of this circumstance, but I forgot it, alas! until – but I am anticipating my story.

His absence was strangely prolonged. I at last seated myself by the fire, and lulled by warmth and the patter of the rain on the window, I fell asleep. I may have dreamt, for during my sleep I had a vague semi-consciousness as of hands being softly pressed on my pockets – no doubt induced by the story of the robbery. When I came fully to my senses, I found Hemlock Jones sitting on the other side of the hearth, his deeply concentrated gaze fixed on the fire.

'I found you so comfortably asleep that I could not bear to waken you,' he said with a smile.

I rubbed my eyes. 'And what news.' I asked. 'How have you succeeded?'

'Better than I expected,' he said, 'and I think,' he added, tapping his notebook – 'I owe much to *you*.'

Deeply gratified, I awaited more. But in vain. I ought to have remembered that in his moods Hemlock Jones was reticence itself. I told him simply of the strange intrusion, but he only laughed.

Later, when I rose to go, he looked at me playfully. 'If you were a married man,' he said, 'I would advise you not to go home until you had brushed your sleeve. There are a few short, brown sealskin hairs on the inner side of the fore-arm – just where they would have adhered if your arm had encircled a sealskin sacque with some pressure!'

'For once you are at fault,' I said triumphantly; 'the hair is my own as you will perceive; I have just had it cut at the hairdressers, and no doubt this arm projected beyond the apron.'

He frowned slightly, yet nevertheless, on my turning to go, he embraced me warmly – a rare exhibition in that man of ice. He even helped me on with my overcoat and pulled out and smoothed down the flaps of my pockets. He was particular, too, in fitting my arm in my overcoat sleeve, shaking the sleeve down from the armhole to the cuff with his deft fingers. 'Come again soon!' he said, clapping me on the back.

'At any and all times,' I said enthusiastically. 'I only ask ten minutes twice a day to eat a crust at my office and four hours' sleep at night, and the rest of my time is devoted to you always – as you know.'

'It is, indeed,' he said, with his impenetrable smile.

Nevertheless I did not find him at home when I next called. One afternoon, when nearing my own home, I met him in one of his favourite disguises – a long, blue, swallow-tailed coat, striped cotton trousers, large turn-over collar, blacked face and white hat, carrying a tambourine. Of course to others the disguise was perfect, although it was known to myself, and I passed him – according to an old understanding between us – without the slightest recognition, trusting to a later explanation. At another time, as I was making a professional visit to the wife of a publican in the East End, I saw him in the disguise of a broken-down artisan looking into the window of an adjacent pawnshop. I was delighted to see that he was evidently following my suggestions, and in my joy I ventured to tip him a wink; it was abstractedly returned.

Two days later I received a note appointing a meeting at his lodgings that night. That meeting, alas! was the one memorable occurrence of my life, and the last meeting I ever had with Hemlock Jones! I will try to set it down calmly, though my pulses still throb with the recollection of it.

I found him standing before the fire with that look upon his face which I had seen only once or twice in our acquaintance – a look which I may call an absolute concatenation of inductive and deductive ratiocination – from which all that was human, tender or sympathetic was absolutely discharged. He was simply an icy, algebraic symbol! Indeed his whole being was concentrated to that extent that his clothes fitted loosely, and his head was absolutely so much reduced in size by his mental compression that his hat tipped back from his forehead and literally hung on his massive ears.

After I had entered, he locked the doors, fastened the windows, and even placed a chair before the chimney. As I watched those significant precautions with absorbing interest, he suddenly drew a revolver and, presenting it to my temple, said in low icy tones: 'Hand over that cigar-case!'

Even in my bewilderment, my reply was truthful, spontaneous, and involuntary. 'I haven't got it,' I said.

He smiled bitterly, and threw down his revolver. 'I expected that reply! Then let me now confront you with something more awful, more deadly, more relentless and convincing than that mere lethal weapon – the damning inductive and deductive proofs of your guilt!' He drew from his pocket a roll of paper and a notebook.

'But surely,' I gasped, 'you are joking! You could not for a moment believe – '

'Silence!' he roared. 'Sit down!'

I obeyed.

'You have condemned yourself,' he went on pitilessly. 'Condemned yourself on my processes – processes familiar to you, applauded by you, accepted by you for years! We will go back to the time when you first saw the cigar-case. Your expressions,' he said in cold, deliberate tones, consulting his paper, 'were: "How beautiful! I wish it were mine." This was your first step in crime – and my first indication. From "I *wish* it were mine" to "I *will* have it mine", and the mere detail, "How *can* I make it mine?", the advance was obvious. Silence! But as in my methods, it was necessary that there should be an overwhelming inducement to the crime, that unholy admiration of yours for the mere trinket itself was not enough. You are a smoker of cigars.'

'But,' I burst out passionately, 'I told you I had given up smoking cigars.'

'Fool!' he said coldly, 'that is the *second* time you have committed yourself. Of course, you *told* me! What more natural than for you to blazon forth that prepared and unsolicited statement to *prevent* accusation. Yet, as I said before, even that wretched attempt to cover up your tracks was not enough. I still had to find that overwhelming, impelling motive necessary to affect a man like you. That motive I found in *passion*, the strongest of all impulses – love, I suppose you would call it,' he added bitterly; 'that night you called, you had brought the damning proof of it in your sleeve.'

'But – ' I almost screamed.

'Silence,' he thundered. 'I know what you would say. You would say that even if you had embraced some young person in a sealskin sacque what had that to do with the robbery. Let me tell you then, that that sealskin sacque represented the quality and character of your fatal entanglement! If you are at all conversant with light sporting literature you would know that a sealskin sacque indicates a love induced by sordid mercenary interests. You bartered your honour for it – that stolen cigar-case was the purchaser of the sealskin sacque! Without money, with a decreasing practice, it was the only way you could ensure your passion being returned by that young person, whom, for your sake, I have not even pursued. Silence! Having thoroughly established your motive, I now proceed to the commission of the crime itself. Ordinary people would have begun with that – with an attempt to discover the whereabouts of the missing object. These are not my methods.'

So overpowering was his penetration, that although I knew myself innocent, I licked my lips with avidity to hear the further details of this lucid exposition of my crime.

'You committed that theft the night I showed you the cigar-case and after I had carelessly thrown it in that drawer. You were sitting in that chair, and I had risen to take something from that shelf. In that instant you secured your booty without rising. Silence! Do you remember when I helped you on with your overcoat the other night? I was particular about fitting your arm in. While doing so I measured your arm with a spring tape measure from the shoulder to the cuff. A later visit to your tailor confirmed that measurement. It proved to be *the exact distance between your chair and that drawer!*'

I sat stunned.

'The rest are mere corroborative details! You were again tampering with the drawer when I discovered you doing so. Do not start! The stranger that blundered into the room with the muffler on – was myself. More, I had placed a little soap on the drawer handles when I purposely left you alone. The soap was on your hand when I shook it at parting. I softly felt your pockets when you were asleep for further developments. I embraced you when you left – that I might feel if you had the cigar-case, or any other articles, hidden on your body. This confirmed me in the belief that you had already disposed of it in the manner and for the purpose I have shown you. As I still believed you capable of remorse and confession, I allowed you to see I was on your track twice, once in the garb of an itinerant negro minstrel, and the second time as a workman looking in the window of the pawnshop where you pledged your booty.'

'But,' I burst out, 'if you had asked the pawnbroker you would have seen how unjust – '

'Fool! he hissed; 'that was one of *your* suggestions to search the pawnshops. Do you suppose I followed any of your suggestions – the suggestions of the thief? On the contrary, they told me what to avoid.'

'And I suppose,' I said bitterly, 'you have not even searched your drawer.'

'No,' he said calmly.

I was for the first time really vexed. I went to the nearest drawer and pulled it out sharply. It stuck as it had before, leaving a part of the drawer unopened. By working it, however, I discovered that it was impeded by some obstacle that had slipped to the upper part of the drawer and held it firmly fast. Inserting my hand, I pulled out the impeding object. It was the missing cigar-case. I turned to him with a cry of joy.

But I was appalled at his expression. A look of contempt was now added to his acute, penetrating gaze. 'I have been mistaken,' he said slowly. 'I had not allowed for your weakness and cowardice. I thought too highly of you even in your guilt; but I see now why you tampered with that drawer the other night. By some incredible means – possibly another theft – you took the cigar-case out of pawn, and like a whipped hound restored it to me in this feeble, clumsy fashion. You thought to deceive me, Hemlock Jones; more, you thought to destroy my infallibility. Go! I give you your liberty. I shall not summon the three policemen who wait in the adjoining room – but, out of my sight for ever!'

As I stood once more dazed and petrified, he took me firmly by the ear and led me into the hall, closing the door behind him. This re-opened presently wide enough to permit him to thrust out my hat, overcoat, umbrella and overshoes, and then closed against me for ever!

I never saw him again. I am bound to say, however, that thereafter my business increased – I recovered much of my old practice – and a few of my patients recovered also. I became rich. I had a brougham and a house in the West End. But I often wondered, pondering on that wonderful man's penetration and insight, if, in some lapse of consciousness, I had not really stolen his cigar-case!

A Princess's Vengeance

C. L. PIRKIS

'The girl is young, pretty, friendless and a foreigner, you say, and has disappeared as completely as if the earth had opened to receive her,' said Miss Brooke, making a résumé of the facts that Mr Dyer had been relating to her. 'Now, will you tell me why two days were allowed to elapse before the police were communicated with?'

'Mrs Druce, the lady to whom Lucie Cunier acted as amanuensis,' answered Mr Dyer, 'took the matter very calmly at first and said she felt sure that the girl would write to her in a day or so, explaining her extraordinary conduct. Major Druce, her son, the gentleman who came to me this morning, was away from home, on a visit, when the girl took flight. Immediately on his return, however, he communicated the fullest particulars to the police.'

'They do not seem to have taken up the case very heartily at Scotland Yard.'

'No, they have as good as dropped it. They advised Major Druce to place the matter in my hands, saying that they considered it a case for private rather than police investigation.'

'I wonder what made them come to that conclusion.'

'I think I can tell you, although the major seemed quite at a loss on the matter. It seems he had a photograph of the missing girl, which he kept in a drawer of his writing-table. (By the way, I think the young man is a good deal "gone" on this Mlle Cunier, in spite of his engagement to another lady.) Well, this portrait he naturally thought would be most useful in helping to trace the girl, and he went to his drawer for it, intending to take it with him to Scotland Yard. To his astonishment, however, it was nowhere to be seen, and, although he at once instituted a rigorous search, and questioned his mother and the servants, one and all, on the matter, it was all to no purpose.'

Loveday thought for a moment.

'Well, of course,' she said presently, 'that photograph must have been stolen by someone in the house, and, equally, of course, that someone must know more on the matter than he or she cares to

avow, and, most probably, has some interest in throwing obstacles
in the way of tracing the girl. At the same time, however, the fact in
no way disproves the possibility that a crime, and a very black one,
may underlie the girl's disappearance.'

'The major himself appears confident that a crime of some sort
has been committed, and he grew very excited and a little mixed in
his statements more than once just now.'

'What sort of woman is the major's mother?'

'Mrs Druce? She is rather a well-known personage in certain sets.
Her husband died about ten years ago, and since his death she has
posed as promoter and propagandist of all sorts of benevolent,
though occasionally somewhat visionary ideas: theatrical missions,
magic-lantern and playing-cards missions, societies for providing
perpetual music for the sick poor, for supplying cabmen with
comforters, and a hundred other similar schemes have in turn
occupied her attention. Her house is a rendezvous for faddists of
every description. The latest fad, however, seems to have put all
others to flight; it is a scheme for alleviating the condition of "our
sisters in the East", so she puts it in her prospectus; in other words a
Harem Mission on somewhat similar, but I suppose broader lines
than the old-fashioned Zenana Mission. This Harem Mission has
gathered about her a number of Turkish and Egyptian potentates
resident in or visiting London, and has thus incidentally brought
about the engagement of her son, Major Druce, with the Princess
Dullah-Veih. This princess is a beauty and an heiress, and although
of Turkish parentage, has been brought up under European influence in Cairo.'

'Is anything known of the antecedents of Mlle Cunier?'

'Very little. She came to Mrs Druce from a certain Lady Gwynne,
who had brought her to England from an orphanage for the
daughters of jewellers and watchmakers at Echâllets, in Geneva.
Lady Gwynne intended to make her governess to her young
children, but when she saw that the girl's good looks had attracted
her husband's attention, she thought better of it, and suggested to
Mrs Druce that mademoiselle might be useful to her in conducting
her foreign correspondence. Mrs Druce accordingly engaged the
young lady to act as her secretary and amanuensis, and appears, on
the whole, to have taken to the girl, and to have been on a pleasant,
friendly footing with her. I wonder if the Princess Dullah-Veih was
on an equally pleasant footing with her when she saw, as no doubt
she did, the attention she received at the major's hands.' (Mr Dyer
shrugged his shoulders.) 'The major's suspicions do not point in

that direction, in spite of the fact which I elicited from him by judicious questioning, that the princess has a violent and jealous temper, and has at times made his life a burden to him. His suspicions centre solely upon a certain Hafiz Cassimi, son of the Turkish-Egyptian banker of that name. It was at the house of these Cassimis that the major first met the princess, and he states that she and young Cassimi are like brother and sister to each other. He says that this young man has had the run of his mother's house and made himself very much at home in it for the past three weeks, ever since, in fact, the princess came to stay with Mrs Druce, in order to be initiated into the mysteries of English family life. Hafiz Cassimi, according to the major's account, fell desperately in love with the little Swiss girl almost at first sight and pestered her with his attentions, and off and on there appear to have passed hot words between the two young men.'

'One could scarcely expect a princess with Eastern blood in her veins to sit a quiet and passive spectator to such a drama of cross purposes.'

'Scarcely. The major, perhaps, hardly takes the princess sufficiently into his reckoning. According to him, young Cassimi is a thoroughgoing Iago, and he begs me to concentrate attention entirely on him. Cassimi, he says, has stolen the photograph. Cassimi has inveigled the girl out of the house on some pretext – perhaps out of the country also, and he suggests that it might be as well to communicate with the police at Cairo with as little delay as possible.'

'And it hasn't so much as entered his mind that his princess might have a hand in such a plot as that!'

'Apparently not. I think I told you that mademoiselle had taken no luggage – not so much as a handbag – with her. Nothing, beyond her coat and hat, has disappeared from her wardrobe. Her writing-desk, and, in fact, all her boxes and drawers, have been opened and searched, but no letters or papers of any sort have been found that throw any light upon her movements.'

'At what hour in the day is the girl supposed to have left the house?'

'No one can say for certain. It is conjectured that it was sometime in the afternoon of the second of this month – a week ago today. It was one of Mrs Druce's big reception days, and with a stream of people going and coming, a young lady, more or less, leaving the house would scarcely be noticed.'

'I suppose,' said Loveday, after a moment's pause, 'this Princess

Dullah-Veih has something of a history. One does not often get a Turkish princess in London.'

'Yes, she has a history. She is only remotely connected with the present reigning dynasty in Turkey, and I dare say her princess-ship has been made the most of. All the same, however, she has had an altogether exceptional career for an Oriental lady. She was left an orphan at an early age, and was consigned to the guardianship of the elder Cassimi by her relatives. The Cassimis, both father and son, seem to be very advanced and European in their ideas, and by them she was taken to Cairo for her education. About a year ago they "brought her out" in London, where she made the acquaintance of Major Druce. The young man, by the way, appears to be rather hot-headed in his lovemaking, for within six weeks of his introduction to her their engagement was announced. No doubt it had Mrs Druce's fullest approval, for knowing her son's extravagant habits and his numerous debts, it must have been patent to her that a rich wife was a necessity to him. The marriage, I believe, was to have taken place this season; but taking into consideration the young man's ill-advised attentions to the little Swiss girl, and the fervour he is throwing into the search for her, I should say it was exceedingly doubtful whether – '

'Major Druce, sir, wishes to see you,' said a clerk at that moment, opening the door leading from the outer office.

'Very good; show him in,' said Mr Dyer. Then he turned to Loveday.

'Of course, I have spoken to him about you, and he is very anxious to take you to his mother's reception this afternoon so that you may have a look round and – '

He broke off, having to rise and greet Major Druce who at that moment entered the room.

He was a tall, handsome young fellow of about seven or eight and twenty, 'well turned out' from head to foot, moustache waxed, orchid in buttonhole, light kid gloves and patent-leather boots. There was assuredly nothing in his appearance to substantiate his statement to Mr Dyer that he hadn't slept a wink all night – that, in fact, another twenty-four hours of this terrible suspense would send him into his grave.

Mr Dyer introduced Miss Brooke, and she expressed her sympathy with him on the painful matter that was filling his thoughts.

'It is very good of you, I'm sure,' he replied, in a slow, soft drawl, not unpleasant to listen to. 'My mother receives this afternoon from half-past four to half-past six, and I shall be very glad if you will allow me to introduce you to the inside of our house, and to the very ill-looking set that we have somehow managed to gather about us.'

'The ill-looking set?'

'Yes. Jews, Turks, heretics and infidels – all there. And they're on the increase too, that's the worst of it. Every week a fresh importation from Cairo.'

'Ah, Mrs Druce is a large-hearted, benevolent woman,' interposed Mr Dyer; 'all nationalities gather within her walls.'

'Was your mother a large-hearted, benevolent woman?' said the young man, turning upon him. 'No! well then, thank providence that she wasn't; and admit that you know nothing at all on the matter. Miss Brooke,' he continued turning to Loveday, 'I've brought round my hansom for you; it's nearly half-past four now, and it's a good twenty minutes drive from here to Portland Place. If you're ready, I'm at your service.'

Major Druce's hansom was, like himself, in all respects 'well turned out', and the india-rubber tyres round its wheels allowed an easy flow of conversation to be kept up during the twenty minutes drive from Lynch Court to Portland Place.

The major led off the talk in frank and easy fashion.

'My mother,' he said, 'prides herself on being cosmopolitan in her tastes, and just now we are very cosmopolitan indeed. Even our servants represent diverse nationalities: the butler is French, the two footmen Italians, the maids, I believe, are some of them German, some Irish; and I've no doubt if you penetrated to the kitchen-quarters, you'd find the staff there composed in part of Scandinavians, in part of South Sea Islanders. The other quarters of the globe you will find fully represented in the drawing room.'

Loveday had a direct question to ask.

'Are you certain that Mlle Cunier had no friends in England?' she said.

'Positive. She hadn't a friend in the world outside my mother's four walls, poor child! She told me more than once that she was *seule sur la terre*. He broke off for a moment, as if overcome by a sad memory, then added: 'but I'll put a bullet into him, take my word for it, if she isn't found within another twenty-four hours. Personally I should prefer settling the brute in that fashion to handing him over to the police.'

His face flushed a deep red and there came a sudden flash to his eye but, for all that, his voice was as soft and slow and unemotional as though he were talking of nothing more serious than bringing down a partridge.

There fell a brief pause; then Loveday asked another question.

'Is mademoiselle Catholic or Protestant, can you tell me?'

The major thought for a moment, then replied: ' 'Pon my word, I don't know. She used sometimes to attend a little church in South Savile Street – I've walked with her occasionally to the church door – but I couldn't for the life of me say whether it was a Catholic, Protestant or pagan place of worship. But – but you don't think those confounded priests have – '

'Here, we are in Portland Place,' interrupted Loveday. 'Mrs Druce's rooms are already full, to judge from that long line of carriages!'

'Miss Brooke,' said the major suddenly, bethinking himself of his responsibilities, 'how am I to introduce you? what role will you take up this afternoon? Pose as a faddist of some sort, if you want to win my mother's heart. What do you say to having started a grand scheme for supplying Hottentots and Kaffirs with eye-glasses? My mother would swear eternal friendship with you at once.'

'Don't introduce me at all at first,' answered Loveday. 'Get me into some quiet corner, where I can see without being seen. Later on in the afternoon when I have had time to look round a little, I'll tell you whether it will be necessary to introduce me or not.'

'It will be a mob this afternoon, and no mistake,' said Major Druce, as, side by side, they entered the house. 'Do you hear that fizzing and clucking just behind us? That's Arabic; you'll get it in whiffs between gusts of French and German all the afternoon. The Egyptian contingent seems to be in full force today. I don't see any Choctaw Indians, but no doubt they'll send their representatives later on. Come in at this side door, and we'll work our way round to that big palm. My mother is sure to be at the principal doorway.'

The drawing rooms were packed from end to end, and Major Druce's progress, as he headed Loveday through the crowd, was impeded by hand-shaking and the interchange of civilities with his mother's guests.

Eventually the big palm standing in a Chinese cistern was reached, and there, half screened from view by its graceful branches, he placed a chair for Miss Brooke.

From this quiet nook, as now and again the crowd parted, Loveday could command a fair view of both drawing-rooms.

'Don't attract attention to me by standing at my elbow,' she whispered to the major.

He answered her whisper with another.

'There's the Beast – Iago, I mean,' he said, 'do you see him? He's standing talking to that fair, handsome woman in pale green, with a picture hat. She's Lady Gwynne. And there's my mother, and there's Dolly – the princess, I mean – alone on the sofa. Ah! you can't see her now for the crowd. Yes, I'll go, but if you want me, just nod to me and I shall understand.'

It was easy to see what had brought such a fashionable crowd to Mrs Druce's rooms that afternoon. Every caller, as soon as she had shaken hands with the hostess, passed on to the princess's sofa, and there waited patiently till opportunity presented itself for an introduction to her Eastern highness.

Loveday found it impossible to get more than the merest glimpse of her, and so transferred her attention to Mr Hafiz Cassimi, who had been referred to in such unceremonious language by Major Druce.

He was a swarthy, well-featured man with bold, black eyes, and lips that had the habit of parting now and again, not to smile, but as if for no other purpose than to show a double row of gleaming white teeth. The European dress he wore seemed to accord ill with the man; and Loveday could fancy that those black eyes and that double row of white teeth would have shown to better advantage beneath a turban or a fez cap.

From Cassimi, her eye wandered to Mrs Druce – a tall stout woman, dressed in black velvet, and with hair, mounted high on her head, that had the appearance of being either bleached or powdered. She gave Loveday the impression of being that essentially modern product of modern society – the woman who combines in one person the hard-working philanthropist with the hard-working woman of fashion. As arrivals began to slacken, she left her post near the door and began to make the round of the room. From snatches of talk that came to her where she sat, Loveday could gather that with one hand, as it were, this energetic lady was organising a grand charity concert, and with the other pushing the interests of a big ball that was shortly to be given by the officers of her son's regiment.

It was a hot June day. In spite of closed blinds and open windows, the rooms were stifling to a degree. The butler, a small, dark, slight Frenchman, made his way through the throng to a window at Loveday's right hand, to see if a little more air could be admitted.

Major Druce followed on his heels to Loveday's side.

'Will you come into the next room and have some tea?' he asked; 'I'm sure you must feel nearly suffocated here.' He broke off, then added in a lower tone: 'I hope you have kept your eyes on the Beast. Did you ever in your life see a more repulsive-looking animal?'

Loveday took his questions in their order.

'No tea, thank you,' she said, 'but I shall be glad if you will tell your butler to bring me a glass of water – there he is, at your elbow. Yes, off and on I have been studying Mr Cassimi, and I must admit I do not like his smileless smile.'

The butler brought the water. The major, much to his annoyance was seized upon simultaneously by two ladies, one eager to know if any tidings had been received of Mlle Cunier, the other anxious to learn if a distinguished president for the Harem Mission had been decided upon.

Soon after six the rooms began to thin somewhat, and presentations to the princess ceasing, Loveday was able to get a full view of her.

She presented a striking picture, seated, half-reclining, on a sofa, with two white-robed, dark-skinned Egyptian maidens standing behind it. A more unfortunate sobriquet than 'Dolly' could scarcely have been found by the major for this Oriental beauty, with her olive complexion, her flashing eyes and extravagant richness of attire.

' "Queen of Sheba" would be far more appropriate,' thought Loveday. 'She turns the commonplace sofa into a throne, and, I should say, makes every one of those ladies feel as if she ought to have donned court dress and plumes for the occasion.'

It was difficult for her, from where she sat, to follow the details of the princess's dress. She could only see that a quantity of soft orange-tinted silk was wound about the upper part of her arms and fell from her shoulders like drooping wings, and that here and there jewels flashed out from its folds. Her thick black hair was loosely knotted, and kept in its place by jewelled pins and a bandeau of pearls; and similar bandeaus adorned her slender throat and wrists.

'Are you lost in admiration?' said the major, once more at her elbow, in a slightly sarcastic tone. 'That sort of thing is very taking and effective at first, but after a time – '

He did not finish his sentence but shrugged his shoulders and walked away. Half-past six chimed from a small clock on a bracket. Carriage after carriage was rolling away from the door now, and progress on the stairs was rendered difficult by a descending crowd.

A quarter to seven struck, the last hand-shaking had been gone through, and Mrs Druce, looking hot and tired, had sunk into a chair at the princess's right hand, bending slightly forward to render conversation with her easy.

On the princess's left hand, Lady Gwynne had taken a chair, and sat in converse with Hafiz Cassimi, who stood beside her.

Evidently these four were on very easy and intimate terms with each other. Lady Gwynne had tossed her big picture hat on a chair at her left hand, and was fanning herself with a palm-leaf. Mrs Druce, beckoning to the butler, desired him to bring them some claret-cup from the refreshment-room.

No one seemed to observe Loveday seated still in her nook beside the big palm.

She signalled to the major, who stood looking discontentedly from one of the windows.

'That is a most interesting group,' she said; 'now, if you like, you may introduce me to your mother.'

'Oh, with pleasure – under what name?' he asked.

'Under my own,' she answered, 'and please be very distinct in pronouncing it; raise your voice slightly so that everyone of those persons may hear it. And then, please add my profession, and say I am here at your request to investigate the circumstances connected with Mlle Cunier's disappearance.'

Major Druce looked astounded.

'But – but,' he stammered, 'have you seen anything – found out anything? If not, don't you think it will be better to preserve your incognito a little longer.'

'Don't stop to ask questions,' said Loveday sharply; 'now, this very minute, do what I ask you, or the opportunity will be gone.'

The major, without further demur, escorted Loveday across the room. The conversation between the four intimate friends had now become general and animated, and he had to wait for a minute or so before he could get an opportunity to speak to his mother.

During that minute Loveday stood a little in his rear, with Lady Gwynne and Cassimi at her right hand.

'I want to introduce this lady to you,' said the major, when a pause in the talk gave him his opportunity. 'This is Miss Loveday Brooke, a lady detective, and she is here at my request to investigate the circumstances connected with the disappearance of Mlle Cunier.'

He said the words slowly and distinctly.

'There!' he said to himself complacently, as he ended; 'if I had been reading the lessons in church, I couldn't have been more emphatic.'

A blank silence for a moment fell upon the group, and even the butler, just then entering with the claret-cup, came to a standstill at the door.

Then, simultaneously, a glance flashed from Mrs Druce to Lady Gwynne, from Lady Gwynne to Mrs Druce, and then, also simultaneously, the eyes of both ladies rested, though only for an instant, on the big picture hat lying on the chair.

Lady Gwynne started to her feet and seized her hat, adjusting it without so much as a glance at a mirror.

'I must go at once; this very minute,' she said. 'I promised Charlie I would be back soon after six, and now it is past seven. Mr Cassimi, will you take me down to my carriage?' And with the most hurried of leave-takings to the princess and her hostess, the lady swept out of the room, followed by Mr Cassimi.

The butler still standing at the door drew back to allow the lady to pass, and then, claret-cup and all, followed her out of the room.

Mrs Druce drew a long breath and bowed formally to Loveday. 'I was a little taken by surprise – ' she began.

But here the princess rose suddenly from the sofa.

'Moi, je suis fatiguée,' she said in excellent French to Mrs Druce, and she too swept out of the room, throwing, as she passed, what seemed to Loveday a slightly scornful glance towards the major.

Her two attendants, one carrying her fan, and the other her reclining cushions, followed.

Mrs Druce again turned to Loveday. 'Yes, I confess I was taken a little by surprise,' she said, her manner thawing slightly. 'I am not accustomed to the presence of detectives in my house. But now tell me what do you propose doing; how do you mean to begin your investigations – by going over the house and looking in all the corners, or by cross-questioning the servants? Forgive my asking, but really I am quite at a loss; I haven't the remotest idea how such investigations are generally conducted.'

'I do not propose to do much in the way of investigation tonight,' answered Loveday, as formally as she had been addressed, 'for I have very important business to transact before eight o'clock this evening. I shall ask you to allow me to see Mlle Cunier's room – ten minutes there will be sufficient – after that I do not think I need further trouble you.'

'Certainly; by all means,' answered Mrs Druce, 'you'll find the room exactly as Lucie left it, nothing has been disturbed.'

She turned to the butler, who had by this time returned and stood presenting the claret-cup, and, in French, desired him to summon her maid, and tell her to show Miss Brooke to Mlle Cunier's room.

The ten minutes that Loveday had said would suffice for her survey of this room extended themselves to fifteen, but the extra five minutes assuredly were not expended by her in the investigation of drawers and boxes. The maid, a pleasant, well-spoken young woman, jingled her keys, and opened every lock, and seemed not at all disinclined to enter into the light gossip that Loveday contrived to set going.

She answered freely a variety of questions that Loveday put to her respecting mademoiselle and her general habits, and from mademoiselle, the talk drifted to other members of Mrs Druce's household.

If Loveday had, as she had stated, important business to transact that evening, she certainly set about it in a strange fashion.

After she quitted mademoiselle's room, she went straight out of the house, without leaving a message of any sort for either Mrs or Major Druce. She walked the length of Portland Place in leisurely fashion, and then, having first ascertained that her movements were not being watched, she called a hansom, and desired the man to drive her to Madame Céline's, a fashionable milliner's in Old Bond Street.

At Madame Céline's she spent close upon half an hour giving many and minute directions for the making of a hat, which assuredly, when finished, would compare with nothing in the way of millinery that she had ever before put upon her head.

From Madame Céline's the hansom conveyed her to an undertaker's shop, at the corner of South Savile Street, and here she spent a brief ten minutes in conversation with the undertaker himself in his little back parlour.

From the undertaker's she drove home to her rooms in Gower Street, and then, before she divested herself of hat and coat, she wrote a brief note to Major Druce, requesting him to meet her on the following morning at Eglacé's, the confectioner's in South Savile Street, at nine o'clock punctually.

This note she committed to the charge of the cab-driver, desiring him to deliver it at Portland Place on his way back to his stand.

'They've queer ways of doing things – these people!' said the major, as he opened and read the note. 'Suppose I must keep the appointment, though, confound it, I can't see that she can possibly have found out anything by just sitting still in a corner for a couple of hours! And I'm confident she didn't give that beast Cassimi one quarter the attention she bestowed on other people.'

In spite of his grumbling, however, the major kept his appointment, and nine o'clock the next morning saw him shaking hands with Miss Brooke on Eglacé's doorstep.

'Dismiss your hansom,' she said to him. 'I only want you to come a few doors down the street, to the French Protestant church, to which you have sometimes escorted Mlle Cunier.'

At the church door Loveday paused a moment.

'Before we enter,' she said, 'I want you to promise that whatever you may see going on there – however greatly you may be surprised – you will make no disturbance, not so much as open your lips till we come out.'

The major, not a little bewildered, gave the required promise; and, side by side, the two entered the church.

It was little more than a big room; at the farther end, in the middle of the nave, stood the pulpit, and immediately behind this was a low platform, enclosed by a brass rail.

Behind this brass rail, in black Geneva gown, stood the pastor of the church and before him, on cushions, kneeled two persons, a man and a woman.

These two persons and an old man, the verger, formed the whole of the congregation. The position of the church, amid shops and narrow back-yards, had necessitated the filling in of every one of its windows with stained glass; it was, consequently, so dim that, coming in from the outside glare of sunlight, the major found it difficult to make out what was going on at the farther end.

The verger came forward and offered to show them to a seat. Loveday shook her head – they would be leaving in a minute, she said, and would prefer standing where they were.

The major began to take in the situation.

'Why they're being married!' he said in a loud whisper. 'What on earth have you brought me in here for?'

Loveday laid her finger on her lips and frowned severely at him.

The marriage service came to an end, the pastor extended his black-gowned arms like the wings of a bat and pronounced the benediction; the man and woman rose from their knees and proceeded to follow him into the vestry.

The woman was neatly dressed in a long dove-coloured travelling cloak. She wore a large hat, from which fell a white gossamer veil that completely hid her face from view. The man was small, dark and slight, and as he passed on to the vestry beside his bride, the major at once identified him as his mother's butler.

'Why, that's Lebrun!' he said in a still louder whisper than before. 'Why, in the name of all that's wonderful, have you brought me here to see that fellow married?'

'You'd better come outside if you can't keep quiet,' said Loveday severely and leading the way out of the church as she spoke.

Outside, South Savile Street was busy with early morning traffic.

'Let us go back to Eglacé's,' said Loveday, 'and have some coffee. I will explain to you there all you are wishing to know.'

But before the coffee could be brought to them, the major had asked at least a dozen questions.

Loveday put them all on one side.

'All in good time,' she said. 'You are leaving out the most important question of all. Have you no curiosity to know who was the bride that Lebrun has chosen?'

'I don't suppose it concerns me in the slightest degree,' he answered indifferently; 'but since you wish me to ask the question – Who was she?'

'Lucie Cunier, lately your mother's amanuensis.'

'The — !' cried the major, jumping to his feet and uttering an exclamation that must be indicated by a blank.

'Take it calmly,' said Loveday; 'don't rave. Sit down and I'll tell you all about it. No, it is not the doing of your friend Cassimi, so you need not threaten to put a bullet into him; the girl has married Lebrun of her own free will—no one has forced her into it.'

'Lucie has married Lebrun of her own free will!' he echoed, growing very white and taking the chair which faced Loveday at the little table.

'Will you have sugar?' asked Loveday, stirring the coffee, which the waiter at that moment brought.

'Yes, I repeat,' she presently resumed, 'Lucie has married Lebrun of her own free will, although I conjecture she might not perhaps have been quite so willing to crown his happiness if the Princess Dullah-Veih had not made it greatly to her interest to do so.'

'Dolly made it to her interest to do so?' again echoed the major.

'Do not interrupt me with exclamations; let me tell the story in my own fashion, and then you may ask as many questions as you please. Now, to begin at the beginning, Lucie became engaged to Lebrun within a month of her coming to your mother's house, but she carefully kept the secret from everyone, even from the servants, until about a month ago, when she mentioned the fact in confidence to Mrs Druce in order to defend herself from the charge of having sought to attract your attention. There was nothing surprising in this engagement; they were both lonely and in a foreign land, spoke the same language, and no doubt had many things in common; and although chance has lifted Lucie somewhat out of her station, she really belongs to the same class in life as Lebrun. Their love-making appears to have run along smoothly enough until you came home on leave, and the girl's pretty face attracted your attention. Your evident admiration for her disturbed the equanimity of the princess, who saw your devotion to herself waning; of Lebrun, who fancied

Lucie's manner to him had changed; of your mother, who was anxious that you should make a suitable marriage. Also additional complications arose from the fact that your attentions to the little Swiss girl had drawn Mr Cassimi's notice to her numerous attractions, and there was the danger of you two young men posing as rivals. At this juncture Lady Gwynne, as an intimate friend, and one who had herself suffered a twinge of heartache on mademoiselle's account, was taken into your mother's confidence, and the three ladies in council decided that Lucie, in some fashion, must be got out of the way before you and Mr Cassimi came to an open breach, or you had spoilt your matrimonial prospects.'

Here the major made a slightly impatient movement.

Loveday went on: 'It was the princess who solved the question how this was to he done. Fair Rosamunds are no longer put out of the way by 'a cup of cold poison' – golden guineas do the thing far more easily and innocently. The princess expressed her willingness to bestow a thousand pounds on Lucie on the day that she married Lebrun, and to set her up afterwards as a fashionable milliner in Paris. After this munificent offer, everything else became mere matter of detail. The main thing was to get the damsel out of the way without your being able to trace her – perhaps work on her feelings, and induce her, at the last moment, to throw over Lebrun. Your absence from home, on a three days' visit, gave them the wished-for opportunity. Lady Gwynne took her milliner into her confidence. Madame Céline consented to receive Lucie into her house, seclude her in a room on the upper floor, and at the same time give her an insight into the profession of fashionable milliner. The rest I think you know. Lucie quietly walks out of the house one afternoon, taking no luggage, calling no cab, and thereby cutting off one very obvious means of being traced. Madame Céline receives and hides her – not a difficult feat to accomplish in London, more especially if the one to be hidden is a foreign amanuensis, who is seldom seen out of doors, and who leaves no photograph behind her.'

'I suppose it was Lebrun who had the confounded cheek to go to my drawer and appropriate that photograph. I wish it had been Cassimi – I could have kicked him, but – but it makes one feel rather small to have posed as rival to one's mother's butler.'

'I think you may congratulate yourself that Lebrun did nothing worse than go to your drawer and appropriate that photograph. I never saw a man bestow a more deadly look of hatred than he threw at you yesterday afternoon in your mother's drawing-room; it was that look of hatred that first drew my attention to the man and set me on the track that has ended in the Swiss Protestant church this morning.'

'Ah! let me hear about that – let me have the links in the chain, one by one, as you came upon them,' said the major.

He was still pale – almost as the marble table at which they sat, but his voice had gone back to its normal slow, soft drawl.

'With pleasure. The look that Lebrun threw at you, as he crossed the room to open the window, was link number one. As I saw that look, I said to myself there is someone in that corner whom that man hates with a deadly hatred. Then you came forward to speak to me, and I saw that it was you that the man was ready to murder, if opportunity offered. After this, I scrutinised him closely—not a detail of his features or his dress escaped me, and I noticed, among other things, that on the fourth finger of his left hand, half hidden by a more pretentious ring, was an old fashioned curious-looking silver one. That silver ring was link number two in the chain.'

'Ah, I suppose you asked for that glass of water on purpose to get a closer view of the ring?'

'I did, I found it was a Genevese ring of ancient make, the like of which I had not seen since I was a child and played with one that my old Swiss *bonne* used to wear. Now I must tell you a little bit of Genevese history before I can make you understand how important a link that silver ring was to me. Echâllets, the town in which Lucie was born and where her father had kept a watchmaker's shop, has long been famous for its jewellery and watchmaking. The two trades, however, were not combined in one until about a hundred years ago, when the corporation of the town passed a law decreeing that they should unite in one guild for their common good. To celebrate this amalgamation of interests, the jewellers fabricated a certain number of silver rings, consisting of a plain band of silver, on which two hands, in relief, clasped each other. These rings were distributed among the members of the guild, and as time has gone on they have become scarce and valuable as relics of the past. In certain families, they have been handed down as heirlooms, and have frequently done duty as betrothal rings—the clasped hands no doubt suggesting their suitability for this purpose. Now, when I saw such a ring on Lebrun's finger, I naturally guessed from whom he had received it, and at once classed his interests with those of your mother and the princess, and looked upon him as their possible coadjutor.'

'What made you throw the brute Cassimi altogether out of your reckoning?'

'I did not do so at this stage of events; only, so to speak, marked him as "doubtful" and kept my eye on him. I determined to try an experiment that I have never before attempted in my work. You know what that experiment was. I saw five persons, Mrs Druce, the princess, Lady Gwynne, Mr Cassimi and Lebrun all in the room within a few yards of each other, and I asked you to take them by surprise and announce my name and profession, so that every one of those five persons could hear you,'

'You did. I could not, for the life of me, make out what was your motive for so doing.'

'My motive for so doing was simply, as it were, to raise the sudden cry, "The enemy is upon you," and to set every one of those five persons guarding their weak point – that is, if they had one. I'll draw your attention to what followed. Mr Cassimi remained nonchalant and impassive; your mother and Lady Gwynne exchanged glances, and then both simultaneously threw a nervous look at Lady Gwynne's hat lying on the chair. Now as I had stood waiting to be introduced to Mrs Druce, I had casually read the name of Madame Céline on the lining of the hat and I at once concluded that Madame Céline must be a very weak point indeed – a conclusion that was confirmed when Lady Gwynne hurriedly seized her hat and as hurriedly departed. Then the princess scarcely less abruptly rose and left the room, and Lebrun on the point of entering, quitted it also. When he returned five minutes later, with the claret-cup, he had removed the ring from his finger, so I had now little doubt where his weak point lay.'

'It's wonderful; it's like a fairy tale,' drawled the major. 'Pray, go on.'

'After this,' continued Loveday, 'my work became very simple. I did not care two straws for seeing mademoiselle's room, but I cared very much to have a talk with Mrs Druce's maid. From her I elicited the important fact that Lebrun was leaving very unexpectedly on the following day, and that his boxes were packed and labelled for Paris. After I left your house, I drove to Madame Céline's, and there, as a sort of entrance fee, ordered an elaborate hat. I praised freely the hats they had on view, and while giving minute directions as to the one I required, I extracted the information that Madame Céline had recently taken on a new milliner who had very great artistic skill. Upon this, I asked permission to see this new milliner and give her special instructions concerning my hat. My request was referred to Madame Céline, who appeared much ruffled by it, and informed me that it would be quite useless for me to see this new milliner; she could execute no more orders, as she was leaving the next day for Paris, where she intended opening an establishment on her own account.

Now you see the point at which I had arrived. There was Lebrun and there was this new milliner each leaving for Paris on the same day; it was not unreasonable to suppose that they might start in company, and that before so doing, a little ceremony might be gone through in the Swiss Protestant church that mademoiselle occasionally attended. This conjecture sent me to the undertaker in South Savile Street, who combines with his undertaking the office of verger to the little church. From him I learned that a marriage was to take place at the church at a quarter to nine the next morning and that the names of the contracting parties were Pierre Lebrun and Lucie Cuénin.'

'Cuénin!'

'Yes, that is the girl's real name; it seems Lady Gwynne rechristened her Cunier, because she said the English pronunciation of Cuénin grated on her ear – people would insist upon adding a g after the n. She introduced her to Mrs Druce under the name of Cunier, forgetting, perhaps, the girl's real name, or else thinking it a matter of no importance. This fact, no doubt, considerably lessened Lebrun's fear of detection in procuring his licence and transmitting it to the Swiss pastor. Perhaps you are a little surprised at my knowledge of the facts I related to you at the beginning of our conversation. I got at them through Lebrun this morning. At half-past eight I went down to the church and found him there, waiting for his bride. He grew terribly excited at seeing me, and thought I was going to bring you down on him and upset his wedding arrangements at the last moment. I assured him to the contrary, and his version of the facts I have handed on to you. Should, however, any details of the story seem to you to be lacking, I have no doubt that Mrs Druce or the princess will supply them now that all necessity for secrecy has come to an end.'

The major drew on his gloves; his colour had come back to him; he had resumed his easy suavity of manner.

'I don't think,' he said slowly, 'I'll trouble my mother or the princess; and I shall be glad, if you have the opportunity, if you will make people understand that I only moved in the matter at all out of – of mere kindness to a young and friendless foreigner.'

The Absent-Minded Coterie

ROBERT BARR

Some years ago I enjoyed the unique experience of pursuing a man for one crime, and getting evidence against him of another. He was innocent of the misdemeanour, the proof of which I sought, but was guilty of another most serious offence, yet he and his confederates escaped scot free in circumstances which I now purpose to relate.

You may remember that in Rudyard Kipling's story, *Dedalia Herodsfoot*, the unfortunate woman's husband ran the risk of being arrested as a simple drunkard, at a moment when the blood of murder was upon his boots. The case of Ralph Summertrees was rather the reverse of this. The English authorities were trying to fasten upon him a crime almost as important as murder, while I was collecting evidence which proved him guilty of an action much more momentous than that of drunkenness.

The English authorities have always been good enough, when they recognise my existence at all, to look down upon me with amused condescension. If today you ask Spenser Hale, of Scotland Yard, what he thinks of Eugène Valmont, that complacent man will put on the superior smile which so well becomes him, and if you are a very intimate friend of his, he may draw down the lip of his right eye, as he replies: 'Oh, yes, a very decent fellow, Valmont, but he's a Frenchman,' as if, that said, there was no need of further enquiry.

Myself, I like the English detective very much, and if I were to be in a *mêlée* tomorrow, there is no man I would rather find beside me than Spenser Hale. In any situation where a fist that can fell an ox is desirable, my friend Hale is a useful companion, but for in-tellectuality, mental acumen, finesse – ah, well! I am the most modest of men, and will say nothing.

It would amuse you to see this giant come into my room during an evening, on the bluff pretence that he wishes to smoke a pipe with me. There is the same difference between this good-natured giant and myself as exists between that strong black pipe of his and my delicate cigarette, which I smoke feverishly when he is present, to protect myself from the fumes of his terrible tobacco. I look with delight upon the huge man, who, with an air of the utmost good humour, and a twinkle in his eye as he thinks he is twisting me about his finger, vainly endeavours to obtain a hint regarding whatever case is perplexing him at that moment. I baffle him with the ease with which an active greyhound eludes the pursuit of a heavy mastiff, then at last I say to him with a laugh: 'Come, *mon ami* Hale, tell me all about it, and I will help you if I can.'

Once or twice at the beginning he shook his massive head, and replied the secret was not his. The last time he did this I assured him that what he said was quite correct, and then I related full particulars of the situation in which he found himself, excepting the names, for these he had not mentioned. I had pieced together his perplexity from scraps of conversation in his half-hour's fishing for my advice, which, of course, he could have had for the plain asking. Since that time he has not come to me except with cases he feels at liberty to reveal, and one or two complications I have happily been enabled to unravel for him.

But, staunch as Spenser Hale holds the belief that no detective service on earth can excel that centring on Scotland Yard, there is one department of activity in which even he confesses that Frenchmen are his masters, although he somewhat grudgingly qualifies his admission by adding that we in France are constantly allowed to do what is prohibited in England. I refer to the minute search of a house during the owner's absence. If you read that excellent story entitled *The Purloined Letter*, by Edgar Allan Poe, you will find a record of the kind of thing I mean, which is better than any description I, who have so often taken part in such a search, can set down.

Now, these people among whom I live are proud of their phrase, 'the Englishman's house is his castle', and into that castle even a policeman cannot penetrate without a legal warrant. This may be all very well in theory, but if you are compelled to march up to a man's house blowing a trumpet and rattling a snare drum, you need not be disappointed if you fail to find what you are in search of when all the legal restrictions are complied with. Of course, the English are a very excellent people, a fact to which I am always proud to bear testimony, but it must be admitted that for cold common sense the French are very much their superiors. In Paris, if I wish to obtain an incriminating document, I do not send the possessor a *carte postale* to inform him of my desire, and in this procedure the French people sanely acquiesce. I have known men who, when they go out to spend an evening on the boulevards, toss their bunch of keys to the concierge, saying: 'If you hear the police rummaging about while

I'm away, pray assist them, with an expression of my distinguished consideration.'

I remember while I was a chief detective in the service of the French government being requested to call at a certain hour at the private *hôtel* of the Minister for Foreign Affairs. It was during the time that Bismarck meditated a second attack upon my country, and I am happy to say that I was then instrumental in supplying the Secret Bureau with documents which mollified that iron man's purpose, a fact which I think entitled me to my country's gratitude; not that I ever even hinted such a claim when a succeeding ministry forgot my services. The memory of a republic, as has been said by a greater man than I, is short. However, all that has nothing to do with the incident I am about to relate. I merely mention the crisis to excuse a momentary forgetfulness on my part which in any other country might have been followed by serious results to myself. But in France – ah, we understand those things, and nothing happened.

I am the last person in the world to give myself away, as they say in the great West. I am usually the calm, collected Eugène Valmont whom nothing can perturb, but this was a time of great tension, and I had become absorbed. I was alone with the minister in his private house, and one of the papers he desired was in his bureau at the Ministry for Foreign Affairs; at least, he thought so, and said: 'Ah, it is in my desk at the bureau. How annoying! I must send for it!'

'No, excellency,' I cried, springing up in a self-oblivion the most complete, 'it is here.' Touching the spring of a secret drawer, I opened it, and taking out the document he wished, handed it to him.

It was not until I met his searching look, and saw the faint smile on his lips, that I realised what I had done.

'Valmont,' he said quietly, 'on whose behalf did you search my house?'

'Excellency,' I replied in tones no less agreeable than his own, 'tonight at your orders I pay a domiciliary visit to the mansion of Baron Dumoulaine, who stands high in the estimation of the President of the French Republic. If either of those distinguished gentlemen should learn of my informal call and should ask me in whose interests I made the domiciliary visit, what is it you wish that I should reply?'

'You should reply, Valmont, that you did it in the interests of the Secret Service.'

'I shall not fail to do so, excellency, and in answer to your question just now, I had the honour of searching this mansion in the interests of the Secret Service of France.'

The Minister for Foreign Affairs laughed; a hearty laugh that expressed no resentment.

'I merely wished to compliment you, Valmont, on the efficiency of your search, and the excellence of your memory. This is indeed the document which I thought was left in my office.'

I wonder what Lord Lansdowne would say if Spenser Hale showed an equal familiarity with his private papers! But now that we have returned to our good friend Hale, we must not keep him waiting any longer.

*   *   *

I well remember the November day when I first heard of the Summertrees case, because there hung over London a fog so thick that two or three times I lost my way, and no cab was to be had at any price. The few cabmen then in the streets were leading their animals slowly along, making for their stables. It was one of those depressing London days which filled me with *ennui* and a yearning for my own clear city of Paris, where, if we are ever visited by a slight mist, it is at least clean, white vapour, and not this horrible London mixture saturated with suffocating carbon. The fog was too thick for any passer-by to read the contents bills of the newspapers plastered on the pavement, and as there were probably no races that day the newsboys were shouting what they considered the next most important event – the election of an American president. I bought a paper and thrust it into my pocket. It was late when I reached my flat, and, after dining there, which was an unusual thing for me to do, I put on my slippers, took an easy-chair before the fire, and began to read my evening journal. I was distressed to learn that the eloquent Mr Bryan had been defeated. I knew little about the silver question, but the man's oratorical powers had appealed to me, and my sympathy was aroused because he owned many silver mines, and yet the price of the metal was so low that apparently he could not make a living through the operation of them. But of course, the cry that he was a plutocrat, and a reputed millionaire over and over again, was bound to defeat him in a democracy where the average voter is exceedingly poor and not comfortably well-to-do as is the case with our peasants in France. I always took great interest in the affairs of the huge republic to the west, having been at some pains to inform myself accurately regarding its politics, and although, as my readers know, I seldom quote anything complimentary that is said of me, never-theless, an American client of mine once admitted that he never knew the true inwardness – I think that was the phrase he used – of American politics until he heard me discourse upon them. But then, he added, he had been a very busy man all his life.

I had allowed my paper to slip to the floor, for in very truth the fog was penetrating even into my flat, and it was becoming difficult to read, notwithstanding the electric light. My man came in, and announced that Mr Spenser Hale wished to see me, and, indeed, any night, but especially when there is rain or fog outside, I am more pleased to talk with a friend than to read a newspaper.

'*Mon Dieu*, my dear Monsieur Hale, it is a brave man you are to venture out in such a fog as is abroad tonight.'

'Ah, Monsieur Valmont,' said Hale with pride, 'you cannot raise a fog like this in Paris!'

'No. There you are supreme,' I admitted, rising and saluting my visitor, then offering him a chair.

'I see you are reading the latest news,' he said, indicating my newspaper. 'I am very glad that man Bryan is defeated. Now we shall have better times.'

I waved my hand as I took my chair again. I will discuss many things with Spenser Hale, but not American politics; he does not understand them. It is a common defect of the English to suffer complete ignorance regarding the internal affairs of other countries.

'It is surely an important thing that brought you out on such a night as this. The fog must be very thick in Scotland Yard.'

This delicate shaft of fancy completely missed him, and he answered stolidly: 'It's thick all over London, and, indeed, through-out most of England.'

'Yes, it is,' I agreed, but he did not see that either.

Still a moment later he made a remark which, if it had come from some people I know, might have indicated a glimmer of compre-hension.

'You are a very, very clever man, Monsieur Valmont, so all I need say is that the question which brought me here is the same as that on which the American election was fought. Now, to a countryman, I should be compelled to give further explanation, but to you, monsieur, that will not be necessary.'

There are times when I dislike the crafty smile and partial closing of the eyes which always distinguishes Spenser Hale when he places on the table a problem which he expects will baffle me. If I said he never did baffle me, I would be wrong, of course, for sometimes the utter simplicity of the puzzles which trouble him leads me into an intricate involution entirely unnecessary in the circumstances.

I pressed my finger tips together, and gazed for a few moments at the ceiling. Hale had lit his black pipe, and my silent servant placed at his elbow the whisky and soda, then tiptoed out of the room. As the door closed my eyes came from the ceiling to the level of Hale's expansive countenance.

'Have they eluded you?' I asked quietly.

'Who?'

'The coiners.'

Hale's pipe dropped from his jaw, but he managed to catch it before it reached the floor. Then he took a gulp from the tumbler.

'That was just a lucky shot,' he said.

'*Parfaitement*,' I replied carelessly.

'Now, own up, Valmont, wasn't it?'

I shrugged my shoulders. A man cannot contradict a guest in his own house.

'Oh, stow that!' cried Hale impolitely. He is a trifle prone to strong and even slangy expressions when puzzled. 'Tell me how you guessed it.'

'It is very simple, *mon ami*. The question on which the American election was fought is the price of silver, which is so low that it has ruined Mr Bryan, and threatens to ruin all the farmers of the west who possess silver mines on their farms. Silver troubled America, *ergo* silver troubles Scotland Yard.'

'Very well, the natural inference is that someone has stolen bars of silver. But such a theft happened three months ago, when the metal was being unloaded from a German steamer at Southampton and my dear friend Spenser Hale ran down the thieves very cleverly as they were trying to dissolve the marks off the bars with acid. Now crimes do not run in series, like the numbers in roulette at Monte Carlo. The thieves are men of brains. They say to themselves, What chance is there successfully to steal bars of silver while Mr Hale is at Scotland Yard? Eh, my good friend?'

'Really, Valmont,' said Hale, taking another sip, 'sometimes you almost persuade me that you have reasoning powers.'

'Thanks, comrade. Then it is not a *theft* of silver we have now to deal with. But the American election was fought on the *price* of silver. If silver had been high in cost, there would have been no silver question. So the crime that is bothering you arises through the low price of silver, and this suggests that it must be a case of illicit coinage, for there the low price of the metal comes in. You have, perhaps, found a more subtle illegitimate act going forward than heretofore. Someone is making your shillings and your half-crowns from real silver, instead of from baser metal, and yet there is a large profit which has not hitherto been possible through the high price of silver. With the old conditions you were familiar, but this new element sets at nought all your previous formulae. That is how I reasoned the matter out.'

'Well, Valmont, you have hit it. I'll say that for you; you have hit it. There is a gang of expert coiners who are putting out real silver money, and making a clear shilling on the half-crown. We can find no trace of the coiners, but we know the man who is shoving the stuff.'

'That ought to be sufficient,' I suggested.

'Yes, it should, but it hasn't proved so up to date. Now I came tonight to see if you would do one of your French tricks for us, right on the quiet.'

'What French trick, Monsieur Spenser Hale?' I enquired with some asperity, forgetting for the moment that the man invariably became impolite when he grew excited.

'No offence intended,' said this blundering officer, who really is a good-natured fellow, but always puts his foot in it, and then apologises. 'I want someone to go through a man's house without a search warrant, spot the evidence, let me know, and then we'll rush the place before he has time to hide his tracks.'

'Who is this man, and where does he live?'

'His name is Ralph Summertrees, and he lives in a very natty little bijou residence, as the advertisements call it, situated in no less a fashionable street than Park Lane.'

'I see. What has aroused your suspicions against him?'

'Well, you know, that's an expensive district to live in; it takes a bit of money to do the trick. This Summertrees has no ostensible business, yet every Friday he goes to the United Capital bank in Piccadilly, and deposits a bag of swag, usually all silver coin.'

'Yes, and this money?'

'This money, so far as we can learn, contains a good many of these new pieces which never saw the British Mint.'

'It's not all the new coinage, then?'

'Oh, no, he's a bit too artful for that. You see, a man can go round London, his pockets filled with new coinage five-shilling pieces, buy this, that and the other, and come home with his change in legitimate coins of the realm – half-crowns, florins, shillings, sixpences and all that.'

'I see. Then why don't you nab him one day when his pockets are stuffed with illegitimate five-shilling pieces?'

'That could be done, of course, and I've thought of it, but, you see, we want to land the whole gang. Once we arrested him, without knowing where the money came from, the real coiners would take flight.'

'How do you know he is not the real coiner himself?'

Now poor Hale is as easy to read as a book. He hesitated before answering this question, and looked confused as a culprit caught in some dishonest act.

'You need not be afraid to tell me,' I said soothingly after a pause. 'You have had one of your men in Mr Summertrees's house, and so learned that he is not the coiner. But your man has not succeeded in getting you evidence to incriminate other people.'

'You've about hit it again, Monsieur Valmont. One of my men has been Summertrees' butler for two weeks, but, as you say, he has found no evidence.'

'Is he still butler?'

'Yes.'

'Now tell me how far you have got. You know that Summertrees deposits a bag of coin every Friday in the Piccadilly bank, and I suppose the bank has allowed you to examine one or two of the bags.'

'Yes, sir, they have, but, you see, banks are very difficult to treat with. They don't like detectives bothering round, and whilst they do not stand out against the law, still they never answer any more questions than they're asked, and Mr Summertrees has been a good customer at the United Capital for many years.'

'Haven't you found out where the money comes from?'

'Yes, we have; it is brought there night after night by a man who looks like a respectable city clerk, and he puts it into a large safe, of which he holds the key, this safe being on the ground floor, in the dining-room.'

'Haven't you followed the clerk?'

'Yes. He sleeps in the Park Lane house every night, and goes up in the morning to an old curiosity shop in Tottenham Court Road, where he stays all day, returning with his bag of money in the evening.'

'Why don't you arrest and question him?'

'Well, Monsieur Valmont, there is just the same objection to his arrest as to that of Summertrees himself. We could easily arrest both, but we have not the slightest evidence against either of them, and then, although we put the go-betweens in clink, the worst criminals of the lot would escape.'

'Nothing suspicious about the old curiosity shop?'

'No. It appears to be perfectly regular.'

'This game has been going on under your noses for how long?'

'For about six weeks.'

'Is Summertrees a married man?'

'No.'

'Are there any women servants in the house.'

'No, except that three charwomen come in every morning to do up the rooms.'

'Of what is his household comprised?'

'There is the butler, then the valet, and last, the French cook.'

'Ah,' cried I, 'the French cook! This case interests me. So Summertrees has succeeded in completely disconcerting your man? Has he prevented him going from top to bottom of the house?'

'Oh, no, he has rather assisted him than otherwise. On one occasion he went to the safe, took out the money, had Podgers – that's my chap's name – help him to count it, and then actually sent Podgers to the bank with the bag of coin.'

'And Podgers has been all over the place?'

'Yes.'

'Saw no signs of a coining establishment?'

'No. It is absolutely impossible that any coining can be done there. Besides, as I tell you, that respectable clerk brings him the money.'

'I suppose you want me to take Podgers' position?'

'Well, Monsieur Valmont, to tell you the truth, I would rather you didn't. Podgers has done everything a man can do, but I thought if you got into the house, Podgers assisting, you might go through it night after night at your leisure.'

'I see. That's just a little dangerous in England. I think I should prefer to assure myself the legitimate standing of being the amiable Podgers' successor. You say that Summertrees has no business?'

'Well, sir, not what you might call a business. He is by way of being an author, but I don't count that any business.'

'Oh, an author, is he? When does he do his writing?'

'He locks himself up most of the day in his study.'

'Does he come out for lunch?'

'No; he lights a little spirit lamp inside, Podgers tells me, and makes himself a cup of coffee, which he takes with a sandwich or two.'

'That's rather frugal fare for Park Lane.'

'Yes, Monsieur Valmont, it is, but he makes it up in the evening, when he has a long dinner with all them foreign kickshaws you people like, done by his French cook.'

'Sensible man! Well, Hale, I see I shall look forward with pleasure to making the acquaintance of Mr Summertrees. Is there any restriction on the going and coming of your man Podgers?'

'None in the least. He can get away either night or day.'

'Very good, friend Hale, bring him here tomorrow, as soon as our author locks himself up in his study, or rather, I should say, as soon as the respectable clerk leaves for Tottenham Court Road, which I should guess, as you put it, is about half an hour after his master turns the key of the room in which he writes.'

'You are quite right in that guess, Valmont. How did you hit it?'

'Merely a surmise, Hale. There is a good deal of oddity about that Park Lane house, so it doesn't surprise me in the least that the master gets to work earlier in the morning than the man. I have also a suspicion that Ralph Summertrees knows perfectly well what the estimable Podgers is there for.'

'What makes you think that?'

'I can give no reason except that my opinion of the acuteness of Summertrees has been gradually rising all the while you were speaking, and at the same time my estimate of Podgers' craft has been as steadily declining. However, bring the man here tomorrow, that I may ask him a few questions.'

*　　*　　*

Next day, about eleven o'clock, the ponderous Podgers, hat in hand, followed his chief into my room. His broad, impassive, immobile smooth face gave him rather more the air of a genuine butler than I had expected, and this appearance, of course, was enhanced by his livery. His replies to my questions were those of a well-trained servant who will not say too much unless it is made worth his while. All in all, Podgers exceeded my expectations, and really my friend Hale had some justification for regarding him, as he evidently did, a triumph in his line.

'Sit down, Mr Hale, and you, Podgers.'

The man disregarded my invitation, standing like a statue until his chief made a motion; then he dropped into a chair. The English are great on discipline.

'Now, Mr Hale, I must first congratulate you on the make-up of Podgers. It is excellent. You depend less on artificial assistance than we do in France, and in that I think you are right.'

'Oh, we know a bit over here, Monsieur Valmont,' said Hale, with pardonable pride.

'Now then, Podgers, I want to ask you about this clerk. What time does he arrive in the evening?'

'At prompt six, sir.'

'Does he ring, or let himself in with a latchkey?'

'With a latchkey, sir.'

'How does he carry the money?'

'In a little locked leather satchel, sir, flung over his shoulder.'

'Does he go direct to the dining-room?'

'Yes, sir.'

'Have you seen him unlock the safe and put in the money?'

'Yes, sir.'

'Does the safe unlock with a word or a key?'

'With a key, sir. It's one of the old-fashioned kind.'

'Then the clerk unlocks his leather money bag?'

'Yes, sir.'

'That's three keys used within as many minutes. Are they separate or in a bunch?'

'In a bunch, sir.'

'Did you ever see your master with this bunch of keys?'

'No, sir.'

'You saw him open the safe once, I am told?'

'Yes, sir.'

'Did he use a separate key, or one of a bunch?'

Podgers slowly scratched his head, then said: 'I don't just remember, sir.'

'Ah, Podgers, you are neglecting the big things in that house. Sure you can't remember?'

'No, sir.'

'Once the money is in and the safe locked up, what does the clerk do?'

'Goes to his room, sir.'

'Where is this room?'

'On the third floor, sir.'

'Where do you sleep?'

'On the fourth floor with the rest of the servants, sir.'

'Where does the master sleep?'

'On the second floor, adjoining his study.'

'The house consists of four storeys and a basement, does it?'

'Yes, sir.'

'I have somehow arrived at the suspicion that it is a very narrow house. Is that true?'

'Yes, sir.'

'Does the clerk ever dine with your master?'

'No, sir. The clerk don't eat in the house at all, sir.'

'Does he go away before breakfast?'

'No, sir.'

'No one takes breakfast to his room?'

'No, sir.'

'What times does he leave the house?'

'At ten o'clock, sir.'

'When is breakfast served?'

'At nine o'clock, sir.'

'At what hour does your master retire to his study?'

'At half-past nine, sir.'

'Locks the door on the inside?'

'Yes, sir.'

'Never rings for anything during the day?'

'Not that I know of, sir.'

'What sort of a man is he?'

Here Podgers was on familiar ground, and he rattled off a description minute in every particular.

'What I meant was, Podgers, is he silent, or talkative, or does he get angry? Does he seem furtive, suspicious, anxious, terrorised, calm, excitable, or what?'

'Well, sir, he is by way of being very quiet, never has much to say for hisself; never saw him angry, or excited.'

'Now, Podgers, you've been at Park Lane for a fortnight or more. You are a sharp, alert, observant man. What happens there that strikes you as unusual?'

'Well, I can't exactly say, sir,' replied Podgers, looking rather helplessly from his chief to myself, and back again.

'Your professional duties have often compelled you to enact the part of butler before, otherwise you wouldn't do it so well. Isn't that the case?'

Podgers did not reply, but glanced at his chief. This was evidently a question pertaining to the service, which a subordinate was not allowed to answer. However, Hale said at once: 'Certainly. Podgers has been in dozens of places.'

'Well, Podgers, just call to mind some of the other households where you have been employed, and tell me any particulars in which Mr Summertrees' establishment differs from them.'

Podgers pondered a long time.

'Well, sir, he do stick to writing pretty close.'

'Ah, that's his profession, you see, Podgers. Hard at it from half-past nine till towards seven, I imagine?'

'Yes, sir.'

'Anything else, Podgers? No matter how trivial.'

'Well, sir, he's fond of reading too; leastways, he's fond of newspapers.'

'When does he read?'

'I've never seen him read 'em, sir; indeed, so far as I can tell, I never knew the papers to be opened, but he takes them all in, sir.'

'What, all the morning papers?'

'Yes, sir, and all the evening papers too.'

'Where are the morning papers placed?'

'On the table in his study, sir.'

'And the evening papers?'

'Well, sir, when the evening papers come, the study is locked. They are put on a side table in the dining-room, and he takes them upstairs with him to his study.'

'This has happened every day since you've been there?'

'Yes, sir.'

'You reported that very striking fact to your chief, of course?'

'No, sir, I don't think I did,' said Podgers, confused.

'You should have done so. Mr Hale would have known how to make the most of a point so vital.'

'Oh, come now, Valmont,' interrupted Hale, 'you're chaffing us. Plenty of people take in all the papers!'

'I think not. Even clubs and hotels subscribe to the leading journals only. You said *all*, I think, Podgers?'

'Well, *nearly* all, sir.'

'But which is it? There's a vast difference.'

'He takes a good many, sir.'

'How many?'

'I don't just know, sir.'

'That's easily found out, Valmont,' cried Hale, with some impatience, 'if you think it really important.'

'I think it so important that I'm going back with Podgers myself. You can take me into the house, I suppose, when you return?'

'Oh, yes, sir.'

'Coming back to these newspapers for a moment, Podgers. What is done with them?'

'They are sold to the ragman, sir, once a week.'

'Who takes them from the study?'

'I do, sir.'

'Do they appear to have been read very carefully?'

'Well, no. sir; leastways, some of them seem never to have been opened, or else folded up very carefully again.'

'Did you notice that extracts have been clipped from any of them?'

'No, sir.'

'Does Mr Summertrees keep a scrapbook?'

'Not that I know of, sir.'

'Oh, the case is perfectly plain,' said I, leaning back in my chair, and regarding the puzzled Hale with that cherubic expression of self-satisfaction which I know is so annoying to him.

'*What's* perfectly plain?' he demanded, more gruffly perhaps than etiquette would have sanctioned.

'Summertrees is no coiner, nor is he linked with any band of coiners.'

'What is he, then?'

'Ah, that opens another avenue of enquiry. For all I know to the contrary, he may be the most honest of men. On the surface it would appear that he is a reasonably industrious tradesman in Tottenham Court Road, who is anxious that there should be no visible connection between a plebeian employment and so aristocratic a residence as that in Park Lane.'

At this point Spenser Hale gave expression to one of those rare flashes of reason which are always an astonishment to his friends.

'That is nonsense, Monsieur Valmont,' he said, 'the man who is ashamed of the connection between his business and his house is one who is trying to get into Society, or else the women of his family are trying it, as is usually the case. Now Summertrees has no family. He himself goes nowhere, gives no entertainments, and accepts no invitations. He belongs to no club, therefore to say that that he is ashamed of his connection with the Tottenham Court Road shop is absurd. He is concealing the connection for some other reason that will bear looking into.'

'My dear Hale, the goddess of wisdom herself could not have made a more sensible series of remarks. Now, *mon ami*, do you want my assistance, or have you enough to go on with?'

'Enough to go on with? We have nothing more than we had when I called on you last night.'

'Last night, my dear Hale, you supposed this man was in league with coiners. Today you know he is not.'

'I know you *say* he is not.'

I shrugged my shoulders, and raised my eyebrows, smiling at him.

'It is the same thing, Monsieur Hale.'

'Well, of all the conceited – ' and the good Hale could get no further.

'If you wish my assistance, it is yours.'

'Very good. Not to put too fine a point upon it, I do.'

'In that case, my dear Podgers, you will return to the residence of our friend Summertrees, and get together for me in a bundle all of yesterday's morning and evening papers that were delivered to the house. Can you do that, or are they mixed up in a heap in the coal cellar?'

'I can do it, sir. I have instructions to place each day's papers in a pile by itself in case they should be wanted again. There is always one week's supply in the cellar, and we sell the papers of the week before to the ragman.'

'Excellent. Well, take the risk of abstracting one day's journals, and have them ready for me. I will call upon you at half-past three o'clock exactly, and then I want you to take me upstairs to the clerk's bedroom in the third storey, which I suppose is not locked during the daytime?'

'No, sir, it is not.'

With this the patient Podgers took his departure. Spenser Hale rose when his assistant left.

'Anything further I can do?' he asked.

'Yes; give me the address of the shop in Tottenham Court Road. Do you happen to have about you one of those new five-shilling pieces which you believe to be illegally coined?'

He opened his pocketbook, took out the bit of white metal, and handed it to me.

'I'm going to pass this off before evening,' I said, putting it in my pocket, 'and I hope none of your men will arrest me.'

'That's all right,' laughed Hale as he took his leave.

At half-past three Podgers was waiting for me, and opened the front door as I came up the steps, thus saving me the necessity of ringing. The house seemed strangely quiet. The French cook was evidently down in the basement, and we had probably all the upper part to ourselves, unless Summertrees was in his study, which I doubted. Podgers led me directly upstairs to the clerk's room on the third floor, walking on tiptoe, with an elephantine air of silence and secrecy combined, which struck me as unnecessary.

'I will make an examination of this room,' I said. 'Kindly wait for me down by the door of the study.'

The bedroom proved to be of respectable size when one considers the smallness of the house. The bed was all nicely made up, and there were two chairs in the room, but the usual washstand and swing-mirror were not visible. However, seeing a curtain at the farther end of the room, I drew it aside, and found, as I expected, a fixed lavatory in an alcove of perhaps four feet deep by five in width. As the room was about fifteen feet wide, this left two-thirds of the space unaccounted for. A moment later, I opened a door which exhibited a closet filled with clothes hanging on hooks. This left a space of five feet between the clothes closet and the lavatory. I thought at first that the entrance to the secret stairway must have issued from the lavatory, but on examining the boards closely, I found that although they sounded hollow to the knuckles, they were quite evidently plain matchboarding, and not a concealed door. The entrance to the stairway, therefore, must issue from the clothes closet. The right-hand wall proved similar to the matchboarding of the lavatory as far as the casual eye or touch was concerned, but I saw at once it was a door. The latch turned out to be somewhat ingeniously operated by one of the hooks which held a pair of old trousers. I found that the hook, if pressed upward, allowed the door to swing outward, over the stairhead. Descending to the second floor, a similar latch let me in to a similar clothes closet in the room beneath. The two rooms were identical in size, one directly above the other, the only difference being that the lower room door gave into the study, instead of into the hall, as was the case with the upper chamber.

The study was extremely neat, either not much used, or the abode of a very methodical man. There was nothing on the table except a pile of that morning's papers. I walked to the farther end, turned the key in the lock, and came out upon the astonished Podgers.

'Well, I'm blowed!' exclaimed he.

'Quite so,' I rejoined, 'you've been tiptoeing past an empty room for the last two weeks. Now, if you'll come with me, Podgers, I'll show you how the trick is done.'

When he entered the study, I locked the door once more, and led the assumed butler, still tiptoeing through force of habit, up the stair into the top bedroom, and so out again, leaving everything exactly as we found it. We went down the main stair to the front hall, and there Podgers had my parcel of papers all neatly wrapped up. This bundle I carried to my flat, gave one of my assistants some instructions, and left him at work on the papers.

*   *   *

I took a cab to the foot of Tottenham Court Road, and walked up that street till I came to J. Simpson's old curiosity shop. After gazing at the well-filled windows for some time, I stepped inside, having selected a little iron crucifix displayed behind the pane – the work of some ancient craftsman.

I knew at once from Podgers' description that I was waited upon by the veritable respectable clerk who brought the bag of money each night to Park Lane, and who I was certain was no other than Ralph Summertrees himself.

There was nothing in his manner differing from that of any other quiet salesman. The price of the crucifix proved to be seven-and-six, and I threw down a sovereign to pay for it.

'Do you mind the change being all in silver, sir?' he asked, and I answered without any eagerness, although the question aroused a suspicion that had begun to be allayed: 'Not in the least.'

He gave me half-a-crown, three two-shilling pieces, and four separate shillings, all the coins being well-worn silver of the realm, the undoubted inartistic product of the reputable British Mint. This seemed to dispose of the theory that he was palming off illegitimate money. He asked me if I were interested in any particular branch of antiquity, and I replied that my curiosity was merely general, and exceedingly amateurish, whereupon he invited me to look round. This I proceeded to do, while he resumed the addressing and stamping of some wrapped-up pamphlets which I surmised to be copies of his catalogue.

He made no attempt either to watch me or to press his wares upon me. I selected at random a little inkstand, and asked its price. It was two shillings, he said, whereupon I produced my fraudulent five-shilling piece. He took it, gave me the change without comment, and the last doubt about his connection with coiners flickered from my mind.

At this moment a young man came in, who, I saw at once, was not a customer. He walked briskly to the farther end of the shop, and disappeared behind a partition which had one pane of glass in it that gave an outlook towards the front door.

'Excuse me a moment,' said the shopkeeper, and he followed the young man into the private office.

As I examined the curious heterogeneous collection of things for sale, I heard the clink of coins being poured out on the lid of a desk or an uncovered table, and the murmur of voices floated out to me. I was now near the entrance of the shop, and by a sleight-of-hand trick, keeping the corner of my eye on the glass pane of the private office, I removed the key of the front door without a sound, and took an impression of it in wax, returning the key to its place unobserved. At this moment another young man came in, and walked straight past me into the private office. I heard him say: 'Oh, I beg pardon, Mr Simpson. How are you, Rogers?'

'Hallo, Macpherson,' saluted Rogers, who then came out, bidding good-night to Mr Simpson, and departed whistling down the street, but not before he had repeated his phrase to another young man entering, to whom he gave the name of Tyrrel.

I noted these three names in my mind. Two others came in together, but I was compelled to content myself with memorising their features, for I did not learn their names. These men were evidently collectors, for I heard the rattle of money in every case; yet here was a small shop, doing apparently very little business, for I had been within it for more than half an hour, and yet remained the only customer. If credit were given one collector would certainly have been sufficient, yet five had come in, and had poured their contributions into the pile Summertrees was to take home with him that night.

I determined to secure one of the pamphlets which the man had been addressing. They were piled on a shelf behind the counter, but I had no difficulty in reaching across and taking the one on top, which I slipped into my pocket. When the fifth young man went down the street Summertrees himself emerged, and this time he carried in his hand the well-filled locked leather satchel, with the straps dangling. It was now approaching half-past five, and I saw he was eager to close up and get away.

'Anything else you fancy, sir?' he asked me.

'No, or rather yes and no. You have a very interesting collection here, but it's getting so dark I can hardly see.'

'I close at half-past five, sir.'

'Ah, in that case,' I said, consulting my watch, 'I shall be pleased to call some other time.'

'Thank you, sir,' replied Summertrees quietly, and with that I took my leave.

From the corner of an alley on the other side of the street I saw him put up the shutters with his own hands, then he emerged with overcoat on, and the money satchel slung across his shoulder. He locked the door, tested it with his knuckles, and walked down the street, carrying under one arm the pamphlets he had been addressing. I followed him some distance, saw him drop the pamphlets into the box at the first post office he passed, and walk rapidly towards his house in Park Lane.

When I returned to my flat and called in my assistant, he said: 'After putting to one side the regular advertisements of pills, soap and what not, here is the only one common to all the newspapers, morning and evening alike. The advertisements are not identical, sir, but they have two points of similarity, or perhaps I should say three. They all profess to furnish a cure for absent-mindedness; they all ask that the applicant's chief hobby shall be stated, and they all bear the same address: Dr Willoughby, in Tottenham Court Road.'

'Thank you,' said I, as he placed the scissored advertisements before me.

I read several of the announcements. They were all small, and perhaps that is why I had never noticed one of them in the newspapers, for certainly they were odd enough. Some asked for lists of absent-minded men, with the hobbies of each, and for these lists, prizes of from one shilling to six were offered. In other clippings Dr Willoughby professed to be able to cure absent-mindedness. There were no fees, and no treatment, but a pamphlet would be sent, which, if it did not benefit the receiver, could do no harm. The doctor was unable to meet patients personally, nor could he enter into correspondence with them. The address was the same as that of the old curiosity shop in Tottenham Court Road. At this juncture I pulled the pamphlet from my pocket, and saw it was entitled *Christian Science and Absent Mindedness* by Dr Stamford Willoughby, and at the end of the article was the statement contained in the advertisements, that Dr Willoughby would neither see patients nor hold any correspondence with them.

I drew a sheet of paper towards me, wrote to Dr Willoughby alleging that I was a very absent-minded man, and would be glad of his pamphlet, adding that my special hobby was the collecting of first editions. I then signed myself, 'Alport Webster, Imperial Flats, London, W'.

I may here explain that it is often necessary for me to see people under some other name than the well-known appellation of Eugène Valmont. There are two doors to my flat, and on one of these is painted, 'Eugène Valmont'; on the other there is a receptacle, into which can be slipped a sliding panel bearing any *nom de guerre* I choose. The same device is arranged on the ground floor, where the names of all the occupants of the building appear on the right-hand wall.

I sealed, addressed and stamped my letter, then told my man to put out the name of Alport Webster, and if I did not happen to be in when anyone called upon that mythical person, he was to make an appointment for me.

It was nearly six o'clock next afternoon when the card of Angus

Macpherson was brought in to Mr Alport Webster. I recognised the young man at once as the second who had entered the little shop carrying his tribute to Mr Simpson the day before. He held three volumes under his arm, and spoke in such a pleasant, insinuating sort of way, that I knew at once he was an adept in his profession of canvasser.

'Will you be seated, Mr Macpherson? In what can I serve you?'

He placed the three volumes, backs upward, on my table.

'Are you interested at all in first editions, Mr Webster?'

'It is the one thing I am interested in,' I replied; 'but unfortunately they often run into a lot of money.'

'That is true,' said Macpherson sympathetically, 'and I have here three books, one of which is an exemplification of what you say. This one costs a hundred pounds. The last copy that was sold by auction in London brought a hundred and twenty-three pounds. This next one is forty pounds, and the third ten pounds. At these prices I am certain you could not duplicate three such treasures in any bookshop in Britain.'

I examined them critically, and saw at once that what he said was true. He was still standing on the opposite side of the table.

'Please take a chair, Mr Macpherson. Do you mean to say you go round London with a hundred and fifty pounds worth of goods under your arm in this careless way?'

The young man laughed.

'I run very little risk, Mr Webster. I don't suppose anyone I meet imagines for a moment there is more under my arm than perhaps a trio of volumes I have picked up in the fourpenny box to take home with me.'

I lingered over the volume for which he asked a hundred pounds, then said, looking across at him: 'How came you to be possessed of this book, for instance?'

He turned upon me a fine, open countenance, and answered without hesitation in the frankest possible manner: 'I am not in actual possession of it, Mr Webster. I am by way of being a connoisseur in rare and valuable books myself, although, of course, I have little money with which to indulge in the collection of them. I am acquainted, however, with the lovers of desirable books in different quarters of London. These three volumes, for instance, are from the library of a private gentleman in the West End. I have sold many books to him, and he knows I am trustworthy. He wishes to dispose of them at something under their real value, and has kindly allowed me to conduct the negotiation. I make it my business to find out those who are interested in rare books, and by such trading I add considerably to my income.'

'How, for instance, did you learn that I was a bibliophile?'

Mr Macpherson laughed genially.

'Well, Mr Webster, I must confess that I chanced it. I do that very often. I take a flat like this, and send in my card to the name on the door. If I am invited in, I ask the occupant the question I asked you just now: "Are you interested in rare editions?" If he says no, I simply beg pardon and retire. If he says yes, then I show my wares.'

'I see,' said I, nodding. What a glib young liar he was, with that innocent face of his, and yet my next question brought forth the truth.

'As this is the first time you have called upon me, Mr Macpherson, you have no objection to my making some further enquiry, I suppose. Would you mind telling me the name of the owner of these books in the West End?'

'His name is Mr Ralph Summertrees, of Park Lane.'

'Of Park Lane? Ah, indeed.'

'I shall be glad to leave the books with you, Mr Webster, and if you care to make an appointment with Mr Summertrees, I am sure he will not object to say a word in my favour.'

'Oh, I do not in the least doubt it, and should not think of troubling the gentleman.'

'I was going to tell you,' went on the young man, 'that I have a friend, a capitalist, who, in a way, is my supporter; for, as I said, I have little money of my own. I find it is often inconvenient for people to pay down any considerable sum. When, however, I strike a bargain, my capitalist buys the book, and I make an arrangement with my customer to pay a certain amount each week and so even a large purchase is not felt, as I make the instalments small enough to suit my client.'

'You are employed during the day, I take it?'

'Yes, I am a clerk in the City.'

Again we were in the blissful realms of fiction!

'Suppose I take this book at ten pounds, what instalment should I have to pay each week?'

'Oh, what you like, sir. Would five shillings be too much?'

'I think not.'

'Very well, sir, if you pay me five shillings now, I will leave the book with you, and shall have pleasure in calling this day week for the next instalment.'

I put my hand into my pocket, and drew out two half-crowns, which I passed over to him.

'Do I need to sign any form or undertaking to pay the rest?'

The young man laughed cordially.

'Oh, no, sir, there is no formality necessary. You see, sir, this is largely a labour of love with me, although I don't deny I have my eye on the future. I am getting together what I hope will be a very valuable connection with gentlemen like yourself who are fond of books, and I trust someday that I may be able to resign my place with the insurance company and set up a choice little business of my own, where my knowledge of values in literature will prove useful.'

And then, after making a note in a little book he took from his pocket, he bade me a most graceful goodbye and departed, leaving me cogitating over what it all meant.

Next morning two articles were handed to me. The first came by post and was a pamphlet on *Christian Science and Absent Mindedness*, exactly similar to the one I had taken away from the old curiosity shop; the second was a small key made from my wax impression that would fit the front door of the same shop – a key fashioned by an excellent anarchist friend of mine in an obscure street near Holborn.

That night at ten o'clock I was inside the old curiosity shop, with a small storage battery in my pocket, and a little electric glow lamp at my buttonhole, a most useful instrument for either burglar or detective.

I had expected to find the books of the establishment in a safe, which, if it was similar to the one in Park Lane, I was prepared to open with the false keys in my possession or to take an impression of the keyhole and trust to my anarchist friend for the rest. But to my amazement I discovered all the papers pertaining to the concern in a desk which was not even locked. The books, three in number, were the ordinary day-book, journal and ledger referring to the shop – book-keeping of the older fashion; but in a portfolio lay half a dozen foolscap sheets, headed 'Mr Rogers's List', 'Mr Macpherson's', 'Mr Tyrrel's' – the names I had already learned and three others. These lists contained in the first column, names; in the second column, addresses; in the third, sums of money; and then in the small, square places following were amounts ranging from two-and-sixpence to a pound. At the bottom of Mr Macpherson's list was the name of Alport Webster, Imperial Flats, £10; then in the small, square place, five shillings. These six sheets, each headed by a canvasser's name, were evidently the record of current collections, and the innocence of the whole thing was so apparent that if it were not for my fixed rule never to believe that I am at the bottom of any case until I have come on something suspicious, I would have gone out empty-handed as I came in.

The six sheets were loose in a thin portfolio, but standing on a shelf above the desk were a number of fat volumes, one of which I took down, and saw that it contained similar lists running back several years. I noticed on Mr Macpherson's current list the name of Lord Semptam, an eccentric old nobleman whom I knew slightly. Then turning to the list immediately before the current one the name was still there; I traced it back through list after list until I found the first entry, which was no less than three years previous, and there Lord Semptam was down for a piece of furniture costing fifty pounds, and on that account he had paid a pound a week for more than three years, totalling a hundred and seventy pounds at the least, and instantly the glorious simplicity of the scheme dawned upon me, and I became so interested in the swindle that I lit the gas, fearing my little lamp would be exhausted before my investigation ended, for it promised to be a long one.

In several instances the intended victim proved shrewder than old Simpson had counted upon, and the word 'Settled' had been written on the line carrying the name when the exact number of instalments was paid. But as these shrewd persons dropped out, others took their places, and Simpson's dependence on their absent-mindedness seemed to be justified in nine cases out of ten. His collectors were collecting long after the debt had been paid. In Lord Semptam's case, the payment had evidently become chronic, and the old man was giving away his pound a week to the suave Macpherson two years after his debt had been liquidated.

From the big volume I detached the loose leaf, dated 1893, which recorded Lord Semptam's purchase of a carved table for fifty pounds on which he had been paying a pound a week from that time to the date of which I am writing, which was November 1896. This single document taken from the file of three years previous, was not likely to be missed, as would have been the case if I had selected a current sheet. I nevertheless made a copy of the names and addresses of Macpherson's present clients; then, carefully placing everything exactly as I had found it, I extinguished the gas, and went out of the shop, locking the door behind me. With the 1893 sheet in my pocket I resolved to prepare a pleasant little surprise for my suave friend Macpherson when he called to get his next instalment of five shillings.

Late as was the hour when I reached Trafalgar Square I could not deprive myself of the felicity of calling on Mr Spenser Hale, who I knew was then on duty. He never appeared at his best during office hours, because officialism stiffened his stalwart frame. Mentally he was impressed with the importance of his position, and added to this he was not then allowed to smoke his big, black pipe and terrible tobacco. He received me with the curtness I had been taught to expect when I inflicted myself upon him at his office. He greeted me abruptly with: 'I say, Valmont, how long do you expect to be on this job?'

'What job?' I asked mildly.

'Oh, you know what I mean: the Summertrees affair.'

'Oh, *that*!' I exclaimed, with surprise. 'The Summertrees case is already completed, of course. If I had known you were in a hurry, I should have finished up everything yesterday, but as you and Podgers, and I don't know how many more, have been at it sixteen or seventeen days, if not longer, I thought I might venture to take as many hours, as I am working entirely alone. You said nothing about haste, you know.'

'Oh, come now, Valmont, that's a bit thick. Do you mean to say you have already got evidence against the man?'

'Evidence absolute and complete.'

'Then who are the coiners?'

'My most estimable friend, how often have I told you not to jump at conclusions? I informed you when you first spoke to me about the matter that Summertrees was neither a coiner nor a confederate of coiners. I have secured evidence sufficient to convict him of quite another offence, which is probably unique in the annals of crime. I have penetrated the mystery of the shop, and discovered the reason for all those suspicious actions which quite properly set you on his trail. Now I wish you to come to my flat next Wednesday night at a quarter to six, prepared to make an arrest.'

'I must know who I am to arrest, and on what counts.'

'Quite so, *mon ami* Hale; I did not say you were to make an arrest, but merely warned you to be prepared. If you have time now to listen to the disclosures, I am quite at your service. I promise you there are some original features in the case. If, however, the present moment is inopportune, drop in on me at your convenience, previously telephoning so that you may know whether I am there or not, and thus your valuable time will not be expended purposelessly.'

With this I presented to him my most courteous bow, and although his mystified expression hinted a suspicion that he thought

I was chaffing him, as he would call it, official dignity dissolved somewhat, and he intimated his desire to hear all about it then and there. I had succeeded in arousing my friend Hale's curiosity. He listened to the evidence with perplexed brow, and at last ejaculated he would be blessed.

'This young man,' I said in conclusion, 'will call upon me at six on Wednesday afternoon, to receive his second five shillings. I propose that you, in your uniform, shall be seated there with me to receive him, and I am anxious to study Mr Macpherson's countenance when he realises he has walked in to confront a policeman. If you will then allow me to cross-examine him for a few moments, not after the manner of Scotland Yard, with a warning lest he incriminate himself, but in the free and easy fashion we adopt in Paris, I shall afterwards turn the case over to you to be dealt with at your discretion.'

'You have a wonderful flow of language, Monsieur Valmont,' was the officer's tribute to me. 'I shall be on hand at a quarter to six on Wednesday.'

'Meanwhile,' said I, 'kindly say nothing of this to anyone. We must arrange a complete surprise for Macpherson. That is essential. Please make no move in the matter at all until Wednesday night.'

Spenser Hale, much impressed, nodded acquiescence, and I took a polite leave of him.

The question of lighting is an important one in a room such as mine, and electricity offers a good deal of scope to the ingenious. Of this fact I have taken full advantage. I can manipulate the lighting of my room so that any particular spot is bathed in brilliancy, while the rest of the space remains in comparative gloom, and I arranged the lamps so that the full force of their rays impinged against the door that Wednesday evening, while I sat on one side of the table in semi-darkness and Hale sat on the other with a light beating down on him from above which gave him the odd, sculptured look of a living statue of Justice, stern and triumphant. Anyone entering the room would be first dazzled by the light, and next would see the gigantic form of Hale in the full uniform of his order.

When Angus Macpherson was shown into this room he was quite visibly taken aback, and paused abruptly on the threshold, his gaze riveted on the huge policeman. I think his first purpose was to turn and run, but the door closed behind him, and he doubtless heard, as we all did, the sound of the bolt being thrust in its place, this locking him in.

'I – I beg your pardon,' he stammered, 'I expected to meet Mr Webster.'

As he said this, I pressed the button under my table, and was instantly enshrouded with light. A sickly smile overspread the countenance of Macpherson as he caught sight of me, and he made a very creditable attempt to carry off the situation with nonchalance.

'Oh, there you are, Mr Webster; I did not notice you at first.'

It was a tense moment. I spoke slowly and impressively.

'Sir, perhaps you are not unacquainted with the name of Eugène Valmont.'

He replied brazenly: 'I am sorry to say, sir, I never heard of the gentleman before.'

At this came a most inopportune 'Haw-haw' from that blockhead Spenser Hale, completely spoiling the dramatic situation I had elaborated with such thought and care. It is little wonder the English possess no drama, for they show scant appreciation of the sensational moments in life.

'Haw-haw,' brayed Spenser Hale, and at once reduced the emotional atmosphere to a fog of commonplace. However, what is a man to do? He must handle the tools with which it pleases providence to furnish him. I ignored Hale's untimely laughter.

'Sit down, sir,' I said to Macpherson, and he obeyed.

'You have called on Lord Semptam this week,' I continued sternly.

'Yes, sir.'

'And collected a pound from him?'

'Yes, sir.'

'In October 1893, you sold Lord Semptam a carved antique table for fifty pounds?'

'Quite right, sir.'

'When you were here last week you gave me Ralph Summertrees as the name of a gentleman living in Park Lane. You knew at the time that this man was your employer?'

Macpherson was now looking fixedly at me, and on this occasion made no reply. I went on calmly: 'You also knew that Summertrees, of Park Lane, was identical with Simpson, of Tottenham Court Road?'

'Well, sir,' said Macpherson, 'I don't exactly see what you're driving at, but it's quite usual for a man to carry on a business under an assumed name. There is nothing illegal about that.'

'We will come to the illegality in a moment, Mr Macpherson. You, and Rogers, and Tyrrel, and three others, are confederates of this man Simpson.'

'We are in his employ; yes, sir, but no more confederates than clerks usually are.'

'I think, Mr Macpherson, I have said enough to show you that the game is, what you call, up. You are now in the presence of Mr Spenser Hale, from Scotland Yard, who is waiting to hear your confession.

Here the stupid Hale broke in with his: 'And remember, sir, that anything you say will be – '

'Excuse me, Mr Hale,' I interrupted hastily, 'I shall turn over the case to you in a very few moments, but I ask you to remember our compact, and to leave it for the present entirely in my hands. Now, Mr Macpherson, I want your confession, and I want it at once.'

'Confession? Confederates?' protested Macpherson with admirably simulated surprise. 'I must say you use extraordinary terms, Mr – Mr What did you say the name was?'

'Haw, haw,' roared Hale. 'His name is Monsieur Valmont.'

'I implore you, Mr Hale, to leave this man to me for a very few moments. Now, Macpherson, what have you to say in your defence?'

'Where nothing criminal has been alleged, Monsieur Valmont, I see no necessity for defence. If you wish me to admit that somehow you have acquired a number of details regarding our business, I am perfectly willing to do so, and to subscribe to their accuracy. If you will be good enough to let me know of what you complain, I shall endeavour to make the point clear to you if I can. There has evidently been some misapprehension, but for the life of me, without further explanation, I am as much in a fog as I was on my way coming here, for it is getting a little thick outside.'

Macpherson certainly was conducting himself with great discretion, and presented, quite unconsciously, a much more diplomatic figure than my friend, Spenser Hale, sitting stiffly opposite me. His tone was one of mild expostulation, mitigated by the intimation that all misunderstanding speedily would be cleared away. To outward view he offered a perfect picture of innocence, neither protesting too much nor too little. I had, however, another surprise in store for him, a trump card, as it were, and I played it down on the table.

'There!' I cried with vim, 'have you ever seen that sheet before?'

He glanced at it without offering to take it in his hand.

'Oh, yes,' he said, 'that has been abstracted from our file. It is what I call my visiting list.'

'Come, come, sir,' I cried sternly, 'you refuse to confess, but I warn you we know all about it. You never heard of Dr Willoughby, I suppose?'

'Yes, he is the author of the silly pamphlet on Christian Science.'

'You are in the right, Mr Macpherson; on Christian Science and absent-mindedness.'

'Possibly. I haven't read it for a long while.'

'Have you ever met this learned doctor, Mr Macpherson?'

'Oh, yes. Dr Willoughby is the pen-name of Mr Summertrees. He believes in Christian Science and that sort of thing, and writes about it.'

'Ah, really. We are getting your confession bit by bit, Mr Macpherson. I think it would be better to be quite frank with us.'

'I was just going to make the same suggestion to you, Monsieur Valmont. If you will tell me in a few words exactly what is your charge against either Mr Summertrees or myself, I will know then what to say.'

'We charge you, sir, with obtaining money under false pretences, which is a crime that has landed more than one distinguished financier in prison.'

Spenser Hale shook his fat forefinger at me, and said: 'Tut, tut, Valmont; we mustn't threaten, we mustn't threaten, you know;' but I went on without heeding him.

'Take, for instance, Lord Semptam. You sold him a table for fifty pounds, on the instalment plan. He was to pay a pound a week, and in less than a year the debt was liquidated. But he is an absent-minded man, as all your clients are. That is why you came to me. I had answered the bogus Willoughby's advertisement. And so you kept on collecting and collecting for something more than three years. Now do you understand the charge?'

Mr Macpherson's head during this accusation was held slightly inclined to one side. At first his face was clouded by the most clever imitation of anxious concentration of mind I had ever seen, and this was gradually cleared away by the dawn of awakening perception. When I had finished, an ingratiating smile hovered about his lips.

'Really, you know,' he said, 'that is rather a capital scheme. The absent-minded league, as one might call them. Most ingenious. Summertrees, if he had any sense of humour, which he hasn't, would be rather taken by the idea that his innocent fad for Christian Science had led him to be suspected of obtaining money under false pretences. But, really, there are no pretensions about the matter at all. As I understand it, I simply call and receive the money through the forgetfulness of the persons on my list, but where I think you

would have both Summertrees and myself, if there was anything in
your audacious theory, would be in an indictment for conspiracy.
Still, I quite see how the mistake arises. You have jumped to the
conclusion that we sold nothing to Lord Semptam except that
carved table three years ago. I have pleasure in pointing out to you
that his lordship is a frequent customer of ours, and has had many
things from us at one time or another. Sometimes he is in our debt;
sometimes we are in his. We keep a sort of running contract with
him by which he pays us a pound a week. He and several other
customers deal on the same plan, and in return for an income that
we can count upon, they get the first offer of anything in which they
are supposed to be interested. As I have told you, we call these
sheets in the office our visiting lists, but to make the visiting lists
complete you need what we term our encyclopaedia. We call it that
because it is in so many volumes; a volume for each year, running
back I don't know how long. You will notice little figures here from
time to time above the amount stated on this visiting list. These
figures refer to the pages of the encyclopaedia for the current year,
and on that page is noted the new sale, and the amount of it, as it
might be set down, say, in a ledger.'

'That is a very entertaining explanation, Mr Macpherson. I
suppose this encyclopaedia, as you call it, is in the shop at
Tottenham Court Road.'

'Oh, no, sir. Each volume of the encyclopaedia is self-locking.
These books contain the real secret of our business, and they are kept
in the safe at Mr Summertrees's house in Park Lane. Take Lord
Semptam's account, for instance. You will find in faint figures under
a certain date, 102. If you turn to page 102 of the encyclopaedia for
that year, you will then see a list of what Lord Semptam has bought,
and the prices he was charged for them. It is really a very simple
matter. If you will allow me to use your telephone for a moment, I
will ask Mr Summertrees, who has not yet begun dinner, to bring
with him here the volume for 1893, and, within a quarter of an hour,
you will be perfectly satisfied that everything is quite legitimate.'

I confess that the young man's naturalness and confidence
staggered me, the more so as I saw by the sarcastic smile on Hale's
lips that he did not believe a single word spoken. A portable
telephone stood on the table, and as Macpherson finished his
explanation, he reached over and drew it towards him. Then
Spenser Hale interfered.

'Excuse me,' he said, 'I'll do the telephoning. What is the call
number of Mr Summertrees?'

'140 Hyde Park.'

Hale at once called up Central, and presently was answered from Park Lane. We heard him say: 'Is this the residence of Mr Summertrees? Oh, is that you, Podgers? Is Mr Summertrees in? Very well. This is Hale. I am in Valmont's flat – Imperial Flats – you know. Yes, where you went with me the other day. Very well, go to Mr Summertrees, and say to him that Mr Macpherson wants the encyclopaedia for 1893. Do you get that? Yes, encyclopaedia. Oh, he'll understand what it is. Mr Macpherson. No, don't mention my name at all. Just say Mr Macpherson wants the encyclopaedia for the year 1893, and that you are to bring it. Yes, you may tell him that Mr Macpherson is at Imperial Flats, but don't mention my name at all. Exactly. As soon as he gives you the book, get into a cab, and come here as quickly as possible with it. If Summertrees doesn't want to let the book go, then tell him to come with you. If he won't do that, place him under arrest, and bring both him and the book here. All right. Be as quick as you can; we're waiting.'

Macpherson made no protest against Hale's use of the telephone; he merely sat back in his chair with a resigned expression on his face which, if painted on canvas, might have been entitled 'The Falsely Accused'. When Hale rang off, Macpherson said: 'Of course you know your own business best, but if your man arrests Summertrees, he will make you the laughing-stock of London. There is such a thing as unjustifiable arrest, as well as getting money under false pretences, and Mr Summertrees is not the man to forgive an insult. And then, if you will allow me to say so, the more I think over your absent-minded theory, the more absolutely grotesque it seems, and if the case ever gets into the newspapers, I am sure, Mr Hale, you'll experience an uncomfortable half-hour with your chiefs at Scotland Yard.'

'I'll take the risk of that, thank you,' said Hale stubbornly.

'Am I to consider myself under arrest?' enquired the young man.

'No, sir.'

'Then, if you will pardon me, I shall withdraw. Mr Summertrees will show you everything you wish to see in his books, and can explain his business much more capably than I, because he knows more about it; therefore, gentlemen, I bid you good-night.'

'No, you don't. Not just yet awhile,' exclaimed Hale, rising to his feet simultaneously with the young man.

'Then I am under arrest,' protested Macpherson.

'You're not going to leave this room until Podgers brings that book.'

'Oh, very well,' and he sat down again.

And now, as talking is dry work, I set out something to drink, a box of cigars and a box of cigarettes. Hale mixed his favourite brew, but Macpherson, shunning the wine of his country, contented himself with a glass of plain mineral water, and lit a cigarette. Then he awoke my high regard by saying pleasantly as if nothing had happened: 'While we are waiting, Monsieur Valmont, may I remind you that you owe me five shillings?'

I laughed, took the coin from my pocket, and paid him, where-upon he thanked me.

'Are you connected with Scotland Yard, Monsieur Valmont?' asked Macpherson, with the air of a man trying to make conversation to bridge over a tedious interval; but before I could reply, Hale blurted out: 'Not likely!'

'You have no official standing as a detective, then, Monsieur Valmont?'

'None whatever,' I replied quickly, thus getting in my oar ahead of Hale.

'That is a loss to our country,' pursued this admirable young man, with evident sincerity.

I began to see I could make a good deal of so clever a fellow if he came under my tuition.

'The blunders of our police,' he went on, 'are something de-plorable. If they would but take lessons in strategy, say, from France, their unpleasant duties would be so much more acceptably performed, with much less discomfort to their victims.'

'France,' snorted Hale in derision, 'why, they call a man guilty there until he's proven innocent.'

'Yes, Mr Hale, and the same seems to be the case in Imperial Flats. You have quite made up your mind that Mr Summertrees is guilty, and will not be content until he proves his innocence. I venture to predict that you will hear from him before long in a manner that may astonish you.'

Hale grunted and looked at his watch. The minutes passed very slowly as we sat there smoking, and at last even I began to get uneasy. Macpherson, seeing our anxiety, said that when he came in the fog was almost as thick as it had been the week before, and that there might be some difficulty in getting a cab. Just as he was speaking the door was unlocked from the outside, and Podgers entered, bearing a thick volume in his hand. This he gave to his superior, who turned over its pages in amazement, and then looked at the spine, crying: *Encyclopae-dia of Sport, 1893*! What sort of a joke is this, Mr Macpherson?'

There was a pained look on Mr Macpherson's face as he reached forward and took the book. He said with a sigh: 'If you had allowed me to telephone, Mr Hale, I should have made it perfectly plain to Summertrees what was wanted. I might have known this mistake was liable to occur. There is an increasing demand for out-of-date books of sport, and no doubt Mr Summertrees thought this was what I meant. There is nothing for it but to send your man back to Park Lane and tell Mr Summertrees that what we want is the locked volume of accounts for 1893, which we call the encyclopaedia. Allow me to write an order that will bring it. Oh, I'll show you what I have written before your man takes it,' he said, as Hale stood ready to look over his shoulder.

On my notepaper he dashed off a request such as he had outlined, and handed it to Hale, who read it and gave it to Podgers.

'Take that to Summertrees, and get back as quickly as possible. Have you a cab at the door?'

'Yes, sir.'

'Is it foggy outside?'

'Not so much, sir, as it was an hour ago. No difficulty about the traffic now, sir.'

'Very well, get back as soon as you can.'

Podgers saluted, and left with the book under his arm. Again the door was locked, and again we sat smoking in silence until the stillness was broken by the tinkle of the telephone. Hale put the receiver to his ear.

'Yes, this is Imperial Flats. Yes. Valmont. Oh, yes; Macpherson is here. What? Out of what? Can't hear you. Out of print. What, the encyclopaedia's out of print? Who is that speaking? Dr Willoughby; thanks.'

Macpherson rose as if he would go to the telephone, but instead (and he acted so quietly that I did not notice what he was doing until the thing was done), he picked up the sheet which he called his visiting list, and walking quite without haste, held it in the glowing coals of the fireplace until it disappeared in a flash of flame up the chimney. I sprang to my feet indignant, but too late to make even a motion towards saving the sheet. Macpherson regarded us both with that self-deprecatory smile which had several times lighted up his face.

'How dared you burn that sheet?' I demanded.

'Because, Monsieur Valmont, it did not belong to you; because you do not belong to Scotland Yard; because you stole it; because you had no right to it; and because you have no official standing in this country. If it had been in Mr Hale's possession I should not have dared, as you put it, to destroy the sheet, but as this sheet was abstracted from my master's premises by you, an entirely unauthorised person, whom he would have been justified in shooting dead if he had found you housebreaking and you had resisted him on his discovery, I took the liberty of destroying the document. I have always held that these sheets should not have been kept, for, as has been the case, if they fell under the scrutiny of so intelligent a person as Eugène Valmont, improper inferences might have been drawn. Mr Summertrees, however, persisted in keeping them, but made this concession, that if I ever telegraphed him or telephoned him the word "encyclopaedia", he would at once burn these records, and he, on his part, was to telegraph or telephone to me "the *encyclopaedia* is out of print", whereupon I would know that he had succeeded.

'Now, gentlemen, open this door, which will save me the trouble of forcing it. Either put me formally under arrest, or cease to restrict my liberty. I am very much obliged to Mr Hale for telephoning, and I have made no protest to so gallant a host as Monsieur Valmont is, because of the locked door. However, the farce is now terminated. The proceedings I have sat through were entirely illegal, and if you will pardon me, Mr Hale, they have been a little too French to go down here in old England, or to make a report in the newspapers that would be quite satisfactory to your chiefs. I demand either my formal arrest, or the unlocking of that door.'

In silence I pressed a button, and my man threw open the door. Macpherson walked to the threshold, paused, and looked back at Spenser Hale, who sat there silent as a sphinx.

'Good-evening, Mr Hale.'

There being no reply, he turned to me with the same ingratiating smile: 'Good-evening, Monsieur Eugène Valmont,' he said, 'I shall give myself the pleasure of calling next Wednesday at six for my five shillings.'

The Swedish Match

ANTON CHEKHOV

On the morning of October 6, 1885, a well-dressed young man presented himself at the office of the police superintendent of the second division of the S district, and announced that his employer, a retired cornet of the guards called Mark Ivanovitch Klyauzov, had been murdered. The young man was pale and extremely agitated as he made this announcement. His hands trembled and there was a look of horror in his eyes.

'To whom have I the honour of speaking?' the superintendent asked him.

'Psyekov, Klyauzov's steward. Agricultural and engineering expert.'

The police superintendent, on reaching the spot with Psyekov and the necessary witnesses, found the position as follows.

Masses of people were crowding about the lodge in which Klyauzov lived. The news of the event had flown round the neighbourhood with the rapidity of lightning, and, thanks to its being a holiday, the people were flocking to the lodge from all the neighbouring villages. There was a regular hubbub of talk. Pale and tearful faces were to be seen here and there. The door into Klyauzov's bedroom was found to be locked. The key was in the lock on the inside.

'Evidently the criminals made their way in by the window,' Psyekov observed, as they examined the door.

They went into the garden into which the bedroom window looked. The window had a gloomy, ominous air. It was covered by a faded green curtain. One corner of the curtain was slightly turned back, which made it possible to peep into the bedroom.

'Has any one of you looked in at the window?' enquired the superintendent.

'No, your honour,' said Yefrem, the gardener, a little, grey-haired old man with the face of a veteran non-commissioned officer. 'No one feels like looking when they are shaking in every limb!'

'Ech, Mark Ivanovitch! Mark Ivanovitch!' sighed the superintendent, as he looked at the window. 'I told you that you would come to
a bad end! I told you, poor dear – you wouldn't listen! Dissipation
leads to no good!'

'It's thanks to Yefrem,' said Psyekov. 'We should never have
guessed it but for him. It was he who first thought that something
was wrong. He came to me this morning and said: "Why is it our
master hasn't waked up for so long? He hasn't been out of his
bedroom for a whole week!" When he said that to me I was struck
all of a heap . . . The thought flashed through my mind at once. He
hasn't made an appearance since Saturday of last week, and today's
Sunday. Seven days is no joke!'

'Yes, poor man,' the superintendent sighed again. 'A clever
fellow, well educated, and so good-hearted. There was no one like
him, one may say, in company. But a rake; the kingdom of heaven
be his! I'm not surprised at anything with him! Stepan,' he said,
addressing one of the witnesses, 'ride off this minute to my house
and send Andryushka to the police captain's, let him report to him.
Say Mark Ivanovitch has been murdered. Yes, and run to the
inspector – why should he sit in comfort doing nothing? Let him
come here. And you go yourself as fast as you can to the examining
magistrate, Nikolay Yermolaitch, and tell him to come here. Wait a
bit, I will write him a note.'

The police superintendent stationed watchmen round the lodge,
and went off to the steward's to have tea. Ten minutes later he was
sitting on a stool, carefully nibbling lumps of sugar, and sipping tea
as hot as a red-hot coal.

'There it is! . . . ' he said to Psyekov, 'there it is! . . . a gentleman,
and a well-to-do one, too . . . a favourite of the gods, one may say,
to use Pushkin's expression, and what has he made of it? Nothing!
He gave himself up to drinking and debauchery, and . . . here
now . . . he has been murdered!'

Two hours later the examining magistrate drove up. Nikolay
Yermolaitch Tchubikov (that was the magistrate's name), a tall,
thick-set old man of sixty, had been hard at work for a quarter of a
century. He was known to the whole district as an honest, intelligent, energetic man, devoted to his work. His invariable
companion, assistant and secretary, a tall young man of six and
twenty, called Dyukovsky, arrived on the scene of action with him.

'Is it possible, gentlemen?' Tchubikov began, going into Psyekov's
room and rapidly shaking hands with everyone. 'Is it possible? Mark
Ivanovitch? Murdered? No, it's impossible! Im–poss–i–ble!'

'There it is,' sighed the superintendent.

'Merciful heavens! Why, I saw him only last Friday. At the fair at Tarabankovo! Saving your presence, I drank a glass of vodka with him!'

'There it is,' the superintendent sighed once more.

They heaved sighs, expressed their horror, drank a glass of tea each, and went to the lodge.

'Make way!' the police inspector shouted to the crowd.

On going into the lodge the examining magistrate first of all set to work to inspect the door into the bedroom. The door turned out to be made of deal, painted yellow, and not to have been tampered with. No special traces that might have served as evidence could be found. They proceeded to break open the door.

'I beg you gentlemen who are not concerned to retire,' said the examining magistrate, when, after long banging and cracking, the door yielded to the axe and the chisel. 'I ask this in the interests of the investigation . . . Inspector, admit no one!'

Tchubikov, his assistant and the police superintendent opened the door and hesitatingly, one after the other, walked into the room. The following spectacle met their eyes. In the solitary window stood a big wooden bedstead with an immense feather bed on it. On the rumpled feather bed lay a creased and crumpled quilt. A pillow, in a cotton pillowcase, also much creased, was on the floor. On a little table beside the bed lay a silver watch, and silver coins to the value of twenty kopecks. Some sulphur matches lay there too. Except the bed, the table and a solitary chair, there was no furniture in the room. Looking under the bed, the superintendent saw two dozen empty bottles, an old straw hat and a jar of vodka. Under the table lay one boot, covered with dust. Taking a look round the room, Tchubikov frowned and flushed crimson.

'The blackguards!' he muttered, clenching his fists.

'And where is Mark Ivanovitch?' Dyukovsky asked quietly.

'I beg you not to put your spoke in,' Tchubikov answered roughly. 'Kindly examine the floor. This is the second case in my experience, Yevgraf Kuzmitch,' he added to the police superintendent, dropping his voice. 'In 1870 I had a similar case. But no doubt you remember it . . . The murder of the merchant Portretov. It was just the same. The blackguards murdered him, and dragged the dead body out of the window.

Tchubikov went to the window, drew the curtain aside and cautiously pushed the window. The window opened.

'It opens, so it was not fastened . . . H'm . . . there are traces on the window-sill. Do you see? Here is the trace of a knee . . . Some-one climbed out . . . We shall have to inspect the window thoroughly.'

'There is nothing special to be observed on the floor,' said Dyukovsky. 'No stains, nor scratches. The only thing I have found is a used Swedish match. Here it is. As far as I remember, Mark Ivanovitch didn't smoke; in a general way he used sulphur ones, never Swedish matches. This match may serve as a clue . . . '

'Oh, hold your tongue, please!' cried Tchubikov, with a wave of his hand. 'He keeps on about his match! I can't stand these excitable people! Instead of looking for matches, you had better examine the bed!'

On inspecting the bed, Dyukovsky reported: 'There are no stains of blood or of anything else . . . Nor are there any fresh rents. On the pillow there are traces of teeth. A liquid, having the smell of beer and also the taste of it, has been spilt on the quilt . . . The general appearance of the bed gives grounds for supposing there has been a struggle.'

'I know there was a struggle without your telling me! No one asked you whether there was a struggle. Instead of looking out for a struggle, you had better be . . . '

'One boot is here, the other one is not on the scene.'

'Well, what of that?'

'Why, they must have strangled him while he was taking off his boots. He hadn't time to take the second boot off when . . . '

'He's off again! . . . And how do you know that he was strangled?'

'There are marks of teeth on the pillow. The pillow itself is very much crumpled, and has been flung to a distance of six feet from the bed.'

'He argues, the chatterbox! We had better go into the garden. You had better look in the garden instead of rummaging about here . . . I can do that without your help.'

When they went out into the garden their first task was the inspection of the grass. The grass had been trampled down under the windows. The clump of burdock against the wall under the window turned out to have been trodden on too. Dyukovsky succeeded in finding on it some broken shoots, and a little bit of wadding. On the topmost burrs, some fine threads of dark blue wool were found.

'What was the colour of his last suit?' Dyukovsky asked Psyekov.

'It was yellow, made of canvas.'

'Capital! Then it was they who were in dark blue . . . '

Some of the burrs were cut off and carefully wrapped up in paper. At that moment Artsybashev-Svistakovsky, the police captain, and Tyutyuev, the doctor, arrived. The police captain greeted the others, and at once proceeded to satisfy his curiosity; the doctor, a tall and extremely lean man with sunken eyes, a long nose and a sharp chin, greeting no one and asking no questions, sat down on a stump, heaved a sigh, and said: 'The Serbians are in a turmoil again! I can't make out what they want! Ah, Austria, Austria! It's your doing!'

The inspection of the window from outside yielded absolutely no result; the inspection of the grass and surrounding bushes furnished many valuable clues. Dyukovsky succeeded, for instance, in detecting a long, dark streak in the grass, consisting of stains, and stretching from the window for a good many yards into the garden. The streak ended under one of the lilac bushes in a big, brownish stain. Under the same bush was found a boot, which turned out to be the fellow to the one found in the bedroom.

'This is an old stain of blood,' said Dyukovsky, examining the stain.

At the word 'blood', the doctor got up and lazily took a cursory glance at the stain.

'Yes, it's blood,' he muttered.

'Then he wasn't strangled, since there's blood,' said Tchubikov, looking malignantly at Dyukovsky.

'He was strangled in the bedroom, and here, afraid he would come to, they stabbed him with something sharp. The stain under the bush shows that he lay there for a comparatively long time, while they were trying to find some way of carrying him, or something to carry him on out of the garden.'

'Well, and the boot?'

'That boot bears out my contention that he was murdered while he was taking off his boots before going to bed. He had taken off one boot; the other – that is, this boot – he had only managed to get half off. While he was being dragged and shaken the boot that was only half on came off of itself . . . '

'What powers of deduction! Just look at him!' Tchubikov jeered. 'He brings it all out so pat! And when will you learn not to put your theories forward? You had better take a little of the grass for analysis instead of arguing!'

After making the inspection and taking a plan of the locality, they went off to the steward's to write a report and have lunch. At lunch they talked.

'Watch, money and everything else . . . all untouched,' Tchubikov began the conversation. 'It is as clear as twice two makes four that the murder was committed not for mercenary motives.'

'It was committed by a man of the educated class,' Dyukovsky put in.

'From what do you draw that conclusion?'

'I base it on the Swedish match, which the peasants about here have not learned to use yet. Such matches are only used by landowners and not by all of them. He was murdered, by the way, not by one but by three, at least: two held him while the third strangled him. Klyauzov was strong and the murderers must have known that.'

'What use would his strength be to him, supposing he were asleep?'

'The murderers came upon him as he was taking off his boots. He was taking off his boots, so he was not asleep.'

'It's no good making things up! You had better eat your lunch!'

'To my thinking, your honour,' said Yefrem, the gardener, as he set the samovar on the table, 'this vile deed was the work of no other than Nikolashka.'

'Quite possible,' said Psyekov.

'Who's this Nikolashka?'

'The master's valet, your honour,' answered Yefrem.

'Who else should it be if not he? He's a ruffian, your honour! A drunkard, and such a dissipated fellow! May the queen of heaven never bring the like again! He always used to fetch vodka for the master, he always used to put the master to bed . . . Who should it be if not he? And what's more, I venture to bring to your notice, your honour, he boasted once in the tavern, the rascal, that he would murder his master. It's all on account of Akulka, on account of a woman . . . He had a soldier's wife . . . The master took a fancy to her and got intimate with her, and he . . . was angered by it, to be sure. He's lolling about in the kitchen now, drunk. He's crying . . . making out he is grieving over the master . . .'

'And anyone might be angry over Akulka, certainly,' said Psyekov. 'She is a soldier's wife, a peasant woman, but . . . Mark Ivanovitch might well call her Nana. There is something in her that does suggest Nana . . . fascinating . . .'

'I have seen her . . . I know . . .' said the examining magistrate, blowing his nose in a red handkerchief.

Dyukovsky blushed and dropped his eyes. The police superintendent drummed on his saucer with his fingers. The police captain coughed and rummaged in his portfolio for something. On the doctor alone the mention of Akulka and Nana appeared to produce no impression. Tchubikov ordered Nikolashka to be fetched. Nikolashka, a lanky young man with a long pock-marked nose and a hollow chest, wearing a reefer jacket that had been his master's, came into Psyekov's room and bowed down to the ground before Tchubikov. His face looked sleepy and showed traces of tears. He was drunk and could hardly stand up.

'Where is your master?' Tchubikov asked him.

'He's murdered, your honour.'

As he said this Nikolashka blinked and began to cry.

'We know that he is murdered. But where is he now? Where is his body?'

'They say it was dragged out of the window and buried in the garden.'

'H'm . . . the results of the investigation are already known in the kitchen then . . . That's bad. My good fellow, where were you on the night when your master was killed? On Saturday, that is?'

Nikolashka raised his head, craned his neck, and pondered.

'I can't say, your honour,' he said. 'I was drunk and I don't remember.'

'An alibi!' whispered Dyukovsky, grinning and rubbing his hands.

'Ah! And why is it there's blood under your master's window!'

Nikolashka flung up his head and pondered.

'Think a little quicker,' said the police captain.

'In a minute. That blood's from a trifling matter, your honour. I killed a hen; I cut her throat very simply in the usual way, and she fluttered out of my hands and took and ran off . . . That's what the blood's from.'

Yefrem testified that Nikolashka really did kill a hen every evening and killed it in all sorts of places, and no one had seen the half-killed hen running about the garden, though of course it could not be positively denied that it had done so.

'An alibi,' laughed Dyukovsky, 'and what an idiotic alibi.'

'Have you had relations with Akulka?'

'Yes, I have sinned.'

'And your master carried her off from you?'

'No, not at all. It was this gentleman here, Mr Psyekov, Ivan Mihalitch, who enticed her from me, and the master took her from Ivan Mihalitch. That's how it was.'

Psyekov looked confused and began rubbing his left eye. Dyukovsky fastened his eyes upon him, detected his confusion, and started. He saw on the steward's legs dark blue trousers which he had not previously noticed. The trousers reminded him of the blue threads found on the burdock. Tchubikov in his turn glanced suspiciously at Psyekov.

'You can go!' he said to Nikolashka. 'And now allow me to put one question to you, Mr Psyekov. You were here, of course, on the Saturday of last week?'

'Yes, at ten o'clock I had supper with Mark Ivanovitch.'

'And afterwards?'

Psyekov was confused, and got up from the table.

'Afterwards ... afterwards ... I really don't remember,' he muttered. 'I had drunk a good deal on that occasion ... I can't remember where and when I went to bed ... Why do you all look at me like that? As though I had murdered him!'

'Where did you wake up?'

'I woke up in the servants' kitchen on the stove ... They can all confirm that. How I got on to the stove I can't say ... '

'Don't disturb yourself ... Do you know Akulina?'

'Oh well, not particularly.'

'Did she leave you for Klyauzov?'

'Yes ... Yefrem, bring some more mushrooms! Will you have some tea, Yevgraf Kuzmitch?'

There followed an oppressive, painful silence that lasted for some five minutes. Dyukovsky held his tongue, and kept his piercing eyes on Psyekov's face, which gradually turned pale. The silence was broken by Tchubikov.

'We must go to the big house,' he said, 'and speak to the deceased's sister, Marya Ivanovna. She may give us some evidence.'

Tchubikov and his assistant thanked Psyekov for the lunch, then went off to the big house. They found Klyauzov's sister, a maiden lady of five and forty, on her knees before a high family shrine of icons. When she saw portfolios and caps adorned with cockades in her visitors' hands, she turned pale.

'First of all, I must offer an apology for disturbing your devotions, so to say,' the gallant Tchubikov began, with a scrape. 'We have come to you with a request. You have heard, of course, already ... There is a suspicion that your brother has somehow been murdered. God's will, you know ... Death no one can escape, neither tsar nor ploughman. Can you not assist us with some fact, something that will throw light?'

'Oh, do not ask me!' said Marya Ivanovna, turning whiter still, and hiding her face in her hands. 'I can tell you nothing! Nothing!

I implore you! I can say nothing. . . . What can I do? Oh no, no . . . not a word . . . of my brother! I would rather die than speak!'

Marya Ivanovna burst into tears and went away into another room. The officials looked at each other, shrugged their shoulders and beat a retreat.

'A devil of a woman!' said Dyukovsky, swearing as they went out of the big house. 'Apparently she knows something and is concealing it. And there is something peculiar in the maidservant's expression too . . . You wait a bit, you devils! We will get to the bottom of it all!'

In the evening, Tchubikov and his assistant were driving home by the light of a pale-faced moon; they sat in their wagonette, summing up in their minds the incidents of the day. Both were exhausted and sat silent. Tchubikov never liked talking on the road. In spite of his talkativeness, Dyukovsky held his tongue in deference to the old man.

Towards the end of the journey, however, the young man could endure the silence no longer, and began: 'That Nikolashka has had a hand in the business,' he said, *'non dubitandum est.* One can see from his mug too what sort of a chap he is . . . His alibi gives him away, hand and foot. There is no doubt either that he was not the instigator of the crime. He was only the stupid hired tool. Do you agree? The discreet Psyekov plays a not unimportant part in the affair too. His blue trousers, his embarrassment, his lying on the stove from fright after the murder, his alibi, and Akulka.'

'Keep it up, you're in your glory! According to you, if a man knows Akulka he is the murderer. Ah, you hot-head! You ought to be sucking your bottle instead of investigating cases! You used to be running after Akulka too; does that mean that you had a hand in this business?'

'Akulka was a cook in your house for a month, too, but . . . I don't say anything. On that Saturday night I was playing cards with you, I saw you, or I should be after you too. The woman is not the point, my good sir. The point is the nasty, disgusting, mean feeling . . . The discreet young man did not like to be cut out, do you see. Vanity, do you see . . . He longed to be revenged. Then . . . His thick lips are a strong indication of sensuality. Do you remember how he smacked his lips when he compared Akulka to Nana? That he is burning with passion, the scoundrel, is beyond doubt! And so you have wounded vanity and unsatisfied passion. That's enough to lead to murder. Two of them are in our hands, but who is the third? Nikolashka and Psyekov held him. Who was it smothered him? Psyekov is timid, easily embarrassed, altogether a coward. People like Nikolashka are not equal to smothering with a pillow, they set to work with an axe or a mallet . . . Some third person must have smothered him, but who?'

Dyukovsky pulled his cap over his eyes, and pondered. He was silent till the wagonette had driven up to the examining magistrate's house.

'Eureka!' he said, as he went into the house, and took off his overcoat. 'Eureka, Nikolay Yermolaitch! I can't understand how it is it didn't occur to me before. Do you know who the third is?'

'Do leave off, please! There's supper ready. Sit down to supper!'

Tchubikov and Dyukovsky sat down to supper. Dyukovsky poured himself out a wine-glassful of vodka, got up, stretched, and with sparkling eyes, said: 'Let me tell you then that the third person who collaborated with the scoundrel Psyekov and smothered him was a woman! Yes! I am speaking of the murdered man's sister, Marya Ivanovna!'

Tchubikov coughed over his vodka and fastened his eyes on Dyukovsky.

'Are you . . . not quite right? Is your head . . . not quite right? Does it ache?'

'I am quite well. Very good, suppose I have gone out of my mind, but how do you explain her confusion on our arrival? How do you explain her refusal to give information? Admitting that that is trivial – very good! All right! – but think of the terms they were on! She detested her brother! She is an Old Believer, he was a profligate, a godless fellow . . . that is what has bred hatred between them! They say he succeeded in persuading her that he was an angel of Satan! He used to practise spiritualism in her presence!'

'Well, what then?'

'Don't you understand? She's an Old Believer, she murdered him through fanaticism! She has not merely slain a wicked man, a profligate, she has freed the world from Antichrist – and that she fancies is her merit, her religious achievement! Ah, you don't know these old maids, these Old Believers! You should read Dostoevsky! And what does Lyeskov say . . . and Petchersky! It's she, it's she, I'll stake my life on it. She smothered him! Oh, the fiendish woman! Wasn't she, perhaps, standing before the icons when we went in to put us off the scent? "I'll stand up and say my prayers," she said to herself, "they will think I am calm and don't expect them." That's the method of all novices in crime. Dear Nikolay Yermolaitch! My dear man! Do hand this case over to me! Let me go through with it to the end! My dear fellow! I have begun it, and I will carry it through to the end.'

Tchubikov shook his head and frowned.

'I am equal to sifting difficult cases myself,' he said. 'And it's your place not to put yourself forward. Write what is dictated to you, that is your business!'

Dyukovsky flushed crimson, walked out, and slammed the door.

'A clever fellow, the rogue,' Tchubikov muttered, looking after him. 'Ve–ery clever! Only inappropriately hasty. I shall have to buy him a cigar-case at the fair for a present.'

Next morning a lad with a big head and a hare lip came from Klyauzovka. He gave his name as the shepherd Danilko, and furnished a very interesting piece of information.

'I had had a drop,' said he. 'I stayed on till midnight at my crony's. As I was going home, being drunk, I got into the river for a bathe. I was bathing and what do I see? Two men coming along the dam carrying something black. "Tyoo!" I shouted at them. They were scared, and cut along as fast as they could go into the Makarev kitchen-gardens. Strike me dead, if it wasn't the master they were carrying!'

Towards evening of the same day Psyekov and Nikolashka were arrested and taken under guard to the district town. In the town they were put in the prison tower.

*   *   *

Twelve days passed.

It was morning. The examining magistrate, Nikolay Yermolaitch, was sitting at a green table at home, looking through the papers relating to the 'Klyauzov case'; Dyukovsky was pacing up and down the room restlessly, like a wolf in a cage.

'You are convinced of the guilt of Nikolashka and Psyekov,' he said, nervously pulling at his youthful beard. 'Why is it you refuse to be convinced of the guilt of Marya Ivanovna? Haven't you evidence enough?'

'I don't say that I don't believe in it. I am convinced of it, but somehow I can't believe it ... There is no real evidence. It's all theoretical, as it were ... Fanaticism and one thing and another ...'

'And you must have an axe and bloodstained sheets! ... You lawyers! Well, I will prove it to you then! Do give up your slipshod attitude to the psychological aspect of the case. Your Marya Ivanovna ought to be in Siberia! I'll prove it. If theoretical proof is

not enough for you, I have something material . . . It will show you
how right my theory is! Only let me go about a little!'

'What are you talking about?'

The Swedish match! Have you forgotten? I haven't forgotten it!
I'll find out who struck it in the murdered man's room! It was not
struck by Nikolashka, nor by Psyekov, neither of whom turned out
to have matches when searched, but a third person, that is Marya
Ivanovna. And I will prove it! . . . Only let me drive about the
district, make some enquiries . . . '

'Oh, very well, sit down . . . Let us proceed to the examination.'

Dyukovsky sat down to the table, and thrust his long nose into the
papers.

'Bring in Nikolay Tetchov!' cried the examining magistrate.

Nikolashka was brought in. He was pale and thin as a chip. He
was trembling.

'Tetchov!' began Tchubikov. 'In 1879 you were convicted of theft
and condemned to a term of imprisonment. In 1882 you were
condemned for theft a second time, and a second time sent to
prison . . . We know all about it . . . '

A look of surprise came up into Nikolashka's face. The examining
magistrate's omniscience amazed him, but soon wonder was replaced by an expression of extreme distress. He broke into sobs, and
asked leave to go to wash, and calm himself. He was led out.

'Bring in Psyekov!' said the examining magistrate.

Psyekov was led in. The young man's face had greatly changed
during those twelve days. He was thin, pale and wasted. There was a
look of apathy in his eyes.

'Sit down, Psyekov,' said Tchubikov. 'I hope that today you will
be sensible and not persist in lying as on other occasions. All this
time you have denied your participation in the murder of Klyauzov,
in spite of the mass of evidence against you. It is senseless.
Confession is some mitigation of guilt. Today I am talking to you
for the last time. If you don't confess today, tomorrow it will be too
late. Come, tell us . . . '

'I know nothing, and I don't know your evidence,' whispered
Psyekov.

'That's useless! Well then, allow me to tell you how it happened.
On Saturday evening, you were sitting in Klyauzov's bedroom
drinking vodka and beer with him.' (Dyukovsky riveted his eyes on
Psyekov's face, and did not remove them during the whole mono-
logue.) 'Nikolay was waiting upon you. Between twelve and one
Mark Ivanovitch told you he wanted to go to bed. He always did go

to bed at that time. While he was taking off his boots and giving you some instruction regarding the estate, Nikolay and you at a given signal seized your intoxicated master and flung him back upon the bed. One of you sat on his feet, the other on his head. At that moment the lady, you know who, in a black dress, who had arranged with you beforehand the part she would take in the crime, came in from the passage. She picked up the pillow, and proceeded to smother him with it. During the struggle, the light went out. The woman took a box of Swedish matches out of her pocket and lighted the candle. Isn't that right? I see from your face that what I say is true. Well, to proceed . . . Having smothered him, and being convinced that he had ceased to breathe, Nikolay and you dragged him out of the window and put him down near the burdocks. Afraid that he might regain consciousness, you struck him with something sharp. Then you carried him, and laid him for some time under a lilac bush. After resting and considering a little, you carried him . . . lifted him over the hurdle . . . Then went along the road . . . Then comes the dam; near the dam you were frightened by a peasant. But what is the matter with you?'

Psyekov, white as a sheet, got up, staggering.

'I am suffocating!' he said. 'Very well . . . So be it . . . Only I must go . . . Please.'

Psyekov was led out.

'At last he has admitted it!' said Tchubikov, stretching at his ease. 'He has given himself away! How neatly I caught him there.'

'And he didn't deny the woman in black!' said Dyukovsky, laughing. 'I am awfully worried over that Swedish match, though! I can't endure it any longer. Goodbye! I am going!'

Dyukovsky put on his cap and went off. Tchubikov began interrogating Akulka.

Akulka declared that she knew nothing about it . . . 'I have lived with you and with nobody else!' she said.

At six o'clock in the evening Dyukovsky returned. He was more excited than ever. His hands trembled so much that he could not unbutton his overcoat. His cheeks were burning. It was evident that he had not come back without news.

'*Veni, vidi, vici!*' he cried, dashing into Tchubikov's room and sinking into an armchair. 'I vow, on my honour, I begin to believe in my own genius. Listen, damnation take us! Listen and wonder, old friend! It's comic and it's sad. You have three in your grasp already . . . haven't you? I have found a fourth murderer, or rather murderess, for it is a woman! And what a woman! I would have given ten years of my life merely to touch her shoulders. But ... listen. I drove to Klyauzovka and proceeded to describe a spiral round it. On the way I visited all the shopkeepers and innkeepers, asking for Swedish matches. Everywhere I was told no. I have been on my round up to now. Twenty times I lost hope, and as many times regained it. I have been on the go all day long, and only an hour ago came upon what I was looking for. A couple of miles from here they gave me a packet of a dozen boxes of matches. One box was missing ... I asked at once: "Who bought that box?" "So-and-so. She took a fancy to them ... They crackle." My dear fellow! Nikolay Yermolaitch! What can sometimes be done by a man who has been expelled from a seminary and studied Gaboriau is beyond all conception! From today I shall begin to respect myself! ... Ough ... Well, let us go!'

'Go where?'

'To her, to the fourth. ... We must make haste, or ... or I shall explode with impatience! Do you know who she is? You will never guess! The young wife of our old police superintendent, Yevgraf Kuzmitch, Olga Petrovna; that's who it is! She bought that box of matches!'

'You ... you ... Are you out of your mind?'

'It's very natural! In the first place she smokes, and in the second she was head over ears in love with Klyauzov. He rejected her love for the sake of an Akulka. Revenge. I remember now, I once came upon them behind the screen in the kitchen. She was cursing him, while he was smoking her cigarette and puffing the smoke into her face. But do come along; make haste, for it is getting dark already ... Let us go!'

'I have not gone so completely crazy yet as to disturb a respectable, honourable woman at night for the sake of a wretched boy!'

'Honourable, respectable ... You are a rag then, not an examining magistrate! I have never ventured to abuse you, but now you force me to it! You rag! you old fogey! Come, dear Nikolay Yermolaitch, I entreat you!'

The examining magistrate waved his hand in refusal and spat in disgust.

'I beg you! I beg you, not for my own sake, but in the interests of justice! I beseech you, indeed! Do me a favour, if only for once in your life!'

Dyukovsky fell on his knees.

'Nikolay Yermolaitch, do be so good! Call me a scoundrel, a worthless wretch, if I am in error about that woman! It is such a case, you know! It is a case! More like a novel than a case. The fame of it will be all over Russia. They will make you examining magistrate for particularly important cases! Do understand, you unreasonable old man!'

The examining magistrate frowned and irresolutely put out his hand towards his hat.

'Well, the devil take you!' he said, 'let us go.'

It was already dark when the examining magistrate's wagonette rolled up to the police superintendent's door.

'What brutes we are!' said Tchubikov, as he reached for the bell. 'We are disturbing people.'

'Never mind, never mind, don't be frightened. We will say that one of the springs has broken.'

Tchubikov and Dyukovsky were met in the doorway by a tall, plump woman of three and twenty, with eyebrows as black as pitch and full red lips. It was Olga Petrovna herself.

'Ah, how very nice,' she said, smiling all over her face. 'You are just in time for supper. My Yevgraf Kuzmitch is not at home . . . He is staying at the priest's. But we can get on without him. Sit down. Have you come from an enquiry?'

'Yes . . . We have broken one of our springs, you know,' began Tchubikov, going into the drawing-room and sitting down in an easy-chair.

'Take her by surprise at once and overwhelm her,' Dyukovsky whispered to him.

'A spring . . . er . . . yes . . . We just drove up . . . '

'Overwhelm her, I tell you! She will guess if you go drawing it out.'

'Oh, do as you like, but spare me,' muttered Tchubikov, getting up and walking to the window. 'I can't! You cooked the mess, you eat it!'

'Yes, the spring,' Dyukovsky began, going up to the superintendent's wife and wrinkling his long nose. 'We have not come in to . . . er–er–er . . . to supper, nor to see Yevgraf Kuzmitch. We have come to ask you, madam, where is Mark Ivanovitch, whom you have murdered?'

'What? What Mark Ivanovitch?' faltered the superintendent's wife, and her full face was suddenly in one instant suffused with crimson. 'I . . . don't understand.'

'I ask you in the name of the law! Where is Klyauzov? We know all about it!'

'Through whom?' the superintendent's wife asked slowly, unable to face Dyukovsky's eyes.

'Kindly inform us where he is!'

'But how did you find out? Who told you?'

'We know all about it. I insist in the name of the law.'

The examining magistrate, encouraged by the lady's confusion, went up to her: 'Tell us and we will go away. Otherwise we . . .'

'What do you want with him?'

'What is the object of such questions, madam? We ask you for information. You are trembling, confused . . . Yes, he has been murdered, and if you will have it, murdered by you! Your accomplices have betrayed you!'

The police superintendent's wife turned pale.

'Come along,' she said quietly, wringing her hands. 'He is hidden in the bathhouse. Only, for God's sake, don't tell my husband! I implore you! It would be too much for him.'

The superintendent's wife took a big key from the wall, and led her visitors through the kitchen and the passage into the yard. It was dark in the yard. There was a drizzle of fine rain. The superintendent's wife went on ahead. Tchubikov and Dyukovsky strode after her through the long grass, breathing in the smell of wild hemp and slops, which made a squelching sound under their feet. It was a big yard. Soon there were no more pools of slops, and their feet felt ploughed land. In the darkness they saw the silhouette of trees, and among the trees a little house with a crooked chimney.

'This is the bathhouse,' said the superintendent's wife, 'but, I implore you, do not tell anyone.'

Going up to the bathhouse, Tchubikov and Dyukovsky saw a large padlock on the door.

'Get ready your candle-end and matches,' Tchubikov whispered to his assistant.

The superintendent's wife unlocked the padlock and let the visitors into the bathhouse. Dyukovsky struck a match and lighted up the entry. In the middle of it stood a table. On the table, beside a podgy little samovar, was a soup tureen with some cold cabbage-soup in it, and a dish with traces of some sauce on it.

'Go on!'

They went into the next room, the bathroom. There, too, was a table. On the table there stood a big dish of ham, a bottle of vodka, plates, knives and forks.

'But where is he . . . where's the murdered man?'

'He is on the top shelf,' whispered the superintendent's wife, turning paler than ever and trembling.

Dyukovsky took the candle-end in his hand and climbed up to the upper shelf. There he saw a long, human body, lying motionless on a big feather bed. The body emitted a faint snore . . .

'They have made fools of us, damn it all!' Dyukovsky cried. 'This is not he! It's some living blockhead lying here. Hi! Who are you, damnation take you!'

The body drew in its breath with a whistling sound and moved. Dyukovsky prodded it with his elbow. It lifted up its arms, stretched, and raised its head.

'Who is that poking?' a hoarse, ponderous bass voice enquired. 'What do you want?'

Dyukovsky held the candle-end to the face of the unknown and uttered a shriek. In the crimson nose, in the ruffled uncombed hair, in the pitch-black moustaches, of which one was jauntily twisted and pointed insolently towards the ceiling, he recognised Cornet Klyauzov.

'You . . . Mark . . . Ivanovitch! Impossible!'

The examining magistrate looked up and was dumbfounded.

'It is I, yes . . . And it's you, Dyukovsky! What the devil do you want here? And whose ugly mug is that down there? Holy saints, it's the examining magistrate! How in the world did you come here?'

Klyauzov hurriedly got down and embraced Tchubikov. Olga Petrovna whisked out of the door.

'However did you come? Let's have a drink! – dash it all! Tra–ta–ti–to–tom . . . Let's have a drink! Who brought you here, though? How did you get to know I was here? It doesn't matter, though! Have a drink!'

Klyauzov lighted the lamp and poured out three glasses of vodka.

'The fact is, I don't understand you,' said the examining magistrate, throwing out his hands. 'Is it you, or not you?'

'Stop that . . . Do you want to give me a sermon? Don't trouble yourself! Dyukovsky boy, drink up your vodka! Friends, let us pass the . . . What are you staring at . . . ? Drink!'

'All the same, I can't understand,' said the examining magistrate, mechanically drinking his vodka. 'Why are you here?'

'Why shouldn't I be here, if I am comfortable here?' Klyauzov sipped his vodka and ate some ham. 'I am staying with the superintendent's wife, as you see. In the wilds, among the ruins, like some house goblin. Drink! I felt sorry for her, you know, old man! I took pity on her, and, well, I am living here in the deserted bathhouse, like a hermit . . . I am well fed. Next week I am thinking of moving on . . . I've had enough of it . . . '

'Inconceivable!' said Dyukovsky.

'What is there inconceivable in it?'

'Inconceivable! For God's sake, how did your boot get into the garden?'

'What boot?'

'We found one of your boots in the bedroom and the other in the garden.'

'And what do you want to know that for? It is not your business. But do drink, dash it all. Since you have waked me up, you may as well drink! There's an interesting tale about that boot, my boy, I didn't want to come to Olga's. I didn't feel inclined, you know, I'd had a drop too much . . . She came under the window and began scolding me . . . You know how women . . . as a rule . . . Being drunk, I up and flung my boot at her . . . Ha-ha! . . . Don't scold, I said. She clambered in at the window, lighted the lamp, and gave me a good drubbing, as I was drunk. I have plenty to eat here . . . Love, vodka, and good things! But where are you off to? Tchubikov, where are you off to?'

The examining magistrate spat on the floor and walked out of the bathhouse. Dyukovsky followed him with his head hanging. Both got into the wagonette in silence and drove off. Never had the road seemed so long and dreary. Both were silent. Tchubikov was shaking with anger all the way. Dyukovsky hid has face in his collar as though he were afraid the darkness and the drizzling rain might read his shame on his face.

On getting home the examining magistrate found the doctor, Tyutyuev, there. The doctor was sitting at the table and heaving deep sighs as he turned over the pages of the *Neva*.

'The things that are going on in the world!' he said, greeting the examining magistrate with a melancholy smile. 'Austria is at it again . . . and Gladstone, too, in a way . . . '

Tchubikov flung his hat under the table and began to tremble.

'You devil of a skeleton! Don't bother me! I've told you a thousand times over, don't bother me with your politics! It's not the time for politics! And as for you,' he turned upon Dyukovsky and shook his fist at him, 'as for you . . . I'll never forget it, as long as I live!'

'But the Swedish match, you know! How could I tell . . . '

'Choke yourself with your match! Go away and don't irritate me, or goodness knows what I shall do to you. Don't let me set eyes on you.'

Dyukovsky heaved a sigh, took his hat, and went out.

'I'll go and get drunk!' he decided, as he went out of the gate, and he sauntered dejectedly towards the tavern.

When the superintendent's wife got back from the bathhouse she found her husband in the drawing-room.

'What did the examining magistrate come about?' asked her husband.

'He came to say that they had found Klyauzov. Only fancy, they found him staying with another man's wife.'

'Ah, Mark Ivanovitch, Mark Ivanovitch!' sighed the police superintendent, turning up his eyes. 'I told you that dissipation would lead to no good! I told you so – you wouldn't heed me!'

The Secrets of the Black Brotherhood

DICK DONOVAN

It was a bitter night in December, now years ago, that a young and handsome man called upon me in great distress, to seek my advice and assistance. It was the third day after Christmas, and having dined, and dined well, I had ensconced myself in my favourite easy-chair, before a cheerful fire, and was engaged in the perusal of Charles Dickens's *The Cricket on the Hearth*, when my visitor was unceremoniously ushered into the room. He held his dripping hat in his hand, and the heavy topcoat he wore was white with snow, which was falling heavily outside. He was well proportioned, of blond complexion, and his face at once attracted me by its frank, open expression. He had clear, honest eyes, and a graceful moustache shaded a well-formed mouth.

'Pardon me for intruding upon you,' he said, in a somewhat excited tone, as he placed his wet hat on the table and began to pull off his thick woollen gloves; 'but the fact is, I am in a frame of mind bordering upon distraction. Let me introduce myself, however. My name is Harold Welldom Kingsley; Welldom being an old family name. I am the son of the late Admiral Kingsley, who, as you may possibly be aware, distinguished himself greatly in the service of his queen and country.'

'Yes,' I answered. 'I knew your father by reputation, and I remember that when he died some years ago his remains were accorded a public funeral. I am pleased to make the acquaintance of the son of so distinguished a man. Pray remove your coat and be seated, and let me know in what way I can serve you.'

'I am in the Admiralty Office,' my visitor continued, as he divested himself of his damp coat and, placing it on the back of a chair, sat down. Thereupon I pushed the shaded lamp that stood on the table nearer to him, tilting the shade slightly so that the light might fall upon his face, for it is my habit always to study the face of the person with whom I am in conversation. 'I live with my mother and two sisters at Kensington. For three years I have been engaged to a young lady, who is, I may venture to say, the sweetest woman who ever drew the breath of life.'

'Ah!' I murmured, with a smile, as I closely watched my visitor, and saw his face light up with enthusiasm as he thus referred to his fiancée, 'it is the old story: love is blind and sees no faults until too late.'

'In my case it is not so,' he exclaimed, with a force of emphasis that carried conviction of his perfect sincerity and a belief in his own infallible judgement. 'But we will not discuss that point,' he continued. 'The business that has brought me here is far too serious for time to be wasted in argument. The young lady who is pledged to me as my wife is, at present, under arrest on the serious charge of having stolen some very valuable jewellery from a well-known firm of jewellers.'

'That is a grave charge, indeed,' I remarked, with growing interest in my visitor; 'but presumably there must have been good *prima-facie* evidence to justify her arrest.'

'Yes,' Mr Kingsley exclaimed, with an agonised expression, 'that is the most terrible part of the whole affair. I am afraid that legally the evidence will go against her; and yet morally I will stake my very soul on her innocence.'

'You speak somewhat paradoxically, Mr Kingsley,' I said, with a certain amount of professional sternness, for it seemed to me he was straining to twist facts to suit his own views.

'To you it will seem so,' he answered; 'but if you have the patience to listen to me I will tell you the whole story, and I think you will say I am right.'

I intimated that I was quite prepared to listen to anything he had to say, and leaning back in my chair with the tips of my fingers together and my eyes half closed – an attitude I always uncon-sciously assume when engaged in trying to dissect some human puzzle – I waited for him to continue.

'The lady's name is Beryl Artois,' he went on. 'She was born in France. Her mother was an English lady highly connected; and her father was a Frenchman of independent means. They lived sur-rounded with every luxury in a small château, on the banks of the Seine, not far from St Germain. Unhappily, Monsieur Artois was fatally fond of a life of ease and pleasure, and dying suddenly after a night of revel in Paris, at a *bal masqué* during the *mi-carême*, it was found that he had dissipated his fortune, and left his widow and child totally unprovided for. Even his château was mortgaged up to the hilt, and on his furniture was a bill of sale. Not wishing to be dependent on his relations, Madame Artois and her daughter came to London. Beryl at that time was only six years of age. She was a delicate girl, and needed all her mother's care and attention. For a few years madame earned her living as a teacher of French, music and drawing, and every spare moment she had she devoted to the education and training of her daughter. Unhappily, before Beryl was twelve years of age her doting mother died, and a bachelor uncle, her mother's only brother, took Beryl under his care, and as he was well off he engaged a highly-qualified governess for her. I first became acquainted with her when she was eighteen years of age. That is now a little over six years ago; and though I have proved the soundness of the old adage which says that the course of true love never did run smooth, I have every reason to congratulate myself, for, as I have before hinted, Beryl is goodness itself.'

'In what way has your wooing been ruffled?' I asked.

'Well, Mr Tamworth, her uncle, refused for some time to countenance our engagement and threw every obstacle in the way; and as Beryl was much under his influence, she struggled between what she considered her duty to her uncle and foster father, and love for me. The love has triumphed, and Mr Tamworth has consented to our union on condition that we wait three years, and I obtain the promotion I hope to obtain in the government service in that time.'

'This is a very pretty, even a romantic, story,' I remarked; 'it is as old as the hills, and yet, like all love stories, ever new. But now for the sequel. How comes it that this well-nurtured and well-cared-for young lady has fallen under the suspicion of being a thief?'

'Ah! that is where the mystery comes in,' exclaimed Mr Kingsley in great distress. 'I ask you now, is it likely that Beryl, who has everything she requires – for her uncle is wealthy – and who would shudder at anything that by any possible means could be construed as wrongdoing, would descend to purloin jewellery from a jeweller's shop?'

I could not help smiling at what seemed to be the sweet simplicity of this love-stricken young man, nor could I refrain from saying: 'In answer to your question, Mr Kingsley, permit me to say that the annals of crime contain many such cases. Unhappily, neither education nor moral training is sufficient safeguard against transgression, where the tendency to wrongdoing exists. In the case in point, it is very possible that the lady's vanity and love of display have tempted her to her fall.'

'For heaven's sake, Mr Donovan, don't drive me mad,' cried my visitor, with an outburst of passionate distress that begot my fullest sympathy. 'If all the angels in heaven were to come down and proclaim Beryl's guilt, I would still believe her innocent.'

'May I venture to remark,' I answered, 'that in all probability this sentiment does more credit to your heart than your head?'

'I tell you, sir,' exclaimed Kingsley, almost fiercely, 'that Beryl Artois is as innocent as you are!'

'Well, now, Mr Kingsley,' I observed, 'as we have had the sentimental and poetical side of the affair, let us go into the more vulgar and prosaic part of the business. Therefore please give me a plain, straightforward answer to the questions I shall put to you. First, where does Mr Tamworth reside?'

'He resides at Linden House, Thames Ditton.'

'You say he is well off?'

'Yes. He keeps numerous servants, rides to hounds, drives his carriage, and is very highly respected.'

'Has he always been kind to his niece?'

'In every possible way, I believe.'

'And has supplied her with all she has wanted?'

'Yes. I do not think any reasonable request of hers has ever been refused.'

'And now, as regards the charge she has to meet. Give me full particulars of that.'

'It appears that the day before yesterday she came up to town in the brougham, and drove to Whitney, Blake and Montague, the well-known jewellers of Regent Street. There she stated that she wished to purchase a diamond bracelet for a New Year's gift, and some costly things were shown to her. But after more than an hour spent in the shop she could not make up her mind, for though she saw what she wanted, the price was higher than she cared to go to; and, before committing herself to the purchase of the article, she was anxious to consult her uncle, since she is necessarily dependent upon him for her pocket-money. Consequently, she told the assistant in the shop that she would call again the next day and decide. She thereupon took her departure, and entered the brougham, but had not proceeded very far before the assistant tore down the street, accompanied by a policeman, overtook the brougham, which had been brought to a standstill owing to the congested traffic, and accused Miss Artois of having purloined a diamond pendant worth nearly a thousand pounds. Of course, she most indignantly denied it. But the shopman insisted on giving her in charge.'

'And was the pendant found either in the brougham or on her person?'

'Oh, dear, no. Miss Artois begged that the policeman and the shopman would get into the brougham, and that they should drive straight to Scotland Yard. This was done; and though the young lady and the brougham were alike searched, the pendant was not forthcoming. Nevertheless, the shopman persisted in his accusation, and so there was no alternative but to place Miss Artois under arrest.'

'This is a very remarkable story,' I answered, 'and may prove a very serious business indeed for the firm of jewellers if they cannot justify their charge.'

'They will never be able to do that,' said Kingsley, warmly, 'and you may depend upon it, they will have to pay dearly for their error. They maintain, however, that they have certainly lost the jewel; that no one else could possibly have taken it except Miss Artois; and that she must have managed to secrete it in some way. The whole charge, however, is preposterous, and I wish you thoroughly to prove the young lady's innocence in order that an action may be commenced against Whitney, Blake and Montague.'

Having secured my promise that I would do my utmost in his interests, my visitor took his departure; whereupon, lighting a cigar, I fell to pondering on this – as I had to admit to myself – very remarkable case, assuming that all the facts were as stated by Mr Kingsley.

It was too late to take any steps that night, but immediately after breakfast the following morning I jumped into a hansom and drove to Whitney, Blake and Montague's place. As everyone knows, they are a firm of world-wide renown, and I could not imagine them committing such a grave error as to accuse a lady of theft, unless they had very strong reasons for believing they were right. I requested an interview with Mr Whitney, and his version of the affair was substantially the same as that told to me by Mr Kingsley.

'Of course,' added Mr Whitney, 'we rely entirely upon the statement of our manager, Mr John Coleman, who attended to the lady. Mr Coleman, I may inform you, has been with the firm since he was seventeen years of age, and he is now over fifty. And as he is a partner in the firm, our faith in him is justified. However, you shall see Coleman and judge for yourself.'

Mr Whitney sounded his bell and requested that Mr Coleman would come to the room. In a few minutes Coleman entered. He at once struck me as being a very shrewd, keen-eyed man of business.

Without any unnecessary verbiage he gave me his account of the affair, according to which he devoted special attention to the young lady as he thought she was going to be a good customer. There were other customers in the shop at the time, but he conducted her to one end of the counter where there was no one else. She caused him a good deal of trouble, and looked at a large number of things, but did not seem to know her own mind; and at last went away without purchasing anything.

For some few moments just before she left, his attention was drawn off by one of the assistants coming to him to ask a question, and during that time he had little doubt she availed herself of the opportunity to abstract the pendant from the jewel tray upon which he had displayed the things for her inspection.

On her deciding not to purchase then, he placed the tray temporarily in the glass case on the counter, locked the case, putting the key in his pocket, and then conducted Miss Artois to her brougham. He was certainly not absent more than five minutes. By the time he returned there were very few people in the shop, and he proceeded immediately to the case, took out the tray and began to sort the jewels preparatory to restoring them to their respective positions amongst the stock. It was then he missed the pendant which Miss Artois had examined with eager interest, asking him many questions about the quality of the stones, their intrinsic value, and their setting. The pendant had originally been made to the order of a lady of title from specially selected stones, but she died before the order was completed; her executors declined to take the pendant, and, therefore, in order to dispose of it quickly, the firm had offered it for sale at the low price of one thousand pounds.

As soon as he discovered the loss Mr Coleman ran out of the shop and down the street, and passing a policeman on the way, he demanded his services. As it was the busiest part of the day there was a great deal of traffic, and Miss Artois's brougham had been unable to proceed very far. So convinced was he in his own mind that she was guilty, that though he was fully alive to the risks he ran— if he made a mistake, he did not hesitate to give her into custody, and he was quite prepared to stand or fall by his act.

Although I subjected Mr Coleman to a very close questioning, I could not shake his evidence in any way. I pointed out to him that there was one serious fact in connection with the case, and that was, he had failed to find the pendant either in the brougham or on Miss Artois's person; and that, however morally certain he might be that the young lady was guilty, no magistrate would convict her on such evidence.

'I am aware of that,' answered Mr Coleman, 'but I have employed Detective Spieglemann, of Scotland Yard, to make some enquiries about the lady, and he informs me that on various occasions when she has visited the shops of well-known tradesmen, goods have afterwards been missed. The victims have almost invariably been jewellers, and the property purloined has generally been of great value.'

'If that is correct there is *prima-facia* evidence,' I answered; 'but still, suspicion is not proof, and unless you have something better to offer, I have no hesitation in saying you will fail to secure a conviction.'

Mr Coleman appeared, for the first time, to be a little disconcerted, and I fancied that I detected signs in his face that he felt he had been somewhat hasty. Nevertheless, he reasserted his belief that the young lady was guilty, though he was utterly unable to suggest what had become of the stolen pendant. Female searchers had subjected Miss Artois to the most rigorous examination, and every nook and cranny of the brougham had been searched.

'May I ask, Mr Coleman, if Spieglemann was present when the search was made?' I enquired pointedly.

'Oh, yes,' exclaimed Coleman. 'He happened to be in the Yard at the time, and conducted the search.'

'Indeed. And did he think of searching the coachman who drove the brougham?'

As I asked this question, a pallor of alarm spread itself over Coleman's face, and he and Mr Whitney looked at each other as each saw, for the first time, that a grave oversight had been committed.

Detective Spieglemann was a German, who had long been attached to the force of Scotland Yard. But though he bore the reputation of being almost preternaturally acute, I had never been able to regard him in any other light than as a very ordinary person, whose German stolidity prevented him from getting out of well-worn grooves.

Of course, this expression of opinion will be denounced as mere professional jealousy, but I shall be able to justify my view by hard and indisputable facts.

I have always maintained that the unravelling of anything like a mystery is capable of being elevated to the position of a fine art. Spieglemann, on the other hand, asserted that the whole process was merely a mechanical one, and that only a mechanical mind could succeed. On these points we totally differed, and as I had frequently had the good fortune to be successful where my rival had failed, I was entitled to claim that my process was the correct one. Mr Coleman's answer was another item of evidence in my favour. He confessed with unmistakable concern that the coachman had not been searched, and that nobody had suggested that he should be. In fact, no suspicion had fallen upon him. I really could not resist something like a smile as I remarked: 'That was really a most extraordinary oversight, and may prove very serious for you. For, assuming that you are right, and that Spieglemann is right in his statement that the lady lies under suspicion of having been concerned in other cases of a similar kind, is it not highly probable that the coachman has been in collusion with her, and she passed the stolen property to him? If this is not so, how did she get rid of the pendant? Nothing is truer than that in criminal cases it is the seemingly improbable that is most probable.

'Certainly, on the face of it nothing could seem more improbable than that a young lady, well connected and well off, afflicted with kleptomania, should make a confidant of her coachman. Yet it is the most probable thing imaginable, but both you and Spieglemann have overlooked it.'

Mr Coleman was perfectly crestfallen, and freely admitted that a very grave oversight had been committed. Thanking him and Mr Whitney I withdrew, and it was perfectly clear to me that I left the two gentlemen in a very different frame of mind from that they had been in when I first saw them.

In passing all the facts, as I now knew them, under review, I could not deny that circumstances looked dark against Miss Artois; and putting aside the possibility that somebody else might have stolen the pendant, I admitted the strong probability that she was in reality the thief. That being so, the idea struck me – and it evidently had not struck anyone else, not even the renowned Spieglemann – that she was a confederate, more likely than not a victim, of the coachman. On this supposition I determined to act, and my next step was to seek an interview with Miss Artois, in order that I might form some opinion of her from personal knowledge. I obtained this interview through the solicitors who had been engaged on her behalf by her devoted lover, Harold Kingsley. Although prepared to find her good looking, I certainly was not prepared for the type of beauty she represented.

I don't think I ever looked upon a more perfect, a sweeter, and I will go so far as to say a more angelic face than she possessed, while her form and mould were such that an artist would have gone into raptures about her. I was informed that she had undergone a preliminary examination before the police magistrate, who had remanded her without bail, although bail had been offered to an unlimited amount by her uncle; but the magistrate had stated that he would consider the question of bail the next time she came before him.

As I entered the little cell she occupied at the police station, and introduced myself, giving her to understand at the same time that I was there by request of Mr Kingsley, she rose from the table at which she had been sitting engaged in the perusal of a book, which I subsequently discovered to be a well-thumbed, dilapidated and somewhat dirty copy of Moore's *Lallah Rookh*, and bowing with exquisite grace she said in a low, musical and touchingly pathetic voice: 'It is good of you to come, and more than kind of Mr Kingsley to send you; but I am sorry that you have come, and I wish that you would leave me without another word.'

Her soft, gazelle-like eyes, although apparently bent upon me, had a far-away look in them; and she spoke as a person in a trance might speak. Altogether there was something about her that at once aroused my curiosity and interest.

'That is a somewhat strange wish, Miss Artois,' I answered. 'I am here in your interest; and surely you cannot be indifferent to the grave charge that is hanging over you.'

'I am not indifferent,' she murmured, with a deep sigh.

'Then let me urge you to confide in your solicitors,' I said, 'and withhold nothing from them that may enable them to prepare your defence.'

'I shall confide in no one,' she replied in the same indifferent, same sweetly pathetic tone.

'But think of the consequences,' I urged.

'I have thought of everything.'

'Remember also, Miss Artois, your silence and refusal to give information will be tantamount to a tacit confession of guilt.'

For a moment her dreamy eyes seemed to lose their dreaminess and to be expressive of an infinite pain, as she answered with quite a fiery energy – 'I am *not* guilty!' She laid peculiar emphasis on the word 'not'.

'Then,' said I, quickly, 'do all you possibly can to prove your guiltlessness;' and, in order that there should be no ambiguity in my meaning, I added, 'If you are the victim of anyone, for heaven's sake let it be known. For the sake of your lover conceal not the truth.'

'For the sake of my lover and the love I bear him, I would die,' she murmured, with the dreaminess which seemed peculiar to her.

'Then withhold nothing from your solicitors,' I repeated.

'Go!' she said, peremptorily, as she sank into her seat again, and resumed her reading.

'Have you no message to send to Mr Kingsley?' I asked.

'Go!' she repeated, without looking at me.

'Let me take some comforting word from you to Mr Kingsley,' I entreated.

She made no reply, but apparently was deeply absorbed in the book. Feeling that it would be useless to remain any longer, I withdrew, and as I did so she did not even look up from the book, nor did she make any response when I bade her adieu.

I had promised to call upon Mr Kingsley and acquaint him with the result of my interview with Miss Artois; and I carried out this promise with a sense of distress that I could hardly describe, because I was quite unable to give him the assurance he so much wanted that his fiancée was guiltless. Guiltless she was, in one sense, I was sure; but I was conscious of the fact that I was confronted with as complicated a human problem as I had ever been called upon to find a solution to.

I put the best face I could on matters while talking to young Kingsley; and on leaving him I felt convinced that my first surmise with reference to the coachman being a party to the robbery was a correct one. I had not been slow to determine that Miss Artois's temperament was one of those deeply sympathetic and poetic ones which are peculiarly subject to the influence of stronger wills.

In short, I came to the conclusion that the coachman was the really guilty person, and Miss Artois was his victim. He – in my opinion – had exercised some strange mesmeric influence over her, and she had been entirely under his sway. I was confirmed in this view when I learnt that the great Spieglemann had gathered up a mass of circumstantial evidence which tended to prove that Miss Artois had been in the habit for a long time of visiting some of the leading tradesmen in all quarters of London, and that these trades-men had been robbed of property which in the aggregate represented many thousands of pounds.

It was altogether a peculiar case, as it presented two startling phases of human nature; and if Miss Artois had sinned, she had sinned not because her inclinations tended that way, but because her non-resisting, sympathetic nature had been made an instrument for the profit and gain of a debased and wicked man who did not scruple to use this beautiful girl as a means to an end.

My next step was to hurry off to Linden House at Thames Ditton, in order that I might get full particulars from Mr Tamworth of his coachman, before having the man arrested. Linden House was a large house, standing in its own grounds, and everything about the place was suggestive of wealth and comfort. I was ushered into an elegantly furnished drawing-room, and a few minutes later the door opened, and a little, podgy, bald-headed man, wearing gold eye-glasses and dressed in a large-patterned dressing-gown and Turkish slippers, entered, and eyed me with a pair of strangely keen and hawk-like eyes. It was Mr Tamworth, and in many respects he was a striking and remarkable man, for his face was strongly marked, his eyes of unusual, almost unnatural brilliancy, the mouth firm, the square jaw indicative of an iron will. He was perfectly clean shaved, so that every feature, every line and angle were thrown into stronger prominence.

I had not sent my name up to him, but simply an urgent message that a gentleman wished to see him on very pressing and important business.

'Whom have I the pleasure to address?' he enquired as he bowed stiffly.

'My name is Dick Donovan,' I answered. 'I am – '

He interrupted me by exclaiming: 'Oh, yes, I have heard of you. You are a detective.' I bowed. 'Presumably,' he continued, 'you have come here in connection with the case of my dear niece?' He seemed to be overcome by emotion, and turning towards the window he applied a large bandana handkerchief to his eyes.

'I am not indifferent to the fact,' I answered, 'that the subject is necessarily a delicate and painful one. But from an interview I had with your niece I am forced to the conclusion that she is only guilty in degree.'

'How do you mean?' he asked, turning quickly towards me, with an expression of mental suffering on his face.

'I mean that she is a victim to the machinations of a villain.'

'A victim,' he echoed, hoarsely. 'A victim to whom?'

'To your coachman.'

He almost reeled at this announcement, and passed his hand over his bald head in a confused, distressed way; and then, with something like a wail he exclaimed: 'My God, this is an awful revelation.'

He rushed towards the bell and was about to ring it when I stopped him by saying: 'What are you going to do?'

'Send for Tupper, the coachman.'

'Wait a bit,' I said. 'I should like to have some particulars of Tupper. What is his Christian name?'

'John.'

'Has he been with you long?'

'Just twelve months, I think.'

'Have you ever had occasion to suspect his honesty?'

'Never for a single instant.'

'Is he married?'

'I cannot tell you. I know absolutely nothing about his family affairs.'

'Well now, I have a suggestion to make, Mr Tamworth. I should like you to send for Tupper, and question him closely about what happened on the day that the pendant was stolen. And particularly I would like you to put this question to him, after you have skilfully led up to it: "Is it possible, Tupper, that my unhappy and mis-guided niece handed you the pendant, and you know what has become of it?" '

'I will do so,' answered Mr Tamworth, as he went towards the bell.

'Stop a minute, sir,' I said. 'There is one other important point. It is desirable that Tupper should not see me. Can you conceal me behind that screen in the corner, and in such a position that I can see without being seen? And you must not forget to place Tupper in such a way that I can get a full view of his face.'

'I don't think there will be any difficulty in that,' Mr Tamworth answered, and he requested me to follow him behind the screen. I did so, and taking out his penknife he bored a hole in one leaf of the screen, so that anyone looking through the hole commanded a full view of the room.

'There,' he said, 'I think that will answer your purpose. And now we will have the old villain here.'

He rang the bell, and a very respectable-looking manservant appeared.

'Robert,' said Mr Tamworth, peremptorily, 'send the coachman here.'

'Tupper's away, sir.'

'Away!'

'Yes. He went out last night and didn't come back.'

'Where has he gone to?' roared Mr Tamworth, in his excitement.

'I haven't the remotest idea, sir,' answered Robert.

'The double-dyed villain,' hissed Mr Tamworth between his

clenched teeth. 'The double-dyed villain,' he repeated. 'But by heaven he shall be brought back, even if it takes all my fortune to effect his capture. That will do, Robert. You may go.'

As the man took his departure and closed the door I stepped from behind the screen. Mr Tamworth seemed terribly distressed.

'This is an awful bit of business,' he exclaimed; 'you see the arch villain has anticipated this discovery and bolted. What is to be done now?'

'We must arrest him in his flight,' was my answer. 'And to facilitate that you must furnish me with a full description of him.'

'Unless the rascal has removed it,' said Mr Tamworth, 'his likeness hangs over the mantelpiece in his room above the stable. I will go and get it. You will excuse me.'

He hurried from the room, and was absent nearly a quarter of an hour. Then he returned bearing a framed photograph in his hand. It was the likeness of a short, thick-set man in coachman's garb. He had grey whiskers and moustache, and grey hair; and rather a scowling expression of face. I asked Mr Tamworth if it was a good likeness of John Tupper, and he assured me it was a most excellent likeness.

Promising Mr Tamworth to do all I could to effect Tupper's arrest, I left Linden House, taking the photograph with me. As soon as I got back to London I hailed a hansom and drove to Whitney, Blake and Montague's.

'My surmise about the coachman is correct,' I said, as I showed them the likeness, and told them that the man had fled. They acknowledged that the likeness was a very striking one, and as I intended to have it reproduced and sent broadcast all over the country, I was hopeful that I should be able speedily to bring about Tupper's arrest.

I lost no time in putting the photo in hand for reproduction; in the meantime Miss Artois was again brought up before the magistrate, and in view of the facts the solicitors were able to lay before him with reference to Tupper's flight, he no longer hesitated to admit the young lady to bail, her uncle being accepted for two thousand pounds. Two days after her release, young Kingsley called upon me again. He was terribly agitated, and throwing himself into a chair he rocked himself to and fro, and groaned with the anguish that tortured him. When he had somewhat calmed down, he exclaimed in a voice that was broken up with the passion of his grief: 'Mr Donovan, help me with your advice, or I think I shall go mad. And above all, do not betray the confidence I am going to repose in you.' I assured him that he might trust me, and he proceeded.

'Miss Artois came to me yesterday, and acknowledged that she was an unconscious victim in this terrible business, and said that I must give her up. In spite of my entreaties, my prayers, my tears, she most resolutely declined to tell me whose victim she was, and with a great shudder she said her lips were sealed with a seal she dare not break. I urged her to fly with me. I told her we would be married at once, and seek some corner of the earth where she would be safe, and her answer was that nowhere in the world would she be safe except in the grave.'

'You did wrong in urging her to fly,' I answered.

'I care not. Wrong, or no wrong, I will take her,' he cried, passionately. 'I tell you, Mr Donovan, that there is some hideous mystery about this affair, and I will move heaven and earth to save Miss Artois from the machination that is destroying her body and soul.'

'Your devotion, your chivalry do you infinite credit,' I replied. 'Miss Artois shall be saved if it is possible to save her, but, believe me, she cannot be saved by flight. She must remain here subject to the law. To defy the law will be a fatal mistake.'

Although he did not seem to be quite convinced of the soundness of my advice, he promised to be entirely guided by me, and in a little while he took his departure, and then I sat down to reflect and ponder, and endeavour to unravel the threads of this tangled skein. One thing I resolved on was to go down to Thames Ditton early on the morrow, and have an interview with Miss Artois in the presence of her uncle. In a little while my servant entered the room and handed me a postal packet, which, on opening, I found was from the lithographers who were reproducing the photograph. It contained the original and a note to say that the reproductions would be ready for distribution the first thing in the morning.

Placing the photo of Tupper on the table, I lit my pipe, and once more throwing myself in my favourite easy-chair, I tried by the aid of smoke to solve the mystery surrounding Miss Artois. Presently I found myself almost unconsciously gazing on the photo that lay on the table, in the full rays of the shaded lamp. Suddenly that face presented itself to me as one I had seen before; and I beat my brains, so to speak, to try and think where and when. 'Whose face is it? Where have I seen it?' This was the question that, mentally, I repeated over and over again.

After much cogitation, I threw away the stump of my cigar, went to my desk, and taking out a powerful magnifying glass, I returned to the table and examined the likeness of John Tupper by means of the glass, until suddenly, like an inspiration, it flashed upon me where and when I had seen the face. It is not often I get excited, but I think I did on that occasion, for I felt certain that I had got hold of a clue to the mystery. I did not sleep much that night, and was up betimes in the morning, and hastened to call upon Mr Kingsley, to assure him that I believed I was in a fair way to solving the mystery, and I hoped all would be well with Miss Artois.

A week later, on a night in January as dark and stormy as any that winter, I was in an upper room in an old, untenanted house in the Borough. The owner of the house was Mr Tamworth, of Thames Ditton. Stretched at full length on the dusty floor, with my eye glued to a hole that enabled me to command a view of the room beneath, I was witness of one of the most remarkable and dramatic scenes I had ever looked upon. Thirteen men were in the room, seated at a long deal table. Six sat on one side, six on the other. The thirteenth sat at the head, and was evidently the president. Every man's face was concealed by a hood that entirely covered up the head, two holes being pierced for the eyes. Before the president was a china bowl, and laid across the bowl was a naked dagger.

A small lamp was suspended from the ceiling and threw a feeble light over the scene. In a few minutes one of the men arose and placed a bull's-eye lantern on a shelf in a corner of the room, in such a position that its rays fell full upon the doorway. That done the president rapped on the table with a wooden mallet. Then the door opened and three men appeared. Two were hooded like the rest. The third was not hooded, and was placed at the end of the table opposite the president, so that the light of the bull's-eye fell full upon his face. It was a cruel, cunning, almost fierce face. The man was without coat or waistcoat, and his shirt was opened and turned down, exposing his breast, while round his neck was a rope with the free end hanging behind. In a few minutes the president rose, and addressing the bareheaded man, said: 'Your name is Henry Beechworth?'

'It is.'

'Are you willing, Henry Beechworth, to join the Black Brother-hood?'

'I am.'

'And you are willing to take the oath that will bind you to us?'

'I am.'

'Then listen, and I will read the oath to you.' Here the president unrolled a little scroll of paper he had held in his hand, and read out as follows: 'I, Henry Beechworth, hereby, of my own free will, join the Black Brotherhood, and I vow solemnly by heaven and earth to be true to it, and never utter a single word or give a sign that would be likely to betray any individual of the Brotherhood, or the Brotherhood collectively. And that at any time, should I be arrested, I will give no information against the Brothers, even though my life is at stake. Everything I obtain I will add to the common treasury, and I will at all times be subject to the ruling of the president, whoever he may be. These things I swear to do; and should at any time I break my oath, I hope that I shall go blind. I am aware that the rope I now have round my neck is a symbol that in the event of my betraying the Brotherhood their vengeance will pursue me to the ends of the earth, and that my life will be forfeited.'

'You have heard what I have read?' asked the president.

'I have,' answered Beechworth.

'And you will subscribe your name to it?'

'I will.'

Here the president made a sign, and one of the two hooded men at the head of the table approached, and receiving the bowl and the dagger, he returned to the novitiate, who, instructed by the president, bent forward. Then the man took up the dagger and with its sharp point made a wound in the fleshy part of the novitiate's breast. Beechworth then bent right over the bowl, so that the blood dropped into it. And when a little had thus been caught, a new quill pen was dipped into it, and handed to Beechworth, who thereupon wrote his name with his own blood on the scroll. This senseless ceremony ended, the wound in the man's breast was sponged, a piece of plaster placed upon it, and he was told that he was now one of the Black Brotherhood, and that his interests were bound up with theirs, and that he must stand or fall with them.

'It only remains now for me to give you the sign,' the president added, 'by which you may always know a Brother. It is changed every month. For the current month it is the index finger of the left hand placed in the palm of the right hand, thus.' Here he gave a practical illustration of how it was to be done. 'Then we have a password, also changed every month. The one in use at present is "Croesus". We meet here again in three weeks' time, when you will be expected to contribute to the common fund value or money to the extent of a hundred pounds.'

The business being ended, all the members of this precious Brotherhood removed their hoods, and the hand of the new member was shaken by the others. Amongst them I recognised the fellow called Robert, who had acted the part of the servant at

Linden House when I went there. In a little while the lights were extinguished and the Brotherhood commenced to leave the house, but as they reached the street, to their utter amazement and consternation, they were arrested, for the house was surrounded by a cordon of policemen.

It will, of course, be asked how it was I managed to unearth the secrets of the strange society, whose members were banded together with the sole object of enriching themselves by plundering their fellow-men. The question is easily answered. On the night when it dawned upon me that I had seen the face represented by the photograph of John Tupper somewhere before, I was enabled to detect by aid of the magnifying glass that the whiskers were not natural. There were two or three places where the hair did not adhere to the face. I came to the conclusion at once that Tupper was none other than Tamworth, disguised by false whiskers and moustache, and a wig. The dark piercing eyes, too, I was perfectly convinced were Tamworth's eyes. It was naturally a very startling discovery, and I immediately took steps to prove it right or wrong. For several days I shadowed Mr Tamworth, and at last followed him to the old house in the Borough.

Later on I obtained entrance to the house by means of a false key. In a drawer in a table I found a written circular summoning a meeting for a certain night; and I resolved not only to witness that meeting, but as there could not be a shadow of a doubt that the Black Brotherhood, as they chose to call themselves, met for an unlawful purpose, I took means to have every man jack of them arrested.

At first when the news leaked out people were inclined to think that the Brotherhood was a hoax, but the revelations that were gradually made of their doings caused intense excitement throughout the country. Not only were they bound together by oath, which each man signed with his blood, but they had a formal set of rules and regulations for their guidance. Tamworth was the president, and he, with two others, took charge of all the things that were stolen.

Periodically this property was conveyed to the Continent by some of the members, and there disposed of, the proceeds of the sales being equally divided. In the event of a man being arrested the Brotherhood secretly provided funds for his defence; and if it was a bailable case the bail was always forthcoming, but the accused invariably disappeared unless he felt pretty sure he would only get a light sentence.

The Brotherhood owed its origin and success entirely to the arch villain Tamworth, who had, by some strange mesmeric influence he possessed, been enabled to obtain entire control over the will of his unfòrtunate niece Beryl Artois. In order to keep up this influence, he drove his own brougham disguised as a coachman, and whatever she obtained she handed to him immediately and he concealed it. Of course, nothing bulky was ever taken on such occasions. The plunder was either precious stones or jewellery.

In spite of their oath, three of the gang turned queen's evidence, and the conviction of the rest was secured. Tamworth, as the ringleader, was sentenced to life, and the others were dealt with only a little less severely. Tamworth was one of the most accomplished and consummate villains I ever had to deal with; his power of acting a part, and of concealing his true feelings, was simply marvellous, and would have enabled him to have made a fortune if he had gone upon the stage.

In the face of the exposure I was thus enabled to make, and which left not the slightest doubt that poor Miss Artois had been an unconscious victim of the strange power possessed by her uncle, she was, after being committed for trial and duly tried, acquitted, and her faithful lover, Kingsley, lost no time in making her his wife. And as great sympathy was shown for him and her, a position was found for him abroad, whither he removed with his beautiful bride until time should have wiped the scandal out of the public memory.

The Episode of the Diamond Links

GRANT ALLEN

'Let us take a trip to Switzerland,' said Lady Vandrift. And anyone who knows Amelia will not be surprised to learn that we *did* take a trip to Switzerland accordingly. Nobody can drive Sir Charles, except his wife. And nobody at all can drive Amelia.

There were difficulties at the outset, because we had not ordered rooms at the hotels beforehand, and it was well on in the season; but they were overcome at last by the usual application of a golden key; and we found ourselves in due time pleasantly quartered in Lucerne, at that most comfortable of European hostelries, the Schweitzerhof.

We were a square party of four – Sir Charles and Amelia, myself and Isabel. We had nice big rooms, on the first floor, overlooking the lake; and as none of us was possessed with the faintest symptom of that incipient mania which shows itself in the form of an insane desire to climb mountain heights of disagreeable steepness and unnecessary snowiness, I will venture to assert we all enjoyed ourselves. We spent most of our time sensibly in lounging about the lake on the jolly little steamers; and when we did a mountain climb, it was on the Rigi or Pilatus – where an engine undertook all the muscular work for us.

As usual, at the hotel, a great many miscellaneous people showed a burning desire to be specially nice to us. If you wish to see how friendly and charming humanity is, just try being a well-known millionaire for a week, and you'll learn a thing or two. Wherever Sir Charles goes he is surrounded by charming and disinterested people, all eager to make his distinguished acquaintance, and all familiar with several excellent investments, or several deserving objects of Christian charity. It is my business in life, as his brother-in-law and secretary, to decline with thanks the excellent investments, and to throw judicious cold water on the objects of charity. Even I myself, as the great man's almoner, am very much sought after. People casually allude before me to artless stories of 'poor curates in Cumberland, you know, Mr Wentworth,' or widows in Cornwall, penniless poets with epics in their desks, and young painters who need but the breath of a patron to open to them the doors of an admiring Academy. I smile and look wise, while I administer cold water in minute doses; but I never report one of these cases to Sir Charles, except in the rare or almost unheard-of event where I think there is really something in them.

Ever since our little adventure with the seer at Nice, Sir Charles, who is constitutionally cautious, had been even more careful than usual about possible sharpers. And, as chance would have it, there sat just opposite us at the *table d'hôte* at the Schweitzerhof – 'tis a fad of Amelia's to dine at the *table d'hôte*; she says she can't bear to be boxed up all day in private rooms with 'too much family' – a sinister-looking man with dark hair and eyes, conspicuous by his bushy overhanging eyebrows. My attention was first called to the eyebrows in question by a nice little parson who sat at our side, and who observed that they were made up of certain large and bristly hairs, which (he told us) had been traced by Darwin to our monkey ancestors. Very pleasant little fellow, this fresh-faced young parson, on his honeymoon tour with a nice wee wife, a bonnie Scotch lassie with a charming accent.

I looked at the eyebrows close. Then a sudden thought struck me. 'Do you believe they're his own?' I asked of the curate; 'or are they only stuck on – a make-up disguise? They really almost look like it.'

'You don't suppose – ' Charles began, and checked himself suddenly.

'Yes, I do,' I answered; 'the seer!' Then I recollected my blunder, and looked down sheepishly. For, to say the truth, Vandrift had straightly enjoined on me long before to say nothing of our painful little episode at Nice to Amelia; he was afraid if she once heard of it, *he* would hear of it for ever after.

'What seer?' the little parson enquired, with parsonical curiosity.

I noticed the man with the overhanging eyebrows give a queer sort of start. Charles's glance was fixed upon me. I hardly knew what to answer.

'Oh, a man who was at Nice with us last year,' I stammered out, trying hard to look unconcerned. 'A fellow they talked about, that's all.' And I turned the subject.

But the curate, like a donkey, wouldn't let me turn it.

'Had he eyebrows like that?' he enquired, in an undertone. I was really angry. If this was Colonel Clay, the curate was obviously giving him the cue, and making it much more difficult for us to catch him, now we might possibly have lighted on the chance to do so.

'No, he hadn't,' I answered testily; 'it was a passing expression.

But this is not the man. I was mistaken, no doubt.' And I nudged him gently.

The little curate was too innocent for anything. 'Oh, I see,' he replied, nodding hard and looking wise. Then he turned to his wife and made an obvious face, which the man with the eyebrows couldn't fail to notice.

Fortunately, a political discussion going on a few places farther down the table spread up to us and diverted attention for a moment. The magical name of Gladstone saved us. Sir Charles flared up. I was truly pleased, for I could see Amelia was boiling over with curiosity by this time.

After dinner, in the billiard-room, however, the man with the big eyebrows sidled up and began to talk to me. If he *was* Colonel Clay, it was evident he bore us no grudge at all for the five thousand pounds he had done us out of. On the contrary, he seemed quite prepared to do us out of five thousand more when opportunity offered; for he introduced himself at once as Dr Hector Macpherson, the exclusive grantee of extensive concessions from the Brazilian government on the Upper Amazon. He dived into conversation with me at once as to the splendid mineral resources of his Brazilian estate – the silver, the platinum, the actual rubies, the possible diamonds. I listened and smiled; I knew what was coming. All he needed to develop this magnificent concession was a little more capital. It was sad to see thousands of pounds' worth of platinum and car-loads of rubies just crumbling in the soil or carried away by the river, for want of a few hundreds to work them with properly. If he knew of anybody, now, with money to invest, he could recommend him – nay, offer him – a unique opportunity of earning, say, forty per cent on his capital, on unimpeachable security.

'I wouldn't do it for every man,' Dr Hector Macpherson remarked, drawing himself up; 'but if I took a fancy to a fellow who had command of ready cash, I might choose to put him in the way of feathering his nest with unexampled rapidity.'

'Exceedingly disinterested of you,' I answered drily, fixing my eyes on his eyebrows.

The little curate, meanwhile, was playing billiards with Sir Charles. His glance followed mine as it rested for a moment on the monkey-like hairs.

'False, obviously false,' he remarked with his lips; and I'm bound to confess I never saw any man speak so well by movement alone; you could follow every word though not a sound escaped him.

During the rest of that evening Dr Hector Macpherson stuck to me as close as a mustard-plaster. And he was almost as irritating. I got heartily sick of the Upper Amazon. I have positively waded in my time through ruby mines (in prospectuses, I mean) till the mere sight of a ruby absolutely sickens me. When Charles, in an un-wonted fit of generosity, once gave his sister Isabel (whom I had the honour to marry) a ruby necklet (inferior stones), I made Isabel change it for sapphires and amethysts, on the judicious plea that they suited her complexion better. (I scored one, incidentally, for having considered Isabel's complexion.) By the time I went to bed I was prepared to sink the Upper Amazon in the sea, and to stab, shoot, poison or otherwise seriously damage the man with the concession and the false eyebrows.

For the next three days, at intervals, he returned to the charge. He bored me to death with his platinum and his rubies. He didn't want a capitalist who would personally exploit the thing; he would prefer to do it all on his own account, giving the capitalist preference debentures of his bogus company, and a lien on the concession. I listened and smiled; I listened and yawned; I listened and was rude; I ceased to listen at all; but still he droned on with it. I fell asleep on the steamer one day, and woke up in ten minutes to hear him droning yet – ' . . . and the yield of platinum per ton was certified to be – ' I forget how many pounds, or ounces, or pennyweights. These details of assays have ceased to interest me: like the man who 'didn't believe in ghosts', I have seen too many of them.

The fresh-faced little curate and his wife, however, were quite different people. He was a cricketing Oxford man; she was a breezy Scotch lass, with a wholesome breath of the Highlands about her. I called her 'White Heather'. Their name was Brabazon. Millionaires are so accustomed to being beset by harpies of every description, that when they come across a young couple who are simple and natural, they delight in the purely human relation. We picnicked and went on excursions a great deal with the honeymooners. They were frank in their young love, and so proof against chaff, that we all really liked them. But whenever I called the pretty girl 'White Heather', she looked quite shocked, and cried: 'Oh, Mr Wentworth!' Still, we were the best of friends. The curate offered to row us in a boat on the lake one day, while the Scotch lassie assured us she could take an oar almost as well as he did. However, we did not accept their offer, as row-boats exert an unfavourable influence upon Amelia's digestive organs.

'Nice young fellow, that man Brabazon,' Sir Charles said to me one day, as we lounged together along the quay; 'never talks about advowsons or next presentations. Doesn't seem to me to care two pins about promotion. Says he's quite content in his country curacy; enough to live upon, and needs no more; and his wife has a little, a very little, money. I asked him about his poor today, on purpose to test him: these parsons are always trying to screw something out of one for their poor; men in my position know the truth of the saying that we have that class of the population always with us. Would you believe it, he says he hasn't any poor at all in his parish! They're all well-to-do farmers or else able-bodied labourers, and his one terror is that somebody will come and try to pauperise them. 'If a philanthropist were to give me fifty pounds today for use at Empingham,' he said, 'I assure you, Sir Charles, I shouldn't know what to do with it. I think I should buy new dresses for Jessie, who wants them about as much as anybody else in the village – that is to say, not at all.' There's a parson for you, Sey, my boy. Only wish we had one of his sort at Seldon.'

'He certainly doesn't want to get anything out of you,' I answered.

That evening at dinner a queer little episode happened. The man with the eyebrows began talking to me across the table in his usual fashion, full of his wearisome concession on the Upper Amazon. I was trying to squash him as politely as possible, when I caught Amelia's eye. Her look amused me. She was engaged in making signals to Charles at her side to observe the little curate's curious cuff-links. I glanced at them, and saw at once they were a singular possession for so unobtrusive a person. They consisted each of a short gold bar for one arm of the link, fastened by a tiny chain of the same material to what seemed – to my tolerably experienced eye – a first-rate diamond. Pretty big diamonds, too, and of remarkable shape, brilliancy and cutting. In a moment I knew what Amelia meant. She owned a diamond *rivière*, said to be of Indian origin, but short by two stones for the circumference of her tolerably ample neck. Now, she had long been wanting two diamonds like these to match her set; but owing to the unusual shape and antiquated cutting of her own gems, she had never been able to complete the necklet, at least without removing an extravagant amount from a much larger stone of the first water.

The Scotch lassie's eyes caught Amelia's at the same time, and she broke into a pretty smile of good-humoured amusement. 'Taken in another person, Dick, dear!' she exclaimed, in her breezy way, turning to her husband. 'Lady Vandrift is observing your diamond cuff-links.'

'They're very fine gems,' Amelia observed incautiously. (A most unwise admission if she desired to buy them.)

But the pleasant little curate was too transparently simple a soul to take advantage of her slip of judgement. 'They *are* good stones,' he replied; 'very good stones – considering. They're not diamonds at all, to tell you the truth. They're best old-fashioned Oriental paste. My great-grandfather bought them, after the siege of Seringapatam, for a few rupees, from a sepoy who had looted them from Tippoo Sahib's palace. He thought, like you, he had got a good thing. But it turned out, when they came to be examined by experts, they were only paste – very wonderful paste; it is supposed they had even imposed upon Tippoo himself, so fine is the imitation. But they are worth – well, say, fifty shillings at the utmost.'

While he spoke Charles looked at Amelia, and Amelia looked at Charles. Their eyes spoke volumes. The *rivière* was also supposed to have come from Tippoo's collection. Both drew at once an identical conclusion. These were two of the same stones, very likely torn apart and disengaged from the rest in the *mêlée* at the capture of the Indian palace.

'Can you take them off?' Sir Charles asked blandly. He spoke in the tone that indicates business.

'Certainly,' the little curate answered, smiling. 'I'm accustomed to taking them off. They're always noticed. They've been kept in the family ever since the siege, as a sort of valueless heirloom, for the sake of the picturesqueness of the story, you know; and nobody ever sees them without asking, as you do, to examine them closely. They deceive even experts at first. But they're paste, all the same; unmitigated Oriental paste, for all that.'

He took them both off, and handed them to Charles. No man in England is a finer judge of gems than my brother-in-law. I watched him narrowly. He examined them close, first with the naked eye, then with the little pocket-lens which he always carries. 'Admirable imitation,' he muttered, passing them on to Amelia. 'I'm not surprised they should impose upon inexperienced observers.'

But from the tone in which he said it, I could see at once he had satisfied himself they were real gems of unusual value. I know Charles's way of doing business so well. His glance to Amelia meant, 'These are the very stones you have so long been in search of.'

The Scotch lassie laughed a merry laugh. 'He sees through them now, Dick,' she cried. 'I felt sure Sir Charles would be a judge of diamonds.'

Amelia turned them over. I know Amelia, too; and I knew from the way Amelia looked at them that she meant to have them. And when Amelia means to have anything, people who stand in the way may just as well spare themselves the trouble of opposing her.

They were beautiful diamonds. We found out afterwards the little curate's account was quite correct: these stones *had* come from the same necklet as Amelia's *rivière*, made for a favourite wife of Tippoo's who had presumably as expansive personal charms as our beloved sister-in-law's. More perfect diamonds have seldom been seen. They have excited the universal admiration of thieves and connoisseurs. Amelia told me afterwards that, according to legend, a sepoy stole the necklet at the sack of the palace, and then fought with another for it. It was believed that two stones got spilt in the scuffle, and were picked up and sold by a third person – a looker-on – who had no idea of the value of his booty. Amelia had been hunting for them for several years to complete her necklet.

'They are excellent paste,' Sir Charles observed, handing them back. 'It takes a first-rate judge to detect them from the reality. Lady Vandrift has a necklet much the same in character, but composed of genuine stones; and as these are so much like them, and would complete her set, to all outward appearances, I wouldn't mind giving you, say, ten pounds for the pair of them.'

Mrs Brabazon looked delighted. 'Oh, sell them to him, Dick,' she cried, 'and buy me a brooch with the money! A pair of common links would do for you just as well. Ten pounds for two paste stones! It's quite a lot of money.'

She said it so sweetly, with her pretty Scotch accent, that I couldn't imagine how Dick had the heart to refuse her. But he did, all the same.

'No, Jess, darling,' he answered. 'They're worthless, I know; but they have for me a certain sentimental value, as I've often told you. My dear mother wore them, while she lived, as ear-rings; and as soon as she died I had them set as links in order that I might always keep them about me. Besides, they have historical and family interest. Even a worthless heirloom, after all, *is* an heirloom.'

Dr Hector Macpherson looked across and intervened. 'There is a part of my concession,' he said, 'where we have reason to believe a perfect new Kimberley will soon be discovered. If at any time you would care, Sir Charles, to look at my diamonds – when I get them – it would afford me the greatest pleasure in life to submit them to your consideration.'

Sir Charles could stand it no longer. 'Sir,' he said, gazing across at him with his sternest air, 'if your concession were as full of diamonds as Sindbad the Sailor's valley, I would not care to turn my head to look at them. I am acquainted with the nature and practice of salting.' And he glared at the man with the overhanging eyebrows as if he would devour him raw. Poor Dr Hector Macpherson subsided instantly. We learnt a little later that he was a harmless lunatic, who went about the world with successive concessions for ruby mines and platinum reefs, because he had been ruined and driven mad by speculations in the two, and now recouped himself by imaginary grants in Burmah and Brazil, or anywhere else that turned up handy. And his eyebrows, after all, were of nature's handicraft. We were sorry for the incident; but a man in Sir Charles's position is such a mark for rogues that, if he did not take means to protect himself promptly, he would be forever overrun by them.

When we went up to our *salon* that evening, Amelia flung herself on the sofa. 'Charles,' she broke out in the voice of a tragedy queen, 'those are real diamonds, and I shall never be happy again till I get them.'

'They are real diamonds,' Charles echoed. 'And you shall have them, Amelia. They're worth not less than three thousand pounds. But I shall bid them up gently.'

So, next day, Charles set to work to higgle with the curate. Brabazon, however, didn't care to part with them. He was no money-grubber, he said. He cared more for his mother's gift and a family tradition than for a hundred pounds, if Sir Charles were to offer it. Charles's eye gleamed. 'But if I give you two hundred!' he said insinuatingly. 'What opportunities for good! You could build a new wing to your village schoolhouse!'

'We have ample accommodation,' the curate answered. 'No, I don't think I'll sell them.'

Still, his voice faltered somewhat, and he looked down at them enquiringly.

Charles was too precipitate.

'A hundred pounds more or less matters little to me,' he said; 'and my wife has set her heart on them. It's every man's duty to please his wife – isn't it, Mrs Brabazon? – I offer you three hundred.'

The little Scotch girl clasped her hands.

'Three hundred pounds! Oh, Dick, just think what fun we could have, and what good we could do with it! Do let him have them.'

Her accent was irresistible. But the curate shook his head.

'Impossible,' he answered. 'My dear mother's ear-rings! Uncle Aubrey would be so angry if he knew I'd sold them. I daren't face Uncle Aubrey.'

'Has he expectations from Uncle Aubrey?' Sir Charles asked of White Heather.

Mrs Brabazon laughed. 'Uncle Aubrey! Oh, dear, no. Poor dear old Uncle Aubrey! Why, the darling old soul hasn't a penny to bless himself with, except his pension. He's a retired post captain.' And she laughed melodiously. She was a charming woman.

'Then I should disregard Uncle Aubrey's feelings,' Sir Charles said decisively.

'No, no,' the curate answered. 'Poor dear old Uncle Aubrey! I wouldn't do anything for the world to annoy him. And he'd be sure to notice it.'

We went back to Amelia. 'Well, have you got them?' she asked.

'No,' Sir Charles answered. 'Not yet. But he's coming round, I think. He's hesitating now. Would rather like to sell them himself, but is afraid what "Uncle Aubrey" would say about the matter. His wife will talk him out of his needless considerations for Uncle Aubrey's feelings; and tomorrow we'll finally clench the bargain.'

Next morning we stayed late in our *salon*, where we always breakfasted, and did not come down to the public rooms till just before *déjeuner*, Sir Charles being busy with me over arrears of correspondence. When we *did* come down, the *concierge* stepped forward with a twisted little feminine note for Amelia. She took it and read it. Her countenance fell. 'There, Charles,' she cried, handing it to him, 'you've let the chance slip. I shall *never* be happy now! They've gone off with the diamonds.'

Charles seized the note and read it. Then he passed it on to me. It was short, but final:

> *Thursday, 6 a.m.*

DEAR LADY VANDRIFT – *Will* you kindly excuse our having gone off hurriedly without bidding you goodbye? We have just had a horrid telegram to say that Dick's favourite sister is *dangerously* ill of fever in Paris. I wanted to shake hands with you before we left – you have all been so sweet to us – but we go by the morning train, absurdly early, and I wouldn't for worlds disturb you. Perhaps someday we may meet again – though, buried as we are in a north-country village, it isn't likely; but in any case, you have secured the grateful recollection of

Yours very cordially,

JESSIE BRABAZON

P.S. Kindest regards to Sir Charles and those *dear* Wentworths, and a kiss for yourself, if I may venture to send you one.

'She doesn't even mention where they've gone,' Amelia exclaimed, in a very bad humour.

'The *concierge* may know,' Isabel suggested, looking over my shoulder.

We asked at his office.

Yes, the gentleman's address was the Reverend Richard Peploe Brabazon, Holme Bush Cottage, Empingham, Northumberland.

Any address where letters might be sent at once, in Paris?

For the next ten days, or till further notice, Hôtel des Deux Mondes, Avenue de l'Opéra.

Amelia's mind was made up at once.

'Strike while the iron's hot,' she cried. 'This sudden illness, coming at the end of their honeymoon, and involving ten days' more stay at an expensive hotel, will probably upset the curate's budget. He'll be glad to sell now. You'll get them for three hundred. It was absurd of Charles to offer so much at first; but offered once, of course we must stick to it.'

'What do you propose to do?' Charles asked. 'Write, or telegraph?'

'Oh, how silly men are! ' Amelia cried. 'Is this the sort of business to be arranged by letter, still less by telegram? No. Seymour must start off at once, taking the night train to Paris; and the moment he gets there, he must interview the curate or Mrs Brabazon. Mrs Brabazon's the best. She has none of this stupid, sentimental nonsense about Uncle Aubrey.'

It is no part of a secretary's duties to act as a diamond broker. But when Amelia puts her foot down, she puts her foot down – a fact which she is unnecessarily fond of emphasising in that identical proposition. So the self-same evening saw me safe in the train on my way to Paris; and next morning I turned out of my comfortable sleeping-car at the Gare de Strasbourg. My orders were to bring back those diamonds, alive or dead, so to speak, in my pocket to Lucerne; and to offer any needful sum, up to two thousand five hundred pounds, for their immediate purchase.

When I arrived at the Deux Mondes I found the poor little curate and his wife both greatly agitated. They had sat up all night, they said, with their invalid sister; and the sleeplessness and suspense had certainly told upon them after their long railway journey. They were pale and tired, Mrs Brabazon, in particular, looking ill and worried – too much like White Heather. I was more than half ashamed of bothering them about the diamonds at such a moment, but it occurred to me that Amelia was probably right – they would now have reached the end of the sum set apart for their Continental trip, and a little ready cash might be far from unwelcome.

I broached the subject delicately. It was a fad of Lady Vandrift's, I said. She had set her heart upon those useless trinkets. And she wouldn't go without them. She must and would have them. But the curate was obdurate. He threw Uncle Aubrey still in my teeth. Three hundred? – no, never! A mother's present; impossible, dear Jessie! Jessie begged and prayed; she had grown really attached to Lady Vandrift, she said; but the curate wouldn't hear of it. I went up tentatively to four hundred. He shook his head gloomily. It wasn't a question of money, he said. It was a question of affection. I saw it was no use trying that tack any longer. I struck out a new line. 'These stones,' I said, 'I think I ought to inform you, are really diamonds. Sir Charles is certain of it. Now, is it right for a man of your profession and position to be wearing a pair of big gems like those, worth several hundred pounds, as ordinary cuff-links? A woman? – yes, I grant you. But for a man, is it manly? And you a cricketer!'

He looked at me and laughed. 'Will nothing convince you?' he cried. 'They have been examined and tested by half a dozen jewellers, and we know them to be paste. It wouldn't be right of me to sell them to you under false pretences, however unwilling on my side. I *couldn't* do it.'

'Well, then,' I said, going up a bit in my bids to meet him, 'I'll put it like this. These gems are paste. But Lady Vandrift has an unconquerable and unaccountable desire to possess them. Money doesn't matter to her. She is a friend of your wife's. As a personal favour, won't you sell them to her for a thousand?'

He shook his head. 'It would be wrong,' he said – 'I might even add, criminal.'

'But we take all risk,' I cried.

He was absolute adamant. 'As a clergyman,' he answered, 'I feel I cannot do it.'

'Will *you* try, Mrs Brabazon?' I asked.

The pretty little Scotchwoman leant over and whispered. She coaxed and cajoled him. Her ways were winsome. I couldn't hear what she said, but he seemed to give way at last. 'I should love Lady Vandrift to have them,' she murmured turning to me. 'She *is* such a dear!' And she took out the links from her husband's cuffs and handed them across to me.

'How much?' I asked.

'Two thousand?' she answered interrogatively. It was a big rise, all at once; but such are the ways of women.

'Done!' I replied. 'Do you consent?'

The curate looked up as if ashamed of himself.

'I consent,' he said slowly, 'since Jessie wishes it. But as a clergyman, and to prevent any future misunderstanding, I should like you to give me a statement in writing that you buy them on my distinct and positive declaration that they are made of paste – old Oriental paste – not genuine stones, and that I do not claim any other qualities for them.'

I popped the gems into my purse, well pleased.

'Certainly,' I said, pulling out a paper. Charles, with his unerring business instinct, had anticipated the request, and given me a signed agreement to that effect.

'You will take a cheque?' I enquired.

He hesitated.

'Notes of the bank of France would suit me better,' he answered.

'Very well,' I replied. 'I will go out and get them.'

How very unsuspicious some are! He allowed me to go off – with the stones in my pocket!

Sir Charles had given me a blank cheque, not exceeding two thousand five hundred pounds. I took it to our agents and cashed it for notes of the bank of France. The curate clasped them with pleasure. And right glad I was to go back to Lucerne that night, feeling that I had got those diamonds into my hands for about a thousand pounds under their real value!

At Lucerne railway station Amelia met me. She was positively agitated.

'Have you bought them, Seymour?' she asked.

'Yes,' I answered, producing my spoils in triumph.

'Oh, how dreadful!' she cried, drawing back. 'Do you think they're real? Are you sure he hasn't cheated you?'

'Certain of it,' I replied, examining them. 'No one can take me in, in the matter of diamonds. Why on earth should you doubt them?'

'Because I've been talking to Mrs O'Hagan, at the hotel, and she says there's a well-known trick just like that – she's read of it in a book. A swindler has two sets – one real, one false; and he makes you buy the false ones by showing you the real, and pretending he sells them as a special favour.'

'You needn't be alarmed,' I answered. 'I am a judge of diamonds.'

'I shan't be satisfied,' Amelia murmured, 'till Charles has seen them.'

We went up to the hotel. For the first time in her life I saw Amelia really nervous as I handed the stones to Charles to examine.

Her doubt was contagious. I half feared, myself, he might break out into a deep monosyllabic interjection, losing his temper in haste, as he often does when things go wrong. But he looked at them with a smile, while I told him the price.

'Eight hundred pounds less than their value,' he answered, well satisfied.

'You have no doubt of their reality?' I asked.

'Not the slightest,' he replied, gazing at them. 'They are genuine stones, precisely the same in quality and type as Amelia's necklet.'

Amelia drew a sigh of relief. 'I'll go upstairs,' she said slowly, 'and bring down my own for you both to compare with them.'

One minute later she rushed down again, breathless. Amelia is far from slim, and I never before knew her exert herself so actively.

'Charles, Charles!' she cried, 'do you know what dreadful thing has happened? Two of my own stones are gone. He's stolen a couple of diamonds from my necklet, and sold them back to me.'

She held out the *rivière*. It was all too true. Two gems were missing – and these two just fitted the empty places!

A light broke in upon me. I clapped my hand to my head. 'By Jove,' I exclaimed, 'the little curate is – Colonel Clay!'

Charles clapped his own hand to his brow in turn. 'And Jessie,' he cried, 'White Heather – that innocent little Scotchwoman! I often detected a familiar ring in her voice, in spite of the charming Highland accent. Jessie is – Madame Picardet!'

We had absolutely no evidence; but, like the commissary at Nice, we felt instinctively sure of it.

Sir Charles was determined to catch the rogue. This second deception put him on his mettle. 'The worst of the man is,' he said, 'he has a method. He doesn't go out of his way to cheat us; he makes us go out of ours to be cheated. He lays a trap, and we tumble headlong into it. Tomorrow, Sey, we must follow him on to Paris.'

Amelia explained to him what Mrs O'Hagan had said. Charles took it all in at once, with his usual sagacity. 'That explains,' he said, 'why the rascal used this particular trick to draw us on by. If we had suspected him he could have shown the diamonds were real, and so escaped detection. It was a blind to draw us off from the fact of the robbery. He went to Paris to be out of the way when the discovery was made, and to get a clear day's start of us. What a consummate rogue! And to do me twice running!'

'How did they get at my jewel-case, though?' Amelia exclaimed.

'That's the question,' Charles answered. 'You *do* leave it about so!'

'And why didn't he steal the whole *rivière* at once, and sell the gems?' I enquired.

'Too cunning,' Charles replied. 'This was much better business. It isn't easy to dispose of a big thing like that. In the first place, the stones are large and valuable; in the second place, they're well known – every dealer has heard of the Vandrift *rivière*, and seen pictures of the shape of them. They're marked gems, so to speak. No, he played a better game – took a couple of them off, and offered them to the only person on earth who was likely to buy them without suspicion. He came here, meaning to work this very trick; he had the links made right to the shape beforehand, and then he stole the stones and slipped them into their places. It's a wonderfully clever trick. Upon my soul, I almost admire the fellow.'

For Charles is a businessman himself, and can appreciate business capacity in others.

How Colonel Clay came to know about that necklet, and to appropriate two of the stones, we only discovered much later. I will not here anticipate that disclosure. One thing at a time is a good rule in life. For the moment he succeeded in baffling us altogether.

However, we followed him on to Paris, telegraphing beforehand to the bank of France to stop the notes. It was all in vain. They had been cashed within half an hour of my paying them. The curate and his wife, we found, quitted the Hôtel des Deux Mondes for parts unknown that same afternoon. And, as usual with Colonel Clay, they vanished into space, leaving no clue behind them. In other words, they changed their disguise, no doubt, and reappeared somewhere else that night in altered characters. At any rate, no such person as the Reverend Richard Peploe Brabazon was ever afterwards heard of – and, for the matter of that no such village exists as Empingham, Northumberland.

We communicated the matter to the Parisian police. They were *most* unsympathetic. 'It is no doubt Colonel Clay,' said the official whom we saw; 'but you seem to have little just ground of complaint against him. As far as I can see messieurs, there is not much to choose between you. You, Monsieur le Chevalier, desired to buy diamonds at the price of paste. You, madame, feared you had bought paste at the price of diamonds. You, monsieur the secretary, tried to get the stones from an unsuspecting person for half their value. He took you all in, that brave Colonel Caoutchouc – it was diamond cut diamond.'

Which was true, no doubt, but by no means consoling.

We returned to the Grand Hôtel. Charles was fuming with

indignation. 'This is really too much,' he exclaimed. 'What an audacious rascal! But he will never again take me in, my dear Sey. I only hope he'll try it on. I should love to catch him. I'd know him another time, I'm sure, in spite of his disguises. It's absurd my being tricked twice running like this. But never again while I live! Never again, I declare to you!'

'*Jamais de la vie!*' a courier in the hall close by murmured responsively. We stood under the verandah of the Grand Hotel, in the big glass courtyard. And I verily believe that courier was really Colonel Clay himself in one of his disguises.

But perhaps we were beginning to suspect him everywhere.

A Clever Capture

GUY CLIFFORD

Turning over the pages of one of my old diaries, I come across notes here and there of many curious riddles – some worked out and ticked off as solved, others still awaiting the fullness of time when all shall be known.

Amongst the former, and perhaps one of the most curious of them all in the manner of its solution, is that which I have chosen as the subject of this remarkable story.

My friend and partner, Robert Graceman, had been almost invisible for several days, shut up in his den engaged on some recondite chemical experiment, appearing only at occasional intervals to restore exhausted nature with a hasty meal. His usually rubicund and jovial face bore evident signs of his continuous and laborious researches. His eyes were heavy and leaden-looking with want of sleep, and his whole demeanour showed most painfully the enormous strain of overwork that he was imposing upon his system.

That evening, at dinner, I took him to task severely on the foolishness of continuing his work without proper relaxation.

'All right, Halton, old fellow,' he replied, 'a few more hours and then I will promise to take a holiday. Your anxiety, however, is quite unnecessary, for I'm as right as a trivet, except that I feel a bit fagged. Tomorrow, however, I will lie in bed all day and catch up on my back sleep.' So with a nod and a smile he left me to return to his crucibles and evil-smelling chemical mixtures.

Next morning his place at the breakfast table was empty, and looking into his den I was glad to find his apparatus put aside as though done with for the present. Evidently the experiments he was engaged on were completed, for the present at any rate, so cautioning our old housekeeper not to disturb him, I descended to the offices to get through my usual morning's work.

On going upstairs to lunch I found Graceman perched on the back of a chair, skimming the *Daily Post*.

'Hullo, my busy bee,' he exclaimed, throwing down the paper, 'I've taken your advice, you see, and kept my promise. Now I'm going to dose you with your own physic. We will take a holiday together, turn up business and chemistry and have a good time.'

'I can't leave the office at present – ' I began, but he broke in.

'Well, you'll have to take the office with you then, for go you do, my boy, so there's no use wasting time in discussing that point; the question is where shall we go and what shall we do?'

'I may as well give in,' I replied, with more pretence of reluctance than I really felt, for his joyous mood was very infectious and a few days off would do us both good.

'Ah! I thought you wouldn't resist the temptation. Shall it be Brighton – no, too crowded – a few days up the river at Sonning, say, wouldn't be half bad if this weather holds, and it looks like keeping up.'

So it was decided that on the following morning we should pack our bags and depart for Sonning-on-Thames, one of the sweetest little spots on our lovely river. We were like a couple of schoolboys all that evening, for it was seldom of late years that we had made holiday together, and it was a matter of some difficulty to unearth our boating flannels, so long had they remained unused. Graceman, who was a fisherman of more than ordinary zeal, spent hours in furbishing up his rods and tackle. However, at last all was ready and everything packed up.

We determined to start early, and before nine o'clock we were on our way to Paddington. Sonning is an out-of-the-way little river village having no station of its own, so it is usually reached by driving from Twyford. As our train drew into Maidenhead, just this side of Twyford, Graceman, who was gazing out of the window, suddenly called out 'Why, there's Layman; I wonder what he's doing down here?' and jumping up he thrust his head out of the window and waved his hand.

Layman, or Inspector Layman of Scotland Yard, to give him his proper title, was somewhat of a favourite of Graceman's.

In a few seconds he was at our door and shaking hands.

'We're playing truant, Layman,' said Graceman. 'Mr Halton and I are on the jaunt for a few days; but what's the matter with you man, you look hipped?'

'I am hipped, sir, and pretty badly, too,' returned the inspector. 'You no doubt saw in the papers yesterday that there had been a burglary at Lord Lipham's house down here the night before last and all her ladyship's jewels stolen except those she had on. The usual thing you know, dinner time – entrance gained by ladder to her ladyship's bedroom – no one about – no trace – no clue . . . no nothing,' wound up the inspector, laconically. 'And the aggravating thing,' he went on, 'is that this is one of five or six burglaries that have occurred during the last six weeks or so that we can find no clue to; first they are down in Surrey at Woking, then Sevenoaks, Bickley, Harpenden and Esher are visited, and now they're here. We feel sure it is the same hand at each of these places, for the work is so clean and not the slightest trace left behind to help us.'

'Poor fellow,' said Graceman, 'it's too bad of them to play you such games. We're off now, but come and see us next week at the office if you don't catch them and we'll put our heads together. Goodbye,' and so saying Graceman resumed his seat as the train moved on.

Our holiday has nothing to do with this adventure, so I will pass over the pleasant days we passed on the bosom of old Father Thames and come to our last night at Sonning. It was Sunday, and we intended returning to London by an early train on Monday morning. We were sitting on the lawn of the White Hart Hotel smoking a final pipe before turning in to bed when Graceman remarked: 'I haven't seen any account of the capture of the Maidenhead burglars in the papers this week; have you?'

'I had forgotten there were such things as burglars,' I replied. 'I've scarcely looked at the *Post* which you so thoughtfully ordered.'

'What a humbug you are, Halton,' he languidly answered. 'When I proposed this little trip, oh! you couldn't leave the office, but since you've been down here I don't believe you've thought once of all your multitudinous business obligations. My professional opinion is that at heart you're a loafer, a perfect loafer. Come on, let's turn in.'

When we arrived at Paddington next morning, Graceman rather surprised me by baying he wanted to send a wire to Inspector Layman, so making his way round to the telegraph office he despatched the following message to that gentleman: 'Come and see me tonight at Fig Buildings if you have not found your Maidenhead friends – Graceman.'

As we bowled along in a hansom I endeavoured, delicately, to pump him on the subject of burglaries in general, and Layman's in particular, but he failed to respond to my insinuating enquiries, and, recognising my want of success, I at last desisted.

Business matters have an awkward way of accumulating during one's holidays, and I was kept busily employed for the rest of the day. I was reminded during the afternoon of Inspector Layman, however, by receiving a telegram saying he would call after dinner. I sent the message upstairs to Graceman but the clerk said he was not at home.

Graceman had returned, however, when I went into the dining-room for dinner.

'You've had Layman's wire?' I asked interrogatively.

'Yes, and I see he is still down at Maidenhead.'

'He didn't say so in his message,' I remarked.

'No, of course not, but the telegram was despatched from Maidenhead if you notice, therefore I think it is a fair inference that the man was there, but we shall presently know what success he has had. Meantime, have you any engagement for Wednesday evening, as I have a little adventure to propose which I think you would like to share?'

As I had nothing special on hand I signified my willingness to participate, and from past experience I refrained from trying to elicit what the adventure was until he was prepared to enlighten me.

When dinner was over we adjourned to the smoking-room, where very shortly afterwards Inspector Layman was announced

'How's Maidenhead looking, Layman?' said Graceman, with a twinkle in his eye as he shook the inspector's hand; 'you're getting quite sunburnt.'

'I was about to make the same remark to you,' returned Layman; 'both you and Mr Halton are looking very fit, but as to Maidenhead it's a jolly enough place if you're down there boating and nothing to worry you, but from a professional point of view I'm just about tired of it.'

'Then you have made little progress?'

'No, we are just where we were when I saw you at the station; in fact, we are worse off, as there is a week's loss of time with absolutely nothing to show for it. We overhauled several suspicious customers during the first day or two after the burglary, but they were not our men. Personally I don't hope to trace them, as I feel convinced they are well out of the neighbourhood; their mode of work shows me that they are too clever to be caught unless we are able to drop on them red-handed. I cannot even form any definite theory as to who the thieves may be, or how they work. You've helped me unravel some tough cases, Mr Graceman, but then we've always had some clue or trace to work on, but now I'm beaten.'

'Never say die,' said Graceman, as the inspector finished speaking; 'you forget the Delford Mystery and the McHenry Will Case, to say nothing of one or two others, where we had as little to guide us, and yet you pulled them off all right.'

'You pulled them off, you should have said,' returned Layman, 'for if you had not put me on the right scent they would have remained mysteries to the present day; but I fear even you cannot pull these chestnuts out of the fire for us.'

'Now you want to nettle me, Layman; you know my weak side and take advantage of it,' replied Graceman with a smile. 'However, I will humour you and accept your challenge, but, mind you, on our usual understanding: my name – I may say our names, for Mr Halton will help me – are not to appear under any circumstances whatever.'

'Of course I shall be charmed to go burglar-catching, but I don't quite see – ' I began, when Graceman stopped me with: 'Wait a bit, Halton. Layman, I want your assurance.'

'If you wish it, of course I promise, sir; but let me tell you frankly I would much sooner you allowed me to inform my chief, for I don't much care for false credit, and praise so gained rather rankles here,' said Layman, striking his clenched hand on his chest.

'It must be as I say,' returned Graceman, 'we cannot be known in the matter; you and I have worked together many times and you have previously tried to overcome my desire for remaining incognito without success, so you must accept the stipulation. And now to business. "From information received," as the newspaper reporters have it, I understand a burglary is to be attempted at Sunbury next Wednesday evening. My information, unfortunately, does not give the address of the victims, nor does it state the numerical strength of the burglars, but I put the number at about three. A very important fact, however, is that the confederates meet at Sunbury railway station at half-past six on Wednesday evening, and they are the same gentlemen you are looking for at Maidenhead.' As Graceman finished speaking he leaned back in his seat and surveyed the inspector, who sat bolt upright in his chair, his face vividly expressing the astonishment he felt at this explicit and detailed exposure of the enemy's plans.

'This beats Maskelyne and Cook; why if I did not know you so well I should believe you were making a fool of me,' exclaimed Layman. 'Here have I been in close communication with all our force, half over England, for more than a week on this job while you return this morning from your holiday, and in a few hours put your hand on the entire band. Yes, it's funny, awfully funny,' he wound up, as I burst into laughter at the comical expression which the inspector wore.

'Excuse me, Layman, it's too bad to laugh at your perplexity,' I said; 'however, I am as much in the dark as you are.'

'Can you inform us, Mr Graceman, the source of this remarkable intelligence?' began Layman.

'I thought I told you, "from information received".'

'Is that all?'

'All that I can tell you for the present, but I should like to ask you how you intend to act in the matter; or perhaps you would prefer to hear my ideas first and then say what you think of them?'

'By all means,' replied Layman.

'Halton,' Graceman commenced, 'please give me your attention, for you are as well acquainted with the ground over which we are to travel as I am;' then turning towards Inspector Layman, he continued: 'Sunbury, you are probably aware, is a small riverside village a couple of miles or so above Hampton Court; the station lies about a mile from the river, and the best part of Sunbury is situated close to the Thames; along the road from the station to the village are also several large detached houses, and I may mention here that this road is exceedingly badly lighted at night. Near the station on the opposite side of the line are a number of houses – in fact, another village – but as these are all small cottages I don't think we need trouble about them. You made the remark when we met at Maidenhead that there had been five or six burglaries, all very similar in character, during the past few weeks around London, and that they occurred during the time the family were at dinner – was this so in each case?'

'There was only one exception, if exception it may be termed,' replied Layman, 'and in that case the thieves are presumed to have entered after dinner, as during dessert the lady of the house sent one of the servants up to her bedroom for her vinaigrette, and the girl noticed nothing unusual in the room; but they must have been just at hand, for within an hour the robbery was discovered by the lady's maid when she went to tidy up her mistress's room. For all practical purposes we may, therefore, say each of these robberies was effected during dinner.'

'Let us assume then that the plans of our friends at Sunbury are laid on the same lines – what I propose is this, that tomorrow you go down to Sunbury with two or three good men and thoroughly investigate the neighbourhood, find out the habits of all the residents in the near vicinity who may be considered worth these fellows' attention, ascertain if there are any strangers recently arrived at any of the hotels and if anyone is giving a dance or a dinner-party on Wednesday evening. You will have but little difficulty in your enquiries, as it is only a one-horse place and everyone knows everybody else's business. You can leave your men down there if you like, but they must be careful to avoid being conspicuous. They should dress like boating men, flannel shirts and serge suits, and go for a row in the day to blind suspicion. By this means you will gain a good knowledge of the locality; and if you will call here tomorrow evening we will make our plans for Wednesday. If you get back in time, come straight on here and have dinner with us.'

As Graceman concluded, he rose and stretched himself by slowly walking up and down the room, while Layman, after asking a few questions about Sunbury and promising to see us again the next evening, lighted up a fresh cigar which I offered him and took his departure.

'If not asking too much, Graceman,' I remarked, when the inspector had gone, 'I should rather like to have one or two little points cleared up on this affair.'

'Say on, my friend.'

'Firstly, then, at what time on Wednesday do you require the pleasure of my company? Secondly, where are *we* – that is, you and I – going to? And, thirdly, what are we going to do when we get there?'

'Concisely put and with commendable moderation,' responded Graceman; 'and I will reply as tersely. Firstly, three p.m.; secondly, Hampton Court; thirdly, go for a row. Having gratified your curiosity I must bid you good-night, for I still feel the effects of the balmy air of Sonning, and am confoundedly sleepy.'

Whether this was an excuse to avoid further questioning or no I cannot say, but I rather think it was, for my friend Robert's custom was rather to sit up till the small hours of the morning.

Graceman, after breakfast next morning, informed our house-keeper that we should probably have a visitor to dinner that evening, and a little later on he joined me in the office, where, somewhat to my surprise he remained the rest of the day, a thing he now rarely did, as I think I have before mentioned.

Inspector Layman, however, did not arrive in time for dinner, and it was past ten o'clock when he appeared. His report of the day's proceedings at Sunbury may be summed up very shortly. As arranged, he had made enquiries as suggested the previous night, and thoroughly surveyed the neighbourhood. The most important facts he had gleaned were that at two houses there would be parties on the Wednesday evening, and that as far as could be learnt there were no persons staying in the village whose movements were at all suspicious. These two houses were both on the road from Sunbury to Hampton, and not more than five minutes apart.

'The chief result attained,' remarked Graceman, 'is that your knowledge of the ground will be of immense advantage to us when we have to work at night. You, of course, particularly observed the situation of the houses which were giving the entertainments?'

Layman signified his assent to this question by a nod.

'Briefly, then,' went on Graceman, 'my proposal is this. You take down three more good men tomorrow afternoon, and have them just outside the station at a quarter-past six. It will be almost dark at that hour. How many men have you there now?'

'Three.'

'Good! Then instruct two of them to proceed, when it gets dark, to watch these houses, and the third man must patrol between the two; if nothing transpires then they are to return to Sunbury station at eleven o'clock. But if the burglars arrive at either house the man must get quietly away and summon his two *confrères*, and they must secure the thieves as best they can. Mr Halton and myself are going down to Hampton Court tomorrow afternoon; we shall row up to Sunbury, and will meet you at the Magpie Hotel. We shall be there just before six o'clock, and we will immediately proceed to the station, where I hope to spot our friends when they meet. I think that provides for everything?' Graceman wound up, interrogatively.

'It's all right if we can recognise the scamps,' replied Layman; 'or if they attack the houses we have under surveillance; but I don't see where we shall come in if we miss them at the station, and they break into some other place.'

'That's certainly the weak part of our chain,' returned Graceman, 'but I will show you how we can strengthen it when we meet at the Magpie. From their method of work, however, I think you will find one or more of these burglars are past masters at their trade, and I shall be more than surprised, Layman, if you don't find them to be old acquaintances, in which case you will recognise one or more of them yourself. I need hardly suggest that all your men and yourself should be disguised, as we do not wish the birds to take flight just when we are about to snare them.'

Discussing various details of the morrow's campaign took time and it was nearly midnight ere the inspector left us.

Graceman and I went down early on the following afternoon to Hampton Court, where we hired a light skiff from the boatyard we usually patronised, and informed the man that we should leave the boat at Sunbury that night and he could send and fetch it back next day.

The distance by river to Sunbury is just about three miles, and

Graceman suggested that pulling easily we could arrive at our destination about five o'clock and have some tea before Layman joined us.

I must not linger over the scenery of the river, which at that season of the year, for it was the end of September, was full of ripe beauty which always held for me a special charm, and the reach below Sunbury I consider one of the most beautiful on the Thames.

For myself I thought it all too soon when we reached the landing-stage of the Magpie Hotel, and the adventurous enterprise on which we were engaged was forcibly thrust upon me by Graceman's remark to hurry up or I wouldn't get any tea. However, he had arranged matters so well that we had finished our meal comfortably and lighted our pipes before the inspector arrived punctually on the stroke of six.

Dusk was fast deepening into the gloom of night as we started for the station, and as soon as we were out of the main street of the village, Layman reported that everything was in order as arranged.

'Good!' remarked Graceman; 'and now I will tell you how I mean to make the weak link in our chain right; but first I must look in here,' and as he spoke he opened the gate of a tiny cottage, and walking up the short path knocked at the door, which was opened almost instantly.

'Ready, Tom?' we heard him say.

'That you, Mr Graceman? Right you are, sir.'

And as the door shut, and the two men came towards us, I remembered that this was the abode of Tom West, a professional fisherman, who had many a time and oft been engaged for a day's fishing by Graceman.

In a few words Graceman told him as we continued our walk what we were down there for, and then, addressing Layman and myself, remarked that Tom knew every man, woman and child in Sunbury, whether villagers or gentlefolk, and that he had written to him to be ready at six o'clock that evening when he called.

'You will see presently that his assistance will be of the utmost service,' said Graceman, and then he continued his remarks which this addition to our party had interrupted.

'You have no doubt noticed the exit from Sunbury station is through a wooden gate at which a porter stands to collect tickets. You remember that I said my information gave the meeting place as Sunbury station at half-past six? A coincidence, or shall I call it a corollary, is the fact that a train arrives here from town at twenty-six minutes past six – what more probable then, that this train brings one or, perhaps, more of the thieves? Now, Tom West can tell us who are natives and who are not, and if there are any strangers on the platform awaiting the train's arrival we must watch them. If, however, there are no suspicious characters about then we must look for them amongst the passengers getting off the train. You must place your men, Layman, outside the gate where they can be talking together obscured in the gloom. They must watch you, who will indicate to them by a nod to follow any person or persons that Tom West does not know and whom he will point out to me, and I will nod to you as the suspected party passes the gate. Your men, after shadowing any suspects, must report to you at the Magpie, where Mr Halton and myself will adjourn as soon as you are engaged on the track. Here we are at the station and the train's signalled too, so look sharp, inspector, and arrange your men. We'll go on the platform.'

As we passed on to the platform Graceman commenced to chat rather loudly with Tom West on the chance of a day's sport on the morrow amongst the barbel. There was apparently no one there besides ourselves, but still laughing and chatting he kept the conversation from flagging until the roar of the quickly approaching train drowned his efforts. Then he said sharply, 'Tom, keep your eye on each person that approaches the exit, and if you don't know him, give me a poke on the arm with your stick. Now look out sharp and keep chattering and laughing at the same time.' There were very few passengers by the train, perhaps a score in all, and several had already passed through the gate when Tom West whispered, 'That fellow in a brown hat, gaping round near the gate, is a stranger to me.'

As I glanced at the man out of the corner of my eye, I saw a look of recognition flash from him, and in a moment another man joined him.

'There's another stranger talking with him,' whispered West again.

Both men now gazed among the quickly-thinning group of passengers; then I noticed one touch the other on the arm, and both moved towards the gate.

'Now, Halton,' said Graceman rapidly, in a low voice, 'you walk off to the gate as if you were going out, and when I call out "Jim", count five then answer back "yes" and return to us.'

Closely following Graceman's instructions, I took the few steps which brought me amongst the last of the people pushing through the gate; the two men I had been watching were just passing the exit, when Graceman called out 'Jim'.

While I was counting five before I replied, another voice outside the gate answered 'Hallo'; at the same moment I shouted 'Yes'. Naturally surprised, I looked towards the spot whence the voice came; I saw the two men we had been watching, together with a third man, all turned towards the spot where Graceman stood; they were just through the gate in front of me, and I could have touched them by putting out my hand. Fortunately I didn't forget Graceman's instructions, and turning sharp round I called out, 'Well, what is it?' As I did so I heard one of the three give a guffaw, and say, 'I thought it was you, Jim, the bloke wanted.'

This little scene took far less time to act than it does to set down here, and half a minute would more than cover the time occupied.

When I got close to Graceman he burst out into a hearty laugh that might have been heard at the end of the road, and Tom West joined him; but what they saw to laugh at beat me. However, they seemed so tickled that I felt compelled to help them and so we laughed at each other.

'Capital, couldn't have been better,' said Graceman, when he had finished making an exhibition of himself.

'I'm glad of that, anyhow,' I replied.

'All right, old man, keep your hair on, what kind of a chap was Jim?'

'Tall, darkish beard and moustache, rough, dark-grey overcoat, brownish softcloth hat, and he had a largish black hand-bag,' I answered somewhat proudly, for I have a woman's knack of taking stock of people at a glance.

'My dear Halton, you're a credit to me. Let us away. Come on Tom, and don't forget we're fishermen only now.'

So saying, we sauntered away from the station into the darkness of the night. We had barely gone thirty or forty yards before a figure advanced from the gloom of the hedge at the roadside.

'It's all right, sir,' said the figure, for it was Layman. 'My three men are shadowing them. We know one of the scamps, the one in the brown hat, so there's not the slightest doubt you've given us the straight tip this time. I must be off now after my men. Are you going on to the Magpie?'

'Yes.'

'Then I'll come on there directly we've located them.' And the inspector walked briskly off ahead of us.

Nothing more was said on the matter as we returned to the hotel. Tom West and Graceman went deep into the merits of trolling and spinning for jack and the subtle niceties of snap-tackle fishing for that same interesting fish.

'Come in, Tom, and have a whisky,' said Graceman, when we arrived at our destination.

When we were seated in a comfortable corner of the smoke-room, Graceman said: 'Would you like to be in at the death, or shall we wait the final act here, Halton?'

'I should rather like to see the capture,' I replied; 'that is, if it's in the neighbourhood.'

'All right, we will decide when Layman returns.'

It was nearly an hour before the inspector appeared. He was beaming and as sprightly as a two-year-old.

Declining my invitation to have a whisky, he drew a chair up to our little table and detailed his movements since he left us. The presumed burglars had walked leisurely down the road we had just come, without any sign of uneasiness; they continued through the village with the same easy indifference until they were close to the first house where a dinner-party was planned; here they loitered a bit, as if to see if the coast were clear, then they disappeared over the wall which shut off the side grounds from the road. One of the detectives followed them and returned in a few minutes to say they were ensconced in a summer-house, at the bottom of the garden. The other two detectives had then got over the wall and hidden themselves in some shrubs near the house, whilst the first went back to watch the summer-house.

'When do you start, Layman?' said Graceman when the inspector had finished.

'As soon as you like, sir; the dinner-party is for eight o'clock, and it's nearly that now, so we ought to be moving.'

'Come on, then, let's be off, Halton, if you're coming.'

'Yes, I've come so far, so I may as well see the finish,' I remarked.

'You must be careful, gentlemen,' said Layman, 'for one man, I know, is a dangerous customer. Is Mr West to join us, too?'

'I should like to uncommonly, if I shan't be in the way,' eagerly remarked Tom.

'All right,' said Graceman, 'you stick close to me; now we're ready.' And so saying, we moved off on our expedition.

The night had closed in pitch dark, a heavy mantle of black rain-clouds obscured the heavens and the wind was beginning to blow with some force.

The road beyond the village was dark and lonesome; some little distance before we arrived at our destination the inspector bade us halt while he went on to see if all was quiet. Returning in about ten minutes he reported all serene, and under his guidance we went forward and clambered over the wall. He hid us away near the two detectives and desired us to remain perfectly quiet unless he called us by name.

The house was a wide two-storeyed building with a verandah over the ground floor; every room downstairs was a blaze of light, but in the top rooms only two rooms showed a full light, whilst in the others there was only a dim twinkle as though the gas burners were turned down low.

We were barely hidden away when we heard eight o'clock strike from some neighbouring church.

Scarcely breathing, we felt the minutes pass like hours, but it could scarcely have been a quarter past eight when I saw three shadowy forms approaching from the opposite corner of the house. They halted close to where I was crouching, with Tom West on the one side and Graceman on the other.

'Keep a sharp look out, Bill,' I heard one whisper, and then the same man said, 'Give me a hoist.'

Clutching hold of one of the pillars that supported the verandah, the other stooped for him to put his feet on his shoulders; then, slowly rising, the climber grasped the edge of the verandah, and drew himself up; a second man followed in the same manner, and when he was up, the other whispered down, 'Now for the bag,' and the fellow below picked up the black bag, and, groping about, presently said in a hoarse whisper, 'All right,' and I saw the bag slowly ascend. It had evidently been tied on to a piece of cord which it was too dark to discern.

From our hiding-place I could see the two men crawl to one of the darkened windows, then, in about a couple of minutes, I heard a faint click, and presently the window was slowly raised and both men disappeared inside the house.

I was quivering with excitement now and breathlessly awaiting the next act in the drama. I had not long to wait. The man watching below stood back a little from the house, where he could command every window. Just behind him was a patch of shrubs, and as I watched him, a dark object crept noiselessly round the bushes; then it straightened itself up and two arms shot out, clutching the watcher by the throat and throwing him on his back on the grass – a dull thud was the only sound that reached me as the body fell. Then another figure joined the first, and in a few seconds the fallen man was drawn out of my sight behind the bushes. Another figure then appeared, and took up the position the captured man had occupied, whilst three other forms crept under the verandah just where the burglars had climbed up.

Ten minutes or so slowly dragged by, then a figure appeared at the opened window, and crawled quietly out, followed by his pal.

When they got to the edge of the verandah, one whispered, 'Here you are, Bill,' and the supposed Bill stepped forward and secured the black bag. Both the men on the roof then lowered themselves over the edge, and dropped right into the arms of those there waiting for them hidden beneath the verandah. There was a bit of a scuffle, and the rest of us rushed up, but the capture was completed without our aid, and without a word having been spoken.

When the handcuffs were on, one of the twain said in a bitter tone: 'Bill's peached, I s'pose, Jim.'

'Yes, damn him,' replied the other.

'Oh, no, he hasn't,' remarked Layman; 'we've got him trussed like a fowl on the grass here. We've had our eyes on you since the Maidenhead affair.'

'Yes, we've done it once too often,' admitted the fellow.

'But let us see what you've got in the bag here,' and Layman as he spoke moved closer towards the window and let the light shine into the opened bag, turning the contents over with his hand. 'Ah,' he ejaculated. 'By Jove! but you made a grand haul; we had better go round to the front door and let them know what's been happening.'

We all marched through the side yard to the front, the prisoners guarded each by two stalwart detectives.

'Let's get in the background – we don't want to be recognised,' said Graceman to me as the inspector knocked at the main entrance.

The servant started back in alarm on beholding the band of men in the porch, but a few words from Layman reassured him somewhat, and closing the door again he went to fetch his master.

'By Jove! it's old Colonel Stanley,' whispered Graceman in my ear as a tall, white-haired man threw the door open wide.

'Well, friends, what's the matter?'

'Fortunately nothing very serious,' replied Layman, 'your house has been broken into while you were dining, but we secured the thieves in the act and have all the plunder here,' tapping the bag.

'Good gracious! are you a police officer?' said the colonel.

Layman nodded and the colonel asked him to go in.

'We may as well toddle,' remarked Graceman, taking my arm. 'Tell the inspector, Tom, that Mr Halton and I have gone back to the Magpie.'

It was not long before the inspector joined us, and when I suggested a whisky this time he did not refuse.

He still retained the black bag.

'I've sent the men up to the railway station,' he said, in answer to Graceman's enquiry, 'and if you don't object we might catch the next train back to town, as I shall feel more comfortable when these jokers are safe under lock and key.'

On our journey to Waterloo, Layman related what had passed when he entered the house at the colonel's invitation. The old man called his son out from the dining-room and Layman related the affair of the capture, and it was agreed that nothing should be said to the guests till after the dinner was finished. Then the story was to be told and the people in the house were each to make a list of what things they missed and the lists were to be sent on to the inspector at Scotland Yard. Layman was to catalogue the contents of the black bag and send the list to the colonel, who was to attend the police-court on the following morning, when no doubt the magistrate would order the things to be handed over to him.

When the inspector had finished relating these arrangements he turned to Graceman and begged him to relate how he had discovered the plans of the burglars which he had forecast so exactly.

Graceman unbuttoned his overcoat, and taking out his pocket-book, handed to Layman a little slip of a newspaper cutting.

'Have you seen that before?' he asked.

'No,' the inspector replied in a hesitating manner; then suddenly, as a remembrance seemed to strike him, 'Yes I have though, by Jove! Didn't it appear in one of the morning papers a few days ago?'

'Quite so; in the *Daily Post* agony column,' returned Graceman.

'But what's it got to do with this affair?'

'That's my "information received", that's all,' said Graceman quietly.

'Do you mean that this is all you had to work on?' quickly demanded Layman.

'Yes.'

'Well I'm – but I won't swear; please explain it and settle me.'

'Don't flurry, there's a good fellow,' returned Graceman, as he handed me the cutting, which was as follows:

O W S N E U H D N A N B L E U F S R P
D Y A A S S Y T T N A S E T I X I X T
                                                          JIM

Then he continued. 'This appeared in the *Daily Post* agony column last Monday, and I read it and solved it as we were returning from Sonning; then I wired you to come and see me. Similar notices had appeared in the same paper at different times during the past two or three months, but you put the clue in my hands at Maidenhead.'

Me! how?'

'When you informed me that similar burglaries had occurred at Woking, Sevenoaks, and the other places. Now these little cryptograms have an attraction for me and I had taken the trouble to decipher them; the answer to this one is found by reading every third letter in rotation, thus,' and so saying he handed us slip of paper on which was pencilled the following.

O W S N E U H D N A N B L E U F S R P
13 26 1 14 27 2 15 28 3 16 29 4 17 30 5 18 31 6 19

D Y A A S S Y T T N A S E T I X I X T
32 7 20 33 8 21 34 9 22 35 10 23 36 11 24 37 12 25 38

JIM

'If you start at number 1 and read the figures in numerical order the translation comes out, "Sunbury station, half-past six Wednesday next, Jim." Those that appeared in the previous weeks solved themselves by the same rule, but each read differently, the difference being in the place and time of meeting. I looked up the file of the papers and found that on each date a burglary took place in the neighbourhood given. But in two cases the name appended to the cryptogram was "Bloater", the others were all "Jim". I concluded that it was the practice of these rascals, when they spotted a suitable crib to crack, to communicate the fact to each other by this means, and I think you will admit my conclusions have justified themselves, and by our joint efforts we have outwitted the enemy.'

'Joint efforts is good, remarkably good,' Layman said, with a half-hearted kind of laugh. 'A pretty tale to pitch to my chief. "How did you manage it, Layman?" he will say. "Joint efforts with a man unknown," I answer. Make him smile, won't it?'

'Pooh, you can put your chief right better than that,' returned Graceman, 'say anything or nothing, but mum's the word as regards Mr Halton and myself, and now good-night to you;' and shaking hands with Layman as the train drew into Waterloo we left him to look after the safe custody of his charges.

It may be well in conclusion to relate that at the trial it was fully proved that the prisoners had been concerned in all the burglaries mentioned in this narrative, and the sentence was ten years penal servitude, the judge commending Inspector Layman for the smart way in which he had secured his captives.

Nine Points of the Law

E. W. HORNUNG

'Well,' said Raffles, 'what do you make of it?'

I read the advertisement once more before replying. It was the last column of the *Daily Telegraph*, and it ran:

> TWO THOUSAND POUNDS REWARD – The above sum may be earned by anyone qualified to undertake delicate mission and prepared to run certain risk – Apply by telegram: Security, London.

'I think,' said I, 'it's the most extraordinary advertisement that ever got into print!'

Raffles smiled.

'Not quite all that, Bunny; still, extraordinary enough, I grant you.'

'Look at the figure!'

'It is certainly large.'

'And the mission – and the risk!'

'Yes; the combination is frank, to say the least of it. But the really original point is requiring applications by telegram to a telegraphic address! There's something in the fellow who thought of that, and something in his game; with one word he chokes off the million who answer an advertisement every day – when they can raise the stamp. My answer cost me five bob; but then I prepaid another.'

'You don't mean to say that you've applied?'

'Rather,' said Raffles. 'I want two thousand pounds as much as any man.'

'Put your own name?'

'Well – no, Bunny, I didn't. In point of fact, I smell something interesting and illegal, and you know what a cautious chap I am. I signed myself Saumarez, care of Hickey, 28 Conduit Street; that's my tailor, and after sending the wire I went round and told him what to expect. He promised to send the reply along the moment it came – and, by Jove, that'll be it!'

And he was gone before a double-knock on the outer door had

done ringing through the rooms, to return next minute with an open telegram and a face full of news.

'What do you think?' said he. 'Security's that fellow Addenbrooke, the police-court lawyer, and he wants to see me *instanter*!'

'And you're going to him now?'

'This minute,' said Raffles, brushing his hat; 'and so are you.'

'But I came in to drag you out to lunch.'

'You shall lunch with me when we've seen this fellow. Come on, Bunny, and we'll choose your name on the way. Mine's Saumarez, and don't you forget it.'

Mr Bennett Addenbrooke occupied substantial offices in Wellington Street, Strand, and was out when we arrived; but he had only just gone 'over the way to the court'; and five minutes sufficed to produce a brisk, fresh-coloured, resolute-looking man, with a very confident, rather festive air, and black eyes that opened wide at the sight of Raffles.

'Mr – Saumarez?' exclaimed the lawyer.

'My name,' said Raffles, with dry effrontery.

'Not up at Lord's, however!' said the other, slyly. 'My dear sir, I have seen you take far too many wickets to make any mistake!'

For a moment Raffles looked venomous; then he shrugged and smiled, and the smile grew into a little cynical chuckle.

'So you have bowled me out in my turn?' said he. 'Well, I don't think there's anything to explain. I am harder up than I wished to admit under my own name, that's all, and I want that thousand pounds reward!'

'Two thousand,' said the solicitor. 'And the man who is not above an alias happens to be just the sort of man I want; so don't let that worry you, my dear sir. The matter, however, is of a strictly private and confidential character.' And he looked very hard at me.

'Quite so,' said Raffles. 'But there was something about a risk?'

'A certain risk is involved.'

'Then surely three heads will be better than two. I said I wanted that thousand pounds; my friend here wants the other. Must you have his name too? Bunny, give him your card.'

Mr Addenbrooke raised his eyebrows over my name, address, and club; then he drummed on my card with his fingernail, and his embarrassment expressed itself in a puzzled smile.

'The fact is, I find myself in a difficulty,' he confessed at last. 'Yours is the first reply I have received; people who can afford to send long telegrams don't rush to the advertisements in the *Daily Telegraph*; but, on the other hand, I was not quite prepared to hear from men like yourselves. Candidly, and on consideration, I am not sure that you *are* the stamp of men for me – men who belong to good clubs! I rather intended to appeal to the – er – adventurous classes.'

'We are adventurers,' said Raffles gravely.

'But you respect the law?'

The black eyes gleamed shrewdly.

'We are not professional rogues, if that's what you mean,' said Raffles calmly. 'But on our beam-ends we are; we would do a good deal for a thousand pounds apiece.'

'Anything,' I murmured.

The solicitor rapped his desk.

'I'll tell you what I want you to do. You can but refuse. It's illegal, but it's illegality in a good cause; that's the risk, and my client is prepared to pay for it. He will pay for the attempt, in case of failure; the money is as good as yours once you consent to run the risk. My client is Sir Bernard Debenham, of Broom Hall, Esher.'

'I know his son,' I remarked.

'Then,' said the solicitor, you have the privilege of knowing one of the most complete young blackguards about town, and the *fons et origo* of the whole trouble. As you know the son, you may know the father also – at all events, by reputation; and in that case I needn't tell you that he is a very peculiar man. He lives alone in a storehouse of treasures which no eyes but his ever behold. He is said to have the finest collection of pictures in the south of England, though nobody ever sees them to judge; pictures, fiddles and furniture are his hobby, and he is undoubtedly very eccentric. Nor can one deny that there has been considerable eccentricity in his treatment of his son. For years Sir Bernard paid his debts, and the other day, without the slightest warning, not only refused to do so any more, but absolutely stopped the lad's allowance. Well, I'll tell you what has happened. But, first of all, you must know, or you may remember, that I appeared for young Debenham in a little scrape he got into a year or two ago. I got him off all right, and Sir Bernard paid me handsomely on the nail. And no more did I hear or see of either of them until one day last week.'

The lawyer drew his chair nearer ours, and leant forward with a hand on either knee.

'On Tuesday of last week I had a telegram from Sir Bernard; I was to go to him at once. I found him waiting for me in the drive; without a word he led me to the picture-gallery, which was locked and darkened, drew up a blind, and stood simply pointing to an empty picture-frame. It was a long time before I could get a word out of him. Then at last he told me that that frame had contained one of the rarest and most valuable pictures in England – in the world – an original Velasquez. I have checked this,' said the lawyer, 'and it seems literally true; the picture was a portrait of the Infanta Maria Theresa, said to be one of the artist's greatest works, and second only to his portrait of one of the popes in Rome – so they told me at the National Gallery, where they had its history by heart. They say there that the picture is practically priceless. And young Debenham has sold it for five thousand pounds!'

'The deuce he has!' said Raffles.

I enquired who had bought it.

'A Queensland legislator of the name of Craggs – the Honourable John Montagu Craggs MLC, to give him his full title. Not that we knew anything about him on Tuesday last; we didn't even know for certain that young Debenham had stolen the picture. But he had gone down for money on the Monday evening, had been refused, and it was plain enough that he had helped himself in this way; he had threatened revenge, and this was obviously it. Indeed, when I hunted him up in town on the Tuesday night, he confessed as much in the most brazen manner imaginable. But he wouldn't tell me who was the purchaser, and finding out that took the rest of the week; but find it out I did, and a nice time I've had of it ever since! Backwards and forwards between Esher and the Metropole, where the Queenslander is staying, sometimes twice a day; threats, offers, prayers, entreaties, not one of them a bit of good!'

'But,' said Raffles, 'surely it's a clear case? The sale was illegal; you can pay him back his money and force him to give the picture up.'

'Exactly; but not without an action and a public scandal, and that my client declines to face. He would rather lose even his picture than have the whole thing get into the papers; he has disowned his son, but he will not disgrace him; yet his picture he must have by hook or crook, and there's the rub! I am to get it back by fair means or foul. He gives me *carte blanche* in the matter, and, I verily believe, would throw in a blank cheque if asked. He offered one to the Queenslander, but Craggs simply tore it in two; the one old boy is as much a character as the other, and between the two of them I'm at my wits' end.'

'So you put that advertisement in the paper?' said Raffles, in the dry tones he had adopted throughout the interview.

'As a last resort, I did.'

'And you wish us to *steal* this picture?'

It was magnificently said; the lawyer flushed from his hair to his collar.

'I knew you were not the men!' he groaned. 'I never thought of men of your stamp! But it's *not* stealing,' he exclaimed heatedly; 'it's recovering stolen property. Besides, Sir Bernard will pay him his five thousand as soon as he has the picture; and, you'll see, old Craggs will be just as loth to let it come out as Sir Bernard himself. No, no – it's an enterprise, an adventure, if you like – but not stealing.'

'You yourself mentioned the law,' murmured Raffles.

'And the risk,' I added.

'We pay for that,' he said once more.

'But not enough,' said Raffles, shaking his head. 'My good sir, consider what it means to us. You spoke of those clubs; we should not only get kicked out of them, but put in prison like common burglars. It's true we're hard up, but it simply isn't worth it at the price – double your stakes, and I for one am your man.'

Addenbrooke wavered.

'Do you think you could bring it off?'

'We could try.'

'But you have no – '

'Experience? No, not as thieves.'

'And you would really run the risk for four thousand pounds?'

Raffles looked at me. I nodded.

'We would,' said he, 'and blow the odds!'

'It's more than I can ask my client to pay,' said Addenbrooke, growing firm.

'Then it's more than you can expect us to risk.'

'You are in earnest?'

'God wot!'

'Say three thousand if you succeed!'

'No, four.'

'Then nothing if you fail – '

'Double or quits?' said Raffles. 'Well, that's sporting. Done!'

Addenbrooke opened his lips, half rose, then sat back in his chair, and looked long and shrewdly at Raffles – never once at me.

'I know your bowling,' said he reflectively. 'I go up to Lord's whenever I want an hour's real rest, and I've seen you bowl again and again – yes, and take the best wickets in England on a plumb pitch. I don't forget the last Gentlemen and Players; I was there. You're up to every trick – every one . . . I'm inclined to think you would bowl out this old Australian if anybody can. Why! I believe you're my very man!'

The bargain was clinched at the Café Royal, where Bennett

Addenbrooke insisted on playing host at an extravagant luncheon. I remember that he took his whack of champagne with the nervous freedom of a man at high pressure, and have no doubt I kept him in countenance by an equal indulgence; but Raffles, ever an exemplar in such matters, was more abstemious even than his wont, and very poor company to boot. I can see him now, his eyes in his plate – thinking – thinking. I can see the solicitor glancing from him to me in an apprehension of which I did my best to disabuse him by reassuring looks. At the close Raffles apologised for his preoccupation, called for an ABC timetable, and announced his intention of catching the 3.02 to Esher.

'You must excuse me, Mr Addenbrooke,' said he, 'but I have my own idea, and for the moment I should much prefer to keep it to myself. It may end in fizzle, so I would rather not speak about it to either of you just yet. But speak to Sir Bernard I must, so will you write me one line to him on your card? Of course, if you wish, you must come down with me and hear what I say; but I really don't see the point.'

And, as usual, Raffles had his way, though Bennett Addenbrooke was visibly provoked, and I myself shared his annoyance to no small extent. I could only tell him that it was in the nature of Raffles to be self-willed and secretive, but that no man of my acquaintance had half his audacity and determination – that I, for my part would trust him through and through, and let him gang his own gait every time. More I dared not say, even to remove those chill misgivings with which I knew that the lawyer went his way.

That day I saw no more of Raffles, but a telegram reached me when I was dressing for dinner:

> Be in your rooms tomorrow from noon and keep rest of day clear.   RAFFLES

It had been sent off from Waterloo at 6.42.

So Raffles was back in town; at an earlier stage of our relations I should have hunted him up then and there, but now I knew better. His telegram meant that he had no desire for my society that night or the following forenoon; that when he wanted me I should see him soon enough.

And see him I did, towards one o'clock next day. I was watching for him from my window in Mount Street when he drove up furiously in a hansom, and jumped out without a word to the man. I met him next minute at the lift gates, and he fairly pushed me back into my rooms.

'Five minutes, Bunny!' he cried. 'Not a second more.'

And he tore off his coat before flinging himself into the nearest chair.

'I'm fairly on the rush,' he panted; 'having the very dickens of a time! Not a word till I tell you all I've done. I settled my plan of campaign yesterday at lunch. The first thing was to get in with this man Craggs; you can't break into a place like the Metropole – it's got to be done from the inside. Problem one, How to get at the fellow. Only one sort of pretext would do – it must be something to do with this blessed picture, so that I might see where he'd got it, and all that. Well, I couldn't go and ask to see it out of curiosity, and I couldn't go as a second representative of the other old chap, and it was thinking how I could go that made me such a bear at lunch. But I saw my way before we got up. If I could only lay hold of a copy of the picture I might ask leave to go and compare it with the original. So down I went to Esher to find out if there was a copy in existence, and was at Broom Hall for one hour and a half yesterday afternoon. There was no copy there, but they must exist, for Sir Bernard himself (such a rum old boy!) has allowed a couple to be made since the picture has been in his possession. He hunted up the painters' addresses, and the rest of the evening I spent in hunting up the painters themselves; but their work had been done on commission – one copy had gone out of the country, and I'm still on the track of the other.'

'Then you haven't seen Craggs yet?'

'Oh yes, I have seen him and made friends with him, and if possible he's the funnier old cuss of the two. I took the bull by the horns this morning, went in and lied like Ananias, and it was just as well I did – the old ruffian sails for Australia by tomorrow's boat. I told him a man wanted to sell me a copy of the celebrated Infanta Maria Theresa of Velasquez, that I'd been down to the supposed owner of the picture, only to find that he had just sold it to him. You should have seen his face when I told him that! He grinned all round his wicked old head. "Did old Debenham admit it?" says he; and when I said he had, he chuckled to himself for about five minutes. He was so pleased that he did just what I hoped he would do; he showed me the great picture – luckily it isn't by any means a large one – and took a special pride in showing me the case he's got it in. It's an iron map-case in which he brought over the plans of his land in Brisbane; he wants to know who would suspect it of containing an Old Master too? But he's had it fitted with a new Chubb's lock, and I managed to take an interest in the key while he was gloating over the canvas. I had the wax in the palm of my hand, and I shall make my duplicate this afternoon.'

Raffles looked at his watch and jumped up, saying he had given me a minute too much.

'By the way,' he added, 'you've got to dine with him at the Metropole tonight.'

'I?'

'Yes; don't look so scared. Both of us are invited – I swore you were dining with me; but I shan't be there.'

His clear eye was upon me, bright with meaning and with mischief. I implored him to tell me what his meaning was.

'You will dine in his private sitting-room,' said Raffles; 'it adjoins his bedroom. You must keep him sitting as long as possible, Bunny, and talking all the time!'

In a flash I saw his plan.

'You're going for the picture while we're at dinner?'

'Exactly.'

'If he hears you!'

'He shan't.'

'But if he did!' And I fairly trembled at the thought.

'If he did,' said Raffles, 'there would be a collision, that's all. You had better take your revolver. I shall certainly take mine.'

'But it's ghastly!' I cried. 'To sit and talk to an utter stranger and know that you're at work in the next room!'

'Two thousand apiece,' said Raffles, quietly.

'Upon my soul, I believe I shall give it away!'

'Not you, Bunny. I know you better than you know yourself.'

He put on his coat and his hat.

'What time have I to be there?' I asked him with a groan.

'Quarter to eight. There will be a telegram from me saying I can't turn up. He's a terror to talk, you'll have no difficulty in keeping the ball rolling; but head him off his picture for all you're worth. If he offers to show it you, say you must go. He locked up the case elaborately this afternoon, and there's no earthly reason why he should unlock it again in this hemisphere.'

'Where shall I find you when I get away?'

'I shall be down at Esher. I hope to catch the 9.55.'

'But surely I can see you again this afternoon?' I cried in a ferment, for his hand was on the door. 'I'm not half coached up yet! I know I shall make a mess of it!'

'Not you,' he said again, 'but *I* shall if I waste any more time. I've got a deuce of a lot of rushing about to do yet. You won't find me at my rooms. Why not come down to Esher yourself by the last train? That's it – down you come with the latest news. I'll tell old

Debenham to expect you; he shall give us both a bed. By Jove! he won't be able to do us too well if he's got his picture!'

'If!' I groaned, as he nodded his adieu; and he left me limp with apprehension, sick with fear, in a perfectly pitiable condition of pure stage-fright.

For, after all, I had only to act my part; unless Raffles failed where he never did fail, unless Raffles the neat and noiseless was for once clumsy and inept, all I had to do was indeed to 'smile and smile and be a villain'. I practised that smile half the afternoon. I rehearsed putative parts in hypothetical conversations. I got up stories. I dipped in a book on Queensland at the club. And at last it was 7.45 and I was making my bow to a somewhat elderly man with a small bald head and a retreating brow.

'So you're Mr Raffles's friend?' said he, overhauling me rather rudely with his light small eyes. 'Have you seen anything of him? I expected him early to show me something, but he's never come.'

No more, evidently, had his telegram, and my troubles were beginning early. I said I had not seen Raffles since one o'clock, telling the truth with unction while I could; even as we spoke there came a knock at the door; it was the telegram at last, and, after reading it himself, the Queenslander handed it to me.

'Called out of town!' he grumbled. 'Sudden illness of near relative! What near relatives has he got?'

Now Raffles had none, and for an instant I quailed before the perils of invention; then I replied that I had never met any of his people, and again felt fortified by my veracity.

'Thought you were bosom pals?' said he, with (as I imagined) a gleam of suspicion in his crafty little eyes.

'Only in town,' said I. 'I've never been to his place.'

'Well,' he growled, 'I suppose it can't be helped. Don't know why he couldn't come and have his dinner first. Like to see the death-bed that *I'd* go to without *my* dinner; it's a full-skin billet, if you ask me. Well, we must just dine without him, and he'll have to buy his pig in a poke after all. Mind touching that bell? Suppose you know what he came to see me about? Sorry I shan't see him again, for his own sake. I liked Raffles – took to him amazingly. He's a cynic. I like cynics. I'm one myself. Rank bad form of his mother or his aunt to go and kick the bucket today.'

I connect these specimens of his conversation, though they were doubtless detached at the time, and interspersed with remarks of mine here and there. They filled the interval until dinner was served, and they gave me an impression of the man which his every subsequent utterance confirmed. It was an impression which did away with all remorse for my treacherous presence at his table. He was that terrible type, the Silly Cynic, his aim a caustic commentary on all things and all men, his achievement mere vulgar irreverence and unintelligent scorn. Ill-bred and ill-informed, he had (on his own showing) fluked into fortune on a rise in land, yet cunning he possessed, as well as malice, and he chuckled till he choked over the misfortunes of less astute speculators in the same boom. Even now I cannot feel much compunction for my behaviour to the Honourable J. M. Craggs MLC.

But never shall I forget the private agonies of the situation, the listening to my host with one ear and for Raffles with the other! Once I heard him – though the rooms were divided by the old-fashioned folding-doors, and though the dividing door was not only shut but richly curtained, I could have sworn I heard him once. I spilt my wine and laughed at the top of my voice at some coarse sally of my host's. And I heard nothing more, though my ears were on the strain. But later, to my horror, when the waiter had finally withdrawn, Craggs himself sprang up and rushed to his bedroom without a word. I sat like stone till he returned.

'Thought I heard a door go,' he said. 'Must have been mistaken ... imagination ... gave me quite a turn. Raffles tell you priceless treasure I got in there?'

It was the picture at last; up to this point I had kept him to Queensland and the making of his pile. I tried to get him back there now, but in vain. He was reminded of his great ill-gotten possession. I said that Raffles had just mentioned it, and that set him off. With the confidential garrulity of a man who has been drinking freely he plunged into his darling topic, and I looked past him at the clock. It was only a quarter to ten.

In common decency I could not go yet. So there I sat (we were still at port) and learnt what had originally fired my host's ambition to possess what he was pleased to call a 'real, genuine, twin-screw, double-funnelled, copper-bottomed Old Master!' it was to 'go one better' than some rival legislator of pictorial proclivities. But even an epitome of his monologue would be so much weariness; suffice it that it ended inevitably in the invitation I had dreaded all the evening.

'But you must see it. Next room. This way.'

'Isn't it packed up?' I enquired hastily.

'Lock and key. That's all.'

'Pray don't trouble,' I urged.

'Trouble be hanged!' said he. 'Come along.'

And all at once I saw that to resist him further would be to heap suspicion upon myself against the moment of impending discovery. I therefore followed him into his bedroom without further protest, and suffered him first to show me the iron map-case which stood in one corner! he took a crafty pride in this receptacle, and I thought he would never cease descanting on its innocent appearance and its Chubb's lock. It seemed an interminable age before the key was in the latter. Then the ward clicked, and my pulse stood still.

'By Jove!' I cried next instant.

The canvas was in its place among the maps!

'Thought it would knock you,' said Craggs, drawing it out and unrolling it for my benefit. 'Grand thing, ain't it? Wouldn't think it had been painted two hundred and thirty years? But it has, my word! Old Johnson's face will be a treat when he sees it! won't go bragging about *his* pictures much more. Why, this one's worth all the pictures in Colony o' Queensland put together. Worth fifty thousand pounds, my boy – and I got it for five!'

He dug me in the ribs, and seemed in the mood for further confidences. My appearance checked him, and he rubbed his hands.

'If you take it like that,' he chuckled, 'how will old Johnson take it? Go out and hang himself from his own picture-rods, I hope!'

Heaven knows what I contrived to say at last. Struck speechless first by my relief, I continued silent from a very different cause. A new tangle of emotions tied my tongue. Raffles had failed – Raffles had failed! Could I not succeed? Was it too late? Was there no way?

'So long,' he said, taking a last look at the canvas before he rolled it up – 'so long till we get to Brisbane.'

The flutter I was in as he closed the case!

'For the last time,' he went on, as his keys jingled back into his pocket. 'It goes straight into the strong-room on board.'

For the last time! If I could but send him out to Australia with only its legitimate contents in his precious map-case! If I could but succeed where Raffles had failed!

We returned to the other room. I have no notion how long he talked, or what about. Whisky and soda-water became the order of the hour. I scarcely touched it, but he drank copiously, and before eleven I left him incoherent. And the last train for Esher was the 11.50 out of Waterloo.

I took a hansom to my rooms.

I was back at the hotel in thirteen minutes. I walked upstairs. The corridor was empty! I stood an instant on the sitting-room threshold, heard a snore within, and admitted myself softly with my master-key.

Craggs never moved! he was stretched on the sofa fast asleep. But not fast enough for me. I saturated my handkerchief with the chloroform I had brought and I laid it gently over his mouth. Two or three stertorous breaths, and the man was a log.

I removed the handkerchief; I extracted the keys from his pocket. In less than five minutes I put them back, after winding the picture about my body beneath my Inverness cape. I took some whisky and soda-water before I went.

The train was easily caught – so easily that I trembled for ten minutes in my first-class smoking carriage, in terror of every footstep on the platform, in unreasonable terror till the end. Then at last I sat back and lit a cigarette, and the lights of Waterloo reeled out behind.

Some men were returning from the theatre. I can recall their conversation even now. They were disappointed with the piece they had seen. It was one of the later Savoy operas, and they spoke wistfully of the days of *Pinafore* and *Patience*. One of them hummed a stave, and there was an argument as to whether the air was out of *Patience* or *The Mikado*. They all got out at Surbiton, and I was alone with my triumph for a few intoxicating minutes. To think that I had succeeded where Raffles had failed! Of all our adventures, this was the first in which I had played a commanding part; and, of them all, this was infinitely the least discreditable. It left me without a conscientious qualm; I had but robbed a robber, when all was said. And I had done it myself, single-handed – *ipse egomet!*

I pictured Raffles, his surprise, his delight. He would think a little more of me in future. And that future, it should be different. We had two thousand pounds apiece – surely enough to start afresh as honest men – and all through me!

In a glow I sprang out at Esher, and took the one belated cab that was waiting under the bridge. In a perfect fever I beheld Broom Hall, with the lower storey still lit up, and saw the front door open as I climbed the steps.

'Thought it was you,' said Raffles cheerily. 'It's all right. There's a bed for you. Sir Bernard's sitting up to shake your hand.'

His good spirits disappointed me. But I knew the man – he was one of those who wear their brightest smile in the blackest hour. I knew him too well by this time to be deceived.

'I've got it!' I cried in his ear – 'I've got it!'

'Got what?' he asked me, stepping back.

'The picture!'

'*What?*'

'The picture. He showed it me. You had to go without it; I saw that. So I determined to have it. And here it is.'

'Let's see,' said Raffles grimly.

I threw off my cape and unwound the canvas from about my body. While I was doing so an untidy old gentleman made his appearance in the hall, and stood looking on with raised eyebrows.

'Looks pretty fresh for an Old Master, doesn't it?' said Raffles.

His tone was strange. I could only suppose that he was jealous of my success.

'So Craggs said. I hardly looked at it myself.'

'Well, look now – look closely. By Jove, I must have faked it better than I thought!'

'It's a copy!' I cried.

'It's *the* copy,' he answered. 'It's the copy I've been tearing all over the country to procure. It's the copy I faked back and front, so that, on your own showing, it imposed upon Craggs, and might have made him happy for life. And you go and rob him of that!'

I could not speak.

'How did you manage it?' enquired Sir Bernard Debenham.

'Have you killed him?' asked Raffles sardonically.

I did not look at him; I turned to Sir Bernard Debenham, and to him I told my story, hoarsely, excitedly, for it was all that I could do to keep from breaking down. But as I spoke I became calmer, and I finished in mere bitterness, with the remark that another time Raffles might tell me what he meant to do.

'Another time!' he cried instantly. 'My dear Bunny, you speak as though we were going to turn burglars for a living!'

'I trust you won't,' said Sir Bernard, smiling, 'for you are certainly two very daring young men. Let us hope our friend from Queensland will do as he said, and not open the case till he gets back there. He will find my cheque awaiting him, and I shall be very much surprised if he troubles any of us again.'

Raffles and I did not speak till I was in the room which had been prepared for me. Nor was I anxious to do so then. But he followed me and took my hand.

'Bunny,' said he, 'don't you be hard on a fellow! I was in the deuce of a hurry, and didn't know that I should ever get what I wanted in time, and that's a fact. But it serves me right that you should have gone and undone one of the best things I ever did. As for *your* handiwork, old chap, you won't mind my saying that I didn't think you had it in you? In future – '

'For God's sake, don't talk about the future!' I cried. 'I hate the whole thing; I'm going to give it up!'

'So shall I,' said Raffles, 'when I've made my pile.'

The Stir Outside the Café Royal

CLARENCE ROOK

Colonel Mathurin was one of the aristocrats of crime; at least Mathurin was the name under which he had accomplished a daring bank robbery in Detroit, which had involved the violent death of the manager, though it was generally believed by the police that the Rossiter who was at the bottom of some long firm frauds in Melbourne was none other than Mathurin under another name, and that the designer and chief gainer in a sensational murder case in the Midlands was the same mysterious and ubiquitous personage.

But Mathurin had for some years successfully eluded pursuit: indeed it was generally known that he was the most desperate among criminals, and was determined never to be taken alive. Moreover, as he invariably worked through subordinates who knew nothing of his whereabouts and were scarcely acquainted with his appearance, the police had but a slender clue to his identity.

As a matter of fact, only two people beyond his immediate associates in crime could have sworn to Mathurin if a they had met him face to face. One of them was the Detroit bank manager whom he had shot with his own hand before the eyes of his fiancée. It was through the other that Mathurin was arrested, extradited to the States, and finally made to atone for his life of crime. It all happened in a distressingly commonplace way, so far as the average spectator was concerned. But the story, which I have pieced together from the details supplied – first, by a certain detective sergeant whom I met in a tavern hard by Westminster; and second, by a certain young woman named Miss van Snoop – has an element of romance, if you look below the surface.

It was about half-past one o'clock, on a bright and pleasant day, that a young lady was driving down Regent Street in a hansom which she had picked up outside her boarding-house near Portland Place Station. She had told the cabman to drive slowly, as she was nervous behind a horse, and so she had leisure to scan, with the curiosity of a stranger, the strolling crowd that at nearly all hours of the day throngs Regent Street. It was sunny and everybody looked cheerful. Ladies were shopping or looking in at the shop windows; men about town were collecting an appetite for lunch; flower girls were selling 'nice vi'lets, sweet vi'lets, penny a bunch'; and the girl in the cab leaned one arm on the apron and regarded the scene with alert attention. She was not exactly pretty, for the symmetry of her features was discounted by a certain hardness in the set of the mouth, but her hair, so dark as to be almost black, and her eyes, of greyish blue, set her beyond comparison with the commonplace.

Just outside the Café Royal there was a slight stir, and a temporary block in the foot traffic. A brougham was setting down, behind it was a victoria, and behind that a hansom; and as the girl glanced round the heads of the pair in the brougham, she saw several men standing on the steps. Leaning back suddenly, she opened the trap-door in the roof.

'Stop here,' she said, 'I've changed my mind.'

The driver drew up by the kerb, and the girl skipped out.

'You shan't lose by the change,' she said, handing him half-a-crown.

There was a tinge of American accent in the voice; and the cabman, pocketing the half-crown with thanks, smiled.

'They may talk about that McKinley tariff,' he soliloquised as he crawled along the kerb towards Piccadilly Circus, 'but it's better 'n free trade!'

Meanwhile the girl walked slowly back towards the Café Royal, and, with a quick glance at the men who were standing there, entered. One or two of the men raised their eyebrows; but the girl was quite unconscious, and went on her way to the luncheon-room.

'American, you bet,' said one of the loungers. 'They'll go anywhere and do anything.'

Just in front of her as she entered was a tall, clean-shaven man, faultlessly dressed in glossy silk hat and frock coat, with a flower in his button-hole. He looked around for a moment in search of a convenient table. As he hesitated, the girl hesitated: but when the waiter waved him to a small table laid for two, the girl immediately sat down behind him at the next table.

'Excuse me, madam,' said the waiter, 'this table is set for four; would you mind – '

'I guess,' said the girl, 'I'll stay where I am.' And the look in her eyes, as well as a certain sensation in the waiter's palm, ensured her against further disturbance.

The restaurant was full of people lunching, singly or in twos, in threes and even larger parties; and many curious glances were directed to the girl who sat at a table alone and pursued her way calmly through the menu. But the girl appeared to notice no one. When her eyes were off her plate they were fixed straight ahead – on the back of the man who had entered in front of her. The man, who had drunk a half-bottle of champagne with his lunch, ordered a liqueur to accompany his coffee. The girl, who had drunk an aerated water, leaned back in her chair and wrinkled her brows. They were very straight brows that seemed to meet over her nose when she wrinkled them in perplexity. Then she called a waiter.

'Bring me a sheet of notepaper, please,' she said, 'and my bill.'

The waiter laid the sheet of paper before her, and the girl proceeded, after a few moments' thought, to write a few lines in pencil upon it. When this was done, she folded the sheet carefully, and laid it in her purse. Then, having paid her bill, she returned her purse to her dress pocket, and waited patiently.

In a few minutes the clean-shaven man at the next table settled his bill and made preparations for departure. The girl at the same time drew on her gloves, keeping her eyes immovably upon her neighbour's back. As the man rose to depart, and passed the table at which the girl had been sitting, the girl was looking into the mirror upon the wall, and patting her hair. Then she turned and followed the man out of the restaurant, while a pair at an adjacent table remarked to one another that it was a rather curious coincidence for a man and woman to enter and leave at the same moment when they had no apparent connection.

But what happened outside was even more curious.

The man halted for a moment upon the steps at the entrance. The porter, who was in conversation with a policeman, turned, whistle in hand.

'Hansom, sir?' he asked.

'Yes,' said the clean-shaven man.

The porter was raising his whistle to his lips when he noticed the girl behind.

'Do you wish for a cab, madam?' he asked, and blew upon his whistle.

As he turned again for an answer, he plainly saw the girl, who was standing close behind the clean-shaven man, slip her hand under his coat, and snatch from his hip pocket something which she quickly transferred to her own.

'Well, I'm – ' began the clean-shaven man, swinging round and feeling in his pocket.

'Have you missed anything, sir?' said the porter, standing full in front of the girl to bar her exit.

'My cigarette case is gone,' said the man making from one side to another.

'What's this?' said the policeman, stepping forward.

'I saw the woman's hand in the gentleman's pocket, plain as a pikestaff,' said the porter.

'Oh, that's it, is it?' said the policeman, coming close to the girl. 'I thought as much.'

'Come now,' said the clean-shaven man, 'I don't want to make a fuss. Just hand back that cigarette-case, and we'll say no more about it.'

'I haven't got it,' said the girl. 'How dare you? I never touched your pocket.'

The man's face darkened.

'Oh, come now!' said the porter.

'Look here, that won't do,' said the policeman, 'you'll have to come along of me. Better take a four-wheeler, eh, sir?'

A knot of loafers, seeing something interesting in the wind, had collected round the entrance.

A four-wheeler was called, and the girl entered, closely followed by the policeman and the clean-shaven man.

'I was never so insulted in my life,' said the girl.

Nevertheless, she sat back quite calmly in the cab, as though she was perfectly ready to face this or any other situation, while the policeman watched her closely to make sure that she did not dispose in any surreptitious way of the stolen article.

At the police-station hard by, the usual formalities were gone through, and the clean-shaven man was constituted prosecutor. But the girl stoutly denied having been guilty of any offence.

The inspector in charge looked doubtful.

'Better search her,' he said, and the girl was led off to a room for an interview with the female searcher.

The moment the door closed, the girl put her hand into her pocket, pulled out the cigarette-case, and laid it upon the table.

'There you are,' she said. 'That will fix matters so far.'

The woman looked rather surprised.

'Now,' said the girl, holding out her arms, 'feel in this other pocket, and find my purse.'

The woman picked out the purse.

'Open it and read the note on the bit of paper inside.'

On the sheet of paper which the waiter had given her, the girl had written these words, which the searcher read in a muttered undertone.

I am going to pick this man's pocket as the best way of getting him into a police-station without violence. He is Colonel Mathurin, alias Rossiter, alias Connell, and he is wanted in Detroit, New York, Melbourne, Colombo and London. Get four men to pin him unawares, for he is armed and desperate. I am a member of the New York Detective Force – Nora van Snoop.

'It's all right,' said Miss van Snoop, quickly, as the searcher looked up at her after reading the note. 'Show that to the boss – right away.'

The searcher opened the door. After whispered consultation the inspector appeared, holding the note in his hand.

'Now then, be spry,' said Miss van Snoop. 'Oh, you needn't worry! I've got my credentials right here,' and she dived into another pocket.

'But do you know – can you be sure,' said the inspector, 'that this is the man who shot the Detroit bank manager?'

'Great heavens! Didn't I see him shoot Will Stevens with my own eyes! And didn't I take service with the police to hunt him out?'

The girl stamped her foot, and the inspector left. For two, three, four minutes, she stood listening intently. Then a muffled shout reached her ears. Two minutes later the inspector returned.

'I think you're right,' he said. 'We have found enough evidence on him to identify him. But why didn't you give him in charge before to the police?'

'I wanted to arrest him myself,' said Miss van Snoop, 'and I have. Oh, Will! Will!'

Miss van Snoop sank into a cane-bottomed chair, laid her head upon the table, and cried. She had earned the luxury of hysterics. In half an hour she left the station, and, proceeding to a post-office, cabled her resignation to the head of the detective force in New York.

The Duchess of Wiltshire's Diamonds

GUY BOOTHBY

To the reflective mind, the rapidity with which the inhabitants of the world's greatest city seize upon a new name or idea and familiarise themselves with it can scarcely prove otherwise than astonishing. As an illustration of my meaning let me take the case of Klimo – the now famous private detective, who has won for himself the right to be considered as great as Lecocq, or even the late lamented Sherlock Holmes.

Up to a certain morning London had never even heard his name, nor had it the remotest notion as to who or what he might be. It was as sublimely ignorant and careless on the subject as the inhabitants of Kamchatka or Peru. Within twenty-four hours, however, the whole aspect of the case was changed. The man, woman or child who had not seen his posters, or heard his name, was counted an ignoramus unworthy of intercourse with human beings.

Princes became familiar with it as their trains tore them to Windsor to luncheon with the Queen; the nobility noticed and commented upon it as they drove about the town; merchants, and businessmen generally, read it as they made their ways by omnibus or Underground to their various shops and counting-houses; street boys called each other by it as a nickname; music-hall artistes introduced it into their patter; and it was even rumoured that the Stock Exchange itself had paused in the full floodtide of business to manufacture a riddle on the subject.

That Klimo made his profession pay him well was certain, first from the fact that his advertisements must have cost a good round sum, and, second, because he had taken a mansion in Belverton Street, Park Lane, next door to Porchester House, where, to the dismay of that aristocratic neighbourhood, he advertised that he was prepared to receive and be consulted by his clients. The invitation was responded to with alacrity, and from that day forward, between the hours of twelve and two, the pavement upon the north side of the street was lined with carriages, every one containing some person desirous of testing the great man's skill.

I must here explain that I have narrated all this in order to show the state of affairs existing in Belverton Street and Park Lane when Simon Carne arrived, or was supposed to arrive, in England. If my memory serves me correctly, it was on Wednesday, the 3rd of May, that the Earl of Amberley drove to Victoria to meet and welcome the man whose acquaintance he had made in India under such peculiar circumstances, and under the spell of whose fascination he and his family had fallen so completely.

Reaching the station, his lordship descended from his carriage and made his way to the platform set apart for the reception of the Continental express. He walked with a jaunty air, and seemed to be on the best of terms with himself and the world in general. How little he suspected the existence of the noose into which he was so innocently running his head!

As if out of compliment to his arrival, the train put in an appearance within a few moments of his reaching the platform. He immediately placed himself in such a position that he could make sure of seeing the man he wanted, and waited patiently until he should come in sight. Carne, however, was not among the first batch, indeed, the majority of passengers had passed before his lordship caught sight of him.

One thing was very certain, however great the crush might have been, it would have been difficult to mistake Carne's figure. The man's infirmity and the peculiar beauty of his face rendered him easily recognisable. Possibly, after his long sojourn in India, he found the morning cold, for he wore a long fur coat, the collar of which he had turned up round his ears, thus making a fitting frame for his delicate face. On seeing Lord Amberley, he hastened forward to greet him.

'This is most kind and friendly of you,' he said as he shook the other by the hand. 'A fine day and Lord Amberley to meet me. One could scarcely imagine a better welcome.'

As he spoke, one of his Indian servants approached and salaamed before him. Carne gave him an order, and received an answer in Hindustani, whereupon he turned again to Lord Amberley.

'You may imagine how anxious I am to see my new dwelling,' he said. 'My servant tells me that my carriage is here, so may I hope that you will drive back with me and see for yourself how I am likely to be lodged?'

'I shall be delighted,' said Lord Amberley, who was longing for the opportunity, and they accordingly went out into the station yard together to discover a brougham, drawn by two magnificent horses, and with Nur Ali, in all the glory of white raiment and crested turban, on the box, waiting to receive them. His lordship dismissed his victoria, and when Jowur Singh had taken his place beside his fellow servant upon the box, the carriage rolled out of the station yard in the direction of Hyde Park.

'I trust her ladyship is quite well,' said Simon Carne politely, as they turned into Gloucester Place.

'Excellently well, thank you,' replied his lordship. 'She bade me welcome you to England in her name as well as my own, and I was to say that she is looking forward to seeing you.'

'She is most kind, and I shall do myself the honour of calling upon her as soon as circumstances will permit,' answered Carne. 'I beg you will convey my best thanks to her for her thought of me.'

While these polite speeches were passing between them they were rapidly approaching a large hoarding on which was displayed a poster setting forth the name of the now famous detective, Klimo.

Simon Carne, leaning forward, studied it, and when they had passed, turned to his friend again.

'At Victoria and on all the hoardings we meet I see an enormous poster bearing the word "Klimo". Pray, what does it mean?'

His lordship laughed.

'You are asking a question which, a month ago, was on the lips of nine out of every ten Londoners. It is only within the last fortnight that we have learned who and what "Klimo" is.'

'And pray what is he?'

'Well, the explanation is very simple. He is neither more nor less than a remarkably astute private detective, who has succeeded in attracting notice in such a way that half London has been induced to patronise him. I have had no dealings with the man myself. But a friend of mine, Lord Orpington, has been the victim of a most audacious burglary, and, the police having failed to solve the mystery, he has called Klimo in. We shall therefore see what he can do before many days are past. But, there, I expect you will soon know more about him than any of us.'

'Indeed! And why?'

'For the simple reason that he has taken No. 1, Belverton Terrace, the house adjoining your own, and sees his clients there.'

Simon Carne pursed up his lips, and appeared to be considering something.

'I trust he will not prove a nuisance,' he said at last. 'The agents who found me the house should have acquainted me with the fact. Private detectives, on however large a scale, scarcely strike one as the most desirable of neighbours – particularly for a man who is so fond of quiet as myself.'

At this moment they were approaching their destination. As the carriage passed Belverton Street and pulled up, Lord Amberley pointed to a long line of vehicles standing before the detective's door.

'You can see for yourself something of the business he does,' he said. 'Those are the carriages of his clients, and it is probable that twice as many supplicants have arrived on foot.'

'I shall certainly speak to the agent on the subject,' said Carne, with a shadow of annoyance upon his face. 'I consider the fact of this man's being so close to me a serious drawback to the house.'

Jowur Singh here descended from the box and opened the door in order that his master and his guest might alight, while portly Ram Gafur, the butler, came down the steps and salaamed before them with Oriental obsequiousness. Carne greeted his domestics with kindly condescension, and then, accompanied by the ex-viceroy, entered his new abode.

'I think you may congratulate yourself upon having secured one of the most desirable residences in London,' said his lordship ten minutes or so later, when they had explored the principal rooms.

'I am very glad to hear you say so,' said Carne. 'I trust your lordship will remember that you will always be welcome in the house as long as I am its owner.'

'It is very kind of you to say so,' returned Lord Amberley warmly. 'I shall look forward to some months of pleasant intercourse. And now I must be going. Tomorrow, perhaps, if you have nothing better to do, you will give us the pleasure of your company at dinner. Your fame has already gone abroad, and we shall ask one or two nice people to meet you, including my brother and sister-in-law Lord and Lady Gelpington, Lord and Lady Orpington and my cousin, the Duchess of Wiltshire, whose interest in Chinese and Indian art, as perhaps you know, is only second to your own.'

'I shall be most glad to come.'

'We may count on seeing you in Eaton Square, then, at eight o'clock?'

'If I am alive you may be sure I shall be there. Must you really go? Then goodbye, and many thanks for meeting me.'

His lordship having left the house, Simon Carne went upstairs to his dressing room, which it was to be noticed he found without enquiry, and rang the electric bell, beside the fireplace, three times. While he was waiting for it to be answered he stood looking out of the window at the long line of carriages in the street below.

'Everything is progressing admirably,' he said to himself. 'Amberley does not suspect any more than the world in general. As a proof he asks me to dinner tomorrow evening to meet his brother and sister-in-law, two of his particular friends and, above all, Her Grace of Wiltshire. Of course I shall go, and when I bid her grace goodbye it will be strange if I am not one step nearer the interest on Liz's money.'

At this moment the door opened, and his valet, the grave and respectable Belton, entered the room. Carne turned to greet him impatiently.

'Come, come, Belton,' he said, 'we must be quick. It is twenty minutes to twelve and if we don't hurry, the folk next door will become impatient. Have you succeeded in doing what I spoke to you about last night?'

'I have done everything, sir.'

'I am glad to hear it. Now lock that door and let us get to work. You can let me have your news while I am dressing.'

Opening one side of a massive wardrobe that completely filled one end of the room, Belton took from it a number of garments. They included a well-worn velvet coat, a baggy pair of trousers – so old that only a notorious pauper or a millionaire could have afforded to wear them – a flannel waistcoat, a Gladstone collar, a soft silk tie, and a pair of embroidered carpet slippers upon which no old-clothes man in the most reckless way of business in Petticoat Lane would have advanced a single halfpenny. Into these he assisted his master to change.

'Now give me the wig and unfasten the snaps of this hump,' said Carne, as the other placed the garments just referred to upon a neighbouring chair.

Belton did as he was ordered, so that there happened a thing the like of which no one would have believed. Having unbuckled a strap on either shoulder and slipped his hand beneath the waistcoat, he withdrew a large *papier-maché* hump, which he carried away and carefully placed in a drawer of the bureau. Relieved of his burden, Simon Carne stood up as straight and well-made a man as any in Her Majesty's dominions. The malformation, for which so many, including the Earl and Countess of Amberley, had often pitied him, was nothing but a hoax intended to produce an effect which would permit him additional facilities of disguise.

The hump discarded, and the grey wig fitted carefully to his head in such a manner that not even a pinch of his own curly locks could be seen beneath it, he adorned his cheeks with a pair of *crépu*-hair whiskers, donned the flannel vest and the velvet coat previously mentioned, slipped his feet into the carpet slippers, placed a pair of smoked glasses upon his nose, and declared himself ready to proceed about his business. The man who would have known him for Simon Carne would have been as astute as, well, shall we say, as the private detective – Klimo himself.

'It's on the stroke of twelve,' he said, as he gave a final glance at himself in the pier-glass above the dressing-table, and arranged his tie to his satisfaction. 'Should anyone call, instruct Ram Gafur to tell them that I have gone out on business, and shall not be back until three o'clock.'

'Very good, sir.'

'Now undo the door and let me go in.'

Thus commanded, Belton went across to the large wardrobe which, as I have already said, covered the whole of one side of the room, and opened the middle door. Two or three garments were seen inside suspended on pegs, and these he removed, at the same time pushing towards the right the panel at the rear. When this was done a large aperture in the wall between the two houses was disclosed. Through this door Carne passed, drawing it behind him.

In No. 1, Belverton Terrace, the house occupied by the detective, whose presence in the street Carne seemed to find so objectionable, the entrance thus constructed was covered by the peculiar kind of confessional box in which Klimo invariably sat to receive his clients, the rearmost panels of which opened in the same fashion as those in the wardrobe in the dressing-room. These being pulled aside, he had but to draw them to again after him, take his seat, ring the electric bell to inform his housekeeper that he was ready, and then welcome his clients as quickly as they cared to come.

Punctually at two o'clock the interviews ceased, and Klimo, having reaped an excellent harvest of fees, returned to Porchester House to become Simon Carne once more.

Possibly it was due to the fact that the Earl and Countess of Amberley were brimming over with his praise, or it may have been the rumour that he was worth as many millions as you have fingers upon your hand that did it; one thing, however, was self-evident, within twenty-four hours of the noble earl's meeting him at Victoria Station, Simon Carne was the talk, not only of fashionable, but also of unfashionable, London.

That his household servants were, with one exception, natives of India, that he had paid a rental for Porchester House which ran into five figures, that he was the greatest living authority upon Chinese and Indian art generally, and that he had come over to England in search of a wife, were among the smallest of the *canards* set afloat concerning him.

During dinner next evening Carne put forth every effort to please. He was placed on the right hand of his hostess and next to the Duchess of Wiltshire. To the latter he paid particular attention, and to such good purpose that when the ladies returned to the drawing-room afterwards her grace was full of his praises. They had discussed china of all sorts. Carne had promised her a specimen which she had longed for all her life, but had never been able to obtain, and in return she had promised to show him the quaintly carved Indian casket in which the famous necklace, of which he had, of course, heard, spent most of its time. She would be wearing the jewels in question at her own ball in a week's time, she informed him, and if he would care to see the case when it came from her bankers on that day, she would be only too pleased to show it to him.

As Simon Carne drove home in his luxurious brougham afterwards, he smiled to himself as he thought of the success which was attending his first endeavour. Two of the guests, who were stewards of the Jockey Club, had heard with delight his idea of purchasing a horse in order to have an interest in the Derby. While another, on hearing that he desired to become the possessor of a yacht, had offered to propose him for the RCYC. To crown it all, however, and much better than all, the Duchess of Wiltshire had promised to show him her famous diamonds.

'By this time next week,' he said to himself, 'Liz's interest should be considerably closer. But satisfactory as my progress has been hitherto it is difficult to see how I am to get possession of the stones. From what I have been able to discover they are only brought from the bank on the day the duchess intends to wear them, and they are taken back by his grace the morning following.

'While she has got them on her person it would be manifestly impossible to get them from her. And as, when she takes them off, they are returned to their box and placed in a safe constructed in the wall of the bedroom adjoining, the bedroom being for the occasion occupied by the butler and one of the under-footmen and the only key of the safe being in the possession of the duke himself, it would be equally foolish to hope to appropriate them. In what manner therefore I am to become their possessor passes my comprehension. However, one thing is certain, obtained they must be and the attempt must be made on the night of the ball if possible. In the meantime I'll set my wits to work upon a plan.'

Next day Simon Carne was the recipient of an invitation to the ball in question, and two days later he called upon the Duchess of Wiltshire at her residence in Belgrave Square with a plan prepared. He also took with him the small vase he had promised her four nights before. She received him most graciously, and their talk fell at once into the usual channel. Having examined her collection and charmed her by means of one or two judicious criticisms, he asked permission to include photographs of certain of her treasures in his forthcoming book, then, little by little, skilfully guided the conversation on to the subject of jewels.

'Since we are discussing gems, Mr Carne,' she said, 'perhaps it would interest you to see my famous necklace. By good fortune I have it in the house now, for the reason that an alteration is being made to one of the clasps by my jewellers.'

'I should like to see it immensely,' answered Carne. 'At one time and another I have had the good fortune to examine the jewels of the leading Indian princes, and I should like to be able to say that I had seen the famous Wiltshire necklace.'

'Then you shall certainly have that honour,' she answered with a smile. 'If you will ring that bell I will send for it.'

Carne rang the bell as requested, and when the butler entered he was given the key of the safe and ordered to bring the case to the drawing-room.

'We must not keep it very long,' she observed while the man was absent. 'It is to be returned to the bank in an hour's time.'

'I am indeed fortunate,' Carne replied, and turned to the description of some curious Indian wood carving, of which he was making a special feature in his book. As he explained, he had collected his illustrations from the doors of Indian temples, from the gateways of palaces, from old brasswork, and even from carved chairs and boxes he had picked up in all sorts of odd corners. Her grace was most interested.

'How strange that you should have mentioned it,' she said. 'If carved boxes have any interest for you, it is possible my jewel case itself may be of use to you. As I think I told you during Lady Amberley's dinner, it came from Benares, and has carved upon it the portraits of nearly every god in the Hindu pantheon.'

'You raise my curiosity to fever heat,' said Carne.

A few moments later the servant returned, bringing with him a wooden box, about sixteen inches long, by twelve wide and eight deep, which he placed upon a table beside his mistress, after which he retired.

'This is the case to which I have just been referring,' said the duchess, placing her hand on the article in question. 'If you glance at it you will see how exquisitely it is carved.'

Concealing his eagerness with an effort, Simon Carne drew his chair up to the table, and examined the box.

It was with justice she had described it as a work of art. What the wood was of which it was constructed Carne was unable to tell. It was dark and heavy, and, though it was not teak, closely resembled it. It was literally covered with quaint carving and of its kind was a unique work of art.

'It is most curious and beautiful,' said Carne when he had finished his examination. 'In all my experience I can safely say I have never seen its equal. If you will permit me I should very much like to include a description and an illustration of it in my book.'

'Of course you may do so; I shall be only too delighted,' answered her grace. 'If it will help you in your work I shall be glad to lend it to you for a few hours in order that you may have the illustration made.'

This was exactly what Carne had been waiting for and he accepted the offer with alacrity.

'Very well, then,' she said. 'On the day of my ball, when it will be brought from the bank again, I will take the necklace out and send the case to you. I must make one proviso, however, and that is that you let me have it back the same day.'

'I will certainly promise to do that,' replied Carne.

'And now let us look inside,' said his hostess.

Choosing a key from a bunch she carried in her pocket, she unlocked the casket and lifted the lid. Accustomed as Carne had all his life been to the sight of gems, what he saw before him then almost took his breath away. The inside of the box, both sides and bottom, was quilted with the softest Russia leather, and on this luxurious couch reposed the famous necklace. The fire of the stones when the light caught them was sufficient to dazzle the eyes, so fierce was it.

As Carne could see, every gem was perfect of its kind, and there were no fewer than three hundred of them; in addition, the setting was a fine example of the jeweller's art; last, but not least, the value of the whole affair was fifty thousand pounds – a mere fleabite to the man who had given it to his wife, but a fortune to any humbler person.

'And now that you have seen my property, what do you think of it?' asked the duchess as she watched her visitor's face.

'It is very beautiful,' he answered, 'and I do not wonder that you are proud of it. Yes, the diamonds are very fine, but I think it is their abiding place that fascinates me more. Have you any objection to my measuring it?'

'Pray do so, if it is likely to be of any assistance to you,' replied her grace.

Carne thereupon produced a small ivory rule, ran it over the box, and the figures he thus obtained he jotted down in his pocket book.

Ten minutes later, when the case had been returned to the safe, he thanked the duchess for her kindness and took his departure, promising to call in person for the empty case on the morning of the ball.

Reaching home he passed into his study, and, seating himself at his writing table, pulled a sheet of notepaper towards him and began to sketch, as well as he could remember it, the box he had seen. Then he leant back in his chair and closed his eyes.

'I have cracked a good many hard nuts in my time,' he said reflectively, 'but never one that seemed so difficult at first sight as this. As far as I see at present, the case stands as follows: the box will be brought from the bank, where it usually reposes, to Wiltshire House on the morning of the dance. I shall be allowed to have possession of it, without the stones of course, for a period possibly extending from eleven o'clock in the morning to four or five, at any rate not later than seven, in the evening. After the ball the necklace will be returned to it, when it will be locked up in the safe, over which the butler and a footman will mount guard.

'To get into the room during the night is not only too risky, but physically out of the question, while to rob her grace of her treasure during the progress of the dance would be equally impossible. The duke fetches the casket and takes it back to the bank himself, so that to all intents and purposes I am almost as far off the solution as ever.'

Half an hour went by and found him still seated at his desk, staring at the drawing on the paper; then an hour. The traffic of the streets rolled past the house unheeded. Finally Jowur Singh announced his carriage, and, feeling that an idea might come to him with a change of scene, he set off for a drive in the park.

By this time his elegant mail phaeton, with its magnificent horses and Indian servant on the seat behind, was as well known as Her Majesty's state equipage, and attracted almost as much attention.

Today, however, the fashionable world noticed that Simon Carne looked preoccupied. He was still working out his problem, but so far without much success. Suddenly something, no one will ever be able to say what, put an idea into his head. The notion was no sooner born in his brain than he left the park and drove quickly home. Ten minutes had scarcely elapsed before he was back in his study again, having ordered that Wajib Baksh be sent to him.

When the man he wanted put in an appearance Carne handed him the paper upon which he had made the drawing of the jewel case.

'Look at that,' he said, 'and tell me what thou see'st there.'

'I see a box,' answered the man, who by this time was well accustomed to his master's ways.

'As thou say'st, it is a box,' said Carne. 'The wood is heavy and thick, though what wood it is I do not know. The measurements are upon the paper below. Within, both the sides and bottom are quilted with soft leather as I have also shown. Think now, Wajib Baksh, for in this case thou wilt need to have all thy wits about thee. Tell me, is it in thy power, O most cunning of all craftsmen, to insert such extra sides within this box that they, being held by a spring, shall lie so snug as not to be noticeable to the ordinary eye? Can it be so arranged that, when the box is locked, they shall fall flat upon the bottom thus covering and holding fast what lies beneath them, and yet making the box appear to the eye as if it were empty. Is it possible for thee to do such a thing?'

Wajib Baksh did not reply for a few moments. His instinct told him what his master wanted, and he was not disposed to answer hastily, for he also saw that his reputation as the most cunning craftsman in India was at stake.

'If the heaven-born will permit me the night for thought,' he said at last, 'I will come to him when he rises from his bed and tell him what I can do, and he can then give his orders as it pleases him.'

'Very good,' said Carne. 'Then tomorrow morning I shall expect thy report. Let the work be good and there will be many rupees for thee to touch in return. As to the lock and the way it shall act, let that be the concern of Hiram Singh.'

Wajib Baksh salaamed and withdrew, and Simon Carne for the time being dismissed the matter from his mind.

Next morning, while he was dressing, Belton reported that the two artificers desired an interview with him. He ordered them to be admitted, and forthwith they entered the room. It was noticeable that Wajib Baksh carried in his hand a heavy box, which, upon Carne's motioning him to do so, he placed upon the table.

'Have ye thought over the matter?' he asked, seeing that the men waited for him to speak.

'We have thought of it,' replied Hiram Singh, who always acted as spokesman for the pair. If the presence will deign to look he will see that we have made a box of the size and shape such as he drew upon the paper.'

'Yes, it is certainly a good copy,' said Carne condescendingly, after he had examined it.

Wajib Baksh showed his white teeth in appreciation of the compliment, and Hiram Singh drew closer to the table.

'And now, if the Sahib will open it, he will in his wisdom be able to tell if it resembles the other that he has in his mind.'

Carne opened the box as requested, and discovered that the interior was an exact counterfeit of the Duchess of Wiltshire's jewel case, even to the extent of the quilted leather lining which had been the other's principal feature. He admitted that the likeness was all that could be desired.

'As he is satisfied,' said Hiram Singh, 'it may be that the protector of the poor will deign to try an experiment with it. See, here is a comb. Let it be placed in the box, so – now he will see what he will see.'

The broad, silver-backed comb, which had been lying upon his dressing-table, was placed on the bottom of the box, the lid was closed, and the key turned in the lock. The case being securely fastened, Hiram Singh laid it before his master.

'I am to open it, I suppose?' said Carne, taking the key and replacing it in the lock.

'If my master pleases,' replied the other.

Carne accordingly turned it in the lock, and, having done so, raised the lid and looked inside. His astonishment was complete. To all intents and purposes the box was empty. The comb was not to be seen, and yet the quilted sides and bottom were, to all appearances, just the same as when he had first looked inside.

'This is most wonderful,' he said. And indeed it was as clever a conjuring trick as any he had ever seen.

'Nay, it is very simple,' Wajib Baksh replied. 'The heaven-born told me that there must be no risk of detection.'

He took the box in his own hands and, running his nails down the centre of the quilting, dividing the false bottom into two pieces; these he lifted out, revealing the comb lying upon the real bottom beneath.

'The sides, as my lord will see,' said Hiram Singh, taking a step forward, 'are held in their appointed places by these two springs.

Thus, when the key is turned the springs relax, and the sides are driven by others into their places on the bottom, where the seams in the quilting mask the join. There is but one disadvantage. It is as follows: when the pieces which form the bottom are lifted out in order that my lord may get at whatever lies concealed beneath, the springs must of necessity stand revealed. However, to anyone who knows sufficient of the working of the box to lift out the false bottom, it will be an easy matter to withdraw the springs and conceal them about his person.'

'As you say that is an easy matter,' said Carne, 'and I shall not be likely to forget. Now one other question. Presuming I am in a position to put the real box into your hands for say eight hours, do you think that in that time you can fit it up so that detection will be impossible?'

'Assuredly, my lord,' replied Hiram Singh with conviction. 'There is but the lock and the fitting of the springs to be done. Three hours at most would suffice for that.'

'I am pleased with you,' said Carne. 'As a proof of my satisfaction, when the work is finished you will each receive five hundred rupees. Now you can go.'

According to his promise, ten o'clock on the Friday following found him in his hansom driving towards Belgrave Square. He was a little anxious, though the casual observer would scarcely have been able to tell it. The magnitude of the stake for which he was playing was enough to try the nerve of even such a past master in his profession as Simon Carne.

Arriving at the house he discovered some workmen erecting an awning across the footway in preparation for the ball that was to take place at night. It was not long, however, before he found himself in the boudoir, reminding her grace of her promise to permit him an opportunity of making a drawing of the famous jewel case. The duchess was naturally busy, and within a quarter of an hour he was on his way home with the box placed on the seat of the carriage beside him.

'Now,' he said, as he patted it good humouredly, 'if only the notion worked out by Hiram Singh and Wajib Baksh holds good, the famous Wiltshire diamonds will become my property before very many hours are passed. By this time tomorrow, I suppose, London will be all agog concerning the burglary.'

On reaching his house he left his carriage and himself carried the box into his study. Once there he rang his bell and ordered Hiram Singh and Wajib Baksh to be sent to him. When they arrived he showed them the box upon which they were to exercise their ingenuity.

'Bring your tools in here,' he said, 'and do the work under my own eyes. You have but nine hours before you, so you must make the most of them.'

The men went for their implements, and as soon as they were ready set to work. All through the day they were kept hard at it, with the result that by five o'clock the alterations had been effected and the case stood ready. By the time Carne returned from his afternoon drive in the park it was quite prepared for the part it was to play in his scheme. Having praised the men, he turned them out and locked the door, then went across the room and unlocked a drawer in his writing table. From it he took a flat leather jewel case which he opened. It contained a necklace of counterfeit diamonds, if anything a little larger than the one he intended to try to obtain. He had purchased it that morning in the Burlington Arcade for the purpose of testing the apparatus his servants had made, and this he now proceeded to do.

Laying it carefully upon the bottom he closed the lid and turned the key. When he opened it again the necklace was gone, and even though he knew the secret he could not for the life of him see where the false bottom began and ended. After that he reset the trap and tossed the necklace carelessly in. To his delight it acted as well as on the previous occasion. He could scarcely contain his satisfaction. His conscience was sufficiently elastic to give him no trouble. To him it was scarcely a robbery he was planning, but an artistic trial of skill, in which he pitted his wits and cunning against the forces of society in general.

At half-past seven he dined and afterwards smoked a meditative cigar over the evening paper in the billiard room. The invitations to the ball were for ten o'clock, and at nine-thirty he went to his dressing-room.

'Make me tidy as quickly as you can,' he said to Belton when the latter appeared, 'and while you are doing so listen to my final instructions.

'Tonight, as you know, I am endeavouring to secure the Duchess of Wiltshire's necklace. Tomorrow morning all London will re-sound with the hubbub, and I have been making my plans in such a way as to arrange that Klimo shall be the first person consulted. When the messenger calls, if call he does, see that the old woman next door bids him tell the duke to come personally at twelve o'clock. Do you understand?'

'Perfectly, sir.'

'Very good. Now give me the jewel case, and let me be off. You need not sit up for me.'

Precisely as the clocks in the neighbourhood were striking ten Simon Carne reached Belgrave Square, and, as he hoped, found himself the first guest.

His hostess and her husband received him in the ante-room of the drawing-room.

'I come laden with a thousand apologies,' he said as he took her grace's hand, and bent over it with that ceremonious politeness which was one of the man's chief characteristics. 'I am most unconscionably early, I know, but I hastened here in order that I might personally return the jewel case you so kindly lent me. I must trust to your generosity to forgive me. The drawings took longer than I expected.'

'Please do not apologise,' answered her grace. 'It is very kind of you to have brought the case yourself. I hope the illustrations have proved successful. I shall look forward to seeing them as soon as they are ready. But I am keeping you holding the box. One of my servants will take it to my room.'

She called a footman to her and bade him take the box and place it upon her dressing-table.

'Before it goes I must let you see that I have not damaged it either externally or internally,' said Carne with a laugh. It is such a valuable case that I should never forgive myself if it had even received a scratch during the time it has been in my possession.'

So saying he lifted the lid and allowed her to look inside. To all appearance it was exactly the same as when she had lent it to him earlier in the day.

'You have been most careful,' she said. And then, with an air of banter, she continued: 'If you desire it I shall be pleased to give you a certificate to that effect.'

They jested in this fashion for a few moments after the servant's departure, during which time Carne promised to call upon her the following morning at eleven o'clock, and to bring with him the illustrations he had made and a queer little piece of china he had had the good fortune to pick up in a dealer's shop the previous afternoon. By this time fashionable London was making its way up the grand staircase, and with its appearance further conversation became impossible.

Shortly after midnight Carne bade his hostess good night and slipped away. He was perfectly satisfied with his evening's entertainment, and if the key of the jewel case were not turned before the jewels were placed in it, he was convinced they would become his property. It speaks well for his strength of nerve when I record the fact that on going to bed his slumbers were as peaceful and untroubled as those of a little child.

Breakfast was scarcely over next morning before a hansom drew up at his front door and Lord Amberley alighted. He was ushered into Carne's presence forthwith, and on seeing that the latter was surprised at his early visit, hastened to explain.

'My dear fellow,' he said as he took possession of the chair the other offered him, 'I have come round to see you on most important business. As I told you last night at the dance, when you so kindly asked me to come and see the steam yacht you have purchased, I had an appointment with Wiltshire at half-past nine this morning. On reaching Belgrave Square, I found the whole house in confusion. Servants were running hither and thither with scared faces, the butler was on the borders of lunacy, the duchess was well-nigh hysterical in her boudoir, while her husband was in his study vowing vengeance against all the world.'

'You alarm me,' said Carne, lighting a cigarette with a hand that was as steady as a rock. 'What on earth has happened?'

'I think I might safely allow you fifty guesses and then wager a hundred pounds you'd not hit the mark; and yet in a certain measure it concerns you.'

'Concerns me? Good gracious. What have I done to bring all this about?'

'Pray do not look so alarmed,' said Amberley. 'Personally you have done nothing. Indeed, on second thoughts, I don't know that I am right in saying that it concerns you at all. The fact of the matter is, Carne, a burglary took place last night at Wiltshire House, *and the famous neckless has disappeared*.'

'Good Heavens! You don't say so?'

'But I *do*. The circumstances of the case are as follows. When my cousin retired to her room last night after the ball, she unclasped the necklace, and, in her husband's presence, placed it carefully in her jewel case, which she locked. That having been done, Wiltshire took the box to the room which contained the safe, and himself placed it therein, locking the iron door with his own key. The room was occupied that night, according to custom, by the butler and one of the footmen, both of whom have been with the family since they were boys.

'Next morning, after breakfast, the duke unlocked the safe and took out the box, intending to convey it to the bank as usual. Before leaving, however, he placed it on his study-table and went upstairs to speak to his wife. He cannot remember exactly how long he was absent, but he feels convinced that he was not gone more than a quarter of an hour at the very utmost.

'Their conversation finished, she accompanied him downstairs, where she saw him take up the case to carry it to his carriage. Before he left the house, however, she said, "I suppose you have looked to see that the necklace is all right?" "How could I do so?" was his reply. "You know you possess the only key that will fit the box."

'She felt in her pockets, but to her surprise the key was not there.'

'If I were a detective I should say that that is a point to be remembered,' said Carne with a smile. 'Pray, where did she find her keys?'

'Upon her dressing-table,' said Amberley. 'Though she has not the slightest recollection of leaving them there.'

'Well, when she had procured the keys, what happened?'

'Why, they opened the box, and to their astonishment and dismay, *found it empty. The jewels were gone!*'

'Good gracious. What a terrible loss! It seems almost impossible that it can be true. And pray, what did they do?'

'At first they stood staring into the empty box, hardly believing the evidence of their own eyes. Stare how they would, however, they could not bring them back. The jewels had without doubt disappeared, but when and where the robbery had taken place it was impossible to say. After that they had up all the servants and questioned them, but the result was what they might have foreseen, no one from the butler to the kitchen-maid could throw any light upon the subject. To this minute it remains as great a mystery as when they first discovered it.'

'I am more concerned than I can tell you,' said Carne. 'How thankful I ought to be that I returned the case to her grace last night. But in thinking of myself I am forgetting to ask what has brought you to me. If I can be of any assistance, I hope you will command me.'

'Well, I'll tell you why I have come,' replied Lord Amberley. 'Naturally they are most anxious to have the mystery solved and the jewels recovered as soon as possible. Wiltshire wanted to send to Scotland Yard there and then, but his wife and I eventually persuaded him to consult Klimo. As you know, if the police authorities are called in first he refuses the business altogether. Now, we thought, as you are his next-door neighbour, you might possibly be able to assist us.

'You may be very sure, my lord, I will do everything that lies in my power. Let us go in and see him at once.'

As he spoke he rose and threw what remained of his cigarette into the fireplace. His visitor having imitated his example, they procured their hats and walked round from Park Lane into Belverton Street to bring up at No. 1. After they had rung the bell the door was opened to them by the old woman who invariably received the detective's clients.

'Is Mr Klimo at home?' asked Carne. 'And, if so, can we see him?'

The old lady was a little deaf, and the question had to be repeated before she could be made to understand what was wanted. As soon, however, as she realised their desire she informed them that her master was absent from town, but would be back as usual at twelve o'clock to meet his clients.

'What on earth's to be done?' said the earl, looking at his companion in dismay. 'I am afraid I can't come back again, as I have a most important appointment at that hour.'

'Do you think you could entrust the business to me?' asked Carne. 'If so, I will make a point of seeing him at twelve o'clock, and could call at Wiltshire House afterwards and tell the duke what I have done.'

'That's very good of you,' replied Amberley. 'If you are sure it would not put you to too much trouble, that would be quite the best solution.'

'I will do it with pleasure,' Carne replied. 'I feel it my duty to help in whatever way I can.'

'You are very kind,' said the other. 'Then, as I understand it, you are to call upon Klimo at twelve o'clock, and afterwards to let my cousin know what you have succeeded in doing. I only hope he will help us to secure the thief. We are having too many of these burglaries just now. I must catch this hansom and be off. Goodbye, and many thanks.

'Goodbye,' said Carne, and shook him by the hand.

The hansom having rolled away, Carne retraced his steps to his own abode.

'It is really very strange,' he muttered as he walked along, 'how often chance condescends to lend her assistance to my little schemes. The mere fact that his grace left the box unwatched in his study for a quarter of an hour may serve to throw the police off on quite another scent. I am also glad that they decided to open the case in the house, for if it had gone to the bankers' and had been placed in the strong-room unexamined, I should never have been able to get possession of the jewels at all.'

Three hours later he drove to Wiltshire House and saw the duke. The duchess was far too much upset by the catastrophe to see anyone.

'This is really most kind of you, Mr Carne,' said his grace when the other had supplied an elaborate account of his interview with Klimo. 'We are extremely indebted to you. I am sorry he cannot come before ten o'clock tonight, and that he makes this stipulation of my seeing him alone, for I must confess I should like to have had someone else present to ask any questions that might escape me. But if that's his usual hour and custom, well, we must abide by it, that's all. I hope he will do some good, for this is the greatest calamity that has ever befallen me. As I told you just now, it has made my wife quite ill. She is confined to her bedroom and is quite hysterical.'

'You do not suspect anyone, I suppose,' enquired Carne.

'Not a soul,' the other answered. 'The thing is such a mystery that we do not know what to think. I feel convinced, however, that my servants are as innocent as I am. Nothing will ever make me think them otherwise. I wish I could catch the fellow, that's all. I'd make him suffer for the trick he's played me.'

Carne offered an appropriate reply, and after a little further conversation upon the subject, bade the irate nobleman goodbye and left the house. From Belgrave Square he drove to one of the clubs of which he had been elected a member, in search of Lord Orpington, with whom he had promised to lunch, and afterwards took him to a ship-builder's yard near Greenwich in order to show him the steam yacht he had lately purchased.

It was close upon dinnertime before he returned to his own residence. He brought Lord Orpington with him, and they dined in state together. At nine the latter bade him goodbye, and at ten Carne retired to his dressing-room and rang for Belton.

'What have you to report,' he asked, 'with regard to what I bade you do in Belgrave Square?'

'I followed your instructions to the letter,' Belton replied. 'Yesterday morning I wrote to Messrs Horniblow and Jimson, the house agents in Piccadilly, in the name of Colonel Braithwaite, and asked for an order to view the residence to the right of Wiltshire House. I asked that the order might be sent direct to the house, where the colonel would get it upon his arrival. This letter I posted myself in Basingstoke, as you desired me to do.

'At nine o'clock yesterday morning I dressed myself as much like an elderly army officer as possible, and took a cab to Belgrave

Square. The caretaker, an old fellow of close upon seventy years of age, admitted me immediately upon hearing my name, and proposed that he should show me over the house. This, however, I told him was quite unnecessary, backing my speech with a present of half-a-crown, whereupon he returned to his breakfast, perfectly satisfied, while I wandered about the house at my own leisure.

'Reaching the same floor as that upon which is situated the room in which the duke's safe is kept, I discovered that your supposition was quite correct, and that it would be possible for a man, by opening the window, to make his way along the coping from one house to the other without being seen. I made certain that there was no one in the bedroom in which the butler slept, and then arranged the long telescope walking-stick you gave me, and fixed one of my boots to it by means of the screw in the end. With this I was able to make a regular succession of footsteps in the dust along the ledge, between one window and the other.

'That done, I went downstairs again, bade the caretaker good morning, and got into my cab. From Belgrave Square I drove to the shop of the pawnbroker who you told me you had discovered was out of town. His assistant enquired my business and was anxious to do what he could for me. I told him, however, that I must see his master personally as it was about the sale of some diamonds I had had left me. I pretended to be annoyed that he was not at home, and muttered to myself, so that the man could hear, something about its meaning a journey to Amsterdam.

'Then I limped out of the shop, paid off my cab, and, walking down a street, removed my moustache, and altered my appearance by taking off my greatcoat and muffler. A few streets farther on I purchased a bowler hat in place of the old-fashioned topper I had hitherto been wearing, and then took a cab from Piccadilly and came home.'

'You have fulfilled my instructions admirably,' said Carne. 'And if the business comes off, as I expect it will, you shall receive your usual percentage. Now I must be turned into Klimo and be off to Belgrave Square to put his grace of Wiltshire upon the track of this burglar.'

Before he retired to rest that night Simon Carne took something wrapped in a red silk handkerchief from the capacious pocket of the coat Klimo had been wearing a few moments before. Having unrolled the covering, he held up to the light the magnificent necklace which for so many years had been the joy and pride of the ducal house of Wiltshire. The electric light played upon it, and touched it with a thousand different hues.

'Where so many have failed,' he said to himself, as he wrapped it in the handkerchief again and locked it in his safe, 'it is pleasant to be able to congratulate oneself on having succeeded. It is without its equal, and I don't think I shall be overstepping the mark if I say that I think when she receives it Liz will be glad she lent me the money.'

Next morning all London was astonished by the news that the famous Wiltshire diamonds had been stolen, and a few hours later Carne learnt from an evening paper that the detectives who had taken up the case, upon the supposed retirement from it of Klimo, were still completely at fault.

That evening he was to entertain several friends to dinner. They included Lord Amberley, Lord Orpington and a prominent member of the Privy Council. Lord Amberley arrived late, but filled to overflowing with importance. His friends noticed his state, and questioned him.

'Well, gentlemen,' he answered, as he took up a commanding position upon the drawing-room hearthrug, 'I am in a position to inform you that Klimo has reported upon the case, and the upshot of it is that the Wiltshire Diamond Mystery is a mystery no longer.'

'What do you mean?' asked the others in a chorus.

'I mean that he sent in his report to Wiltshire this afternoon, as arranged. From what he deduced the other night, after being alone in the room with the empty jewel case and a magnifying glass for two minutes or so, he was in a position to describe the *modus operandi* and, what is more, to put the police on the scent of the burglar.'

'And how *was* it worked?' asked Carne.

'From the empty house next door,' replied the other. 'On the morning of the burglary a man, purporting to be a retired army officer, called with an order to view, got the caretaker out of the way, clambered along to Wiltshire House by means of the parapet outside, reached the room during the time the servants were at breakfast, opened the safe, and abstracted the jewels.'

'But how did Klimo find all this out?' asked Lord Orpington.

'By his own inimitable cleverness,' replied Lord Amberley. 'At any rate, it has been proved that he was correct. The man *did* make his way from next door, and the police have since discovered that an individual, answering to the description given, visited a pawn-broker's shop in the city about an hour later and stated that he had diamonds to sell.'

'If that is so, it turns out to be a very simple mystery after all,' said Lord Orpington as they began their meal.

'Thanks to the ingenuity of the cleverest detective in the world,' remarked Amberley.

'In that case here's a good health to Klimo,' said the privy councillor, raising his glass.

'I will join you in that,' said Simon Carne. 'Here's a very good health to Klimo and his connection with the Duchess of Wiltshire's diamonds. May he always be equally successful!'

'Hear, hear to that,' replied his guests.

The Problem of Dressing Room A

JACQUES FUTRELLE

It was absolutely impossible. Twenty-five chess masters from the world at large, forgathered in Boston for the annual championships, unanimously declared it impossible, and unanimity on any given point is an unusual mental condition for chess masters. Not one would concede for an instant that it was within the range of human achievement. Some grew red in the face as they argued it, others smiled loftily and were silent; still others dismissed the matter in a word as wholly absurd.

A casual remark by the distinguished scientist and logician, Professor van Dusen, provoked the discussion. He had, in the past, caused bitter disputes by chance remarks; in fact, he had once been a sort of controversial centre of the sciences. It had been due to his modest announcement of a startling and unorthodox hypothesis that he had been asked to vacate the chair of philosophy in a great university; later that university had been honoured when he accepted its degree of LL.D.

For a score of years now educational and scientific institutions of the world had amused themselves by crowding degrees upon him. He had initials that stood for things he could not pronounce: degrees from England, Russia, Germany, Italy, Sweden and Spain. These were expressed recognition of the fact that he was the foremost brain in science. The imprint of his crabbed personality lay heavily on half a dozen of its branches. Finally there came a time when argument was respectfully silent in the face of one of his conclusions.

The remark which had arrayed the chess masters of the world in so formidable and unanimous a dissent was made by Professor van Dusen in the presence of three other gentlemen of standing. One of these, Dr Charles Elbert, happened to be a chess enthusiast.

'Chess is a shameless perversion of the functions of the brain,' was Professor van Dusen's declaration in his perpetually irritated voice. 'It is a sheer waste of effort, greater because it is possibly the most difficult of all fixed abstract problems. Of course logic will solve it.

Logic will solve any problem – not *most* of them, but *any* problem. A thorough understanding of its rules would enable anyone to defeat your greatest chess players. It would be inevitable, just as inevitable as that two and two make four, not sometimes, but always. I don't know chess, because I never do useless things; but I could take a few hours of competent instruction and defeat a man who has devoted his life to it. His mind is cramped – bound down to the logic of chess. Mine is not, mine employs logic in its widest scope.'

Dr Elbert shook his head vigorously. 'It is impossible,' he asserted.

'Nothing is impossible,' snapped the scientist. 'The human mind can do anything. It is all we have to lift us above the brute creation. For heaven's sake leave us that.'

'Do you know the purposes of chess – its countless combinations?' asked Dr Elbert.

'No,' was the crabbed reply. 'I know nothing whatever of the game beyond the general purpose which, I understand, is to move certain pieces in certain directions to stop an opponent from moving his king. Is that correct?'

'Yes,' said Dr Elbert, slowly, 'but I never heard it stated just that way before.'

'Then, if that is correct, I maintain that the true logician can defeat the chess expert by the pure mechanical rule of logic. I'll take a few hours some time, acquaint myself with the moves of the pieces, and defeat you to convince you.'

Professor van Dusen glared savagely into the eyes of Dr Elbert.

'Not me,' said Dr Elbert. 'You say anyone – you, for instance – might defeat the greatest chess player. Would you be willing to meet the greatest chess player after you "acquaint" yourself with the game?'

'Certainly,' said the scientist. 'I have frequently found it necessary to make a fool of myself to convince people. I'll do it again.'

This, then, was the acrimonious beginning of the discussion which aroused chess masters and brought open dissent from eminent men who had not dared for years to dispute any assertion by the distinguished Professor van Dusen. It was arranged that at the conclusion of the championships Professor van Dusen should meet the winner. This happened to be Tschaikowsky, the Russian, who had been chess champion for half a dozen years.

After this expected result of the tournament, Hillsbury, a noted American master, spent a morning with Professor van Dusen in the latter's modest apartments on Beacon Hill. He left there with a sadly puzzled face. That afternoon Professor van Dusen met the

Russian champion. The newspapers had said a great deal about the affair, and hundreds were present to witness the game.

There was a little murmur of astonishment when Professor van Dusen appeared. He was slight, to the point of childishness, and his thin shoulders seemed to droop beneath the weight of his enormous head. He wore a No. 8 hat. His brow rose straight and dome-like, and a heavy shock of long yellow hair gave him almost a grotesque appearance. The eyes were narrow slits of blue, squinting eternally through thick glasses; the face was small, clean shaven and white, with the pallor of the student; his lips made a perfectly straight line; his hands were remarkable for their whiteness, their flexibility, and for the length of the slender fingers. One glance showed that physical development had never entered into the schedule of the scientist's fifty years of life.

The Russian smiled at he sat down at the chess table. He felt that he was humouring a crank. The other masters were grouped near by, curiously expectant. Professor van Dusen began the game, opening with a queen's gambit. At his fifth move, made without the slightest hesitation, the smile left the Russian's face. At the tenth the masters grew tensely eager. The Russian champion was playing for honour now. Professor van Dusen's fourteenth move was king's castle to queen's four.

'Check,' he announced.

After a long study of the board the Russian protected his king with a knight. Professor van Dusen noted the play, then leaned back in his chair with fingertips pressed together. His eyes left the board, and dreamily studied the ceiling.

For at least fifteen minutes there was no sound, no movement then: 'Mate in fifteen moves,' he said quietly.

There was a quick gasp of astonishment. It took the practised eyes of the masters several minutes to verify the announcement. But the Russian champion saw, and leaned back in his chair a little white and dazed. He was not astonished; he was helplessly floundering in a maze of incomprehensible things. Suddenly he arose and grasped the slender hand of his conqueror.

'You have never played chess before?' he asked.

'Never.'

'*Mon Dieu!* You are not a man; you are a brain – a machine – a thinking machine.'

'It is a child's game,' said the scientist abruptly. There was no note of exultation in his voice; it was still the irritable, impersonal tone which was habitual.

This, then, was Professor van Dusen. This is how he came to be known to the world at large as The Thinking Machine. The Russian's phrase had been applied to the scientist as a title by a newspaper reporter, Hutchinson Hatch. It had stuck.

* * *

That strange, seemingly inexplicable chain of circumstances which had to do with the mysterious disappearance of a famous actress, Miss Irene Wallack, from her dressing-room in a Springfield theatre during a performance, while the echo of tumultuous appreciation still rang in her ears, was perhaps the first problem not purely scientific that The Thinking Machine was ever asked to solve. The scientist's aid was enlisted in this baffling case by Hutchinson Hatch, reporter.

'But I am a scientist, a logician,' The Thinking Machine had protested. 'I know nothing whatever of crime.'

'No one knows that a crime has been committed,' the reporter hastened to say. 'There is something far beyond the ordinary in this affair. A woman has disappeared, evaporated into thin air in the hearing, almost in sight, of her friends. The police can make nothing of it. It is a problem for a greater mind than theirs.'

Professor van Dusen waved the newspaper man to a seat, and himself sank back into a great cushioned chair in which his diminutive figure seemed even more childlike than it really was.

'Tell me the story,' he said petulantly. 'All of it.'

'Miss Wallack is thirty years old, and beautiful,' the reporter began. 'As an actress she has won recognition not only in this country, but in England. You may have read something of her in the daily papers, and if – '

'I never read the papers,' the other interrupted curtly. 'Go on.'

'She is unmarried, and, so far as anyone knows, had no immediate intention of changing her condition,' Hatch resumed, staring curiously at the thin face of the scientist. 'I presume she had admirers – most beautiful women of the stage have – but she is one whose life has been perfectly good, whose record is an open book. I tell you this because it might have a bearing on your conclusion as to a possible reason for her disappearance.

'Now for the actual circumstances of that disappearance. Miss Wallack has been playing in Shakespearean repertoire. Last week she was in Springfield. On Saturday night, which concluded her engagement there, she appeared as Rosalind in *As You Like It*. The house was crowded. She played the first two acts amid great enthusiasm, and this despite the fact that she was suffering intensely from one of the headaches to which she was subject at times. After the second act she returned to her dressing-room and just before the curtain went up for the third the stage-manager called her. She replied that she would be out immediately. There seems no possible shadow of a doubt but that it was her voice.

'Rosalind does not appear in the third act until the curtain has been up for six minutes. When Miss Wallack's cue came she did not answer it. The stage-manager rushed to her door and again called her. There was no answer. Then, fearing that she might have fainted, he went in. She was not there. A hurried search was made without result, and the stage-manager finally was compelled to announce to the audience that the sudden illness of the star would make it impossible to finish the performance.

'The curtain was lowered, and the search resumed. Every nook and corner back of the footlights was gone over. The stage-door keeper, William Meegan, had seen no one go out. He and a policeman had been standing at the stage-door talking for at least twenty minutes. It is, therefore, conclusive that Miss Wallack did not leave by the stage-door. The only other way it was possible to leave the stage was over the footlights. Of course she didn't go that way. Yet no trace of her has been found. Where is she?'

'The windows?' asked The Thinking Machine.

'The stage is below the street level,' Hatch explained. 'The window of her dressing-room, room A, is small, and barred with iron. It opens into an air shaft that goes straight up for ten feet, and that is covered with an iron grating fixed in the granite. The other windows on the stage are not only inaccessible, but are also barred with iron. She could not have approached either of these windows without being seen by other members of the company or the stage hands.'

'Under the stage?' suggested the scientist.

'Nothing,' the reporter went on. 'It is a large cemented basement, which was vacant. It was searched, because there was, of course, a chance that Miss Wallack might have become temporarily unbalanced, and wandered down there. There was even a search made of the 'flies' – that is, the galleries over the stage, where the men who work the drop-curtains are stationed.'

'How was Miss Wallack dressed at the time of her disappearance?'

'In doublet and hose – that is tights,' the newspaper man responded. 'She wears that costume from the second act until practically the end of the play.'

'Was all her street clothing in her room?'

'Yes, everything, spread across an unopened trunk of costumes. It was all as if she had left the room to answer her cue – all in order, even to an open box of chocolate-cream on her table.'

'No sign of a struggle, nor any noise heard?'

'No.'

'Nor trace of blood?'

'Nothing.'

'Her maid? Did she have one?'

'Oh, yes. I neglected to tell you that the maid, Gertrude Manning, had gone home immediately after the first act. She grew suddenly ill, and was excused.'

The Thinking Machine turned his squint eyes on the reporter for the first time.

'Ill?' he repeated. 'What was the matter?'

'That I can't say,' replied the reporter.

'Where is she now?'

'I don't know. Everyone forgot all about her in the excitement about Miss Wallack.'

'What kind of chocolate-cream was it?'

'I'm afraid I don't know that either.'

'Where was it bought?'

The reporter shrugged his shoulders; that was something else he didn't know. The Thinking Machine shot out the questions aggressively, staring meanwhile steadily at Hatch, who squirmed uncomfortably.

'Where is the chocolate now?' demanded the scientist; and again Hatch shrugged his shoulders.

'How much did Miss Wallack weigh?'

The reporter was willing to guess at this. He had seen her half a dozen times.

'Between a hundred and thirty and a hundred and forty,' he ventured.

'Does there happen to be a hypnotist connected with the company?'

'I don't know,' Hatch replied.

The Thinking Machine waved his slender hands impatiently; he was annoyed.

'It is perfectly absurd, Mr Hatch,' he expostulated, 'to come to me with only a few facts, and ask advice. If you had *all* the facts I might be able to do something, but this – '

The newspaper man was nettled. In his own profession he was accredited a man of discernment and acumen. He resented the tone, the manner, even the seemingly trivial questions which the other asked.

'I don't see,' he began, 'that the chocolate, even if it had been poisoned, as I imagine you think possible, or a hypnotist, could have had anything to do with Miss Wallack's disappearance. Certainly neither poison nor hypnotism would have made her invisible.'

'Of course you don't see,' blazed The Thinking Machine. 'If you did you wouldn't have come to me. When did this thing happen?'

'Saturday night, as I said,' the reporter informed him a little more humbly. 'It closed the engagement in Springfield. Miss Wallack was to have appeared here in Boston tonight.'

'When did she disappear – by the clock, I mean?'

'Oh,' said the reporter. 'The stage-manager's time-slip shows that the curtain for the third act went up at 9.41 – he spoke to her, say, one minute before, or at 9.40. The action of the play before she appears in the third act takes six minutes, therefore – '

'In precisely seven minutes a woman, weighing more than a hundred and thirty pounds, certainly not dressed for the street, disappeared completely from her dressing-room. It is now 5.18, Monday afternoon. I think we may solve this crime within a few hours.'

'Crime?' Hatch repeated eagerly. 'Do you imagine there is a crime, then?'

Professor van Dusen did not heed the question. Instead he rose and paced back and forth across the reception-room half a dozen times, his hands behind his back, and his eyes cast down. At last he stopped and faced the reporter, who had also risen.

'Miss Wallack's company, I presume, with the baggage, is now in Boston,' he said. 'See every male member of the company, talk to them, and particularly *study their eyes*. Don't overlook anyone, however humble. Also find out what became of the box of chocolate, and if possible how many pieces are out of it. Then report here to me. Miss Wallack's safety may depend upon your speed and accuracy.'

Hatch was frankly startled.

'How – ' he began.

'Don't stop to talk – hurry,' commanded The Thinking Machine. 'I will have a cab waiting when you come back. We must get to Springfield.'

The newspaper man rushed away to obey orders. He did not understand them at all. Studying men's eyes was not in his line, but he obeyed nevertheless. An hour and a half later he returned, to be thrust unceremoniously into a waiting cab by The Thinking

Machine. The cab rattled away toward South Station, where the two men caught a train, just about to move out for Springfield. Once settled in their seats, the scientist turned to Hatch, who was nearly suffocating with suppressed information.

'Well?' he asked.

'I found out several things,' the reporter burst out. 'First, Miss Wallack's leading man, Langdon Mason, who has been in love with her for three years, bought the chocolate at Schuyler's in Springfield, early Saturday evening, before he went to the theatre. He told me so himself, rather reluctantly, but I – I made him say it.'

'Ah!' exclaimed The Thinking Machine. It was a most unequivocal ejaculation. 'How many pieces are out of the box?'

'Only three,' replied Hatch. 'Miss Wallack's things were packed into the open trunk in her dressing-room, the chocolate with them. I induced the manager – '

'Yes, yes, yes,' interrupted The Thinking Machine impatiently. 'What sort of eyes has Mason? What colour?'

'Blue, frank in expression, nothing unusual at all,' said the reporter.

'And the others?'

'I didn't quite know what you meant by studying their eyes, so I got a set of photographs. I thought perhaps they might help.'

'Excellent! Excellent!' commented The Thinking Machine. He shuffled the pictures through his fingers, stopping now and then to study one and to read the name printed below.

'Is that the leading man?' he asked at last, and handed one to Hatch.

'Yes.'

Professor van Dusen did not speak again. The train pulled up at Springfield at 9.20. Hatch followed the scientist out of the station and, without a word, into a cab.

'Schuyler's shop,' commanded The Thinking Machine. 'Hurry.'

The cab rushed off through the night. Ten minutes later it stopped before a brilliantly lighted confectionery shop. The Thinking Machine led the way inside, and approached the girl behind the chocolate counter.

'Will you please tell me if you remember this man's face?' he asked as he produced Mason's photograph.

'Oh, yes, I remember him,' the girl replied. 'He's an actor.'

'Did he buy a small box of chocolates from you early on Saturday evening?' was the next question.

'Yes. I recall it because he seemed to be in a hurry – in fact, I believe he said he was anxious to get to the theatre to pack.'

'And do you recall that this man ever bought chocolates here?' asked the scientist. He produced another photograph, and handed it to the girl. She studied it a moment, while Hatch craned his neck, vainly, to see.

'I don't recall that he ever did,' the girl answered finally.

The Thinking Machine turned away abruptly and disappeared into a public telephone booth. He remained there for five minutes, then rushed out to the cab again, with Hatch following closely.

'City Hospital,' he commanded.

Again the cab dashed away. Hatch was dumb; there seemed to be nothing to say. The Thinking Machine was plainly pursuing some definite line of enquiry, yet the reporter did not know what. The case was getting kaleidoscopic. This impression was strengthened when he found himself standing beside The Thinking Machine in City Hospital conversing with the house surgeon, Dr Carlton.

'Is there a Miss Gertrude Manning here?' was the scientist's first question.

'Yes,' replied the surgeon. 'She was brought here on Saturday night suffering from – '

'Strychnine poisoning; yes, I know,' interrupted the other. 'Picked up in the street, probably. I am physician. If she is well enough I should like to ask her a couple of questions.'

Dr Carlton agreed and Professor van Dusen, still followed faithfully by Hatch, was ushered into the ward where Miss Wallack's maid lay pallid and weak. The Thinking Machine picked up her hand, and his slender finger rested for a minute on her pulse. He nodded as if satisfied.

'Miss Manning, can you understand me?' he asked.

The girl nodded weakly.

'How many pieces of chocolate did you eat?'

'Two,' she replied. She stared into the face above her with dull eyes.

'Did Miss Wallack eat any of it up to the time you left the theatre?'

'No.'

If The Thinking Machine had been in a hurry previously, he was racing now. Hatch trailed dutifully behind, down the stairs and into the cab, whence Professor van Dusen shouted a word of thanks to Dr Carlton. This time their destination was the stage-door of the theatre from which Miss Wallack had disappeared.

The reporter was muddled. He did not know anything very clearly except that three pieces of chocolate were missing from the box. Of these the maid had eaten only two. She had been poisoned. Therefore it seemed reasonable to suppose that if Miss Wallack had eaten the third piece she also would be poisoned. But poison would not make her invisible. At this point the reporter shook his head hopelessly.

William Meegan, the stage-door keeper, was easily found.

'Can you inform me, please,' began The Thinking Machine, 'if Mr Mason left a box of chocolate with you last Saturday night for Miss Wallack?'

'Yes,' Meegan replied good-naturedly. He was amused at the little man. 'Miss Wallack hadn't arrived. Mason brought a box of chocolate for her nearly every night, and usually left it here. I put the one Saturday night on the shelf here.'

'Did Mr Mason come to the theatre before or after the others on Saturday night?'

'Before,' replied Meegan. 'He was unusually early, presumably to pack.'

'And the other members of the company coming in stop here, I imagine, to get their letters?' and the scientist squinted up at the correspondence box above the shelf.

'Always.'

The Thinking Machine drew a long breath. Up to this time there had been little perplexed wrinkles in his brow. Now they disappeared.

'Now, please,' he went on, 'was any package or box *of any kind* taken from the stage on Saturday night between nine and eleven o'clock?'

'No,' said Meegan, positively. 'Nothing at all until the company's baggage was removed at midnight.'

'Miss Wallack had two trunks in her dressing-room?'

'Yes. Two whacking big ones, too.'

'How do you know?'

'Because I helped put 'em in, and helped take 'em out,' replied Meegan sharply. 'What's it to you?'

Suddenly The Thinking Machine turned and ran out to the cab, with Hatch, his shadow, close behind.

'Drive, drive as fast as you know how to the nearest long-distance telephone,' the scientist instructed the cabby. 'A woman's life is at stake.'

*   *   *

Half an hour later Professor van Dusen and Hutchinson Hatch

were on a train rushing back to Boston. The Thinking Machine had been in the telephone booth for fifteen minutes. When he came out Hatch had asked several questions, to which the scientist vouchsafed no answer. They were perhaps thirty minutes out of Springfield before the scientist showed any disposition to talk. Then he began, without preliminary, much as if he were resuming a former conversation.

'Of course, if Miss Wallack didn't leave the theatre, she was there,' he said. 'We will admit that she did not become invisible. The problem therefore was to find her. The fact that no violence was used against her was conclusively proven by half a dozen instances. No one heard her scream, there was no struggle, no trace of blood. *Ergo*, we assume in the beginning that she must have consented to the first steps which led to her disappearance. Remember her attire was wholly unsuited to the street.

'Now let's shape a hypothesis which will fit all the circumstances. Miss Wallack has a severe headache. Hypnotic influence will cure headaches. Was there a hypnotist to whom Miss Wallack would have submitted herself? Assume there was. Then would that hypnotist take advantage of his control to place her in a cataleptic condition? Assume a motive, and he would. Then, how would he dispose of her?

'From this point questions radiate in all directions. We will confine ourselves to the probable, granting for the moment that this hypothesis – the only one which fits all the circumstances – is correct. Obviously a hypnotist would not have attempted to get her out of the dressing-room. What remains? One of the two trunks in her room.'

Hatch gasped.

'You mean you think it possible that she was hypnotised and placed in that second trunk, the one that was strapped and locked?' he asked.

'It's the only thing that *could* have happened,' said The Thinking Machine emphatically, 'therefore that is just what *did* happen.'

'Why, it's horrible,' exclaimed Hatch. 'A live woman in a trunk for forty-eight hours? Even if she were alive then, she must be dead now.'

The reporter shuddered a little, and gazed curiously at the inscrutable face of his companion. He saw no pity, no horror there; there was merely the reflection of brain workings.

'It does not necessarily follow that she is dead,' explained The Thinking Machine. 'If she ate that third piece of chocolate *before* she was hypnotised she is probably dead. If it were placed in her mouth after she was in a cataleptic condition the chances are that she is not dead. The chocolate would not melt, and her system could not absorb the poison.'

'But she would be suffocated – her bones would be broken by the rough handling of the trunk – there are a hundred possibilities,' the reporter suggested.

A person in a cataleptic condition is singularly impervious to injury,' replied the scientist 'There is, of course, a chance of suffocation, but a great deal of air may enter a trunk.'

'And the chocolate?' Hatch asked.

'Yes, the chocolate. We know that two pieces of chocolate nearly killed the maid. Yet Mr Mason admitted having bought it. This admission indicated that this poisoned chocolate is not the chocolate he bought. Is Mr Mason a hypnotist? No. He hasn't the eyes. His picture tells me that. We know that Mr Mason did buy chocolate for Miss Wallack on several occasions. We know that sometimes he left it with the stage-door keeper. We know that members of the company stopped there for their letters. We instantly see that it was possible for one to take away that box and substitute poisoned chocolate.

'Madness and the cunning of madness lie at the back of all this. It was a deliberate attempt to murder Miss Wallack, due, perhaps, to unrequited or hopeless infatuation. It began with the poisoned chocolate, and that failing, went to a point immediately following the moment when the stage-manager last spoke to the actress. The hypnotist was probably in her room then.'

'Is Miss Wallack still in the trunk?' Hatch asked at last.

'No,' replied The Thinking Machine. 'She is out now, dead or alive – I am inclined to believe alive.'

'And the man?'

'I will turn him over to the police in half an hour after we reach Boston.'

From South Station the scientist and Hatch were driven immediately to the police headquarters. Detective Mallory, whom Hatch knew well, received them.

'We got your phonecall from Springfield,' he began.

'Was she dead?' interrupted the scientist.

'No,' Mallory replied. 'She was unconscious when we took her out of the trunk, but no bones are broken. She is badly bruised. The doctor says she's hypnotised.'

'Was the piece of chocolate taken from her mouth?'

'Yes, a piece of chocolate-cream. It hadn't melted.'

'I'll come back here in a few minutes and awake her,' said The Thinking Machine. 'Come with us now, and get the man.'

Wonderingly the detective entered the cab, and the three were driven to a big hotel a dozen streets away. Before they entered, The Thinking Machine handed a photograph to Mallory, who studied it under an electric light.

'That man is upstairs with several others,' explained the scientist. 'Pick him out, and get behind him when we enter the room. He may attempt to shoot. Don't touch him until I say so.'

In a large room on the fifth floor manager Stanfeld had assembled the Irene Wallack company. There were no preliminaries when Professor van Dusen entered. He squinted comprehensively about him, then went straight to Langdon Mason, staring deeply into his eyes for a moment.

'Were you on the stage, in the third act of your play, before Miss Wallack was to appear – I mean the play last Saturday night?' he asked.

'I was,' Mason replied, 'for at least three minutes.'

'Mr Stanfeld, is that correct?'

'Yes,' replied the manager.

There was a long tense silence, broken only by the steps of Mallory as he walked toward a distant corner of the room. A faint flush crept into Mason's face as he realised that the questions were almost an accusation. He started to speak, but the steady, impassive voice of The Thinking Machine stopped him.

'Mr Mallory, take your prisoner,' it said.

Instantly there was a fierce, frantic struggle, and those present turned to see Detective Mallory with his great arms locked about Stanley Wightman, the melancholy Jacques of *As You Like It.* By a sudden movement Mallory threw Wightman down and manacled his hands, then looked up to find The Thinking Machine peering over his shoulder into the eyes of the prostrate man.

'Yes; he's a hypnotist,' the scientist remarked in self-satisfied conclusion. 'It always tells in the pupils of the eyes.'

Miss Wallack, when revived, told a story almost identical to that of The Thinking Machine, and three months later resumed her tour.

Meanwhile Stanley Wightman, whose brooding over a hopeless love for her made a maniac of him, raves and shrieks the lines of Jacques in the seclusion of a padded cell. Mental experts pronounce him incurable.

The Hundred-Thousand-Dollar Robbery

HESKETH PRITCHARD

'I want the whole affair kept unofficial and secret,' said Harris, the bank manager.

November Joe nodded. He was seated on the extreme edge of a chair in the manager's private office, looking curiously out of place in that prim, richly furnished room.

'The truth is,' continued Harris, 'we bankers cannot afford to have our customers' minds unsettled. There are, as you know, Joe, numbers of small depositors, especially in the rural districts, who would be scared out of their seven senses if they knew that this infernal Cecil James Atterson had made off with a hundred thousand dollars. They'd never trust us again.'

'A hundred thousand dollars is a wonderful lot of money,' agreed Joe.

'Our reserve is over twenty millions, two hundred times a hundred thousand,' replied Harris grandiloquently.

Joe smiled in his pensive manner. 'That so? Then I guess the bank won't be hurt if Atterson escapes,' said he.

'I shall be bitterly disappointed if you permit him to do so,' returned Harris. 'But here, let's get down to business.'

On the previous night, Harris, the manager of the Quebec branch of the Grand Banks of Canada, had rung me up to borrow November Joe, who was at the time building a log camp for me on one of my properties. I sent Joe a telegram, with the result that within five hours of its receipt he had walked the twenty miles into Quebec, and was now with me at the bank ready to hear Harris's account of the robbery.

The manager cleared his throat and began with a question: 'Have you ever seen Atterson?'

'No.'

'I thought you might have. He always spends his vacations in the woods – fishing, usually. The last two years he has fished Red River. This is what happened. On Saturday I told him to go down to the strong-room to fetch up a fresh batch of dollar and five-dollar bills, as we were short. It happened that in the same safe there were a number of bearer securities. Atterson soon brought me the notes I had sent him for, with the keys. That was about noon on Saturday. We closed at one o'clock. Yesterday, Monday, Atterson did not turn up. At first I thought nothing of it, but when it came to afternoon, and he had neither come nor sent any reason for his absence, I began to smell a rat. I went down to the strong-room and found that over one hundred thousand dollars in notes and bearer securities were missing.

'I communicated at once with the police and they started in to make enquiries. I must tell you that Atterson lived in a boarding-house behind the Frontenac. No one had seen him on Sunday, but on Saturday night a fellow boarder, called Collings, reports Atterson as going to his room about 10.30. He was the last person who saw him. Atterson spoke to him and said he was off to spend Sunday on the south shore. From that moment Atterson has vanished.'

'Didn't the police find out anything further?' enquired Joe.

'Well, we couldn't trace him at any of the railway stations.'

'I s'pose they wired to every other police-station within a hundred miles?'

'They did, and that is what brought you into it.'

'Why?'

'The constable at Roberville replied that a man answering to the description of Atterson was seen by a farmer walking along the Stoneham road, and heading north, on Sunday morning, early.'

'No more facts?'

'No.'

'Then let's get back to the robbery. Why are you so plum sure Atterson done it?'

'The notes and securities were there on Saturday morning.'

'How do you know?'

'It's my business to know. I saw them myself.'

'Huh! . . . And no one else went down to the strong-room?'

'Only Atterson. The second clerk – it is a rule that no employee may visit the strong-room alone – remained at the head of the stairs while Atterson descended.'

'Who keeps the key?'

'I do.'

'And it was never out of your possession?'

'Never.'

November was silent for a few moments.

'How long has Atterson been with the bank?'

'Two years odd.'

'Anything against him before?'

'Nothing.'

At this point a clerk knocked at the door and, entering, brought in some letters. Harris stiffened as he noticed the writing on one of them. He cut it open and, when the clerk was gone out, he read aloud:

'DEAR HARRIS – I hereby resign my splendid and lucrative position in the Grand Banks of Canada. It is a dog's dirty life – anyway it is so for a man of spirit. You can give the week's screw that's owing to me to buy milk and bath buns for the next meeting of directors.

Yours truly,

C. J. ATTERSON.'

'What's the postmark?' asked Joe.

'Rimouski. Sunday, 9.30 a.m.'

'It looks like Atterson's the thief,' remarked Joe.

'I've always been sure of it!' cried Harris.

'I wasn't,' said Joe.

'Are you sure of it now?'

'I'm inclined that way because Atterson had that letter posted by a con–con–what's the word?'

'Confederate?'

'You've got it. He was seen here in town on Saturday at 1.30, and he couldn't have posted no letter in Rimouski in time for the 9.30 a.m. on Sunday unless he'd gone there on the 7 o'clock express on Saturday evening. Yes, Atterson's the thief, all right. And if that really was him they saw Stoneham ways, he's had time to get thirty mile of bush between us and him, and he can go right on till he's in Labrador. I doubt you'll see your hundred thousand dollars again. Mr Harris.'

'Bah! You can trail him easily enough?'

Joe shook his head. 'If you was to put me on his tracks I could,' said he, 'but up there in the Laurentides he'll sure pinch a canoe and make along a waterway.'

'H'm!' coughed Harris. 'My directors won't want to pay you two dollars a day for nothing.'

'Two dollars a day?' said Joe in his gentle voice, 'I shouldn't a' thought the two hundred times a hundred thousand dollars could stand a *strain* like that!'

I laughed. 'Look here, November, I think I'd like to make this bargain for you.'

'Yes, sure,' said the young woodsman.

'Then I'll sell your services to Mr Harris here for five dollars a day if you fail, and twenty per cent of the sum you recover if you succeed.'

Joe looked at me with wide eyes, but he said nothing.

'Well, Harris, is it on or off?' I asked.

'Oh, on, I suppose, confound you!' said Harris.

November looked at both of us with a broad smile.

*   *   *

Twenty hours later, Joe, a police trooper named Hobson and I were deep in the woods. We had briefly paused to interview the farmer at Roberville, and then had passed on down the old deserted roads until at last we entered the forest, or as it is locally called, the 'bush'.

'Where are you heading for?' Hobson had asked Joe.

'Red River, because if it was really Atterson the farmer saw, I guess he'll have gone up there.'

'Why do you think that?'

'Red River's the overflow of Snow Lake, and there is several trappers has canoes on Snow Lake. There's none of them trappers there now in July month, so he can steal a canoe easy. Besides, a man who fears pursuit always likes to get into a country he knows, and you heard Mr Harris say how Atterson had fished Red River two vacations. Besides . . . ' here Joe stopped and pointed to the ground, 'them's Atterson's tracks,' he said. 'Leastways, it's a black fox to a lynx pelt they are his.'

'But you've never seen him. What reason have you . . . ?' demanded Hobson.

'When first we come on them about four hours back, while you was lightin' your pipe,' replied Joe, 'they come out of the bush, and when we come near Cartier's place they went back into the bush again. Then a mile beyond Cartier's out of the bush they come on to the road. What can that circumventin' mean? Feller who made the tracks don't want to be seen. No. 8 boots, city-made, nails in 'em, rubber heels. Come on.'

I will not attempt to describe our journey hour by hour, nor tell how November held to the trail, following it over areas of hard ground and rock, noticing a scratch here and a broken twig there. The trooper, Hobson, proved to be a good track-reader, but he thought himself a better and, it seemed to me, was a little jealous of Joe's obvious superiority.

We slept that night beside the trail. According to November, the thief was now not many hours ahead of us. Everything depended upon whether he could reach Red River and a canoe before we caught up with him. Still it was not possible to follow a trail in the darkness, so perforce we camped. The next morning November wakened us at daylight and once more we hastened forward.

For some time we followed Atterson's footsteps and then found that they left the road. The police officer went crashing along till Joe stopped him with a gesture.

'Listen!' he whispered.

We moved on quietly and saw that, not fifty yards ahead of us, a man was walking excitedly up and down. His face was quite clear in the slanting sunlight, a resolute face with a small, dark moustache and a two-days' growth of beard. His head was sunk upon his chest in an attitude of the utmost despair, he waved his hands, and on the still air there came to us the sound of his monotonous muttering.

We crept upon him. As we did so Hobson leapt forward and, snapping his handcuffs on the man's wrists, cried: 'Cecil Atterson, I've got you!'

Atterson sprang like a man on a wire, his face went dead white. He stood quite still for a moment as if dazed, then he said in a queer voice: 'Got me, have you? Much good may it do you!'

'Hand over that packet you're carrying,' answered Hobson.

There was another pause.

'By the way, I'd like to hear exactly what I'm charged with,' said Atterson.

'Like to hear!' said Hobson. 'You know! Theft of one hundred thousand dollars from the Grand Banks. May as well hand them over and put me to no more trouble!'

'You can take all the trouble you like,' said the prisoner.

Hobson plunged his hand into Atterson's pockets, and searched him thoroughly, but found nothing.

'They are not on him,' he cried. 'Try his pack.'

From the pack November produced a square bottle of whisky, some bread, salt, a slab of mutton – that was all.

'Where have you hidden the stuff,' demanded Hobson.

Suddenly Atterson laughed.

'So you think I robbed the bank?' he said. 'I've my own down on them, and I'm glad they've been hit by someone, though I'm not the man. Anyway, I'll have you and them for wrongful arrest with violence.' Then he turned to us. 'You two are witnesses.'

'Do you deny you're Cecil Atterson?' said Hobson.

'No, I am Atterson right enough.'

'Then look here, Atterson, your best chance is to show us where you've hid the stuff. Your counsel can put that in your favour at your trail.'

'I'm not taking any advice just now, thank you. I have said I know nothing of the robbery.'

Hobson looked him up and down.

'You'll sing another song by and by,' he said ironically. 'We may as well start in now, Joe, and find where he's cached that packet.'

November was fingering over the pack which lay open on the ground, examining it and its contents with concentrated attention. Atterson had sunk down under a tree like a man wearied out.

Hobson and Joe made a rapid examination of the vicinity. A few yards brought them to the end of Atterson's tracks.

'Here's where he slept,' said Hobson. 'It's all pretty clear. He was dog-tired and just collapsed. I guess that was last night. It's an old camping place this.' The policeman pointed to weathered beds of balsam and the scars of several camp-fires. 'Yes,' he continued, 'that's what it is. But the trouble is where has he cached the bank's property?'

For upwards of an hour Hobson searched every conceivable spot, but not so November Joe, who, after a couple of quick casts down to the river, made a fire, put on the kettle, and lit his pipe. Atterson, from under his tree, watched the proceedings with a drowsy lack of interest that struck me as being particularly well simu!ated.

At length Hobson ceased his exertions, and accepted a cup of the tea Joe had brewed.

'There's nothing cached round here,' he said in a voice low enough to escape the prisoner's ear, 'and his' – he indicated Atterson's recumbent form with his hand – 'trail stops right where he slept. He never moved a foot beyond that nor went down to the river fifty yards away. I guess what he's done is clear enough.'

'Huh!' said Joe. 'Think so?'

'Yep! The chap's either cached them or handed them to an accomplice on the back trail.'

'That so? And what are you going to do next?'

'I'm thinking he'll confess all right when I get him alone.' He stood up as November moved to take a cup of tea over to Atterson.

'No, you don't,' he cried. 'Prisoner Atterson neither eats not drinks between here and Quebec unless he confesses where he has got the stuff hid.'

'We'd best be going now,' he continued as November, shrugging, came back to the fireside. 'You two walk on and let me get a word quiet with the prisoner.'

'I'm staying here,' said Joe.

'What for?' cried Hobson.

'I'm employed by bank manager Harris to recover stolen property,' replied Joe.

'But,' expostulated Hobson, 'Atterson's trail stops right here where he slept. There are no other tracks, so no one could have visited him. Do you think he's got the bills and papers hid about here after all?'

'No,' said Joe.

Hobson stared at the answer, then turned to go. 'Well,' said he, 'you take your way and I'll take mine. I reckon I'll get a confession out of him before we reach Quebec. He's a pretty tired man, and he don't rest nor sleep, no, nor sit down, till he's put me wise as to where he's hid the stuff he stole.'

'He won't ever put you wise,' said Joe definitely.

'Why do you say that?'

''Cause he can't. He don't know himself.'

'Bah!' was all Hobson's answer as he turned on his heel.

*   *   *

November Joe did not move as Hobson, his wrist strapped to Atterson's, disappeared down the trail by which we had come.

'Well,' I said, 'what next?'

'I'll take another look around.' Joe leapt to his feet and went quickly over the ground. I accompanied him.

'What do you make of it?' he said at last.

'Nothing,' I answered. 'There are no tracks nor other signs at all, except these two or three places where old logs have been lying – I expect Atterson picked them up for his fire. I don't understand what you are getting at any more than Hobson does.'

'Huh!' said Joe, and led the way down to the river, which, though not more than fifty yards away, was hidden from us by the thick trees.

It was a slow-flowing river, and in the soft mud of the margin I saw, to my surprise, the quite recent traces of a canoe having been beached. Beside the canoe, there was also on the mud the faint mark of a paddle having lain at full length.

Joe pointed to it. The paddle had evidently, I thought, fallen from the canoe, for the impression it had left on the soft surface was very slight.

'How long ago was the canoe here?'

'At first light – maybe between three and four o'clock,' replied Joe.

'Then I don't see how it helps you at all. Its coming can't have anything to do with the Atterson robbery, for the distance from here to the camp is too far to throw a packet, and the absence of tracks makes it clear that Atterson cannot have handed the loot over to a confederate in the canoe. Isn't that right?'

'Looks that way,' admitted Joe.

'Then the canoe can be only a coincidence.'

November shook his head. 'I wouldn't go so far as to say that, Mr Quaritch.'

Once again he rapidly went over the ground near the river, then returned to the spot where Atterson had slept, following a slightly different track to that by which we had come. Then taking the hatchet from his belt, he split a dead log or two for a fire and hung up the kettle once more. I guessed from this that he had seen at least some daylight in a matter that was still obscure and inexplicable to me.

'I wonder if Atterson has confessed to Hobson yet,' I said, meaning to draw Joe.

'He may confess about the robbery, but he can't tell anyone where the bank property is.'

'You said that before, Joe. You seem very sure of it.'

'I am sure. Atterson doesn't know, because *he's* been robbed in his turn.'

'Robbed!' I exclaimed.

Joe nodded.

'And the robber?'

' 'Bout five foot eight, lightweight, very handsome, has black hair, is, I think, under twenty-five years old, and lives in Lendeville, or near it.'

'Joe, you've nothing to go on!' I cried. 'Are you sure of this? How can you know?'

'I'll tell you when I've got those bank bills back. One thing's sure – Atterson'll be better off doing five years' hard than if he'd – But here, Mr Quaritch, I'm going too fast. Drink your tea, and then let us make Lendeville. It's all of eight miles upstream.'

It was still early afternoon when we arrived in Lendeville, which could hardly be called a village, except in the Canadian acceptance of that term. It was composed of a few scattered farms and a single general store. Outside one of the farmhouses Joe paused.

'I know the chap that lives in here,' he said. 'He's a pretty mean kind of a man, Mr Quaritch. I may find a way to make him talk – though if he thought I wanted information he'd not part with it.'

We found the farmer at home, a dour fellow, whose father had emigrated from the north of Scotland half a century earlier.

'Say, McAndrew,' began Joe, 'there's a chance I'll be bringing a party up on to Red River month after next for the moose-calling. What's your price for hiring two strong horses and a good buckboard to take us and our outfit on from here to the Burnt Lands by Sandy Pond?'

'Twenty dollars.'

'Huh!' said Joe, 'we don't want to buy the old horses!'

The Scotchman's shaven lips (he wore a chin-beard and whiskers) opened. 'It wouldna' pay to do it for less.'

'Then there's others as will.'

'And what might their names be?' enquired McAndrew ironically.

'Them as took up bank-clerk Atterson when he was here six weeks back.'

'Weel, you're wrang!' cried McAndrew, 'for bank-clerk Atterson juist walked in with young Simon Pointarré and lived with the family at their new mill. So the price is twenty, or I'll nae harness a horse for ye!'

'Then I'll have to go on to Simon Pointarré. I've heard him well spoken of.'

'Have ye now? That's queer for he . . . '

'Maybe then it was his brother,' said Joe, quickly.

'Which?'

'The other one that was with Atterson at Red River.'

'There was nae one, only the old man, Simon and the two girls.'

'Well, anyway I've got my sportsmen's interests to mind,' said November, 'and I'll ask the Pointarrés' price before I close with yours.'

'I'll make a reduce to seventeen dollars if ye agree here and now.'

November said something further of Atterson's high regard for Simon Pointarré, which goaded old McAndrew to fury.

'And I'll suppose it was love of Simon that made him employ that family,' he snarled. 'Oh yes, that's comic. 'Twas Simon and no that grinning lassie they call Phèdre! . . . Atterson? Tush! I tell ye if ever a man made a fule o' himself . . . '

But here, despite McAndrew's protests, Joe left the farm.

At the store, which was next visited, we learned the position of the Pointarré steading and the fact that old Pointarré, the daughters,

Phèdre and Claire, and one son, Simon, were at home while the other sons were on duty at the mill.

Joe and I walked together along various trails until from a hillside we were able to look down upon the farm, and in a few minutes we were knocking at the door.

It was opened by a girl of about twenty years of age; her bright brown eyes and hair made her very good-looking. Joe gave her a quick glance.

'I came to see your sister,' said he.

'Simon,' called the girl, 'here's a man to see Phèdre.'

'What's his business?' growled a man's voice from the inner room.

'I've a message for Miss Pointarré,' said Joe.

'Let him leave it with you, Claire,' again growled the voice.

'I was to give it to her and no one else,' persisted Joe.

This brought Simon to the door. He was a powerful young French-Canadian with up-brushed hair and a dark moustache. He stared at us.

'I've never seen you before,' he said at last.

'No, I'm going south and I promised I'd leave a message passing through,' replied Joe.

'Who sent you?'

'Can't tell that, but I guess Miss Pointarré will know when I give her the message.'

'Well, I suppose you'd best see her. She's down bringing in the cows. You'll find her below there in the meadow,' he waved his arm to where we could see a small stream that ran under wooded hills at a distance of about half a mile. 'Yes, you'll find her there below.'

Joe thanked him and we set off.

It did not take us long to locate the cows, but there was no sign of the girl. Then, taking up a well-marked trail which led away into the bush, we advanced upon it in silence till, round a clump of pines, it debouched upon a large open shed or byre. Two or three cows stood at the farther end of it, and near them with her back to us was a girl with the sun shining on the burnished coils of her black hair.

A twig broke under my foot and she swung round at the noise.

'What do you want?' she asked.

She was tall and really gloriously handsome.

'I've come from Atterson. I've just seen him,' said November.

I fancied her breath caught for the fraction of a second, but only a haughty surprise showed in her face.

'There are many people who see him every day. What of that?' she retorted.

'Not many have seen him today, or even yesterday.'

Her dark blue eyes were fixed on November. 'Is he ill? What do you mean?'

'Huh! Don't they read the newspaper in Lendeville? There's something about him going round. I came thinking you'd sure want to hear,' said November.

The colour rose in Phèdre's beautiful face.

'They're saying,' went on Joe, 'that he robbed the bank where he was employed of a hundred thousand dollars, and instead of trying to get away on the train or by one of the steamers, he made for the woods. That was all right if a Roberville farmer hadn't seen him. So they put the police on his track and I went with the police.'

Phèdre turned away as if bored. 'What interest have I in this? It *ennuies* me to listen.'

'Wait!' replied November. 'With the police I went, and soon struck Atterson's trail on the old Colonial Post Road, and in time come up with Atterson himself, nigh Red River. The police takes Atterson prisoner and searches him.'

'And got the money back!' she said scornfully. 'Well, it sounds silly enough. I don't want to hear more.'

'The best is coming, Miss Pointarré. They found nothing. Though they searched him and all round about the camp, they found nothing.'

'He had hidden it I suppose.'

'So the police thought. And I thought so too, till . . . ' (November's gaze never left her face) 'till I see his eyes. The pupils was like pinpoints in his head.' He paused and added, 'I got the bottle of whisky that was in his pack. It'll go in as evidence.'

'Of what?' she cried impatiently.

'That Atterson was drugged and the bank property stole from him. You see,' continued Joe, 'this robbery wasn't altogether Atterson's own idea.'

'Ah!'

'No, I guess he had the first notion of it when he was on his vacation six weeks back. He was in love with a wonderful handsome girl. Blue eyes she had and black hair, and her teeth was as good as yours. She pretended to be in love with him, but all along she was in love with – well, I can't say who she was in love with – herself likely. Anyway, I expect she used all her influence to make Atterson rob the bank and then light out for the woods with the stuff. He does all she wants. On his way to the woods she meets him with a pack of food and necessaries. In that pack was a bottle of drugged whisky. She asks him where he's going to camp that night, he suspects nothing and tells her, and off she goes in a canoe up Red Rover till she comes to opposite where he's lying drugged. She lands and robs him, but she don't want him to know who done that, so she plays an old game to conceal her tracks. She's a rare active young woman, so she carries out her plan, gets back to her canoe and home to Lendeville . . . Need I tell any more about her?'

During Joe's story Phèdre's colour had slowly died away.

'You are very clever!' she said bitterly. 'But why should you tell *me* all this?'

'Because I'm going to advise you to hand over the hundred thousand dollars you took from Atterson. I'm in this case for the bank.'

'I?' she exclaimed violently. 'Do you dare to say that I had anything whatever to do with this robbery, that I have the hundred thousand dollars . . . Bah! I know nothing about it. How should I?'

Joe shrugged his shoulders. 'Then I beg your pardon, Miss Pointarré, and I say goodbye. I must go and make my report to the police and let them act their own way.' He turned, but before he had gone more than a step or two, she called to him.

'There is one point you have missed for all your cleverness,' she said. 'Suppose what you have said is true, may it not be that the girl who robbed Atterson took the money just to return it to the bank?'

'Don't seem to be that way, for she has just denied all knowledge of the property, and denied she had it before two witnesses. Besides, when Atterson comes to know that he's been made a cat's-paw of, he'll be liable to turn king's evidence. No, miss, your only chance is to hand over the stuff – here and now.'

'To you!' she scoffed. 'And who are you? What right have you . . . '

'I'm in this case for the bank. Old McAndrew knows me well and can tell you my name.'

'What is it?'

'People mostly call me November Joe.'

She threw back her head – every attitude, every movement of hers was wonderful.

'Now supposing that the money could be found . . . what would you do?'

'I'd go to the bank and tell them I'd make shift to get every cent back safe for them if they'd agree not to prosecute . . . anybody.'

'So you're man enough not to wish to see me in trouble?'

November looked at her. 'I was sure not thinking of you at all,' he said simply, 'but of bank-clerk Atterson, who's lost the girl he robbed for and ruined himself for. I'd hate to see that chap over-punished with a dose of gaol too . . . But the bank people only wants their money, and I guess if they get that they'll be apt to think the less said about the robbery the better. So if you take my advice – why, now's the time to see old McAndrew. You see, Miss Pointarré, I've got the cinch on you.'

She stood still for a while. 'I'll see old man McAndrew,' she cried suddenly. 'I'll lead. It's near enough this way.'

Joe turned after her, and I followed. Without arousing McAndrew's suspicions, Joe satisfied the girl as to his identity.

Before dark she met us again. 'There!' she said, thrusting a packet into Joe's hand, 'But look out for yourself! Atterson isn't the only man who'd break the law for love of me. Think of that at night in the lonely bush!'

'My!' ejaculated November as he looked after her receding figure, 'she's a bad loser, ain't she, Mr Quaritch?'

*   *   *

We went back into Quebec, and Joe made over to the bank the amount of their loss as soon as Harris the manager (rather against his will) agreed that no questions should be asked nor action taken.

The same evening I, not being under the same embargo regarding questions, enquired from Joe how in the world the fair Phèdre covered her tracks from the canoe to where Atterson was lying.

'That was simply for an active girl. She walked ashore along the paddle, and after her return to the canoe threw water upon the mark it made in the mud. Didn't you notice how faint it was?'

'But when she got on shore – how did she hide her trail then?'

'It's not a new trick. She took a couple of short logs with her in the canoe. First she put one down and stepped on to it, then she'd put the other one farther and step on to that. Next she'd lift the one behind, and so on. Why did she do that? Well, I reckon she thought the trick good enough to blind Atterson. If he'd found a woman's tracks after being robbed he'd have suspected.'

'But you said before we left Atterson's camp that whoever robbed him was middle height, a lightweight and had black hair.'

'Well, hadn't she? Lightweight because the logs wasn't much drove into the ground, not tall since the marks of them was so close together.'

'But the black hair?'

Joe laughed. 'That was the surest thing of the lot, and put me wise to it and Phèdre at the start. Twisted up in the buckle of the pack she gave Atterson I found several strands of splendid black hair. She must 'a' caught her hair in the buckles while carrying it.'

'But, Joe, you also said at Red River that the person who robbed Atterson was not more than twenty-five years old?'

'Well, the hair proved it was a woman, and what but being in love with her face would make a slap-up bank-clerk like Atterson have any truck with a settler's girl? And them kind are early ripe and go off their looks at twenty-five. I guess, Mr Quaritch, her age was a pretty safe shot.'

The Surrey Cattle-Maiming Mystery

HERBERT JENKINS

'Disguise,' Malcolm Sage had once remarked, 'is the chief characteristic of the detective of fiction. In actual practice it is rarely
possible. I am a case in point. No one but a builder, or an engineer,
could disguise the shape of a head like mine;' as he spoke he had
stroked the top of his head, which rose above his strongly marked
brows like a down-covered cone.

He maintained that a disguise can always be identified, although
not necessarily penetrated. This in itself would be sufficient to
defeat the end of the disguised man by rendering him an object of
suspicion. Few men can disguise their walk or bearing, no matter
how clever they might be with false beards, grease-paint and wigs.

In this Malcolm Sage was a bitter disappointment to William
Johnson, the office junior. His conception of the sleuth hound had
been tinctured by the vivid fiction with which he beguiled his
spare time. In the heart of William Johnson there were three great
emotions: his hero-worship of Malcolm Sage, his romantic devotion to Gladys Norman and his wholesome fear of the
rumbustious humour of Tims. In his more imaginative moments
he would create a world in which he was the recognised colleague
of Malcolm Sage, the avowed admirer of Miss Norman and the
austere employer of Tims – chauffeurs never took liberties with
the hair of their employers, no matter how knut-like it might be
worn.

It was with the object of making sure of the first turret of his
castle in Spain, that William Johnson devoted himself to the earnest
study of what he conceived to be his future profession. He read
voraciously all the detective stories and police reports he came
across. Every moment he could snatch from his official duties he
devoted to some scrap of paper, booklet or magazine. He strove to
cultivate his reasoning powers. Never did a prospective client enter
the Malcolm Sage Bureau without automatically setting into operation William Johnson's mental induction-coil. With eyes that were
covertly keen, he would examine the visitor as he sat waiting for the

two sharp buzzes on the private telephone which indicated that Malcolm Sage was at liberty.

It mattered little to William Johnson that error seemed to dog his footsteps: that he had 'deduced' a famous pussyfoot admiral as a comedian addicted to drink; a lord, with a ten-century lineage, as a man selling something or other; a cabinet minister as a company promoter in the worst sense of the term; nothing could damp his zeal.

Malcolm Sage's 'cases' he studied as intimately as he could from his position as junior; but they disappointed him. They seemed lacking in that element of drama he found so enthralling in the literature he read and the films he saw.

Malcolm Sage would enter the office as Malcolm Sage, and leave it as Malcolm Sage, as obvious and as easily recognisable as St Paul's Cathedral. He seemed indifferent to the dramatic possibilities of disguise.

William Johnson longed for some decrepit and dirty old man or woman to enter the bureau, selling bootlaces or bananas, and, on being peremptorily ordered out, suddenly to straighten itself, and in his chief's well-known voice remark, 'So you don't recognise me, Johnson – good.' There was romance.

He yearned for a 'property-room', where executive members of the staff would disguise themselves beyond recognition. In his more imaginative moments he saw come out from that mysterious room a full-blooded Kaffir, whereas he knew that only Thompson had entered. He would have liked to see Miss Norman shed her pretty brunetteness and reappear as an old apple-woman, who besought him to buy of her wares. He even saw himself being transformed into a hooligan, or a smart RAF officer, complete with a tooth-brush moustache and 'swish'.

In his own mind he was convinced that, given the opportunity, he could achieve greatness as a master of disguise, rivalling the highly coloured exploits of Charles Peace. He had even put his theories to the test.

One evening as Miss Norman, who had been working late, was on her way to Charing Cross Underground Station, she was accosted by a youth with upturned collar, wearing a shabby cap and a queer Charlie Chaplain moustache that was not on straight. In a husky voice he enquired his way to the Strand.

'Good gracious, Johnnie!' she cried involuntarily. 'What on earth's the matter?'

A moment later, as she regarded the vanishing form of William Johnson, she wanted to kill herself for her lack of tact.

'Poor little innocent!' she had murmured as she continued down Villiers Street, and there was in her eyes a reflection of the tears she had seen spring to those of William Johnson, whose first attempt at disguise had proved so tragic a failure.

Neither ever referred to the incident subsequently – although for days William Johnson experienced all the unenviable sensations of Damocles.

From that moment his devotion to Gladys Norman had become almost worship.

But William Johnson was not deterred, either by his own initial failure or his chief's opinion. He resolutely stuck to his own ideas, and continued to expend his pocket-money upon tinted glasses, false-moustaches and grease-paint; for hidden away in the inner recesses of his mind was the conviction that it was not quite playing the game, as the game should be played, to solve a mystery or bring a criminal to justice without having recourse to disguise.

It was to him as if Nelson had won the Battle of Trafalgar in a soft hat and a burberry, or Wellington had met Blucher in flannels and silk socks.

Somewhere in the future he saw himself the head of a 'William Johnson Bureau', and in the illustrated papers a portrait of 'Mr William Johnson as he is', and beneath it a series of characters that would rival a Dickens novel with another legend reading, 'Mr William Johnson as he appears'.

With these daydreams, the junior at the Malcolm Sage Bureau would occupy the time when not actually engaged either in the performance of his by no means arduous duties, or in reading the highly coloured detective stories from which he drew his inspiration.

From behind the glass-panelled door would come the ticktack of Miss Norman's typewriter, whilst outside droned the great symphony of London, growing into a crescendo as the door was opened, dying away again as it fell to once more, guided by an automatic self-closer.

From these reveries William Johnson would be aroused either by peremptory blasts upon the buzzer of the private telephone, or by the entry of a client.

One morning, as he was hesitating between assuming the disguise of a naval commander and a street-hawker, a florid little man with purple jowl and a white, bristling moustache hurtled through the swing-door, followed by a tall, spare man, whose clothing indicated his clerical calling.

'Mr Sage in?' demanded the little man fiercely.

'Mr Sage is engaged, sir,' said the junior, his eyes upon the clergyman, in whose appearance there was something that caused William Johnson to like him on the spot.

'Take my card in to him,' said the little, bristly man. 'Tell him that general Sir John Hackblock wishes to see him immediately.' The tone was suggestive of the parade-ground rather than a London office.

At that moment Gladys Norman appeared through the glass-panelled door. The clergyman immediately removed his hat, the general merely turned as if changing front to receive a new foe.

'Mr Sage will be engaged for about a quarter of an hour. I am his secretary,' she explained. She, also, looked at the general's companion, wondering what sort of teeth were behind that gentle, yet firm mouth. 'Perhaps you will take a seat,' she added.

This time the clergyman smiled, and Gladys Norman knew that she too liked him. Sir John looked about him aggressively, blew out his cheeks several times, then flopped into a chair. His companion also seated himself, and appeared to become lost in a fit of abstraction.

William Johnson returned to his table and became engrossed, ostensibly in the exploits of an indestructible trailer of men, but really in a surreptitious examination of the two callers.

He had just succeeded in deducing from their manner that they were father and son, and from the boots of the younger that he was low church and a bad walker, when two sharp blasts on the telephone-buzzer brought him to his feet and half-way across the office in what was practically one movement. With Malcolm Sage there were two things to be avoided, delay in answering a summons, and unnecessary words.

'This way, sir,' he said, and led them through the glass-panelled door to Malcolm Sage's private room.

With a short, jerky movement of his head Malcolm Sage motioned his visitors to be seated. In that one movement his steel-coloured eyes had registered a mental photograph of the two men. That glance embraced all the details; the dark hair of the younger, greying at the temples, the dreamy grey eyes, the gentle curves of a mouth that was, nevertheless, capable of great sternness, and the spare, almost lean frame; then the self-important, over-bearing manner of the older man. 'High Anglican, ascetic, out-of-doors,' was Malcolm Sage's mental classification of the one, thus unconsciously reversing William Johnson's verdict. The other he dismissed as a pompous ass.

'You Mr Sage?' Sir John regarded the bald conical head and gold-rimmed spectacles as if they had been unpolished buttons on parade.

Malcolm Sage inclined his head slightly, and proceeded to gaze down at his fingers spread out on the table before him. After the first appraising glance he rarely looked at a client.

'I am Sir John Hackblock; this is my friend, the Reverend Geoffrey Callice.'

Again a slight inclination of the head indicated that Malcolm Sage had heard.

Mr Llewellyn John would have recognised in Sir John Hackblock the last man in the world who should have been brought into contact with Malcolm Sage. The prime minister's own policy had been to keep Malcolm Sage from contact with other ministers, and thus reduce the number of embarrassing resignations.

'I want to consult you about a most damnable outrage,' exploded the general. 'It's inconceivable that in this – '

'Will you kindly be as brief as possible?' said Malcolm Sage, fondling the lobe of his left ear. 'I can spare only a few minutes.'

Sir John gasped, glared across at him angrily then, seeming to take himself in hand, continued: 'You've heard of the Surrey cattle-maiming outrages?'

Malcolm Sage nodded.

'Well, this morning a brood-mare of mine was found hacked about in an unspeakable manner. Oh, the damn scoundrels!' he burst out as he jumped from his chair and began pacing up and down the room.

'I think it will be better if Mr Callice tells me the details,' said Malcolm Sage, evenly. 'You seem a little over-wrought.'

'Overwrought!' cried Sir John. 'Overwrought! Dammit, so would you be if you had lost over a dozen beasts.' In the army he was known as 'Dammit Hackblock'.

Mr Callice looked across to the general, who, nodding acquiescence, proceeded to blow his nose violently, as if to bid Malcolm Sage defiance.

'This morning a favourite mare belonging to Sir John was found mutilated in a terrible manner – ' Mr Callice paused; there was something in his voice that caused Malcolm Sage to look up. The gentle look had gone from his face, his eyes flashed, and his mouth was set in a stern, severe line.

'Good preacher,' Malcolm Sage decided as he dropped his eyes once more, and upon his blotting pad proceeded to develop the Pons Asinorum into a church.

In a voice that vibrated with feeling and suggested great self-restraint, Mr Callice proceeded to tell the story of the latest outrage. How when found that morning the mare was still alive, of the terrible nature of her injuries, and how the perpetrator had disappeared leaving no trace.

'Her look, sir! Dammit!' the general broke in. 'Her eyes have haunted me ever since. They – ' His voice broke, and he proceeded once more to blow his nose violently.

Mr Callice went on to explain that after having seen the mare put out of her misery, Sir John had motored over to his lodgings and insisted that they should go together to Scotland Yard and demand that something be done.

'Callice is Chairman of the Watchers' Committee,' broke in Sir John.

'I should explain,' proceeded Mr Callice, 'that some time ago we formed ourselves into a committee to patrol the neighbourhood at night in the hope of tracing the criminal. On the way up Sir John remembered hearing of you in connection with Department Z, and as he was not satisfied with his call at Scotland Yard, he decided to come on here and place the matter in your hands.'

'This is the twenty-ninth maiming?' Malcolm Sage remarked, as he proceeded to add a graveyard to the church.

'Yes, the first occurred some two years ago.' Then, as if suddenly realising what Malcolm Sage's question implied, he added: 'You have interested yourself in the affair?'

'Yes,' was the reply. 'Tell me what has been done.'

'The police seem utterly at fault,' continued Mr Callice. 'Locally we have organised watch-parties. My boys and I have been out night after night; but without result. I am a scoutmaster,' he explained. 'The poor beasts' sufferings are terrible,' he continued after a slight pause. 'It is a return to barbarism;' again there was the throb of indignation in his voice.

'You have discovered nothing?'

'Nothing,' was the response, uttered in a tone of deep despondency. 'We have even tried bloodhounds; but without result.'

'And now I want you to take up the matter, and don't spare expense,' burst out Sir John, unable to contain himself longer.

'I will consider the proposal and let you know,' said Malcolm Sage, evenly. 'As it is, my time is fully occupied at present; but later – ' He never lost an opportunity of resenting aggression by emphasising the democratic tendency of the times. Mr Llewellyn John had called it 'incipient Bolshevism'.

'Later!' cried Sir John in consternation. 'Why, dammit, sir! there won't be an animal left in the county. This thing has been going on for two years now, and those damn fools at Scotland Yard – '

'If it were not for Scotland Yard,' said Malcolm Sage quietly, as he proceeded to shingle the roof of the church, the graveyard having proved a failure, 'we should probably have to sleep at night with pistols under our pillows.'

'Eh!' Sir John looked across at him with a startled expression.

'Scotland Yard is the headquarters of the most efficient and highly organised police force in the world,' was the quiet reply.

'But, dammit! if they're so clever why don't they put a stop to this torturing of poor dumb beasts?' cried the general indignantly. 'I've shown them the man. It's Hinds; I know it. I've just been to see that fellow Wensdale. Why, dammit! he ought to be cashiered, and I told him so.'

'Who is Hinds?' Malcolm Sage addressed the question to Mr Callice.

'He used to be Sir John's head gamekeeper – '

'And I discharged him,' exploded the general. 'I'll shoot a poacher or his dog; but, dammit! I won't set traps for them,' and he puffed out his cheeks aggressively.

'Hinds used to set traps to save himself the trouble of patrolling the preserves,' explained Mr Callice, 'and one day Sir John discovered him actually watching the agonies of a dog caught across the hind-quarters in a man-trap.' Again there was a wave of feeling in the voice, and a stern set about the mouth.

'It's Hinds right enough,' cried the general with conviction. 'The man's a brute. Now will you – ?'

'I will let you know as soon as possible whether or no I can take up the enquiry,' said Malcolm Sage, rising. 'I fear that is the best I can promise.'

'But – ' began Sir John; then he stopped and stared at Malcolm Sage as he moved towards the door. 'Dammit! I don't care what it costs,' he spluttered explosively. 'It'll be worth five hundred pounds to the man who catches the scoundrel. Poor Betty,' he added in a softer tone.

'I will write to you shortly,' said Malcolm Sage. There was dismissal in his tone.

With darkened jowl and bristling moustache Sir John strutted towards the door. Mr Callice paused to shake hands with Malcolm

Sage, and then followed the general, who, with a final glare at William Johnson, as he held open the swing-door, passed out into the street, convinced that now the country was no longer subject to conscription it would go rapidly to the devil.

For the next half-hour Malcolm Sage pored over a volume of press-cuttings containing accounts of previous cattle-maimings.

Following his usual custom in such matters, he had caused the newspaper accounts of the various mutilations to be collected and pasted in a press-cutting book. Sooner or later he had determined to devote time to the affair.

Without looking up from the book he pressed three times in rapid succession a button of the private-telephone. Instantly Gladys Norman appeared, notebook in hand. She had been heard to remark that if she were dead 'three on the buzzer' would bring her to life again.

'*Whitaker's* and Inspector Wensdale,' said Malcolm Sage, his eyes still on the book before him.

When deep in a problem, Malcolm Sage's economy in words made it difficult for anyone but his own staff to understand his requirements.

Without a word the girl vanished and, a moment later, William Johnson placed *Whitaker's Almanack* on the table, then he in turn disappeared as silently as Gladys Norman.

Malcolm Sage turned to the calendar, and for some time studied the pages devoted to the current month – June – and July. As he closed the book there were three buzzes from the house-telephone, the signal that he was through to the number required. Drawing the pedestal-instrument towards him, he put the receiver to his ear.

'That Inspector Wensdale? – Yes! Mr Sage speaking. It's about the cattle-maiming business. – I've just heard of it. – I've not decided yet. I want a large-scale map of the district, with the exact spot of each outrage indicated, and the date. – Tomorrow will do. – Yes, come round. Give me half an hour with the map first.'

Malcolm Sage replaced the receiver as the buzzer sounded, announcing another client.

*   *   *

'So there is nothing?' Malcolm Sage looked up enquiringly from the map before him.

'Nothing that even a stage detective could turn into a clue,' said Inspector Wensdale, a big, clean-shaven man with hard, alert eyes.

Malcolm Sage continued his study of the map.

'Confound those magazine detectives!' the inspector burst out explosively. 'They've always got a dustpan full of clues ready made for 'em.'

'To say nothing of fingerprints,' said Malcolm Sage dryly. He never could resist a sly dig at Scotland Yard's faith in fingerprints as clues instead of means of identification.

'It's a bit awkward for me, too, Mr Sage,' continued the inspector, confidentially. 'Last time, the *Daily Telegram* went for us because – '

'You haven't found a dustpan full of clues?' suggested Malcolm Sage, who was engaged in forming geometrical designs with spent matches.

'They're getting a bit restive, too, at the Yard,' he continued. He was too disturbed in mind for flippancy. 'It was this cattle-maiming business that sent poor old Scott's number up,' he added, referring to Detective Inspector Scott's failure to solve the mystery. 'Now the general's making a terrible row. Threatens me with the commissioner.'

For some seconds Malcolm Sage devoted himself to his designs.

'Any theory?' he enquired at length, without looking up.

'I've given up theorising,' was the dour reply.

In response to a further question as to what had been done, the inspector proceeded to detail how the whole neighbourhood had been scoured after each maiming, and how, night after night, watchers had been posted throughout the district, but without result.

'I have had men out night and day,' continued the inspector gloomily. 'He's a clever devil, whoever he is. It's my opinion the man's a lunatic,' he added.

Malcolm Sage looked up slowly.

'What makes you think that?' he asked.

'His cunning, for one thing,' was the reply. 'Then, it's so senseless. No,' he added with conviction, 'he's no more an ordinary man than Jack the Ripper was.'

He went on to give details of his enquiries among those living in the district. There was absolutely nothing to attach even the remotest suspicion to any particular person. Rewards had been offered for information; but all without producing the slightest evidence or clue.

'This man Hinds?' enquired Malcolm Sage, looking about for more matches.

'Oh! the general's got him on the brain. Absolutely nothing in it. I've turned him inside out. Why, even the deputy commissioner had a go at him, and if he can get nothing out of a man, there's nothing to get out.'

'Well,' said Malcolm Sage rising, 'keep the fact to yourself that I am interested. I suppose, if necessary, you could arrange for twenty or thirty men to run down there?' he queried.

'The whole blessed Yard if you like, Mr Sage,' was the feeling reply.

'We'll leave it at that for the present then. By the way, if you happen to think you see me in the neighbourhood you needn't remember that we are acquainted.'

The inspector nodded comprehendingly and, with a heart lightened somewhat of its burden, he departed. He had an almost childlike faith in Malcolm Sage.

For half an hour Malcolm Sage sat engrossed in the map of the scene of the maimings. On it were a number of red ink crosses with figures beneath In the left-hand bottom corner was a list of the various outrages, with the date and the time, as near as could be approximated, against each.

The numbers in the bottom corner corresponded with those beneath the crosses.

From time to time he referred to the two copies of *Whitaker's Almanack* open before him, and made notes upon the writing-pad at his side. Finally he ruled a square upon the map in red ink, and then drew two lines diagonally from corner to corner. Then without looking up from the map, he pressed one of the buttons of the private-telephone. 'Tims,' he said through the mouthpiece.

Five minutes later Malcolm Sage's chauffeur was standing opposite his chief's table, ready to go anywhere and do anything.

'Tomorrow will be Sunday, Tims.'

'Yessir.'

'A day of rest.'

'Yessir!'

'We are going out to Hempdon, near Selford,' Malcolm Sage continued, pointing to the map. Tims stepped forward and bent over to identify the spot. 'The car will break down. It will take you or any other mechanic two hours to put it right.'

'Yessir,' said Tims, straightening himself.

'You understand,' said Malcolm Sage, looking at him sharply, 'you *or any other mechanic*?'

'Yessir,' repeated Tims, his face sphinx-like in its lack of expression.

He was a clean-shaven, fleshless little man who, had he not been a chauffeur, would probably have spent his life with a straw between his teeth, hissing lullabies to horses.

'I shall be ready at nine,' said Malcolm Sage, and with another 'Yessir' Tims turned to go.

'And Tims.'

'Yessir.' He about-faced smartly on his right heel. 'You might apologise for me to Mrs Tims for depriving her of you on Sunday. Take her out to dinner on Monday and charge it to me.'

'Thank you, sir, very much, sir,' said Tims, his face expressionless.

'That is all, Tims, thank you.'

Tims turned once more and left the room. As he walked towards the outer door he winked at Gladys Norman and, with a sudden dive, made a frightful riot of William Johnson's knut-like hair. Then, without change of expression, he passed out to tune up the car for its run on the morrow.

Malcolm Sage's staff knew that when 'the chief' was what Tims called 'chatty' he was beginning to see light, so Tims whistled loudly at his work: for he, like all his colleagues, was pleased when 'the chief' saw reason to be pleased.

The following morning, as they trooped out of church, the inhabitants of Hempdon were greatly interested in the breakdown of a large car, which seemed to defy the best efforts of the chauffeur to coax into movement The owner drank cider at the Spotted Woodpigeon and talked pleasantly with the villagers, who, on learning that he had never even heard of the Surrey cattle-maimings, were at great pains to pour information and theories into his receptive ear.

The episode quite dwarfed the remarkable sermon preached by Mr Callice, in which he exhorted his congregation to band themselves together to track down whoever was maiming and torturing God's creatures and defying the Master's merciful teaching.

It was Tom Hinds, assisted by a boy scout, who conducted Malcolm Sage to the scene of the latest outrage. It was Hinds who described the position of the mare when she was discovered, and it was he who pocketed two half-crowns as the car moved off Londonwards.

That evening Malcolm Sage sat long and late at his table, engrossed in the map that Inspector Wensdale had sent him.

Finally he subjected to a thorough and exhaustive examination the thumb-nail of his right hand. It was as if he saw in its polished surface the tablets of destiny.

The next morning he wrote a letter that subsequently caused Sir John Hackblock to explode into a torrent of abuse against detectives in general, and one investigator in particular. It stated in a few words that, owing to circumstances over which he had no control, Malcolm Sage would not be able to undertake the enquiry with which Sir John Hackblock had honoured him until the end of the month following. He hoped, however, to communicate further with his client soon after the twenty-third of that month.

*   *   *

Nearly a month had elapsed, and the cattle-maiming mystery seemed as far off solution as ever. The neighbourhood in which the crimes had been committed had once more settled down to its usual occupations, and Scotland Yard had followed suit.

Sir John Hackblock had written to the chief commissioner and a question had been asked in the House.

Inspector Wensdale's colleagues had learned that it was dangerous to mention in his presence the words 'cattle' or 'maiming'. The inspector knew that the affair was referred to as 'Wensdale's Waterloo', and his failure to throw light on the mystery was beginning to tell upon his nerves.

For three weeks he had received no word from Malcolm Sage. One morning on his arrival at Scotland Yard he was given a telephone message asking him to call round at the bureau during the day.

'Nothing new?' queried Malcolm Sage ten minutes later, as the inspector was shown into his room by Thompson.

The inspector shook a gloomy head and dropped his heavy frame into a chair.

Malcolm Sage indicated with a nod that Thompson was to remain.

'Can you borrow a couple of covered government lorries?' queried Malcolm Sage.

'A couple of hundred if necessary,' said the inspector dully.

'Two will be enough,' was the dry rejoinder. 'Now listen carefully, Wensdale. I want you to have fifty men housed some ten miles away from Hempdon on the afternoon of the twenty-second. Select men who have done scouting, ex-boy scouts, for preference. Don't choose any with bald heads or with very light hair. See that they are wearing dark clothes and dark shirts and, above all, no white collars. Take with you a good supply of burnt cork such as is used by nigger minstrels.'

Malcolm Sage paused, and for the fraction of a second there was a curious fluttering at the corners of his mouth.

Inspector Wensdale was sitting bolt upright in his chair, gazing at Malcolm Sage as if he had been requested to supply two lorry-loads of archangels.

'It will be moonlight, and caps might fall off,' explained Malcolm Sage. 'You cannot very well ask a man to black his head. Above all,' he continued evenly, 'be sure you give no indication to anyone why you want the men, and tell them not to talk. You follow me?' he queried.

'Yes,' said the inspector, 'I – I follow.'

'Don't go down Hempdon way again, and tell no one in the neighbourhood; *no one*, you understand, is to know anything about it. Don't tell the general, for instance.'

'Him!' There was a world of hatred and contempt in the inspector's voice. Then he glanced a little oddly at Malcolm Sage.

Malcolm Sage went on to elaborate his instructions. The men were to be divided into two parties, one to form a line north of the scene of the last outrage, and the other to be spread over a particular zone some three miles the other side of Hempdon. They were to blacken their faces and hands, and observe great care to show no light colouring in connection with their clothing. Thus they would be indistinguishable from their surroundings.

'You will go with one lot,' said Malcolm Sage to the inspector, 'and my man Finlay with the other. Thompson and I will be somewhere in the neighbourhood. You will be given a password for purposes of identification. You understand?'

'I think so,' said the inspector in a tone which was suggestive that he was very far from understanding.

'I'll have everything typed out for you, and scale-plans of where you are to post your men. Above all, don't take anyone into your confidence.'

Inspector Wensdale nodded and looked across at Thompson, as if to assure himself that after all it really was not some huge joke.

'If nothing happens on the twenty-second, we shall carry on the second, third and fourth nights. In all probability we shall catch our man on the twenty-third.'

'Then you know who it is?' spluttered the inspector in astonishment.

'I hope to know on the twenty-third,' said Malcolm Sage dryly, as he rose and walked towards the door. Directness was his strong point. Taking the hint, Inspector Wensdale rose also and, with the air of a man not yet quite awake, passed out of the room.

'You had better see him tomorrow, Thompson,' said Malcolm Sage, 'and explain exactly how the men are to be disposed. Make it clear that none must show themselves. If they actually see anyone in the act, they must track him, not try to take him.'

Thompson nodded his head comprehendingly.

'Make it clear that they are there to watch; but I doubt if they'll see anything,' he added.

*   *   *

At eleven o'clock on the night of July the twenty-third, two motor lorries glided slowly along some three miles distant from one another. From their interiors silent forms dropped noiselessly on to the moon-white road. A moment later, slipping into the shadow of the hedge, they disappeared. All the previous night men had watched and waited; but nothing had happened. Now they were to try again.

Overhead the moon was climbing the sky, struggling against masses of cloud that from time to time swung themselves across her disc.

In the village of Hempdon all was quiet. The last light had been extinguished, the last dog had sent forth a final challenging bark, hoping that some neighbouring rival would answer and justify a volume of canine protest.

On the western side of the highway, and well behind the houses, two figures were standing in the shadow cast by a large oak. Their faces and hands were blackened, rendering them indistinguishable from their surroundings.

One wore a shade over a pair of gold-rimmed spectacles, a precaution against the moonlight being reflected on the lenses.

Half an hour, an hour, an hour and a half passed. They waited. Presently one gripped the arm of the other and pointed. At the back of the house immediately opposite there was a slight movement in the shade cast by a hedge. Then the line readjusted itself and the shadow vanished. A moment later it reappeared in a patch of moonlight, looking like a large dog.

Stooping low Malcolm Sage and Thompson followed the dog-like form, themselves taking advantage of every patch of shadow and cover that offered.

The mysterious form moved along deliberately and without haste, now disappearing in the shadow cast by some tree or bush, now reappearing once more on the other side.

It was obviously taking advantage of everything that tended to conceal its movements.

Once it disappeared altogether, and for five minutes the two trackers lay on their faces and waited.

'Making sure he's not being followed,' whispered Thompson, and Malcolm Sage nodded.

Presently the figure appeared once more and, as if reassured, continued its slow and deliberate way.

Once a dog barked, a short, sharp bark of uncertainty. Again there was no sign of the figure for some minutes. Then it moved out from the surrounding shadows and continued its stealthy progress.

Having reached the outskirts of the village, it continued its crouching course along the western side of the hedge flanking the roadside.

Malcolm Sage and Thompson followed under the shadow of a hedge running parallel.

For a mile the slow and laborious tracking continued. Suddenly Malcolm Sage stopped. In the field on their right two horses were grazing in the moonlight. It was the scene of the tragedy of the previous month!

For some minutes they waited expectantly. Suddenly Malcolm Sage gripped Thompson's arm and pointed. From under the hedge a dark patch was moving slowly towards the nearer of the two animals. It was apparently the form of a man, face downwards, wriggling along inch by inch without bending a limb.

'Get across. Cut off his retreat,' whispered Sage. 'Look out for the knife.'

Thompson nodded and slid away under cover of the hedge separating the field in which the horses were from that along which the watchers had just passed.

Slowly the form approached its quarry. Once the horse lifted its head as though scenting danger; but the figure was approaching up-wind.

Suddenly it raised itself, appearing once more like a large dog. Then with a swift, panther-like movement it momentarily disappeared in the shadow cast by the horse.

There was a muffed scream and a gurgle, as the animal collapsed, then silence.

A minute later the form seemed to detach itself from the carcase and wriggled along towards the hedge, a dark patch upon the grass.

Malcolm Sage was already half-way through the second field, keeping well under the shelter of the hedge. He reached a spot where the intersecting hedge joined that running parallel with the highroad. There was a hole sufficiently large for a man to crawl through from one field to the other. By this Malcolm Sage waited, a life-preserver in his hand.

At the sound of the snapping of a twig, he gripped his weapon; a moment later a round, dark shape appeared through the hole in the hedge. Without hesitating Malcolm Sage struck.

There was a sound, half grunt, half sob, and Malcolm Sage was on his feet gazing down at the strangest creature he had ever encountered.

Clothed in green, its face and hands smeared with some pigment of the same colour, lay the figure of a tall man. Round the waist was a belt from which was suspended in its case a Gurkha's kukri.

Malcolm Sage bent down to unbuckle the belt. He turned the man on his back. As he did so he saw that in his hand was a small, collapsible tin cup covered with blood, which also stained his lips and chin, and dripped from his hands, whilst the front of his clothing was stained in dark patches.

'I wonder who he is,' muttered Thompson, as he gazed down at the strange figure.

'Locally he is known as the Reverend Geoffrey Callice,' remarked Malcolm Sage quietly.

And Thompson whistled.

*   *   *

'And that damned scoundrel has been fooling us for two years.' Sir John Hackblock glared at Inspector Wensdale as if it were he who was responsible for the deception.

They were seated smoking in Sir John's library after a particularly early breakfast.

'I always said it was the work of a madman,' said the inspector in self-defence.

'Callice is no more mad than I am,' snapped Sir John. 'I wish I were going to try him,' he added grimly. 'The scoundrel! To think – ' His indignation choked him.

'He is not mad in the accepted sense,' said Malcolm Sage, as he sucked meditatively at his pipe. 'I should say that it is a case of race-memory.'

'Race-memory! Dammit! What's that?' Sir John Hackblock snapped out the words in his best parade-ground manner. He was more purple than ever about the jowl, and it was obvious that he was prepared to disagree with everyone and everything. As Lady Hackblock and her domestics would have recognised without difficulty, Sir John was angry.

'How the devil did you spot the brute?' he demanded, as Malcolm Sage did not reply immediately.

'Race-memory,' he remarked, ignoring the question, 'is to man what instinct is to animals; it defies analysis or explanation.'

Sir John stared; but it was Inspector Wensdale who spoke.

'But how did you manage to fix the date, Mr Sage?' he enquired.

'By the previous outrages,' was the reply.

'The previous outrages!' cried Sir John. 'Dammit! how did they help you?'

'They all took place about the time the moon was full. There were twenty-eight in all.' Malcolm Sage felt in his pocket and drew out a paper. 'These are the figures.'

In his eagerness Sir John snatched the paper from his hand, and with Inspector Wensdale looking over his shoulder, read:

Day before full moon	4
Full moon	15
Day after	7
Second day after	2
Total	28

'Well, I'm damned!' exclaimed Sir John, looking up from the paper at Malcolm Sage, as if he had solved the riddle of the universe.

The inspector's only comment was a quick indrawing of breath.

Sir John continued to stare at Malcolm Sage, the paper still held in his hand.

'That made matters comparatively easy,' continued Malcolm Sage. 'The outrages were clearly not acts of revenge upon any particular person; for they involved nine different owners. They were obviously the work of someone subject to a mania, or obsession, which gripped him when the moon was at the full.'

'But how did you fix the actual spot?' burst out Inspector Wensdale excitedly.

'Each of the previous acts had been either in a diametrically opposite direction from that immediately preceding it, or practically on the same spot. For instance, the first three were north, east and south of Hempdon, in the order named. Then the cunning of the perpetrator prompted him to commit a fourth, not to the west but to the south, within a few yards of the previous act. The criminal argued, probably subconsciously, that he would be expected to complete the square.'

'But what made you fix on Hempdon as the headquarters of the blackguard?' enquired Sir John.

'That was easy,' remarked Malcolm Sage, polishing the thumb-nail of his left hand upon the palm of his right.

'Easy!' The exclamation burst involuntarily from the inspector.

'You supplied me with a large-scale map showing the exact spot where each of the previous maimings had taken place. I drew a square to embrace the whole. Lines drawn diagonally from corner to corner gave me the centre of gravity.'

'But – ' began the inspector.

Ignoring the interruption Malcolm Sage continued.

'A man committing a series of crimes from a given spot was bound to spread his operations over a fairly wide area in order to minimise the chance of discovery. The longer the period and the larger the number of crimes, the greater the chance of his being located somewhere near the centre of his activities.'

'Well, I'm damned!' remarked Sir John for the second time. Then suddenly turning to Inspector Wensdale, 'Dammit!' he exploded, 'why didn't you think of that?'

'There was, of course, the chance of his striking in another direction,' continued Malcolm Sage, digging into the bowl of his pipe with a penknife, 'so I placed the men in such a way that if he did so he was bound to be seen.'

Inspector Wensdale continued to gaze at him, eager to hear more.

'But what was that you said about race-memory?' Sir John had quietened down considerably since Malcolm Sage had begun his explanation.

'I should describe it as a harking back to an earlier phase. It is to the mind what atavism is to the body. In breeding, for instance' – Malcolm Sage looked across to Sir John – 'you find that an offspring will manifest characteristics, or a taint, that is not to be found in either sire or dam.'

Sir John nodded.

'Well, race-memory is the same thing in regard to the mental plane, a sort of subconscious wave of reminiscence. In Callice's case it was in all probability the memory of some sacrificial rite of his ancestors centuries ago.'

'A case of heredity.'

'Broadly speaking, yes. At the full moon this particular tribe, whose act Callice has reproduced, was in the habit of slaughtering some beast, or beasts, and drinking the blood, probably with the idea of absorbing their strength or their courage. Possibly the surroundings at Hempdon were similar to those where the act of sacrifice was committed in the past.

'It must be remembered that Callice was an ascetic, and consequently highly subjective. Therefore when the wave of reminiscence is taken in conjunction with the surroundings, the full moon and his high state of subjectivity, it is easy to see that material considerations might easily be obliterated. That is why I watched the back entrance to his lodgings.'

'And all the time we were telling him our plans,' murmured the inspector half to himself.

'Yes, and he would go out hunting himself,' said Sir John. 'Damn funny, I call it. Anyway, he'll get seven years at least.'

'When he awakens he will remember nothing about it. You cannot punish a man for a subconscious crime.'

Sir John snorted indignantly; but Inspector Wensdale nodded his head slowly and regretfully.

'Anyway, I owe you five hundred pounds,' said Sir John to Malcolm Sage; 'and, dammit! it's worth it,' he added.

Malcolm Sage shrugged his shoulders as he rose to go.

'I was sorry to have to hit him,' he said regretfully, 'but I was afraid of that knife. A man can do a lot of damage with a thing like that. That's why I told you not to let your men attempt to take him, Wensdale.'

'How did you know what sort of knife it was?' asked the inspector.

'Oh! I motored down here, and the car broke down. Incidentally I made a lot of acquaintances, including Callice's patrol-leader, a bright lad. He told me a lot of things about Callice and his ways. A remarkable product the boy scout,' he added. 'Kipling calls him "the friend of all the world".'

Sir John looked across at Inspector Wensdale, who was strongly tempted to wink.

'Don't think too harshly of Callice,' said Malcolm Sage as he shook hands with Sir John. 'It might easily have been you or I, had we been a little purer in mind and thought.'

And with that he passed out of the room with Inspector Wensdale, followed by Sir John Hackblock, who was endeavouring to interpret the exact meaning of the remark.

'They said he was a clever devil,' he muttered as he returned to the library after seeing his guests off, 'and, dammit! they were right.'

The Ghost at Massingham Mansions

GRANT RICHARDS

'Do you believe in ghosts, Max?' enquired Mr Carlyle.

'Only as ghosts,' replied Carrados with decision.

'Quite so,' assented the private detective with the air of acquiescence with which he was wont to cloak his moments of obfuscation. Then he added cautiously: 'And how don't you believe in them, pray?'

'As public nuisances – or private ones for that matter,' replied his friend. 'So long as they are content to behave as ghosts I am with them. When they begin to meddle with a state of existence that is outside their province – to interfere in business matters and depreciate property – to rattle chains, bang doors, ring bells, predict winners and to edit magazines – and to attract attention instead of shunning it, I cease to believe. My sympathies are entirely with the sensible old fellow who was awakened in the middle of the night to find a shadowy form standing by the side of his bed and silently regarding him. For a few minutes the disturbed man waited patiently, expecting some awful communication, but the same profound silence was maintained. "Well," he remarked at length, "if you have nothing to do, I have," and turning over went to sleep again.'

'I have been asked to take up a ghost,' Carlyle began to explain.

'Then I don't believe in it,' declared Carrados.

'Why not?'

'Because it is a pushful, notoriety-loving ghost, or it would not have gone so far. Probably it wants to get into the *Daily Mail*. The other people, whoever they are, don't believe in it either, Louis, or they wouldn't have called you in. They would have gone to Sir Oliver Lodge for an explanation, or to the nearest priest for a stoup of holy water.'

'I admit that I shall direct my researches towards the forces of this world before I begin to investigate any other,' conceded Louis Carlyle. 'And I don't doubt,' he added, with his usual bland complacence, 'that I shall hale up some mischievous or aggrieved individual before the ghost is many days older. Now that you have brought me so far, do you care to go on round to the place with me, Max, to hear what they have to say about it?'

Carrados agreed with his usual good nature. He rarely met his friend without hearing the details of some new case, for Carlyle's practice had increased vastly since the night when chance had led him into the blind man's study. They discussed the cases according to their interest, and there the matter generally ended so far as Max Carrados was concerned, until he casually heard the result subsequently from Carlyle's lips or learned the sequel from the newspaper. For the occasional case that Carrados completed for his friend there must be assumed the unchronicled scores which the inquiry agent dealt capably with himself. This reminder is perhaps necessary to dissipate the impression that Louis Carlyle was a pretentious humbug. He was, as a matter of fact, in spite of his amiable foibles and the self-assurance that was, after all, merely an asset of his trade, a shrewd and capable business man of his world, and behind his office manner nothing concerned him more than to pocket fees for which he felt that he had failed to render value.

Massingham Mansions proved to be a single block of residential flats overlooking a recreation ground. It was, as they afterwards found, an adjunct to a larger estate of similar property situated down another road. A porter, residing in the basement, looked after the interests of Massingham Mansions; the business office was placed among the other flats. On that morning it presented the appearance of a well-kept, prosperous enough place, a little dull, a little unfinished, a little depressing perhaps; in fact, faintly reminiscent of the superfluous mansions that stand among broad, weedy roads on the outskirts of overgrown seaside resorts; but it was persistently raining at the time when Mr Carlyle had his first view of it.

'It is early to judge,' he remarked, after stopping the car in order to verify the name on the brass plate, 'but, upon my word, Max, I really think that our ghost might have discovered more appropriate quarters.'

At the office, to which the porter had directed them, they found a managing clerk and two coltish youths in charge. Mr Carlyle's name produced an appreciable flutter.

'The governor isn't here just now, but I have this matter in hand,' said the clerk with an easy air of responsibility – an effect unfortunately marred by a sudden irrepressible giggle from the least overawed of the colts. 'Will you kindly step into our private room?' He turned at the door of the inner office and dropped a freezing eye on the offender. 'Get those letters copied before you go out to lunch, Binns,' he remarked in a sufficiently loud voice. Then he closed the door quickly, before Binns could find a suitable retort.

So far it had been plain sailing, but now, brought face to face with the necessity of explaining, the clerk began to develop some hesitancy in beginning.

'It's a funny sort of business,' he remarked, skirting the difficulty.

'Perhaps,' admitted Mr Carlyle; 'but that will not embarrass us. Many of the cases that pass through my hands are what you would call "funny sorts of business".'

'I suppose so,' responded the young man, 'but not through ours. Well, this is at 11 Massingham. A few nights ago – I suppose it must be more than a week now – Willett, the estate porter, was taking up some luggage to 75 Northanger for the people there when he noticed a light in one of the rooms at 11 Massingham. The backs face, though about twenty or thirty yards away. It struck him as curious, because 11 Massingham is empty and locked up. Naturally he thought at first that the porter at Massingham or one of us from the office had gone up for something. Still it was so unusual – being late at night – that it was his business to look into it. On his way round – you know where Massingham Mansions are? – he had to pass here. It was dark, for we'd all been gone hours, but Willett has duplicate keys and he let himself in. Then he began to think that something must be wrong, for here, hanging up against their number on the board, were the only two keys of 11 Massingham that there are supposed to be. He put the keys in his pocket and went on to Massingham. Green, the resident porter there, told him that he hadn't been into No. 11 for a week. What was more, no one had passed the outer door, in or out, for a good half-hour. He knew that, because the door "springs" with a noise when it is opened, no matter how carefully. So the two of them went up. The door of No. 11 was locked and inside everything was as it should be. There was no light then, and after looking well round with the lanterns that they carried, they were satisfied that no one was concealed there.'

'You say lanterns,' interrupted Mr Carlyle. 'I suppose they lit the gas, or whatever it is there, as well?'

'It is gas, but they could not light it because it was cut off at the meter. We always cut it off when a flat becomes vacant.'

'What sort of a light was it, then, that Willett saw?'

'It was gas, Mr Carlyle. It is possible to see the bracket in that room from 75 Northanger. He saw it burning.'

'Then the meter had been put on again?'

'It is in a locked cupboard in the basement. Only the office and the porters have keys. They tried the gas in the room and it was dead out; they looked at the meter in the basement afterwards and it was dead off.'

'Very good,' observed Mr Carlyle, noting the facts in his pocket-book. 'What next?'

'The next,' continued the clerk, 'was something that had really happened before. When they got down again – Green and Willett – Green was rather chipping Willett about seeing the light, you know, when he stopped suddenly. He'd remembered something. The day before, the servant at 12 Massingham had asked him who it was that was using the bathroom at No. 11 – she of course knowing that it was empty. He told her that no one used the bathroom. "Well," she said, "we hear the water running and splashing almost every night and it's funny with no one there." He had thought nothing of it at the time, concluding – as he told her – that it must be the water in the bathroom of one of the underneath flats that they heard. Of course, he told Willett then and they went up again and examined the bathroom more closely. Water had certainly been run there, for the sides of the bath were still wet. They tried the taps and not a drop came. When a flat is empty we cut off the water like the gas.'

'At the same place – the cupboard in the basement?' enquired Carlyle.

'No; at the cistern in the roof. The trap is at the top of the stairs and you need a longish ladder to get there. The next morning Willett reported what he'd seen and the governor told me to look into it. We didn't think much of it so far. That night I happened to be seeing some friends to the station here – I live not so far off – and I thought I might as well take a turn round here on my way home. I knew that if a light was burning, I should be able to see the window lit up from the yard at the back, although the gas itself would be out of sight. And, sure enough, there was the light blazing out of one of the windows of No. 11. I won't say that I didn't feel a bit homesick then, but I'd made up my mind to go up.'

'Good man,' murmured Mr Carlyle approvingly.

'Wait a bit,' recommended the clerk, with a shamefaced laugh. 'So far I had only had to make my mind up. It was then close on midnight and not a soul about. I came here for the keys, and I also had the luck to remember an old revolver that had been lying about in a drawer of the office for years. It wasn't loaded, but it didn't seem quite so lonely with it. I put it in my pocket and went on to

Massingham, taking another turn into the yard to see that the light was still on. Then I went up the stairs as quietly as I could and let myself into No. 11.'

'You didn't take Willett or Green with you?'

The clerk gave Mr Carlyle a knowing look, as of one smart man who will be appreciated by another.

'Willett's a very trustworthy chap,' he replied, 'and we have every confidence in him. Green also, although he has not been with us so long. But I thought it just as well to do it on my own, you understand, Mr Carlyle. You didn't look in at Massingham on your way? Well, if you had you would have seen that there is a pane of glass above every door, frosted glass to the hall doors and plain over each of those inside. It's to light the halls and passages, you know. Each flat has a small square hall and a longish passage leading off it. As soon as I opened the door I could tell that one of the rooms down the passage was lit up, though I could not see the door of it from there. Then I crept very quietly through the hall into the passage. A regular stream of light was shining from above the end door on the left. The room, I knew, was the smallest in the flat – it's generally used for a servant's bedroom or sometimes for a box-room. It was a bit thick, you'll admit – right at the end of a long passage and midnight, and after what the others had said.'

'Yes, yes,' assented the inquiry agent. 'But you went on?'

'I went on, tiptoeing without a sound. I got to the door, took out my pistol, put my hand almost on the handle and then – '

'Well, well,' prompted Mr Carlyle, as the narrator paused provokingly, with the dramatic instinct of an expert raconteur, 'what then?'

'Then the light went out; while my hand was within an inch of the handle the light went out, as clean as if I had been watched all along and the thing timed. It went out all at once, without any warning and without the slightest sound from the beastly room beyond. And then it was as black as hell in the passage and something seemed to be going to happen.'

'What did you do?'

'I did a slope,' acknowledged the clerk frankly. 'I broke all the records down that passage, I bet you. You'll laugh, I dare say, and think you would have stood, but you don't know what it was like. I'd been screwing myself up, wondering what I should see in that lighted room when I opened the door, and then the light went out like a knife, and for all I knew the next second the door would open on me in the dark and Christ only knows what would come out.'

'Probably I should have run also,' conceded Mr Carlyle tactfully. 'And you, Max?'

'You see, I always feel at home in the dark,' apologised the blind man. 'At all events, you got safely away, Mr – ?'

'My name's Elliott,' responded the clerk. 'Yes, you may bet I did. Whether the door opened and anybody or anything came out or not, I can't say. I didn't look. I certainly did get an idea that I heard the bath water running and swishing as I snatched at the hall door, but I didn't stop to consider that either, and if it was, the noise was lost in the slam of the door and my clatter as I took about twelve flights of stairs six steps at a time. Then when I was safely out I did venture to go round to look up again, and there was that damned light full on again.'

'Really?' commented Mr Carlyle. 'That was very audacious of him.'

'Him? Oh, well, yes, I suppose so. That's what the governor insists, but he hasn't been up there himself in the dark.'

'Is that as far as you have got?'

'It's as far as we can get. The bally thing goes on just as it likes. The very next day we tied up the taps of the gas-meter and the water cistern and sealed the string. Bless you, it didn't make a ha'peth of difference. Scarcely a night passes without the light showing, and there's no doubt that the water runs. We've put copying ink on the door handles and the taps and got into it ourselves until there isn't a man about the place that you couldn't implicate.'

'Has anyone watched up there?'

'Willett and Green together did one night. They shut themselves up in the room opposite from ten till twelve and nothing happened. I was watching the window with a pair of opera-glasses from an empty flat here – 85 Northanger. Then they chucked it, and before they could have been down the steps the light was there – I could see the gas as plain as I can see this inkstand. I ran down and met them coming to tell me that nothing had happened. The three of us sprinted up again and the light was out and the flat as deserted as a churchyard. What do you make of that?'

'It certainly requires looking into,' replied Mr Carlyle diplomatically.

'Looking into! Well, you're welcome to look all day and all night too, Mr Carlyle. It isn't as though it was an old baronial mansion, you see, with sliding panels and secret passages. The place has the date over the front door, 1882 – 1882 and haunted, by gosh! It was built for what it is, and there isn't an inch unaccounted for between the slates and the foundations.'

'These two things – the light and the water running – are the only indications there have been?' asked Mr Carlyle.

'So far as we ourselves have seen or heard. I ought perhaps to tell you of something else, however. When this business first started, I made a few casual enquiries here and there among the tenants.

Among others I saw Mr Belting, who occupies 9 Massingham – the flat directly beneath No. 11. It didn't seem any good making up a cock and bull story, so I put it to him plainly – had he been annoyed by anything unusual going on at the empty flat above?

' "If you mean your confounded ghost up there, I have not been particularly annoyed," he said at once, "but Mrs Belting has, and I should advise you to keep out of her way, at least until she gets another servant." Then he told me that their girl, who slept in the bedroom underneath the little one at No. 11, had been going on about noises in the room above – footsteps and tramping and a bump on the floor – for some time before we heard anything of it. Then one day she suddenly said that she'd had enough of it and bolted. That was just before Willett first saw the light.'

'It is being talked about, then – among the tenants?'

'You bet!' assented Mr Elliott pungently. 'That's what gets the governor. He wouldn't give a continental if no one knew, but you can't tell where it will end. The people at Northanger don't half like it either. All the children are scared out of their little wits and none of the slaveys will run errands after dark. It'll give the estate a bad name for the next three years if it isn't stopped.'

'It shall be stopped,' declared Mr Carlyle impressively. 'Of course, we have our methods for dealing with this sort of thing, but in order to make a clean sweep it is desirable to put our hands on the offender *in flagrante delicto*. Tell your – er – principal not to have any further concern in the matter. One of my people will call here for any further details that he may require during the day. Just leave everything as it is in the meanwhile. Good-morning, Mr Elliott, good-morning . . . A fairly obvious game, I imagine, Max,' he commented as they got into the car, 'although the details are original and the motive not disclosed as yet. I wonder how many of them are in it?'

'Let me know when you find out,' said Carrados, and Mr Carlyle promised.

Nearly a week passed and the expected revelation failed to make its appearance. Then, instead, quite a different note arrived:

My dear Max – I wonder if you formed any conclusion of that Massingham Mansions affair from Mr Elliott's refined narrative of the circumstances?

I begin to suspect that Trigget, whom I put on, is somewhat of an ass, though a very remarkable circumstance has come to light which might – if it wasn't a matter of business – offer an explanation of the whole affair by stamping it as inexplicable.

You know how I value your suggestions. If you happen to be in the neighbourhood – not otherwise, Max, I protest – I should be glad if you would drop in for a chat.

Yours sincerely,

LOUIS CARLYLE

Carrados smiled at the ingenuous transparency of the note. He had thought several times of the case since the interview with Elliott, chiefly because he was struck by certain details of the manifestation that divided it from the ordinary methods of the bogy-raiser, an aspect that had apparently made no particular impression on his friend. He was sufficiently interested not to let the day pass without 'happening' to be in the neighbourhood of Bampton Street.

'Max,' exclaimed Mr Carlyle, raising an accusing forefinger, 'you have come on purpose.'

'If I have,' replied the visitor, 'you can reward me with a cup of that excellent beverage that you were able to conjure up from somewhere down in the basement on a former occasion. As a matter of fact, I have.'

Mr Carlyle transmitted the order and then demanded his friend's serious attention.

'That ghost at Massingham Mansions – '

'I still don't believe in that particular ghost, Louis,' commented Carrados in mild speculation.

'I never did, of course,' replied Carlyle, 'but, upon my word, Max, I shall have to very soon as a precautionary measure. Triggett has been able to do nothing and now he has as good as gone on strike.'

'Downed tools? – now what on earth can an inquiry man down to go on strike, Louis? Notebooks? So Trigget has got a chill, like our candid friend Elliott, eh?'

'He started all right – said that he didn't mind spending a night or a week in a haunted flat, and, to do him justice, I don't believe he did at first. Then he came across a very curious piece of forgotten local history, a very remarkable – er – coincidence in the circum-stances, Max.'

'I was wondering,' said Carrados, 'when we should come up against that story, Louis.'

'Then you know of it?' exclaimed the inquiry agent in surprise.

'Not at all. Only I guessed it must exist. Here you have the manifestation associated with two things which in themselves are neither usual nor awe-inspiring – the gas and the water. It requires some association to connect them up, to give them point and force. That is the story.'

'Yes,' assented his friend, 'that is the story, and, upon my soul, in the circumstances – well, you shall hear it. It comes partly from the newspapers of many years ago, but only partly, for the circumstances were successfully hushed up in a large measure and it required the stimulated memories of ancient scandalmongers to fill in the details. Oh yes, it was a scandal, Max, and would have been a great sensation too, I do not doubt, only they had no proper pictorial press in those days, poor beggars. It was very soon after Massingham Mansions had been erected – they were called Enderby House in those days, by the way, for the name was changed on account of this very business. The household at No. 11 consisted of a comfortable, middle-aged married couple and one servant, a quiet and attractive young creature, one is led to understand. As a matter of fact, I think they were the first tenants of that flat.'

'The first occupants give the soul to a new house,' remarked the blind man gravely. 'That is why empty houses have their different characters.'

'I don't doubt it for a moment,' assented Mr Carlyle in his incisive way, 'but none of our authorities on this case made any reference to the fact. They did say, however, that the man held a good and responsible position – a position for which high personal character and strict morality were essential. He was also well known and regarded in quiet but substantial local circles where serious views prevailed. He was, in short, a man of notorious "respectability".

'The first chapter of the tragedy opened with the painful death of the prepossessing handmaiden – suicide, poor creature. She didn't appear one morning and the flat was full of the reek of gas. With great promptitude the master threw all the windows open and called up the porter. They burst open the door of the little bedroom at the end of the passage, and there was the thing as clear as daylight for any coroner's jury to see. The door was locked on the inside and the extinguished gas was turned full on. It was only a tiny room, with no fireplace, and the ventilation of a closed well-fitting door and window was negligible in the circumstances. At all events the girl was proved to have been dead for several hours when they reached her, and the doctor who conducted the autopsy crowned the convincing fabric of circumstances when he mentioned as delicately as possible that the girl had a very pressing reason for dreading an inevitable misfortune that would shortly overtake her. The jury returned the obvious verdict.

'There have been many undiscovered crimes in the history of mankind, Max, but it is by no means every ingenious plot that works. After the inquest, at which our gentleman doubtless cut a very proper and impressive figure, the barbed whisper began to insinuate and to grow in freedom. It is sheerly impossible to judge how these things start, but we know that when once they have been begun they gather material like an avalanche. It was remembered by someone at the flat underneath that late on the fatal night a window in the principal bedroom above had been heard to open, top and bottom, very quietly. Certain other sounds of movement in the night did not tally with the tale of sleep-wrapped innocence. Sceptical busybodies were anxious to demonstrate practically to those who differed from them on this question that it was quite easy to extinguish a gas-jet in one room by blowing down the gas-pipe in another; and in this connection there was evidence that the lady of the flat had spoken to her friends more than once of her sentimental young servant's extravagant habit of reading herself to sleep occasionally with the light full on. Why was nothing heard at the inquest, they demanded, of the curious fact that an open novelette lay on the counterpane when the room was broken into? A hundred trifling circumstances were adduced – arrangements that the girl had been making for the future down to the last evening of her life – interpretable hints that she had dropped to her acquaintances – her views on suicide and the best means to that end: a favourite topic, it would seem, among her class – her possession of certain comparatively expensive trinkets on a salary of a very few shillings a week, and so on. Finally, some rather more definite and important piece of evidence must have been conveyed to the authorities, for we know now that one fine day a warrant was issued. Somehow rumour preceded its execution. The eminently respectable gentleman with whom it was concerned did not wait to argue out the merits of the case. He locked himself in the bathroom, and when the police arrived they found that instead of an arrest they had to arrange the details for another inquest.'

'A very convincing episode,' conceded Carrados in response to his friend's expectant air. 'And now her spirit passes the long winter evenings turning the gas on and off, and the one amusement of his consists in doing the same with the bath-water – or the other way, the other way about, Louis. Truly, one half the world knows not how the other half lives!'

'All your cheap humour won't induce Trigget to spend another night in that flat, Max,' retorted Mr Carlyle. 'Nor, I am afraid, will it help me through this business in any other way.'

'Then I'll give you a hint that may,' said Carrados. 'Try your respectable gentleman's way of settling difficulties.'

'What is that?' demanded his friend.

'Blow down the pipes, Louis.'

'Blow down the pipes?' repeated Carlyle.

'At all events try it. I infer that Mr Trigget has not experimented in that direction.'

'But what will it do, Max?'

'Possibly it will demonstrate where the other end goes to.'

'But the other end goes to the meter.'

'I suggest not – not without some interference with its progress. I have already met your Mr Trigget, you know, Louis. An excellent and reliable man within his limits, but he is at his best posted outside the door of a hotel waiting to see the co-respondent go in. He hasn't enough imagination for this case – not enough to carry him away from what would be his own obvious method of doing it to what is someone else's equally obvious but quite different method. Unless I am doing him an injustice, he will have spent most of his time trying to catch someone getting into the flat to turn the gas and water on and off, whereas I conjecture that no one does go into the flat because it is perfectly simple – ingenious but simple – to produce these phenomena without. Then when Mr Trigget has satisfied himself that it is physically impossible for anyone to be going in and out, and when, on the top of it, he comes across this romantic tragedy – a tale that might psychologically explain the ghost, simply because the ghost is moulded on the tragedy – then, of course, Mr Trigget's mental process is swept away from its moorings and his feet begin to get cold.'

'This is very curious and suggestive,' said Mr Carlyle. 'I certainly assumed – But shall we have Trigget up and question him on the point? I think he ought to be here now – if he isn't detained at the Bull.'

Carrados assented, and in a few minutes Mr Trigget presented himself at the door of the private office. He was a melancholy-looking middle-aged little man, with an ineradicable air of being exactly what he was, and the searcher for deeper or subtler indications of character would only be rewarded by a latent pessimism grounded on the depressing probability that he would never be anything else.

'Come in, Trigget,' called out Mr Carlyle when his employee diffidently appeared. 'Come in. Mr Carrados would like to hear some of the details of the Massingham Mansions case.'

'Not the first time I have availed myself of the benefit of your enquiries, Mr Trigget,' nodded the blind man. 'Good-afternoon.'

'Good-afternoon, sir,' replied Trigget with gloomy deference. 'It's very handsome of you to put it in that way, Mr Carrados, sir. But this isn't another Tarporley-Templeton case, if I may say so, sir. That was as plain as a pikestaff after all, sir.'

'When we saw the pikestaff, Mr Trigget; yes, it was,' admitted Carrados, with a smile. 'But this is insoluble? Ah, well. When I was a boy I used to be extraordinarily fond of ghost stories, I remember, but even while reading them I always had an uneasy suspicion that when it came to the necessary detail of explaining the mystery I should be defrauded with some subterfuge as "by an ingenious arrangement of hidden wires the artful Muggles had contrived", etc., or "an optical illusion effected by means of concealed mirrors revealed the *modus operandi* of the apparition". I thought that I had been swindled. I think so still. I hope there are no ingenious wires or concealed mirrors here, Mr Trigget?'

Mr Trigget looked mildly sagacious but hopelessly puzzled. It was his misfortune that in him the necessities of his business and the proclivities of his nature were at variance, so that he ordinarily presented the curious anomaly of looking equally alert and tired.

'Wires, sir?' he began, with faint amusement.

'Not only wires, but anything that might account for what is going on,' interposed Mr Carlyle. 'Mr Carrados means this, Trigget: you have reported that it is impossible for anyone to be concealed in the flat or to have secret access to it – '

'I have tested every inch of space in all the rooms, Mr Carrados, sir,' protested the hurt Trigget. 'I have examined every board and, you may say, every nail in the floor, the skirting-boards, the window frames and in fact wherever a board or a nail exists. There are no secret ways in or out. Then I have taken the most elaborate precautions against the doors and windows being used for surreptitious ingress and egress. They have not been used, sir. For the past week I am the only person who has been in and out of the flat, Mr Carrados, and yet night after night the gas that is cut off at the meter is lit and turned out again, and the water that is cut off at the cistern splashes about in the bath up to the second I let myself in. Then it's as quiet as the grave and everything is exactly as I left it. It isn't human, Mr Carrados, sir, and flesh and blood can't stand it – not in the middle of the night, that is to say.'

'You see nothing further, Mr Trigget?'

'I don't indeed, Mr Carrados. I would suggest doing away with the gas in that room altogether. As a box-room it wouldn't need one.'

'And the bathroom?'

'That might be turned into a small bedroom and all the water fittings removed. Then to provide a bathroom – '

'Yes, yes,' interrupted Mr Carlyle impatiently; 'but we are retained to discover who is causing this annoyance and to detect the means, not to suggest structural alterations in the flat, Trigget. The fact is that after having put in a week on this job you have failed to bring us an inch nearer its solution. Now Mr Carrados has suggested' – Mr Carlyle was not usually detained among the finer shades of humour, but some appreciation of the grotesqueness of the advice required him to control his voice as he put the matter in its baldest form – 'Mr Carrados has suggested that instead of spending the time measuring the chimneys and listening to the wallpaper, if you had simply blown down the gas-pipe – '

Carrados was inclined to laugh, although he thought it rather too bad of Louis.

'Not quite in those terms, Mr Trigget,' he interposed.

'Blow down the gas-pipe, sir?' repeated the amazed man. 'What for?'

'To ascertain where the other end comes out,' replied Carlyle.

'But don't you see, sir, that that is a detail until you ascertain how it is being done? The pipe may be tapped between the bath and the cistern. Naturally, I considered that. As a matter of fact, the water-pipe isn't tapped. It goes straight up from the bath to the cistern in the attic above, a distance of only a few feet, and I have examined it. The gas-pipe, it is true, passes through a number of flats, and without pulling up all the floors it isn't practicable to trace it. But how does that help us, Mr Carrados? The gas-tap has to be turned on and off; you can't do that with these hidden wires. It has to be lit. I've never heard of lighting gas by optical illusions, sir. Somebody must get in and out of the flat or else it isn't human. I've spent a week, a very trying week, sir, in endeavouring to ascertain how it could be done. I haven't shirked cold and wet and solitude, sir, in the discharge of my duty. I've freely placed my poor gifts of observation and intelligence, such as they are, sir, at the service – '

'Not "freely", Trigget,' interposed his employer with decision.

'I am speaking under a deep sense of injury, Mr Carlyle,' retorted Mr Trigget, who, having had time to think it over, had now come to the conclusion that he was not appreciated. 'I am alluding to a moral attitude such as we all possess. I am very grieved by what has been suggested. I didn't expect it of you, Mr Carlyle, sir; indeed I did not. For a week I have done everything that it has been possible to do, everything that a long experience could suggest, and now, as I understand it, sir, you complain that I didn't blow down the gas-pipe, sir. It's hard, sir; it's very hard.'

'Oh, well, for heaven's sake don't cry about it, Trigget,' exclaimed Mr Carlyle. 'You're always sobbing about the place over something or other. We know you did your best – God help you!' he added aside.

'I did, Mr Carlyle; indeed I did, sir. And I thank you for that appreciative tribute to my services. I value it highly, very highly indeed, sir.' A tremulous note in the rather impassioned delivery made it increasingly plain that Mr Trigget's regimen had not been confined entirely to solid food that day. His wrongs were forgotten and he approached Mr Carrados with an engaging air of secrecy.

'What is this tip about blowing down the gas-pipe, sir?' he whispered confidentially. 'The old dog's always willing to learn something new.'

'Max,' said Mr Carlyle curtly, 'is there anything more that we need detain Trigget for?'

'Just this,' replied Carrados after a moment's thought. 'The gas-bracket – it has a mantle attachment on?'

'Oh no, Mr Carrados,' confided the old dog with the affectation of imparting rather valuable information, 'not a mantle on. Oh, certainly no mantle. Indeed – indeed, not a mantle at all.'

Mr Carlyle looked at his friend curiously. It was half evident that something might have miscarried. Furthermore, it was obvious that the warmth of the room and the stress of emotion were beginning to have a disastrous effect on the level of Mr Trigget's ideas and speech.

'A globe?' suggested Carrados.

'A globe? No, sir, not even a globe, in the strict sense of the word. No globe, that is to say, Mr Carrados. In fact nothing like a globe.'

'What is there, then?' demanded the blind man without any break in his unruffled patience. 'There may be another way – but surely – surely there must be some attachment?'

'No,' said Mr Trigget with precision, 'no attachment at all; nothing at all; nothing whatsoever. Just the ordinary or common or penny-plain gas-jet, and above it the whatyoumaycallit thingamabob.'

'The shade – gas consumer – of course!' exclaimed Carrados. 'That is it.'

'The tin thingamabob,' insisted Mr Trigget with slow dignity. 'Call it what you will. Its purpose is self-evident. It acts as a dispirator – a distributer, that is to say – '

'Louis,' struck in Carrados joyously, 'are you good for settling it tonight?'

'Certainly, my dear fellow, if you can really give the time.'

'Good; it's years since I last tackled a ghost. What about – ?' His look indicated the other member of the council.

'Would he be of any assistance?'

'Perhaps – then.'

'What time?'

'Say eleven-thirty.'

'Trigget,' rapped out his employer sharply, 'meet us at the corner of Middlewood and Enderby Roads at half-past eleven sharp tonight. If you can't manage it I shall not require your services again.'

'Certainly, sir; I shall not fail to be punctual,' replied Trigget without a tremor. The appearance of an almost incredible sobriety had possessed him in the face of warning, and both in speech and manner he was again exactly the man who had entered the room. 'I regard it as a great honour, Mr Carrados, to be associated with you in this business, sir.'

'In the meanwhile,' remarked Carrados, 'if you find the time hang heavy on your hands you might look up the subject of "platinum black". It may be the new tip you want.'

'Certainly, sir. But do you mind giving me a hint as to what "platinum black" is?'

'It is a chemical that has the remarkable property of igniting hydrogen or coal gas by mere contact,' replied Carrados. 'Think how useful that may be if you haven't got a match!'

To mark the happy occasion Mr Carlyle had insisted on taking his friend off to witness a popular musical comedy. Carrados had a few preparations to make, a few accessories to procure for the night's work, but the whole business had come within the compass of an hour and the theatre spanned the interval between dinner at the Palm Tree and the time when they left the car at the appointed meeting-place. Mr Trigget was already there, in an irreproachable state of normal dejection. Parkinson accompanied the party, bringing with him the baggage of the expedition.

'Anything going on, Trigget?' enquired Mr Carlyle.

'I've made a turn round the place, sir, and the light was on,' was the reply. 'I didn't go up for fear of disturbing the conditions before you saw them. That was about ten minutes ago. Are you going into the yard to look again? I have all the keys, of course.'

'Do we, Max?' queried Mr Carlyle.

'Mr Trigget might. We need not all go. He can catch us up again.'

He caught them up again before they had reached the outer door.

'It's still on, sir,' he reported.

'Do we use any special caution, Max?' asked Carlyle.

'Oh, no. Just as though we were friends of the ghost, calling in the ordinary way.'

Trigget, who retained the keys, preceded the party up the stairs till the top was reached. He stood a moment at the door of No. 11 examining, by the light of the electric lamp he carried, his private marks there and pointing out to the others in a whisper that they had not been tampered with. All at once a most dismal wail, lingering, piercing and ending in something like a sob that died away because the life that gave it utterance had died with it, drawled forebodingly through the echoing emptiness of the deserted flat. Trigget had just snapped off his light and in the darkness a startled exclamation sprang from Mr Carlyle's lips.

'It's all right, sir,' said the little man, with a private satisfaction that he had the diplomacy to conceal. 'Bit creepy, isn't it? Especially when you hear it by yourself up here for the first time. It's only the end of the bath-water running out.'

He had opened the door and was conducting them to the room at the end of the passage. A faint aurora had been visible from that direction when they first entered the hall, but it was cut off before they could identify its source.

'That's what happens,' muttered Trigget.

He threw open the bedroom door without waiting to examine his marks there and they crowded into the tiny chamber. Under the beams of the lamps they carried it was brilliantly though erratically illuminated. All turned towards the central object of their quest, a tarnished gas-bracket of the plainest description. A few inches

above it hung the metal disc that Trigget had alluded to, for the
ceiling was low and at that point it was brought even nearer to the
gas by corresponding with the slant of the roof outside.

With the prescience so habitual with him that it had ceased to
cause remark among his associates, Carrados walked straight to the
gas-bracket and touched the burner.

'Still warm,' he remarked. 'And so are we getting now. A
thoroughly material ghost, you perceive, Louis.'

'But still turned off, don't you see, Mr Carrados, sir,' put in
Trigget eagerly. 'And yet no one's passed out.'

'Still turned off – and still turned on,' commented the blind man.

'What do you mean, Max?'

'The small screwdriver, Parkinson,' requested Carrados.

'Well, upon my word!' dropped Mr Carlyle expressively. For in
no longer time than it takes to record the fact, Max Carrados had
removed a screw and then knocked out the tap. He held it up
towards them and they all at once saw that so much of the metal had
been filed away that the gas passed through no matter how the tap
stood. 'How on earth did you know of that?'

'Because it wasn't practicable to do the thing in any other way.
Now unhook the shade, Parkinson – carefully.'

The warning was not altogether unnecessary, for the man had to
stand on tiptoes before he could comply. Carrados received the
dingy metal cone and lightly touched its inner surface.

'Ah, here, at the apex, to be sure,' he remarked. 'The gas is bound
to get there. And there, Louis, you have an ever-lit and yet a truly
"safety" match – so far as gas is concerned. You can buy the thing
for a shilling, I believe.'

Mr Carlyle was examining the tiny apparatus with interest. So
small that it might have passed for the mummy of a midget hanging
from a cobweb, it appeared to consist of an insignificant black pellet
and an inch of the finest wire.

'Um, I've never heard of it. And this will really light the gas?'

'As often as you like. That is the whole bag of tricks.'

Mr Carlyle turned a censorious eye upon his lieutenant, but
Trigget was equal to the occasion and met it without embarrassment.

'I hadn't heard of it either, sir,' he remarked conversationally.
'Gracious, what won't they be getting out next, Mr Carlyle!'

'Now for the mystery of the water.' Carrados was finding his way
to the bathroom and they followed him down the passage and
across the hall. 'In its way I think that this is really more ingenious
than the gas, for, as Mr Trigget has proved for us, the water does

not come from the cistern. The taps, you perceive, are absolutely dry.'

'It is forced up?' suggested Mr Carlyle, nodding towards the outlet.

'That is the obvious alternative. We will test it presently.' The blind man was down on his hands and knees following the lines of the different pipes. 'Two degrees more cold are not conclusive, because in any case the water has gone out that way. Mr Trigget, you know the ropes; will you be so obliging as to go up to the cistern and turn the water on?'

'I shall need a ladder, sir.'

'Parkinson.'

'We have a folding ladder out here,' said Parkinson, touching Mr Trigget's arm.

'One moment,' interposed Carrados, rising from his investigation among the pipes; 'this requires some care. I want you to do it without making a sound or showing a light, if that is possible. Parkinson will help you. Wait until you hear us raising a diversion at the other end of the flat. Come, Louis.'

The diversion took the form of tapping the wall and skirting-board in the other haunted room. When Trigget presented himself to report that the water was now on Carrados put him to continue the singular exercise with Mr Carlyle while he himself slipped back to the bathroom.

'The pump, Parkinson,' he commanded in a brisk whisper to his man, who was waiting in the hall.

The appliance was not unlike a powerful tyre pump with some modifications. One tube from it was quickly fitted to the outlet pipe of the bath, another trailed a loose end into the bath itself, ready to take up the water. There were a few other details, the work of moments. Then Carrados turned on the tap, silencing the inflow by the attachment of a short length of rubber tube. When the water had risen a few inches he slipped off to the other room, told his rather mystified confederates there that he wanted a little more noise and bustle put into their performance, and was back again in the bathroom within seconds.

'Now, Parkinson,' he directed, and turned off the tap. There was about a foot of water in the bath.

Parkinson stood on the broad base of the pump and tried to drive down the handle. It scarcely moved.

'Harder,' urged Carrados, interpreting every detail of sound with perfect accuracy.

Parkinson set his teeth and lunged again. Again he seemed to come up against a solid wall of resistance.

'Keep trying; something must give,' said his master encouragingly. 'Here, let me – ' He threw his weight into the balance and for a moment they hung like a group poised before action. Then, somewhere, something did give and the sheathing plunger 'drew'.

'Now like blazes till the bath is empty. Then you can tell the others to stop hammering.' Parkinson, looking round to acquiesce, found himself alone, for with silent step and quickened senses Carrados was already passing down the dark flights of the broad stone stairway.

It was perhaps three minutes later when an excited gentleman, in the state of disrobement that is tacitly regarded as falling upon the *punctum caecum* in times of fire, flood and nocturnal emergency, shot out of the door of No. 7 and, bounding up the intervening flights of steps, pounded with the knocker on the door of No. 9. As someone did not appear with the instantaneity of a jack-in-the-box, he proceeded to repeat the summons, interspersing it with an occasional 'I say!' shouted through the letter-box.

The light above the door made it unconvincing to affect that no one was at home. The gentleman at the door trumpeted the fact through his channel of communication and demanded instant attention. So immersed was he with his own grievance, in fact, that he failed to notice the approach of someone on the other side, and the sudden opening of the door, when it did take place, surprised him on his knees on his neighbour's doorstep, a large and consequential-looking personage as revealed in the light from the hall, wearing the silk hat that he had instinctively snatched up, but with his braces hanging down.

'Mr Tupworthy of No. 7, isn't it?' quickly interposed the new man before his visitor could speak. 'But why this – homage? Permit me to raise you, sir.'

'Confound it all,' snorted Mr Tupworthy indignantly, 'you're flooding my flat. The water's coming through my bathroom ceiling in bucketfuls. The plaster'll fall next. Can't you stop it. Has a pipe burst or something?'

'Something, I imagine,' replied No. 9 with serene detachment. 'At all events it appears to be over now.'

'So I should hope,' was the irate retort. 'It's bad enough as it is. I shall go round to the office and complain. I'll tell you what it is, Mr Belting: these mansions are becoming a pandemonium, sir, a veritable pandemonium.'

'Capital idea; we'll go together and complain: two will be more effective,' suggested Mr Belting. 'But not tonight, Mr Tupworthy. We should not find anyone there. The office will be closed. Say tomorrow – '

'I had no intention of anything so preposterous as going there tonight. I am in no condition to go. If I don't get my feet into hot water at once, I shall be laid up with a severe cold. Doubtless you haven't noticed it, but I am wet through to the skin, saturated, sir.'

Mr Belting shook his head sagely.

'Always a mistake to try to stop water coming through the ceiling,' he remarked. 'It will come, you know. Finds its own level and all that.'

'I did not try to stop it – at least not voluntarily. A temporary emergency necessitated a slight rearrangement of our accommodation. I – I tell you this in confidence – I was sleeping in the bathroom.'

At the revelation of so notable a catastrophe Mr Belting actually seemed to stagger. Possibly his eyes filled with tears; certainly he had to turn and wipe away his emotion before he could proceed.

'Not – not right under it?' he whispered.

'I imagine so,' replied Mr Tupworthy. 'I do not conceive that I could have been placed more centrally. I received the full cataract in the region of the ear. Well, if I may rely on you that it has stopped, I will terminate our interview for the present.'

'Good-night,' responded the still tremulous Belting. 'Good-night – or good-morning, to be exact.' He waited with the door open to light the first flight of stairs for Mr Tupworthy's descent. Before the door was closed another figure stepped down quietly from the obscurity of the steps leading upwards.

'Mr Belting, I believe?' said the stranger. 'My name is Carrados. I have been looking over the flat above. Can you spare me a few minutes?'

'What, Mr Max Carrados?'

'The same,' smiled the owner of the name.

'Come in, Mr Carrados,' exclaimed Belting, not only without embarrassment, but with positive affection in his voice. 'Come in by all means. I've heard of you more than once. Delighted to meet you. This way. I know – I know.' He put a hand on his guest's arm and insisted on steering his course until he deposited him in an easy-chair before a fire. 'This looks like being a great night. What will you have?'

Carrados put the suggestion aside and raised a corner of the situation.

'I'm afraid that I don't come altogether as a friend,' he hinted.

'It's no good,' replied his host. 'I can't regard you in any other light after this. You heard Tupworthy? But you haven't seen the man, Mr Carrados. I know – I've heard – but no wealth of the imagination can ever really quite reconstruct Tupworthy, the shoddy magnifico, in his immense porcine complacency, his monumental self-importance. And sleeping right underneath! Gods, but we have lived tonight! Why – whyever did you stop?'

'You associate me with this business?'

'Associate you! My dear Mr Carrados, I give you the full glorious credit for the one entirely successful piece of low-comedy humour in real life that I have ever encountered. Indeed, in a legal and pecuniary sense, I hold you absolutely responsible.'

'Oh!' exclaimed Carrados, beginning to laugh quietly. Then he continued: 'I think that I shall come through that all right. I shall refer you to Mr Carlyle, the private inquiry agent, and he will doubtless pass you on to your landlord, for whom he is acting, and I imagine that he in turn will throw all the responsibility on the ingenious gentleman who has put them to so much trouble. Can you guess the result of my investigation in the flat above?'

'Guess, Mr Carrados? I don't need to guess: I know. You don't suppose I thought for a moment that such transparent devices as two intercepted pipes and an automatic gas-lighter would impose on a man of intelligence? They were only contrived to mystify the credulous imagination of clerks and porters.'

'You admit it, then?'

'Admit! Good gracious, of course I admit it, Mr Carrados. What's the use of denying it?'

'Precisely. I am glad you see that. And yet you seem far from being a mere practical joker. Does your confidence extend to the length of letting me into your object?'

'Between ourselves,' replied Mr Belting, 'I haven't the least objection. But I wish that you would have – say a cup of coffee. Mrs Belting is still up, I believe. She would be charmed to have the opportunity – No? Well, just as you like. Now, my object? You must understand, Mr Carrados, that I am a man of sufficient leisure and adequate means for the small position we maintain. But I am not unoccupied – not idle. On the contrary, I am always busy. I don't approve of any man passing his time aimlessly. I have a number of interests in life – hobbies, if you like. You should appreciate that, as you are a private criminologist. I am – among other things which don't concern us now – a private retributionist.

On every side people are becoming far too careless and negligent. An era of irresponsibility has set in. Nobody troubles to keep his word, to carry out literally his undertakings. In my small way I try to set that right by showing them the logical development of their ways. I am, in fact, the sworn enemy of anything approaching sloppiness. You smile at that?'

'It is a point of view,' replied Carrados. 'I was wondering how the phrase at this moment would convey itself, say, to Mr Tupworthy's ear.'

Mr Belting doubled up.

'But don't remind me of Tupworthy or I can't get on,' he said. 'In my method I follow the system of Herbert Spencer towards children. Of course you are familiar with his treatise "On Education"? If a rough boy persists, after warnings, in tearing or soiling all his clothes, don't scold him for what, after all, is only a natural and healthy instinct overdone. But equally, of course, don't punish yourself by buying him other clothes. When the time comes for the children to be taken to an entertainment, little Tommy cannot go with them. It would not be seemly, and he is too ashamed, to go in rags. He begins to see the force of practical logic. Very well. If a tradesman promises – promises explicitly – delivery of his goods by a certain time and he fails, he finds that he is then unable to leave them. I pay on delivery, by the way. If a man undertakes to make me an article like another – I am painstaking, Mr Carrados: I point out at the time how exactly like I want it – and it is (as it generally is) on completion something quite different, I decline to be easy-going and to be put off with it. I take the simplest and most obvious instances; I could multiply indefinitely. It is, of course, frequently inconvenient to me, but it establishes a standard.'

'I see that you are a dangerous man, Mr Belting,' remarked Carrados. 'If most men were like you our national character would be undermined. People would have to behave properly.'

'If most men were like me we should constitute an intolerable nuisance,' replied Belting seriously. 'A necessary reaction towards sloppiness would set in and find me at its head. I am always with minorities.'

'And the case in point?'

'The present trouble centres round the kitchen sink. It is cracked and leaks. A trivial cause for so elaborate an outcome, you may say, but you will doubtless remember that two men quarrelling once at a spring as to who should use it first involved half Europe in a war, and the whole tragedy of *Lear* sprang from a silly business round a word. I hadn't noticed the sink when we took this flat, but the landlord had solemnly sworn to do everything that was necessary. Is a new sink necessary to replace a cracked one? Obviously. Well, you know what landlords are: possibly you are one yourself. They promise you heaven until you have signed the agreement and then they tell you to go to hell. Suggested that we'd probably broken the sink ourselves and would certainly be looked to to replace it. An excellent servant caught a cold standing in the drip and left. Was I to be driven into paying for a new sink myself? Very well, I thought, if the reasonable complaint of one tenant is nothing to you, see how you like the unreasonable complaints of fifty. The method served a useful purpose too. When Mrs Belting heard that old tale about the tragedy at No. 11 she was terribly upset; vowed that she couldn't stay alone in here at night on any consideration.

' "My dear," I said, "don't worry yourself about ghosts. I'll make as good a one as ever lived, and then when you see how it takes other people in, just remember next time you hear of another that someone's pulling the string." And I really don't think that she'll ever be afraid of ghosts again.'

'Thank you,' said Carrados, rising. 'Altogether I have spent a very entertaining evening, Mr Belting. I hope your retaliatory method won't get you into serious trouble this time.'

'Why should it?' demanded Belting quickly.

'Oh, well, tenants are complaining, the property is being depreciated. The landlord may think that he has legal redress against you.'

'But surely I am at liberty to light the gas or use the bath in my own flat when and how I like?'

A curious look had come into Mr Belting's smiling face; a curious note must have sounded in his voice. Carrados was warned and, being warned, guessed.

'You are a wonderful man,' he said with upraised hand. 'I capitulate. Tell me how it is, won't you?'

'I knew the man at No. 11. His tenancy isn't really up till March, but he got an appointment in the north and had to go. His two unexpired months weren't worth troubling about, so I got him to sublet the flat to me – all quite regularly – for a nominal consideration, and not to mention it.'

'But he gave up the keys?'

'No. He left them in the door and the porter took them away. Very unwarrantable of him; surely I can keep my keys where I like? However, as I had another . . . Really, Mr Carrados, you hardly imagine that unless I had an absolute right to be there I should penetrate into a flat, tamper with the gas and water, knock the place about, tramp up and down – '

'I go,' said Carrados, 'to get our people out in haste. Good-night.'

'Good-night, Mr Carrados. It's been a great privilege to meet you. Sorry I can't persuade you . . .'

Sexton Blake and the Time-Killer

ANONYMOUS

Midnight! Midnight underground in London!

It sounds romantic. There is a suggestion of sinister happenings in the time and place, and yet, curiously enough, it is merely a matter of phrasing. If one places it thus – Midnight in the Underground – the thing becomes commonplace, and yet, to Sexton Blake, the celebrated criminal investigator, not even the platform of the Piccadilly Circus tube station, with its crowd of homeward-bound theatregoers, was devoid of interest.

In spite of years of experience of the seamy side of life, in spite of his keen analytic and sometimes ruthlessly scientific mind, there was a deep strain of the romantic in the character of the celebrated detective.

He walked leisurely up and down the platform, his shrewd grey eyes scanning the little crowd of people who were waiting for the last tube train. A suspicion of a smile lurked round his finely chiselled lips as he noticed Tinker's frantic efforts to extract a packet from an automatic machine. Tinker's smooth, boyish face was flushed with exercise, his opera-hat was pushed back from his forehead.

They had both been to a sparkling revue at the Pavilion, and, after an excellent supper at a discreet little Soho restaurant, the two were returning home to Baker Street.

Tinker pushed the chocolate furtively into his mouth and glanced rather impatiently at the electric clock in the tube station.

'It's a confounded nuisance waiting for the train!' he said. 'As it's the last one, I bet it'll be packed.'

'We shall soon see, my lad,' consoled Blake.

There came a long, hooting wail from the blackness of the tube tunnel. The people on the platform, some of them in evening dress, moved forward expectantly. The train at last! Tinker instinctively stood back as he visualised the long roaring carriages. But no train appeared. Again the faint, hooting sound, as if some goblin of the Underground was chuckling in unholy glee.

Then Tinker gasped, and stabbed a trembling forefinger in the direction of the tunnel.

'Look, guv'nor – look!'

A woman screamed hysterically.

Sexton Blake craned forward, and even his immobile face betrayed momentary wonder. Framed at the entrance of the tunnel was the weird figure of an enormous hound. A strange, phosphorescent glow seemed to emanate from the steaming shanks of the brute. It seemed to be running along noiselessly, with its great, yellow tongue flaming, and its cruel teeth seeming to drip with froth.

'Great Scott, guv'nor, what is it?' Tinker's voice was hoarse, and he clutched at Blake's sleeve.

The crowd on the platform seemed frozen with fear at the sight of that amazing apparition. No one moved. Everyone stared as if hypnotised as the uncanny monster advanced. It did not seem to touch the ground, but floated through the air in horrible, nerve-racking silence. Far away in the bowels of the tube came another long-drawn hoot.

Silent as a shadow, the flaming phantom hound glided straight through the tube station and disappeared before the astonished stare of nearly a hundred people.

They stood there an instant like living statues, then the spell was broken. A woman sobbed hysterically, and covered up her face with trembling, bejewelled fingers.

Blake's face was strained and set. His grey eyes grew steely, and his pupils seemed to narrow to a pinpoint.

Tinker licked his dry lips.

'I – I say, guv'nor. Did you see it?'

'I saw it, Tinker,' said Blake gravely.

Immediately there came a shrill babble of voices. Men argued and women chattered. The detective frowned thoughtfully. What was the meaning of this amazing phenomenon – a ghost in the Underground? Impossible – and yet he had seen the hound, an unearthly creature of no known breed.

Tinker watched him anxiously.

'What do you think – ' He broke off with a start, for suddenly, with a dull, reverberating roar and a long hoot, the train roared into the station.

The rush of that throbbing, pulsating, familiar thing seemed to have broken the strained, unnatural atmosphere, and as they pushed forward into the carriage, and heard the clang! cling clang! go echoing down the carriages, and the sudden roar of the motor, Tinker was inclined to regard the apparition as an evil dream.

They were silent on the journey homeward. At Baker Street the two got out. It was a crisp evening in December, and the stars twinkled frostily bright in the indigo sky above their heads.

Tinker took in great, deep gulps of the fresh night air. There was a note of thankfulness in his voice as he said: 'I am glad to get out from that ghastly place underground.'

Blake nodded.

They turned into their famous chambers in Baker Street. A cheerful fire was blazing in Blake's consulting room, and Tinker was glad to divest himself of what he inelegantly termed his 'glad rags'.

Blake himself removed his cloak and opera-hat, and, with a sigh of relief, snuggled into his stained and tattered dressing-gown.

Bed, Tinker, my lad! Don't worry about this hound business. You couldn't have a nightmare worst than the reality.

The famous detective filled up his blackened briar, and curled himself comfortably in his favourite attitude before the glowing fire.

Tinker glanced a little wistfully at the opposite chair, but he was too used to his beloved governor's moods to intrude. Very softly he closed the door and wish him good-night.

For hours Sexton Blake was wrapped in thought and tobacco smoke. It was nearly three when he knocked out the dead ashes from his pipe, but the problem of the phantom hound was solved an hour before.

*　　*　　*

'Which I sez to the gent, don't you go casting no nastershuns on my character. I am a honest woman, I am, I sez, and I don't 'old with microbes a-crawlin' all over my 'ouse. Fresh air I believes in, I sez, and if yer want to see Mr Sexton Blake in his insulting-room, you can – '

Mrs Bardell, Sexton Blake's worthy and incomparable house-keeper, was indignant – very indignant. It was nine o'clock next morning.

Blake, in spite of his late hour of retirement the night before, looked fresh, and seemed to have a hearty appetite as he punished the inevitable eggs and bacon.

Tinker grinned. His round, boyish face was, even now, red with the brisk towelling after his morning tub.

'Quite, quite!' said Sexton Blake, waving a deprecatory hand.

There were times when the garrulity of the good lady jarred upon him. And it gave Tinker a good deal of delight to watch the stifled groans of his governor when Mrs Bardell grew more than usually loquacious.

'Shall we begin at the beginning again, Mrs Bardell?' he said patiently. 'Last evening, I gather, when Tinker and I left for the Pavilion, a gentleman called who claimed to be a professor. He wanted to see me urgently, but would leave no card or name and address. He mentioned something about microbes – something with which, I can vouch, you are entirely unfamiliar?'

Tinker grinned behind a large piece of buttered toast.

Mrs Bardell flushed at Blake's tribute to her spotless housekeeping.

'Which I sez, Mr Blake, 'e's a nasty-tempered, ginger fellow, with a foreign accent. I sent 'im away, and 'e was waggling his beard like a man possessed. He was observed – utterly observed!'

With difficulty Blake repressed a smile.

'I am sure it was absurd, Mrs Bardell,' he said gravely, 'However, as he did not steal the doormat I don't think we need worry about him.'

'I ain't so sure, Mr Blake. I don't think that there foreigner could be trusted even with the doormat. Begging your pardon for interrupting your breakfasts, but I thought you'd like to know.'

'It was very kind of you, Mrs Bardell.'

Blake's voice was as courteous as if he was talking to a duchess, and the worthy landlady, as she withdrew, muttered audibly to the cat, which had crawled up from the nether regions of the house: 'A nicer man than Mr Blake I never wish to see. He may be a defective, but he's a gent – a perfect gent!'

Judging by the contented purr of the cat she also was in complete agreement.

'Well, Tinker, my lad, did you dream about the hound last night?' Tinker smiled.

'No, guv'nor, but I got a nasty shock this morning when Pedro put his paws on my bed and woke me up. I thought it was that horrible hound for one dreadful moment.'

Blake smiled whimsically.

'I wonder who our red-headed visitor was last night, Tinker?' He idly ripped open a pile of correspondence on his breakfast plate. His mail was always heavy, and this morning was no exception. After wading through about a dozen charity letters, invitations to suppers and dances, and the usual kind notes from the inevitable Mr Isaac MacPherson, who was willing to lend him five thousand pounds on note of hand alone, Blake came across a letter which seemed to interest him. He read it through carefully, instinctively noticing the texture of the paper and ink.

'Anything doing, guv'nor?' Tinker's voice was hopeful.

'We are to receive a visitor this morning, Tinker, and the identity of our excitable professor is solved.'

Tinker's eyebrows arched into interrogation.

'Oh! Who is he?'

'Professor Rufus Llewellyn, the man who invented the new Z tubes for overcoming atmospherics in wireless,' said Blake gravely.

Tinker gasped.

'Great Scott, guv'nor! The man the papers all went crazy about a few months ago? They say he's half-mad!'

'That is the man, Tinker,' said Blake. 'One must forgive much to genius. Professor Rufus Llewellyn is one of the most amazing men alive. He is certainly one of the most distinguished scientists that has ever appeared upon this planet. He is brusque, excitable, I grant you. But a man who has done such a lot for the advancement of science can be forgiven trifles like that.'

'But what does he want to see you about?' Tinker's voice was interested.

Blake handed over the letter, which was written on flimsy, green paper, as if it had been hurriedly torn off from some wrapping round a package.

Tinker looked at the small, cramped handwriting, and it was with difficulty he deciphered it.

The letter ran:

SIR – I must see you. Your dolt of a landlady was most offensive. Sir, I must see you. Be in tomorrow, I crave. It is important. You are a detective. I hope you are.

RUFUS LLEWELLYN

'Well, I'm hanged!' Tinker's voice held a note of disgust. 'If that's a specimen of the letter-writing of England's greatest scientist, I'll go back to school!'

Blake pointed to a copy of the *Daily Mail* on the table, and Tinker stared at the heavily inked lines:

PHANTOM HOUND IN THE UNDERGROUND!
MIDNIGHT TUBE MYSTERY!
WHAT IS IT?

'Blowed if I know how these newspaper guys do it!' said Tinker, as he read the account of the strange midnight occurrence of the night before. No explanation was offered of the mystery. The report simply concluded with the words – 'What is this ghastly hound? Is it supernatural, or is it some strange trick of the imagination? Watch out for the Werewolf of Piccadilly!'

Then followed exclusive interviews with about a dozen people who had been eye-witnesses of the occurrence. Blake groaned as the telephone receiver jarred suddenly.

The voice of a smart young reporter on the *Daily Mail* twanged over the wires.

Blake's voice was icily incisive.

'Yes, I did see the hound,' he said slowly. 'What's that – any theories? Yes, rather! Will I give them to you? With pleasure!'

A delighted chuckle came from the other end of the wire.

'Do you think it is supernatural, Mr Blake?'

Blake deliberately winked at Tinker.

'No. It was the salmon for supper!'

Very gently he replaced the receiver.

'One thing about newspaper men is that they're too quick. I don't give any theories until I have established at least a few facts. Pass me the newspaper-cutting book, Tinker.'

Tinker took out the latest volume from Blake's library of press cuttings. They were neatly indexed and cross-indexed. It was a task that Tinker loathed, but he did it conscientiously and well. Without it much of Blake's efficiency would have been impaired, and it was with a grunt of approval that the famous detective noted that the book was practically up-to-date.

He lit his battered pipe and leant thoughtfully over the volume of clippings. His long, slender, nervous fingers turned over the leaves rapidly, then he gave a grunt of satisfaction.

'Found anything, guv'nor?' Tinker's voice was gruff.

Blake grunted.

'Remember a few weeks ago, Tinker, a little dog was lost in the Underground? Here's an account of it in the *Daily Mail*. It seemed that the poor little animal leapt on to the permanent way from its mistress's arms. In spite of frantic efforts on the part of the station officials, the poor little brute dashed like a mad thing into the tunnel. Its body has never been recovered. Whether it was electrocuted by touching the live rail, or whether it crawled out again, no one is able to say. It might have been crushed to death by an on-coming train. In any case, it has not been seen since.'

Tinker's eyes grew very round. He hesitated a little before enquiring: 'I – I say guv'nor, you don't seriously mean to think that this ghastly-looking hound is the ghost of that poor little dog? Why, it's utterly absurd. The little dog was a Pekingese, while that ghastly creature we saw last night was more like a wolf-hound.'

Blake smiled enigmatically.

'There are more things in heaven and earth, Tinker, than are dreamed of in your philosophy.'

'Look you, it's all right, indeed to goodness, my good woman. I will go and see Mr Sexton Blake myself. I haven't seen him this long time since, whateffer.'

Tinker started to his feet with a cry of amazement, while Blake hastily rose from his chair.

A loud, not unpleasant voice, with an appalling Welsh accent, boomed from behind the door of the consulting-room.

'Who on earth is that?' gasped Tinker hoarsely.

Blake chuckled as he heard a muffled remark about 'imperence' in Mrs Bardell's throaty voice.

'Show Professor Llewellyn in at once, my lad,' he said.

Tinker opened the door and said civilly: 'Mr Blake will see you, professor.'

A tall, raw-boned man, well over six feet in height, entered the room with a strange, shambling gait. His shoulders sloped like the neck of a bottle, while his long, lean legs, with their corrugated trousers reminded one forcibly of hair-pins with wavy centres. A flaming mass of orange-coloured hair clustered about his face, which was almost hidden by a tangled mass of red whiskers.

Tinker had to check a tendency to grin outright as the extra-ordinary apparition entered the room, casting a glance of disdain at the disgusted Mrs Bardell.

Blake stepped forward courteously, and bowed.

'My dear Professor Llewellyn, this is indeed a pleasure,' he said.

'Indeed, yes. You got my letter, I suppose, Mr Blake?'

Sexton Blake nodded and waved his strange visitor into an armchair.

Tinker hung about in an undecided fashion by the door and almost trembled as the professor's beady eyes transfixed him with a glance. Then he smiled for the eyes of the professor were of a vivid blue, and shone with kindliness and good humour.

'Bright boy, Mr Blake – bright boy. Extraordinarily well-developed cerebrum, look you.'

Tinker flushed slightly. There had been many curious visitors from time to time in Sexton Blake's world-famous consulting-room, but seldom one quite like this, who referred in such an easy manner to his forehead development.

Blake waited until his visitor chose to speak. He knew Rufus Llewellyn of old. He had met him once or twice at various scientific gatherings, and his respect for the red-headed Welshman's amazing genius was tempered by his knowledge of the professor's weaknesses.

'Look you here, Mr Blake; you are a good fellow. I know you; I have seen you; I trust you! Some scoundrel has stolen something of the most inestimable value from my laboratory. I cannot tell you what it is. Mind you, it is not because I do not think you are an honest man. Whateffer else you are, you are that – whateffer!'

'Quite!'

Sexton Blake's face was as inscrutable as a sphinx. He knew that the appalling accent used by the professor was simply one of his mannerisms. Rufus Llewellyn was inordinately proud of his Welsh descent and in his spare time wrote the most fiery speeches, calling upon Wales to revolt against the accursed English. Nobody ever took him seriously as a Welsh patriot, but as scientist his name was revered and respected all over the world.

'I suppose you criminologists must be as exact in your own way as we scientists. After all criminology is a science, look you!'

'Yes,' said Blake quietly, 'though hardly an exact science.'

The professor produced an enormous black cigar, which, large as it was, was almost lost in his tangle of beard, so that Tinker dreaded to see him set fire to his whiskers as he lit the fragrant weed with a match held in his acid-stained fingers.

'Well, briefly it is this, Mr Blake. Let us assume that you are not interested in the contents of the box which has been stolen from my laboratory. Whatever it contains, you may take it from me, mind you, that it is valuable. Here is a photograph of the box.'

From his pocket the professor produced a quarter-plate photograph of a wooden box, about a foot square, with handles of brass and let into the top a plaque, also of brass.

'Did you photograph this before it was stolen?' asked Blake swiftly.

The professor smiled.

'Diawch, that was smart of you – indeed to goodness it was! No, I photographed the box after it had been stolen!'

Tinker gasped. Was the professor mad?

'You see,' continued Rufus Llewellyn puffing violently at his cigar. 'I had two boxes. I always keep my germ culture in boxes like these. So, to save time, I photographed a box identical to the stolen one, and brought it along for you to see. I know nothing except that the box has disappeared. How, or why, I don't know. I can only tell you that inside were millions of deadly germs.'

'H'm!' said Sexton Blake non-committally. 'What kind of germs were in this box?'

Professor Llewellyn hesitated for a fraction of a second.

'Mr Blake, that I cannot tell you. I am bound by a promise not to tell. The germs are not entirely my own discovery: half the credit belongs to a colleague of mine who is at present in South America, hunting up an orchid.'

'Answer me one question,' said Sexton Blake. 'Would these germs, if released, cause a pestilence, like plague, cholera or consumption?'

'I will answer that at once, look you,' replied the professor promptly. 'They will not cause a pestilence, but it is extraordinarily important that they should be returned to me. If you can find that box I shall be everlastingly grateful to you.'

Sexton Blake tapped the photograph with the stem of his briar pipe.

'I notice that on this plaque you have your name engraved. I presume the same thing applies to the stolen box of bacilli?'

'That is so, Mr Blake.'

'How many people, beside myself, know about these germs?'

'Myself and one other – Professor Menkin, who left for America two months ago. That is the situation, Mr Blake. I must have the germs safe before Menkin arrives back. If not, there will be terrible trouble. I suspect no one. My laboratory is burglar-proof. You have plenty of time. Menkin will not return for one month.'

He rose to his feet with a swift, ungainly gesture.

'Goodbye, Mr Blake. I am very glad – indeed to goodness, I am – to have seen you! Come over and make all the investigations you can as soon as you can. I will help you to the best of my ability. Good-morning, and a very good-morning to you, and whatever you do, say nothing to anybody.'

With a quick, jerky stride the professor left the room, without even the formality of shaking hands with Blake.

Tinker grinned a cheerful 'good-morning!' and the extraordinary professor dug him playfully in the ribs with a lean forefinger, and then clattered down the stairs.

'Good heavens, guv'nor, I hate to say anything about your red-headed pal, but don't you think he's got bats in his belfry – a little bit barmy on the crumpet?'

Sexton Blake smiled.

'In spite of the inelegance of your diction, my boy, I think I gather your meaning. But if you imagine that Professor Rufus

Llewellyn is not quite *compos mentis*, you are vastly mistaken. The question that now remains is whether I shall take up the case of the stolen bacilli?'

*   *   *

'I suppose, my dear Tinker, that it would be best to run over and see whether the professor is still keen on recovering his mysterious box of microbes?' said Sexton Blake, a little later in the day, after he had finished his correspondence.

Tinker nodded.

'I bet the silly old ass has mislaid it somewhere. All professors are absent-minded, you know guv'nor. It's probably in his lab all the time, hidden away behind a few test-tubes.'

Down traffic-laden Baker Street came the shrill, piping call of the newsboys. In the quaint jargon of the tribe they called out loudly: 'Extraspeshul! Amazing Disappearance!'

Tinker pricked up his ears.

'I say, guv'nor, looks like a sensational stunt,' he said. And he dashed downstairs, to return a few minutes later flourishing a copy of the *Evening News*, still warm and damp from the press. He pushed the newspaper before Blake's eyes, and pointed to the extra-bold splash headlines.

Blake's usually inscrutable face betrayed a more than ordinary interest as he read the heavily leaded lines:

AMAZING DISAPPEARANCE OF
LORD AND LABOUR LEADER!
MYSTERY OF LORD LAVENDALE AND
MR TOM GUNN! IS IT A BOLSHEVIK PLOT?

A most astounding and inexplicable mystery has been reported to Scotland Yard. It transpires that Lord Lavendale, the well-known sporting peer, and Mr Tom Gunn, the equally well-known Labour leader, lunched together at Pomano's on Monday last. The jovial leader of the National Union of Steel Workers was invited by Lord Lavendale, whose sympathy with Labour is well known, to discuss matters of a general nature with him. The luncheon-party was purely informal, and broke up shortly after 2 p.m. From that moment nothing has been heard of either Lord Lavendale or Mr Tom Gunn.

They have dis-appeared utterly.

Lord Lavendale, who was to have attended the Stadium Club this evening to witness the Bencham–Briskett fight, has not put in an appearance at his town residence, and enquiries at his club have elicited no information as to his whereabouts.

Mr Tom Gunn MP, who was to introduce an important Bill in the House tonight, is also missing. He is a bachelor MP, and lives in Kensington. His house is kept for him by his sister, who is almost distracted at his non-appearance.

Scotland Yard are making diligent enquiries into the affair, but no details are forthcoming.

'What d'you make of that, guv'nor?' said Tinker triumphantly.

Sexton Blake pursed his lips thoughtfully.

'It's impossible to say, my lad. From this meagre, and obviously hurriedly written report, one can glean little, save that both the noble lord and the genial MP have disappeared. It is certainly remarkable, but I do not see any cause for suspecting a sensational Bolshevik plot.

'If they had not both been well-known public men, their disappearance would have excited little comment. What is to prevent them going for a little holiday jaunt together, free for a while from the cares of office? I admit it is remarkable that they have not informed their relatives of their whereabouts, but perhaps they are tired of this interminable newspaper publicity.'

'Then you don't think, guv'nor, that this is in our line?' Tinker's voice was disappointed.

'I cannot tell you, my boy. If Scotland Yard needs any help, I'm always ready to do everything in my power. For the moment I must just Asquithise.'

' "Wait and see!" ' said Tinker, with a grin.

Sexton Blake nodded.

There came a tap at the door, which Tinker rose to open.

Mrs Bardell entered.

'There is a gentleman to see you urgently, Mr Blake,' she said. 'This is his card.'

She handed over a slip of gilt-edged pasteboard.

The detective scanned it swiftly.

'Show him in, please!' he said.

A moment later a tall young man stood on the threshold. He had an olive face, with dark, oily hair, brushed smoothly back from a rather high and slanting forehead. His nose jutted out like a crag above firm, straight lips, and a small, waxed, black moustache.

The newcomer was obviously flurried, for he coughed nervously and fingered his tie in an impatient manner.

'Mr Sexton Blake?' he asked, with a faint hint of a foreign accent in his voice.

Blake nodded. 'What can I do for you?' he asked courteously.

'You are the celebrated detective, is it not,' returned the other. 'Pray pardon my intrusion without an appointment, but the matter is of the most urgent nature. I am Alexis, King of Rosario!'

The criminologist's eyebrows arched a little.

'You will pardon me if I am curious – I thought that Rosario was a republic?'

The young man seated himself in the armchair.

'That is the point, Mr Blake. I am the rightful King of Rosario. It was, until the year 1879, a little separate kingdom. Then came a revolution, and a republic was established. I am the descendant of Alexis III, of the royal line, and I am in peril of my life.'

'H'm!' Sexton Blake nodded. 'You will pardon me,' he said courteously, and signed to Tinker. 'The *Gazetteer*, please!' he said.

The stranger started, and he lowered his voice. 'I beg your pardon, Mr Blake, but the business I have in hand is most urgent and confidential.'

'You may speak freely in front of my assistant,' said Blake. 'He is the soul of discretion.'

Tinker handed the criminologist a leather-bound *Gazetteer*.

Blake's long, nervous fingers flicked over the leaves. His eyes narrowed.

'It is as well to make sure of one's facts,' he explained. 'Ah! Here we are! "Rosario, a small island republic, situated in the Mediterranean Sea, thirty miles from the mainland, off the Italian Riviera. It is noted for its mild and temperate climate. Its quaint villages are relics of a medieval civilisation. The chief industries are – in the winter, sardine fishing, and, in the summer, the tourist traffic. Formerly a tiny independent kingdom, it is now a republic under a federal government. The president, Guido Marinetti, is the principal hotel proprietor of the island."

'H'm! Meagre, but nevertheless illuminating,' said Sexton Blake. 'Perhaps you would tell me precisely what are the facts of your case.'

'Well, Mr Blake, the Rosarians have grown tired of Marinetti. He is a clod – a dull, hopeless tradesman. Since the war things have gone from bad to worse. There have been strikes, and there is much poverty in my island kingdom. The tourist industry has been practically nil, and there is a strong feeling in favour of a revolution and the re-establishment of a monarchy.

'I have come to England to see certain financiers. I believe that
with the aid of a quarter of a million pounds I will set Rosario in her
place again among the nations of Europe. True, we are only a small
island but we have a history, Mr Blake. A history, if I may say so, as
rich in heroism as this island of England!'

Sexton Blake nodded slowly.

'I confess that this is indeed news to me,' he said. 'Why have you
sought my aid.'

'Listen, Mr Blake! My life is in danger. Marinetti is an unscrupulous man. He does not wish to release his hand from the
government. He is aware of the royalist plans to place me back upon
the thrown of Rosario. I was educated here in England. I am a
democrat at heart, but I think that my country will be served better
by a monarch than the present corrupt government.'

'Then you have been followed to London?' said Blake.

The other nodded.

'Twice my life has been attempted,' he said. 'I carry a revolver
always. The last attempt upon my life occurred last night. Returning from the theatre, I was set upon by a gang of roughs – at least,
they appeared roughs at the first glance, but one of them spoke in
the Rosarian dialect, and I guessed that they were emissaries of
Marinetti.'

Sexton Blake nodded thoughtfuly. He was keenly interested in
the strange story of the man who called himself the King of
Rosario.

'What is required,' he said, 'is not the service of a private
detective, but the care and vigilance of Scotland Yard. I have so
many cases on hand at the moment that I am afraid I cannot
undertake the business myself. I advise you, however, to return to
your hotel. By the way, where are you staying?'

'The Hotel Olympic,' replied the visitor promptly.

'Excellent!' said Blake. 'Tompkins, the hotel detective of the
Olympic is known to me. It is purely a question of guarding you,
and I think you could not leave it in more efficient hands. You will
excuse me, won't you?' said Sexton Blake.

Very courteously, he rose to his feet and held out a slim, brown
hand.

The young man seemed to be somewhat crestfallen.

'I am sorry, Mr Blake, but I am obliged to you for your advice. It
is not a question, I see, of deduction, but only one of protection. I
will take your advice and inform the police. I hope to negotiate the
loan by next week. Then, *Viva la Revolution!*'

He took up his hat, and his cheeks flushed with excitement.

Tinker opened the door, and bowed the visitor out.

'My stars, guv'nor!' he said presently. 'We're getting a rum lot of visitors this morning. What d'you make of that guy?'

'Quick!' snapped Sexton Blake. 'Shadow him, Tinker! I believe there will be interesting developments.'

Tinker seized his hat, his eyes sparkled with excitement. He stepped noiselessly down the steps of the house in Baker Street, and followed the unsuspecting King of Rosario into the street.

* * *

It was not very difficult for Tinker, after his years of experience in the underworld of London, to shadow the king to the Hotel Olympic, in Piccadilly.

As he swung through the plate-glass doors of the hotel about two minutes after the entrance of the King of Rosario, Tinker glanced swiftly at the indicator. The hall-porter was busily engaged in telephoning, and he did not notice the youngster's well-dressed figure as it stepped into the waiting lift.

As he shot up soundlessly to the fourth floor of the hotel, Tinker wondered what was going to happen. Why had Blake ordered him to follow the self-styled king? He wondered if the man was staying incognito in the hotel.

The lift deposited him on the fourth floor, and a perky page-boy enquired his business.

Tinker, wise to the ways of page-boys, tipped him half-a-crown and murmured something about catching up his friend. He walked briskly down the thick-pile carpeted corridor. He was just in time to see the figure of the king disappearing into a room at the end of the corridor, which overlooked the fire-escape.

Noiseless as a cat, Tinker stepped out on to the iron ladder. To his delight, he saw that it overlooked the window of the bedroom. He peered in. The man who had called himself the King of Rosario was sitting down before a mirror. Tinker noticed that he had taken off his coat. As he continued to watch, to his astonishment, he saw the man in the room carefully detach a beautiful, close-fitting wig.

Tinker could hardly suppress a cry of astonishment, for the red head that was disclosed gave the man in the room an appearance that was vaguely familiar.

Tinker noted that the other, with a few deft touches of grease-paint, accentuated the sallowness of his complexion. He then carefully adjusted his sleek black wig, and, as if satisfied with his renewed disguise, put on his coat, took up a small leather attaché case and left the room.

Tinker waited until he heard the slam of the lift-gates at the end of the passage. The coast was clear. Very cautiously he raised the sash of the window. It was ticklish work – it was tantamount to housebreaking. Yet the boy felt instinctively that something was very wrong about the so-called King of Rosario.

Tinker's deftness of touch served him in good stead as he noiselessly raised the sash and entered the bedroom of the king.

It was quite plainly furnished. Two trunks, one of them locked, were placed neatly against the wall. On a desk was a sheaf of papers, and Tinker examined them carefully. There were two or three letters addressed to Michael Malone.

'H'm! So his majesty's real name is Mike,' mused Tinker. 'Pretty good name for a king,' he grinned. 'I wonder what the deuce made the guv'nor suspect.'

He broke off suddenly for his keen eyes spotted a sheet of blue linen-faced paper stamped with a coronet.

'My stars! It's from Lord Lavendale to Mr Mike Malone, alias the King of Rosario!'

It was very brief, and read simply:

> DEAR MR MALONE – I have pleasure in accepting your kind invitation. Mr Gunn and myself would be delighted to join you at Pomana's for lunch today.
> Sincerely,   LAVENDALE

Tinker whistled. The date on the letter was December 5th, the last time the sporting peer and the well-known Labour leader had been seen alive! Since then they had utterly disappeared.

What had they in common with the mysterious Michael Malone, King of Rosario?

For some time the young detective remained lost in thought as he gripped the missive in his hand. It was obvious from Sexton Blake's peremptory command that the criminologist had already suspected that the sleek, olive young man was not all that he should have been.

A cursory search round the room elicited very little, and Tinker debated the advisability of taking the letter along with him or merely memorising its contents. He resolved finally to trust to luck that the pseudo king would not notice the disappearance of the document, and he folded it up carefully and slipped it into his pocket.

He reclosed the window and noiselessly slipped the catch of the bedroom door and closed it gently behind him. He nonchalantly lit a cigarette, humming a gay little tune as he stepped along the soft pile carpet of the corridor in the direction of the elevator.

Once outside the hotel Tinker took a taxi straight to Baker Street. Sexton Blake was seated in his customary attitude in his luxurious armchair before the consulting-room fire, his fingertips pressed lightly together, and an abstracted look in his keen, grey eyes.

'I say, guv'nor, how on earth did you spot that the king was a dud?'

Blake raised his eyebrows.

'Hallo, Tinker! You're back soon! Have you found anything?'

'Sure.'

With a little grin of triumph the youngster handed over Lord Lavendale's letter.

Blake frowned thoughtfully as he lit his battered briar. After reading the brief message, he held the notepaper up to the light and scrutinised keenly the watermark.

'H'm! Seems genuine enough, Tinker. Tell me, where did you find this?'

Tinker briefly explained all he had seen in the king's suite at the Olympic Hotel.

Blake took long, reflective puffs on his pipe, and his fingers drummed nervously on the arms of his chair.

'It was obvious, my dear Tinker, that our engaging visitor was an impostor. You know that I am no mean master of the art of disguise, and I am afraid that our visitor's make-up, while no doubt excellent for a passing glance, was not quite natural enough to deceive a trained observer. Wigs are difficult things to adjust, and I noticed a tuft of red hair on his left temple, emerging coyly from beneath his black wig. Then again, a carmine liner must be handled with dexterity and skill; the crow's-feet round the eyes were far too heavy. It was a simple little piece of observation, and I acted at once on my suspicions, though why or wherefore a man should pretend to be a non-existent king of a tenth-rate island, I cannot for the life of me imagine.'

'Do you think that he might be a spy or some Secret Service merchant, guv'nor?' asked Tinker. 'It's obvious that he is a friend of Lord Lavendale's from this letter. Look at the date – December 5th. I'll hike along to Pomano's and find out whom they lunched with, unless, of course, this Mike Malone is another person altogether, and the faked king pinched the letter from him.'

Blake smiled inscrutably.

'I'm beginning to see a little more daylight, Tinker,' he said, with a smile. 'That hound which startled you so in the tube last night – the problem is solved. You remember my talking to you about the little dog that disappeared in the tunnel the other day? A little association of ideas put me on the right trail, though I must admit this late edition of the *Evening News* has helped me considerably.'

He pointed to the theatrical column of the paper, and there boldly outlined in black and white was a picture of a spectral hound.

Tinker gasped as he saw it.

'Why guv'nor, it's a bloomin' cinema film!'

Blake laughed shortly.

'Yes. Some advertising genius has certainly managed to hit the public right in the eye, as the saying is. This is an American super-film to be shown at the West End tonight for the first time. The method of advertising was characteristically Yankee. Bold and effective, if a little blatant. Probably the publicity man read the account of the little dog's disappearance in the tube tunnel, and that suggested to his inventive brain a remarkable scheme to advertise the phantom hound.'

'Anyway, I rang up a reporter on the *Mail*, and suggested this theory to him, and it seems that the whole thing was a clever optical illusion run by the cinema as a stunt. There was a kind of cinema projector hidden above the signal-cabin in the tube station, which directed the image of the hound on to the whitewashed walls of the tube tunnel. Midnight, the uncanniness of the apparition, and the glamour of the Underground did the rest. So there's one little problem solved at least!'

Tinker glanced admiringly at Sexton Blake.

'What a stunt, guv'nor! It fairly took me in, and you solved the whole business without shifting from your armchair!'

Blake smiled.

'It was simple enough, Tinker. One simply needs to study the methods of the average journalist and publicity man to know that they get their ideas from the same source – popular and sensational articles in the newspapers, However, there is still the mystery of Professor Llewellyn's microbes, and, on top of that, the affair of his pseudo majesty. You had better run along to Pomano's and get as much information as you can regarding the little luncheon party the other morning.'

'Right you are, guv'nor! It's a mighty puzzling business to me altogether. Do you think – '

Sexton Blake grinned.

'I must have more data, my lad,' he said. 'Leave this letter with me. Probably I shall be able to account for the King of Rosario's most intriguing visit.'

The youngster adjusted his hat at its customary rakish tilt, and left the famous consulting-room. It was nearly five o'clock when he finally reached Pomano's.

Luigi, the manager of the famous restaurant, knew Tinker well. Blake and he often used to dine at a discreet little table in the palm lounge.

The little Italian rushed up to Tinker with his brown eyes full of concern.

'There is nothing wrong, is there, sare?' he said, shrugging his shoulders, and extending the palms of his hands with a deprecatory gesture.

Tinker smiled.

'No, Luigi; but I should like a few words with you in your private office.'

'Certainly! Come this way, Mistaire Tinker!' The manager grabbed the young detective by the coat-sleeve, and swept him hurriedly into his private sanctum.

'You know Lord Lavendale well, do you not, Luigi?' he enquired.

'But certainly, sare, I am za most grieved that he disappeared in so very extraordinaire a fashion. Last Monday night he and two friends lunched at the very table I reserve for you and Mistaire Blake.'

Tinker's eyes sparkled.

'Oh, did you recognise his two companions?' he asked.

'One, I know him by sight only. It is Mr Tom Gunn, the Labour MP. The other gentleman, who was the host, I have never seen him here before.'

'What was he like?' demanded Tinker crisply.

'Oh, a young man with the most charming smile, and the hair vat you call gingaire.'

'H'm!' Tinker frowned. A man with red hair. It was fairly obvious, therefore, that on Monday the mysterious person who claimed to be King of Rosario had been the host of Lord Lavendale and the well-known Labour leader. He thanked Luigi courteously, and the olive-skinned little manager lowered his voice.

'I pray you will forgeeve, Mistaire Tinker, if I seem to – how do you call it in Engleesh? – violate ze confidence of my customaires. But I think that it is a great shame that Lord Lavendale should so completely disappear. I am a Sicilian myself, but I know a little island close by our country called Rosario, and when I supervised the table I overheard the Lord Lavendale accept ze invitation of the young man with the gingaire hair to visit Rosario on zat day. I think ze young man is an aviator, or something, but at the time I did not consider ze conversation important. Perhaps you and ze so great Mistaire Sexton Blake will be able to put two and two together. As for me, I am *maître d'hôtel* and *hélas* – no detective.'

Tinker smiled. The information he had gleaned, although meagre, was interesting. The fate of the missing man was undoubtedly linked up in some mysterious fashion with the tiny little island republic in the Mediterranean. He pondered deeply over the problem as he was whirled back in a taxi to Baker Street.

Blake seemed not to have moved a muscle during the whole time of his absence, but sat smoking with calm reflection his battered briar pipe.

Tinker told him briefly the facts that he had gathered.

Sexton Blake remained thoughtful.

'H'm! I think a little trip would be good for us, Tinker. I have a certain instinct, a certain intuition – call it what you will – that this case is going to be simpler than it appears on the surface. Ring up the Croydon aerodrome, and book two seats for ten o'clock tomorrow by the De Lesseps air taxi. A change of air would do us good.'

Tinker grinned

'Where are you thinking of going to, guv'nor?'

Blake smiled inscrutably.

'Rosario, my boy.'

'Are you going to look for Lord Lavendale?' asked Tinker, in amazement.

Blake nodded

'Yes, and maybe Professor Llewellyn's missing microbres.'

* * *

The next morning Sexton Blake and Tinker were abroad at nine o'clock, after retiring at an unusually early hour the previous evening.

Mrs Bardell, Blake's worthy housekeeper, raised up her hands in horror as Tinker explained that they were going for a little flying trip to the Continent.

'Lawks amercy, Mr Tinker!' she said. 'They aerioplanes ain't safe, what with them electric currents, sideskids and therms, which float about the atmosphere – which, as I used to say to the late Mr Bardell, if Nature had intended a man to smoke she wud have provided him with a chimbley. The same if we were expected to fly,

we wud have 'ad wings. However, poor dear Bardell 'as got 'is now,
I 'opes, and an 'arp as well.'

Tinker smiled. He as genuinely fond of Mrs Bardell and her
motherly concern. While it amused him, it also heightened the
bond of affection which had existed for so many years between the
housekeeper and himself.

'Don't you worry about us, Mrs Bardell. We shall be as right as
trivets. Four hours. Think of it. That's all it will take us to the coast
of Italy, and then for the sunshine after this grisly London weather.'

He glanced thought the window at the misty murk of a typical
morning in late winter.

'Captain Briscoe, of the Aero-Taxi Company, is going to pilot us,
guv'nor,' he said, as Sexton Blake hurried into the room, his tall,
athletic frame warmly wrapped in a leather coat.

'Good!' The great detective nodded his approval. 'He's a capable
man – Briscoe. It should not take us more than four hours to get
across. Got the bags?'

Tinker nodded.

'They're in the car outside, guv'nor.'

A moment later there came the wheezy, discordant wail of some
long-forgotten Neapolitan tune from the street below.

'There's that dratted Eyetalian again, Mr Blake! Three times this
morning e's been round to this 'ouse, a-churnin' out of his macaroni
'n' spaghetti tunes. What with their monkeys and their ice-creams
and their anchovists, they ought to be conported, every one of
them!'

The suspicion of a smile lurked round the corners of Sexton
Blake's firm, well-chiselled lips, and he glanced casually out of the
window to where the Italian organ-grinder, dressed in a faded
velveteen jacket and a black, low-crowned hat, was standing.

'We'll shoo him away for you, Mrs Bardell,' grinned Tinker, as he
seized the travelling-rug. 'Goodbye! We'll be back in a few days.'

Mrs Bardell, as behoved the housekeeper of a world-renowned
detective, was used to Blake's erratic ways, and, with a final
injunction to Tinker to take care in 'them dratted aerioplanes', she
disappeared into the dim, mysterious quarters in the basement, over
which she reigned supreme.

Sexton Blake took the wheel, and a moment later the car slid
forward in the direction of Croydon.

Tinker was silent as his governor threaded his way through the
traffic at the end of Baker Street. If he had not been so preoccupied
with conjecture regarding the outcome of Blake's hurried dash to

Croydon, he would have noticed that, as the car left the house in Baker Street, the Italian organ-grinder began to play the little lilting Neapolitan tune in quick tempo. The gay, catchy little air, redolent of the sunny south, seemed to be a little out of place in the busy but drab thoroughfare of Baker Street.

With a final flourish of his handle, and a jerk at the chain that held the gibbering monkey on the edge of the organ, the Italian moved on after one slow, keen glance up at the windows of Blake's consulting-room. Then he trudged on, but there was a glint of quiet satisfaction in his shifty, black eyes as he noticed a motorcyclist, heavily goggled, speeding through the roaring traffic in a seeming endeavour to overtake Sexton Blake's car.

Little did Blake or Tinker realise what tangled skein of mystery lay behind the visit of Professor Llewellyn and the disreputable organ grinder who trudged on his way with the decrepit barrel-organ and a mangy monkey.

*   *   *

It was punctually at ten o'clock when Blake drew up at the Croydon aerodrome. Captain Briscoe, the once famous flying ace, and now the crack pilot of the Aero-Taxi Company, greeted Blake warmly as the detective stepped out of his motor car, accompanied by Tinker.

'Good-morning, Briscoe!' said Blake cordially. 'All fit and ready for our little trip?'

'Quite OK, Mr Blake! We should reach Rosario, all being well, by two-thirty, or thereabouts. We'll get there via Marseilles, and pass over the seaport about twelve. I'll be glad to get out of this foggy weather.' He coughed and tapped his chest. 'A little of the sunny Riviera air would do the old lungs good.'

Blake nodded, while Tinker attended to the luggage and garaged the motor car at an adjacent hangar.

'You, of course, want a return trip, do you not, Mr Blake?' said Briscoe.

Sexton Blake took out a cigarette-case and proffered it to the flying officer. 'Very probably, we shall return tomorrow. I don't think my enquiries will take long. On the other hand, there is no knowing what will happen. Is anyone else accompanying you on this journey?'

'No, Mr Blake; you're my only passengers. Rosario is such an out-of-the way place that I get very little demand for trips there.'

Tinker, having emerged victorious from a wordy tussle with the Customs authorities, appeared at this point and followed Blake and the airman as they climbed aboard the plane.

As the mechanics swung the propeller, a motorcyclist, dressed in a close-fitting Burberry and a leather cap, glared at them from the safe seclusion of a wooden hut, just beyond the railed-off public enclosure. Unnoticed by anybody, he dismounted from the machine, kicked down the rear wheel stand, and watched the preparations that were being made for the flight in the middle of the grassy aerodrome.

The propeller was revving erratically by this time, and the engine emitting a series of loud and irregular explosions. Soon the engine warmed to its work, and the revolutions became steady and constant. Then, with an increasing roar, the machine lurched and bumped across the uneven ground, skimmed the surface, rose clear and began to climb, circling for height.

Those below watched it as it dwindled steadily into the blue above, and only ceased interest in it when it had diminished to a little speck, and had headed on its course for the south.

There was a grim smile about the lips of the mysterious motorcyclist as he looked earthwards again. Then, leaving his machine propped up in the roadway, he sauntered across to the aerodrome post-office, an unambitious structure that was concerned not only with His Majesty's mail, but also with the retailing of fruit, sweets and postcards.

'Now, Mr Sexton Blake,' he muttered, as he approached the wire-grilled counter at the end of the shop, 'we'll see if the speed of an aeroplane can be outmatched. We've long memories, you know.'

Then, asking for a foreign telegram form, he set to work composing a very cryptic telegram.

* * *

Tinker was no flying novice, but he was still young enough to gaze down with delight at the foam-capped breakers of the English Channel as the plane skimmed southwards under the capable hands of the pilot. Soon the sea gave place to land again. They were flying an even seventy miles an hour, but when the coast of France was reached the throbbing engines took on a more sonorous tone.

Down below them stretched the rich brown earth of France, fresh from the plough's blade, specked here and there by the brilliant red roofs of little hamlets and villages. Then, eventually, came the sea again, and Tinker gazed down with interest at the congested harbour of Marseilles, with the foreshortened masts of tall-topped ships.

In the distance across the harbour loomed the rugged grim pile of

Château d'If, that romantic prison from which the Count of Monte Cristo escaped after fourteen weary years.

Blake pointed out various places rich in historical associations to the lad as the aeroplane hummed southwards on the Riviera coast.

Tinker gazed down at the broad, smooth, white walks of Monte Carlo, bounded by green-fronded palms. They were flying at too great an altitude to recognise any ordinary buildings, but the shining domes of the casino glittered like golden apples in the sun.

Blake glanced at his watch as the aeroplane hummed over a stretch of some thirty miles of Mediterranean sea, which shimmered and glowed like a gigantic sapphire.

'Soon be there now, Tinker, my lad,' he said. 'I believe that although the country has fallen into decay since the war, there are still one or two decent hotels there.'

His dexterous hands on the controls, Captain Briscoe, with the ease born of long practice, spiralled, then volplaned gracefully downwards to what seemed a facet of purest green set in that sapphire sea.

The landing was perfect, and Tinker stepped out of the aeroplane, followed by Sexton Blake, as a scurry of excited Rosarians surrounded the machine.

'You'd better come along and have lunch with us,' said Blake to Briscoe, as a fat little gendarme bustled forward. 'I suppose no one will pinch the bus.' He turned to the gendarme and spoke rapidly in French. The policeman nodded vigorously several times.

'But certainly, m'sieur, I can quite understand. In a few minutes I will put a guard round the aeroplane.' Very tactfully Blake thrust a French note into the gendarme's podgy palm.

Tinker stared down the quaint, white roadway that twisted and turned like a dragon's writhing tail up and down the rocky slopes of Rosario. Perched upon the rock were buildings that seemed to have been carved out of ivory, so glittering white they seemed against the turquoise sky. A thousand feet below the Mediterranean wish-washed against the rugged boulders of the foreshore.

'We're not far from the town, I imagine,' said Sexton Blake. 'The domes over there are, I think, part of the casino. This used to be a very popular pleasure resort before the war. Crowds who had grown blasé with Monte Carlo came over to this little island. It has had a remarkable history, and the scenery on the other side is really superb. The vineyards are rich, and semi-tropical fruit grows in abundance.'

They walked about a quarter of a mile down the roadway, and soon entered the outskirts of Rosario's one and only town. It was the poorer quarter of the city, and Tinker was reminded vaguely of the mean quarters of Veracruz, or the native bazaars of old Damascus. The shops were huddled together in astonishing confusion. There did not seem to be any windows, although great piles and pyramids of apples, golden oranges and luscious purple grapes lent vivid patches of colour to their sombre background.

'My, it has changed!' said Briscoe, as he lit a cigarette. 'Before the war the promenade on the other side of the city was thronged with the most fashionable people in society.'

'I hope the hotels are existent, at least,' said Sexton Blake. 'Ah, I know where we are now!' The narrow street turned abruptly into a series of steps, hewn out of the solid rock. They climbed these laboriously, and approached a smooth, gleaming promenade. Its surface of granite glistened with facets, as if from a million diamonds, in the warm Riviera sun. The promenade was flanked by waving masses of palms and imposing casinos and hotels rose above green lawns.

'We'll try the Hôtel Splendide,' said Briscoe. 'I stayed here about seven years ago.' He led the way up a flight of steps on to an awning-covered terrace crowded with a gay, laughing throng of chattering Rosarians.

Blake's keen eyes noticed that there seemed to be no Englishmen present, and as they entered the hotel the proprietor gazed at the three with a look of mingled surprise and delight.

Blake ordered lunch without vouchsafing any further information regarding the length of his stay. As they sat down to an excellent repast in the crowded palm court, Tinker stared across the room, then gave vent to a cry of astonishment.

'Good Lord, guv'nor! Look, there is Mr Tom Gunn, and, as I live, with him is Lord Lavendale!'

Blake looked up, and instantly recognised the sturdy Labour MP and the well-known sporting peer. Then he chuckled quietly.

'That solves mystery number two, Tinker,' he said. 'I think I'll invite his lordship and his friend to lunch with us.'

He rose to his feet and strode across to the two Britishers.

'This is an unexpected pleasure,' he drawled, and held out his hand.

'Great Scott! It's Sexton Blake! What on earth are you doing in Rosario?'

The detective laughed.

'Considering that the whole of England has been talking about your disappearance, I think the answer is self-evident.'

'Our disappearance?' The peer's voice was puzzled, and he arched his eyebrows interrogatively. 'What do you mean?'

Sexton Blake piloted them across to the luncheon-table, and as the two sat down he drew from his pocket a copy of that morning's paper.

Lord Lavendale and his friend scanned the heavily inked lines with a look of blank astonishment on their faces.

'B–but, great heavens, Mr Blake,' said Tom Gunn explosively. 'What is the meaning of all this rot? We left London Monday night. We've been in Rosario less than forty-eight hours.'

Sexton Blake smiled inscrutably, and there was a gleam of mischief in his grey eyes.

'I am sorry to contradict you gentlemen but you left London six days ago.' He leant forward confidentially. 'May I ask you, what you have been doing since then?'

*   *   *

For a moment the peer gazed at Blake with a look of hopeless bewilderment in his rather dreamy blue eyes.

'Look here, Mr Blake,' broke in the bluff Labour leader gruffly. 'Do you mean to insinuate that we are lying?'

Sexton Blake coughed.

'I should hesitate a good deal before coming to that conclusion,' he said, 'but there you have the facts. You are quite at liberty to affirm or deny them.'

Lord Lavendale read the news item, then replaced the paper on the table with a weary gesture.

'We arrived here last night Mr Blake, by one of the Continental airlines – ' He broke off suddenly and viewed the newspaper again and glanced at the date. 'Great heavens, it's Saturday! I was under the impression that today was Wednesday.' The peer ran his fingers in a puzzled fashion through his mop of curly chestnut hair.

Sexton Blake frowned thoughtfully and scanned the peer's face shrewdly. Was the nobleman lying to cover up some secret plan?

'Where is the aeroplane now, Lord Lavendale?' he asked at length.

'It returned to San Remo this morning. We intended to cross over to the mainland by the packet-boat tonight, and then catch the PLM express to Paris.'

Tinker and Briscoe looked at each other in bewilderment, and then the youngster rose to his feet. 'If you will excuse us, guv'nor, Captain Briscoe and I feel like a little stroll,' he said, with a meaning glance.

Blake nodded as Tinker strolled down the terrace with his thoroughly mystified companion.

'Have you any theory to account for this amazing state of affairs, Mr Blake?' pleaded the Labour MP. 'Surely it is preposterous to imagine a man losing four whole days out of his life without noticing it. I could understand it if we had been ill or unconscious.' He thumped his chest aggressively. 'I feel as fit as a fiddle, and Lord Lavendale here – well, does he look like an invalid?'

Blake smiled faintly. It was difficult to imagine one less like an invalid than the beefy, good-humoured peer.

'If it is not violating any confidence, may I ask you what brought you to Rosario, gentlemen!' he said.

Lord Lavendale coughed and paused for a moment.

'As a matter of fact, Mr Blake, we're here partly on business and partly on pleasure. I brought my very good friend Mr Tom Gunn with me, because he had certain plans to discuss, and I thought he would appreciate a couple of days of southern sunshine, after a very strenuous session.'

'H'm!' Sexton Blake pursed his lips thoughtfully. 'Had your visit any connection with Mr Mike Malone's luncheon party at Pomano's?'

Lord Lavendale's jaw dropped and his prominent eyes almost goggled as he gasped out in astonishment, 'Great Scott, Blake you're uncanny! However did you discover that Malone was our host, or that he had anything to do with Rosario?'

The criminologist smiled enigmatically.

'Nevertheless, I'm afraid the connection is my secret for the moment,' went on Lord Lavendale.

Blake's manner changed abruptly

'Come, gentlemen, put your cards on the table. On Monday last you lunched with Mr Michael Malone. You state that you have been here just forty-eight hours. The problem is – where were you on Tuesday, Wednesday, Thursday and Friday?'

'Blessed if I know,' said Lavendale. 'I could have sworn today was Tuesday.'

'Precisely,' continued Blake. He half closed his eyes and pressed the tips of his long, lean fingers together. 'I think it is obvious that some person, or persons, has an interest in keeping you in Rosario longer than you intended to stay. I have not sufficient data as yet to elucidate the mystery, unless you inform me why you came to Rosario.'

Lord Lavendale glanced enquiringly at Gunn, who nodded assent.

'Well Mr Blake, Michael Malone in the accredited agent of the Rosarian government. He approached me six months ago with a scheme for exploiting Rosario as a pleasure resort, and restoring its pre-war gaiety so as to rival Monte Carlo. After thoroughly going into the financial side of the question, I invested a quarter of a million pounds in Rosarian government securities. The casinos, promenades and hotels have already been renovated, and we are about to launch an immense publicity scheme throughout the world.'

Blake was thoughtful.

'I see. Then you simply came here on Monday last to confer with the directors of the casino.'

'That is all, Mr Blake, and just to look round and see how the place was progressing,' said Lord Lavendale. 'After all one is rather interested as to whether one's money is being handled properly.'

'Quite. And you, Mr Gunn?' Blake turned to the Labour leader.

Tom Gunn coughed.

'Well, I am here purely as a guest of Lord Lavendale,' he said. 'I felt a little run-down, and I thought that two days in the south, here, would do me good. As a Socialist, I must admit that I am not in favour of some of his schemes, but as a friend I have the very heartiest admiration for Lord Lavendale.'

Blake nodded.

'Would you mind telling me whether Mr Michael Malone accompanied you on this trip?'

'No; he stayed in London. He is acting as a kind of unofficial consul at the moment,' said the peer.

'Thank you, gentlemen!' Sexton Blake rose to his feet. 'I think I shall be able to give you some interesting information shortly. I suppose you intend to return tonight? The boat leaves, I believe, at six o'clock.'

'Most decidedly!' said Tom Gunn. 'Why, they will be frantic at my absence.'

'Say, Lord Lavendale, how goes it?' drawled a nasal, trans-Atlantic voice.

Blake swung round on his heel and faced a burly, broad-shouldered man, dressed in white ducks, with a dazzlingly white topee. The stranger's face was tanned, and his shrewd eyes peered in an oddly bird-like fashion through an enormous pair of tortoiseshell-rimmed spectacles.

The peer smiled, and shook hands with the stranger.

'Pray meet Mr Brian Bruce, Mr Blake. He is our publicity expert, and the only American citizen in Rosario.'

'I am glad to meet you, Mr Blake because the whole world has heard about you. You don't need a publicity man.'

Blake smiled, and extended his hand courteously. 'That is very kind of you,' he said.

'What do you think of our li'l old island, Mr Blake?' asked Bruce.

'I hardly know,' Blake shrugged his shoulders. 'I have been here just an hour or two.'

'I am calling this "The Island Where Time Stood Still" in my next posters, Mr Blake. Gee-whiz! The days here pass as swift as highballs down a man's throat in a Prohibition country.'

Lavendale laughed. 'Well, there's something in that, Bruce. Look here, when did we arrive here?'

For a fraction of a second the publicity man hesitated. 'Why, two days ago, I guess. Or was it yesterday? One day is so like another in this place. Guess this is the only original Garden of Eden, Mr Blake.'

Tom Gunn guffawed heartily.

'You can't keep Mr Bruce from boosting Rosario, Mr Blake. He has certainly got his heart in the job!'

Sexton Blake glanced keenly at the square, rugged face of the American. 'It's rather curious that you should mention the passage of time in this island, Mr Bruce,' he said thoughtfully. 'As a matter of fact, there's no little mystery attached to the time element here.'

'Why, what do you mean, Mr Blake?' The publicity man's voice was startled.

'It looks as if,' broke in Lord Lavendale, 'the whole of England is upset about our absence. Do you know what day it is today?'

The American scratched his chin thoughtfully.

'I'm durned if I do. I feel rather like that guy Robinson Crusoe, on his island. He never seemed to realise what the date was, and it's kind of afflicted me in the same way.'

'Take a look at that,' said Sexton Blake, and handed him a copy of the morning paper.

The American scanned the scare headlines, his eyes agleam.

'Say, some story, Mr Blake. Durned if I know how it happened, but I'll git the cables right now. It'll be a fine publicity stunt for Rosario. Excuse me!' He touched his topee, and swung on his heel.

The trio watched the broad-shouldered athletic figure as he strode down the terrace on to the promenade.

'He's a rum bird, but very efficient,' said Lavendale.

'Yes – very!' Blake's eyes narrowed a little. He had made a pretty shrewd estimate of the American's character.

'Are you going to stay here, Mr Blake, or will you return with us?' asked Tom Gunn.

Blake yawned.

'As a matter of fact, there is more than one reason for my visit to Rosario, gentlemen,' he said. 'The mystery of your whereabouts has happily been solved, but there is yet much work to be done.'

Lavendale glanced curiously at the criminologist.

'Ah, well, Mr Blake, it's a puzzling business, but do you know, ever since I've been in Rosario I have felt that nothing much matters. I feel rather like a lotus-eater.'

'And – and I, too,' added the Labour leader. 'Somehow, the prospect of returning to England is not particularly alluring. However, our duty is clear, and this evening we shall return by the packet-boat to the mainland.

Blake noticed the slim young figure of Tinker, accompanied by Briscoe, at the end of the terrace.

'Pardon me, gentlemen,' he said. 'I will see you later.'

He strolled over to where the lad was sitting, sipping a huge iced drink, in the shadow of a green palm tree.

'Hallo, guv'nor!' Tinker looked up. 'What's all the giddy mystery?'

Blake shook his head and sat down. He was more than usually thoughtful. Suddenly he turned to the lad. 'What time is it now, Tinker?'

The boy looked at his wristwatch. 'Why, it's nearly four o'clock! I thought it was about two,' he added, in surprise.

Sexton Blake glanced sharply at the boy.

'Do you experience any curious sensation here, Tinker?' he said.

'No, nothing at all, gov'nor.' Tinker looked up puzzled. 'We've just been having a stroll round. We called at the pump-house at the back of the hotel and had a drink of that messy water, and just strolled back here.'

'Pump-house?' said Sexton Blake.

'Yes,' put in Briscoe. 'One of the main attractions before the war in Rosario was the wonderful chalybeate springs. They have some of the strongest natural waters in the world. Tinker and I sampled one a little while ago.'

'H'm!' Sexton Blake frowned and lit his pipe.

Suddenly there came a whining sound, and something whizzed past his head with a flash, and buried itself in the palm tree.

Blake jerked to his feet. Then he started, for quivering in the trunk of the palm was a thin, pointed dagger.

'Great Scott, guv'nor! What the – '

Blake took the blade in his long sensitive fingers, and saw that a slip of paper was attached to the hilt. He unrolled it slowly. On it, scrawled in blood-red letters, were the words:

We have long memories. This is our first and final warning.

Beneath this cryptic message was the rude symbol of a black hand.

* * *

'Good heavens, guv'nor!' Tinker's face was serious and sober as he read the message over Blake's shoulders. 'What's the idea of all this mystery? Who on earth knows that you have arrived in Rosario?'

Blake's lips set grimly, and his lean jaw tensed like a steel trap.

'I don't know, Tinker,' he said gruffly, 'but it is evidently someone who is pretty daring.'

No one seemed to have noticed the swift flight of the blade on the terrace except the trio, for the crowd of gaily dressed Rosarians went on drinking and chattering without concern.

Blake glanced at the tree, and then at the crowd of people. He took a sheet of paper out of his pocket and rapidly scribbled a diagram on it. Then he smiled a little bitterly.

'H'm! The fellow got away quickly. Call the waiter, Tinker!'

'Why, do you know who threw the knife, guv'nor?' asked the youngster in bewilderment. 'Why, you had your back to the terrace! How on earth did you – ? Have you got eyes at the back of your head?'

'Bring the waiter over here!' snapped Blake crisply.

Wondering, Tinker crossed over to where a waiter was busy dispensing drinks.

Captain Briscoe looked concerned.

'You're having a fine start, Mr Blake. It's hardly what I'd call a nice welcome to Rosario.'

Blake smiled grimly.

'I don't fear this unknown marksman, Briscoe,' he said. 'I'm not to be terrorised by childish threats like these.'

'Yes, sare?' The Rosarian waiter rubbed his hands obsequiously as he came up to Blake.

'Ah!' Blake spoke rapidly in French. 'You were serving a gentleman at that table over there?' He pointed to a little marble-topped table on which reposed an empty absinthe glass.

'*Mais oui!*' replied the waiter.

'Is he a regular customer?'

'He comes here sometimes, sare, but not very often.'

'Do you happen to know his name?'

'It is Pedro Negretti, sare. He is the keeper of the Fan-tan Saloon in the Rue Scribe.'

'H'm! Thank you!' Blake's voice was stern.

'Stay here, Tinker. I shall be back shortly. I'm going to take a little stroll,' he said.

The youngster looked mystified, but he was too used to Blake's habits to question him.

'Right you are, guv'nor,' he assented cheerfully. 'Captain Briscoe and I will go and smoke in the lounge.'

Blake strode swiftly down the terrace on to the promenade, after enquiring the way to the Rue Scribe.

'Wonder what the guv'nor's up to now?' said Tinker to Briscoe. 'It's been nothing but one maze of puzzles for the last two days.'

Captain Briscoe nodded. He was a typical bluff Britisher, and the whole thing to him seemed fantastic and unreal.

Sexton Blake, his face grim and purposeful, strode swiftly down the promenade until he approached the straggling native quarter of the Rue Scribe. The shopkeepers looked curiously at him, but he did not pause until he neared a garishly painted cabaret, sandwiched between a dingy-looking café and a curiosity shop. Over the door, in letters of faded gold, were the words, 'Fan-tan Saloon'.

Blake entered. The place was full of evil-looking Rosarians of the lower class, and the room was thick with clouds of rank tobacco smoke. The customers slammed dominos and dice in little staccato raps on the dingy, marble-topped tables, and at Blake's entrance there fell a sudden silence.

'Where is Monsieur Negretti?' the detective demanded of a slant-eyed waiter, who hovered at the entrance.

The Chinaman jerked his head towards the counter at the other end of the saloon.

'Him in there, sir,' he said.

'Right, I'll go and see him.'

Blake strode down the aisle, heedless of the malevolent glances of the tough looking mob of Rosarians.

'Monsieur Negretti?' he snapped.

The man behind the counter was a fat, bloated person, with a stubble of beard ornamenting his oily, unhealthy face.

'Vell, vot do you want? Monsieur Negretti is busy,' said the barman.

'Tell him Sexton Blake wishes to see him!' snapped the criminologist. 'And quick about it!'

The barman's three chins quivered, jelly-like, at the rasping command. 'Certainly, sare!' He slipped down with an unaccustomed agility from his bar stool, opened the curtained doorway at the back of the bar and disappeared for a few minutes.

Sexton Blake glanced contemptuously at the drink-sodden riffraff in the saloon; a little later the fat barman returned.

'Monsieur Negretti presents his compliments, and would you be so good as to join him in a little drink in his private saloon. It is so crowded here.'

He pulled aside the curtain. Blake squared his shoulders and entered a long narrow passage. There was a thin beam of amber light, filtering from an open doorway, which illuminated a luxuriously furnished room.

'Come right in, Mr Blake,' called a voice in English, with a faint hint of a foreign accent.

'I'm coming in, Mr Negretti. I want a word with you!' said Blake.

As he did so he felt a staggering blow at the back of his head. His hand flew to his hip-pocket, but before he could withdraw his revolver he felt a second crashing blow over the side of his temple. His senses reeled, he clutched convulsively at some unseen assailant. A red mist, flecked with violet spots, danced before his eyes, and a great roaring sounded in his ears. Then consciousness left him, snapped out as one snaps out an electric-light switch.

*   *   *

'What's happened to everybody?'

Tinker looked at his watch in alarm. It was three hours after Blake's sudden departure from the hotel terrace. He and Captain Briscoe had taken a walk to the beautiful mediaeval castle that crowned the rocky peak of Rosario, and they were now in evening-dress awaiting Blake's belated return to the hotel.

'The guv'nor should have been back some time ago, I should think,' said Tinker. 'It isn't like him to be away so long without letting me know. And where the deuce are Lord Lavendale and Mr Tom Gunn?'

Captain Briscoe shook his head.

'I don't know. I haven't seen Mr Blake, but I understand that his lordship and the Labour leader returned to the mainland by the six o'clock packet-boat.'

'Blessed if I can make it out,' said Tinker. 'There'll be a rare old how-d'ye-do when they get back to England, after playing truant for nearly a week.'

Captain Briscoe smiled.

'That's the penalty of being famous, Tinker, my lad,' he said. 'If it was you or me now, the papers wouldn't kick up any fuss.'

'Don't you be too sure of that,' smiled Tinker. He puffed his chest out and laughed. 'England 'ud be up in arms if they lost me.'

Briscoe snorted.

'Who's the American guy over there?' he said, as the portly figure of Brian Bruce crossed the palm court of the hotel.

'Blessed if I know,' said Tinker. 'He was talking to the guv'nor a little while ago.'

'Good-evening, gentlemen,' drawled Brian Bruce. 'Have you seen anything of Mr Sexton Blake?'

Tinker shook his head. 'No. I was just wondering what had become of him. I'm getting rather hungry. It's about time we had dinner.'

'You're Mr Tinker, I presume?' said Brian Bruce, with a smile.

Tinker nodded, and introduced his companion.

'Say, will you have a cigar?' said the American, proffering his case. 'Come up to my room for a chat and an appetiser before dinner?'

Tinker accepted. 'Thanks very much!' And, accompanied by Briscoe, they followed the American up the wide staircase to a suite on the first floor that was almost regal in its magnificence.

Bruce brought out a decanter and a syphon, and Briscoe helped himself.

'What brings you to this part of the world, Mr Tinker?' Bruce asked.

Tinker looked at him keenly, and said, very cautiously: 'Oh, I – I'm here with Mr Blake on just a short visit.'

'Wal,' drawled the American, 'I hope when you get back to England you will give our little island a good boost. I'm a publicity man myself, and I believe in advertising. This place'll be like fairyland in a few months' time, when we get busy with our improvements.'

'Tell me,' said Tinker abruptly, 'do you know anything about the King of Rosario?'

Brian Bruce started.

'Nope. I guess Rosario's like God's own country – a republic. We don't have much truck with royalty.'

'Oh, I was just wondering,' said Tinker.

The American looked at him keenly through his horn-rimmed spectacles. 'That's a curious kind of question to ask, young man,' he said. 'Where'd you get that idea?'

Tinker smiled. 'Oh, I don't know much about the customs of this country. I thought maybe you had a monarchy here.'

He changed the conversation adroitly, but there lurked at the back of his mind a vague suspicion of the plausible, smooth-tongued American. A few minutes later there came the sound of a gong, and the American rose to his feet.

'Guess I can do with a bite to eat, young fellow,' he said. 'Will you both join me at dinner?'

'Delighted,' murmured the others.

The American led the way. Tinker's keen young eyes took a final rapid survey of the room. He paused for a fraction of a second at an open writing-desk, for on the pad of blotting-paper reposed an unstamped, addressed envelope. The youngster whistled below his breath, for the address on the letter was:

MR MICHAEL MALONE
Hotel Olympic
London, Angleterre

'H'm, Mr Bloomin' Bruce! So you're at the back of this business?' muttered Tinker, as he followed his host down to the dining-room.

He looked anxiously in the hall way for Sexton Blake's familiar figure, but the manager shrugged his shoulders politely.

'No, Mr Blake has not returned, sare. I expect he will be back shortly.'

The three sat down to dine. Tinker watched the American narrowly, but Brian Bruce seemed to be full of good spirits, and bubbled over with light and amusing conversation. In spite of a vague anxiety, Tinker was forced to laugh at the quaint, trans-atlantic stories which Bruce told with immense vim and zest. He was watching him carefully, however.

Dinner over, there was still no sign of Sexton Blake. By this time Tinker was thoroughly alarmed.

'Say, Briscoe, I don't like the look of this at all,' he said. 'Let's go and see if we can find the guv'nor.'

The young airman nodded.

'I'm quite game. You surely don't suspect any foul play, Tinker? Where did he go!'

Tinker pursed his lips thoughtfully. 'I'll ask the waiter. I've forgotten,' he said and crossed over. Then, 'Come on, Briscoe. Have you got your gun? It looks as if it's a tough joint, from what the waiter says.'

Briscoe patted his hip-pocket.

'Sure, I never go without it. It's as well to be prepared for a scrap.'

By now night had fallen. A warm, tropical evening, languorous with the odours of the Mediterranean. The sky was like a robe of violet velvet, on which the stars glittered and twinkled like golden sequins.

Tinker took in deep gulps of the air and sighed. 'Gee! It's a wonderful evening, Briscoe. Think of it – it's probably foggy and raining in good old London now.'

The young airman smiled. 'Yes, I suppose it is. It's a nasty-looking quarter this,' he added, as they approached the Rue Scribe.

Tinker advanced cautiously, and halted suddenly outside the illuminated entrance to the Fan-tan Saloon.

'This is the place the waiter said,' he remarked. 'If the guv'nor's in there we'll probably have to fight to get him out.'

As they entered the vile atmosphere of the gambling saloon there came a murmur of conversation.

'In we get,' said Tinker briskly, 'and we'll ask for the jolly old proprietor.'

At their approach, a tall man with sleek, oily hair plastered low over his forehead, and a pair of heavy golden earrings, barred their entrance.

'Vot is it you vant, messieurs?' he asked.

Tinker looked defiantly at him.

'Has Mr Sexton Blake been here?'

'Sexton Blake – who is he?' demanded the other, who was obviously the proprietor.

'He's a friend of ours,' said Tinker, somewhat nonplussed.

The other's shifty eyes looked at him with an evil glance.

'I ask again. Vot can I do for you, young gentlemen?'

'Is your name Negretti?' demanded Tinker.

'Yes, that is my name. I am the proprietor of this saloon.'

'Then you lie!' said Tinker, chancing all on a bold shot. 'What have you done with Mr Blake? We won't leave here until you tell us where he has gone.'

'That's the stuff to give 'em youngster,' whispered Captain Briscoe, his eyes sparkling with excitement, his muscles nerved and tense for the inevitable scrap.

'I tell you, I know no one of that name,' replied Negretti vehemently. 'You – you must get outside if you do not want to drink or gamble.'

A party of evil-looking Rosarians had stopped their chatter at an adjacent table, and were staring at the two Britishers with avaricious eyes.

Tinker cautiously drew out his automatic and pressed it against the proprietor's stomach.

'Now will you answer?' he said.

Negretti's unwholesome face grew pasty. He shrieked out: 'Miguel, Car – '

Then things happened. A glass whizzed past Tinker's head, missing him by a fraction of an inch, and crashed into a thousand silvery splinters on the opposite wall, leaving a crimson mark of wine that ran down in an ominous blood-red stream. With a howl of fury the group of employees whirled themselves upon the two Britishers.

'Shoot at the lights!' gasped Tinker.

Bang, bang!

Immediately his automatic began to crack out in a swift fusillade of shots, and two lights out of four went out. Presently the other two winked out also – the targets of Tinker's friend.

The saloon became one shrieking pandemonium of sound. There came groans and shrill screams, punctuated by the staccato crack-crack of the Britishers' guns.

'Stick by me, Tinker!' said Briscoe, as he hurled his broad shoulders against a struggling mass of Rosarians in the darkness; 'Come on, laddie, let 'em have it!'

Crash! They lurched against a table. The marble slab broke in pieces on the asphalt floor.

Tinker had fired all his cartridges, and he picked up a broken fragment of stone and hurled it with all his force at where he believed the fighting Rossarians to be.

Suddenly Briscoe jerked out. 'It's our bare fists now. My gun's empty. Let 'em have it, laddie!'

Tinker, panting and dishevelled, was struggling furiously with some unseen assailant in the darkness. He felt a vicious slash at his shins, and then he grunted as he felt the crunch of a skull against the butt of his revolver.

'O–ouch!' He could hear the sudden cry of his assailant as he dropped limply to the floor, and he smiled grimly.

Briscoe was acquitting himself well. His arms whirled like flails, and his knuckles were torn and bleeding from contact with many unshaven Rosarian chins.

Suddenly another revolver-shot sounded through the darkness. Tinker felt a stab of pain in his left shoulder. 'Gosh! They've got me, Briscoe!' he shouted.

Then his heart gave a sudden leap of joy, for a deep, familiar voice shouted out: 'Hold on Tinker, I'm coming!'

'The guv'nor!' gasped the lad. 'The guv'nor!' There was a sob of thankfulness in his voice.

'Sexton Blake!' said Briscoe. It was impossible to distinguish in that roaring dark friend from foe, but suddenly a great yellow beam of light flashed out, cutting through the gloom like a golden dagger. In its rays Tinker caught a fleeting glimpse of Sexton Blake's tall, athletic figure and a swift glance of a struggling mass of humanity. He crashed his fists into the face of one man, grabbed him by the throat and flung him off.

A moment later Sexton Blake was at his side. 'This way!' said Blake. 'I still have four chambers left.'

Bang!

The automatic spurted a tongue of flame through the darkness, and the three Britishers, wedged firmly together, cut their way through the struggling Rosarians until they reached the doorway. As he felt the cool night air fanning his face, Tinker breathed a sob of thankfulness.

In the street outside there was a frenzied crowd, and the shrill pheep of police whistles.

Sexton Blake shrugged his shoulders.

'The fight'll die down shortly. Let 'em beat each other up in the darkness, Tinker,' he said. 'I, for one, will be glad of a wash and something to eat.'

'Thank heavens you're alive, guv'nor!' said Tinker gaspingly.

Blake's face was white and strained. There was an ugly patch of dried blood on his temple, and he smiled wanly. Then his face grew concerned again.

'Good heavens, laddie, you're hit!' he said, and put an arm tenderly round Tinker's shoulders. By the light of a street lamp he took off the youngster's coat and tore away his blood-stained dress-shirt.

'Ah, thank goodness! It's only a flesh wound. I bet it aches abominably, but it will soon heal, my lad,' he said.

'I seem to be the only one unscathed,' said Briscoe with a smile. 'Gee, it was some scrap, Mr Blake! I don't know what it's about, but then I'm Irish, you see, and I like scraps where everyone can join in.'

Sexton Blake laughed

'Thank you both,' he said simply. 'Let us go back to the hotel, and I will tell you all that has happened.'

*　　*　　*

An hour later, refreshed by a warm bath and the ministrations of the hotel doctor, Sexton Blake sat back in a comfortable armchair.

Tinker, clad in a borrowed silk dressing-gown of a weird and wonderful pattern, his wounded shoulder still throbbing painfully beneath the tight white bandages, listened with eager interest as the detective gave an account of his visit to the Fan-tan Saloon.

Captain Briscoe's bronzed face was still flushed after the fray, but he followed Blake's story with keen appreciation as he puffed at a cigar.

'It was really quite a simple piece of deduction,' explained the criminologist easily. 'It was not a particularly difficult feat to discover who hurled that murderous-looking dagger at my head.'

'But, guv'nor, how on earth did you manage to spot him?' queried Tinker. 'You had your back to the hotel terrace, and – '

Sexton Blake smiled.

'When I was at school, Tinker,' he said reminiscently, 'we had an old mathematics master who was as blind as a bat without his spectacles. One day, when he was drawing a diagram on a blackboard, a boy threw a piece of chalk at him – and missed. The chalk hit the blackboard and left a mark. Immediately the master turned round and roared out, "You threw that chalk!" and pointed at the guilty boy. At the time I was just as mystified as you are now, but later I learnt that it was just a question of geometry. It is possible, by a little thought, to trace the angle of a thrown object straight to the thrower. The rest is elementary.'

'Well I'm blessed, Mr Blake!' broke in Briscoe heartily. 'I'm pretty good at geometry myself, but I never thought it could be applied to crime.'

Sexton Blake leant back in his chair. His eyelids drooped for a fleeting instant.

'The really successful criminologist, my dear Briscoe,' he said, 'is one that can apply any art or science to deductive reasoning. I have, on occasion, found *Mrs Beeton's Cookery Book* extremely helpful when unravelling a poison mystery.'

Briscoe laughed shortly.

'But what on earth was that murderous ruffian's idea, Mr Blake?' he asked. 'However did he develop such a fanatical hatred of you all at once? You had only been in Rosario a few hours!'

'I learnt all about Negretti's grievance in the course of a somewhat one-sided discussion in his back parlour,' replied Sexton Blake. 'I'm afraid I must admit I was a bit careless. Some ruffian caught me unawares as I entered Negretti's sanctum, and I was knocked out. When I came to it was to find myself securely tied to a dirty camp bedstead, and entirely at the mercy of the villainous proprietor of the Fan-tan Saloon. He informed me, in far from honeyed accents, that I was to be murdered that evening by order of the Mafia, to avenge the imprisonment of Manuel Lopez. Does that name convey anything to you, Tinker, my boy?' Blake arched his eyebrows into interrogation.

'I seem to have heard it before guv'nor, wasn't he the Italian merchant that – ' He paused uncertainly.

'It was four years ago,' continued Sexton Blake. 'I was instrumental in putting the villain behind prison bars for a richly deserved stretch of penal servitude. He swore to get even with me – and this is the result. The Mafia, as you know, is one of the most remorseless and relentless secret societies on earth. Lopez, I knew, was a member, and after his release he probably awaited a favourable opportunity to get me.'

Tinker started.

'But, I say, guv'nor, how could this secret society know you were in Rosario? Why didn't they get you in London? It's absurd – nobody knew we were leaving Baker Street today. Certainly, no Italian could – ' He broke off as a sudden light dawned on him. 'I've just remembered, guv'nor – there was that organ-grinder Mrs Bardell complained about. Perhaps he was a spy in the society.'

'Precisely!' Sexton Blake rammed a wad of tobacco into his stained and blackened pipe. 'They have evidently been watching my movements. It is a comparatively simple thing to send a Marconigram to Rosario. Don't forget that the members of the Mafia are distributed all over the globe – and each one is pledged to avenge an injury to the society.

'But, by Jove, Blake,' said Briscoe, 'it's a pretty serious business for you, isn't it? You might be knifed before you can say er –' He hesitated.

'Knife!' replied Blake laconically, while his keen, grey eyes twinkled. 'Don't worry about that. Threatened men live long. Negretti is just an agent of the Mafia. It was lucky for me that I managed to unloose my hands while the villain was at the cash desk, or assuredly I should have been murdered. The scoundrel meant business – and evidently intended to carry out the Mafia's death sentence. He told me as much, believing that I was entirely at his mercy. Then you arrived, my friends.'

Blake took a sip of his wine and patted Tinker affectionately on the shoulder.

'Gee, guv'nor, I was glad to hear your voice. It's one of the toughest scraps you've ever taken a hand in.'

Briscoe yawned slightly.

'I hope you don't mind, Mr Blake. I've had a pretty strenuous day – and if we're flying home tomorrow, I think I'll turn in. You're not expecting any night visits from your engaging Mafia friend?' he asked, and gazed ruminatively at his knuckles.

Blake laughed.

'No, I don't think so. The amiable Negretti is in the custody of the police, at the local calaboose. The gendarme rang me up a little while ago, and I shall charge him in the morning.'

Briscoe nodded goodnight, and passed through the swing-doors of the hotel. As he did so Tinker leant across to Blake. 'I didn't have a chance to tell you before, guv'nor, but that fellow Bruce' – he paused impressively – 'he's in league with his spoofing majesty, Mr Mike Malone!'

Briefly Tinker related what had transpired in the American's room, and how he had noticed the letter on the bureau.

Blake pursed his lips thoughtfully and blew a thin blue spiral of tobacco smoke.

'H'm! That's extraordinarily interesting. I wonder whether – ' He broke off abruptly. 'You'd better clear off to bed, Tinker, my lad,' he said suddenly. 'That shoulder of yours will be all the better for a good long rest. You have done very well – very well, indeed!'

Tinker flushed with pleasure. It was not often that Sexton Blake condescended to praise him, and the youngster felt supremely content with his night's work. He rose to his feet.

'Goodnight, guv'nor! Blowed if I can see any daylight in this business. The whole thing seems crazy to me – what with spoof kings, lords who lose their memories, and Italian assassins – to say nothing of old Llewellyn's missing microbes!'

He shook his head regretfully as Sexton Blake, oblivious of his departure, curled his long, lean body into a more comfortable attitude, and gazed with brooding eyes across the deserted terrace.

For nearly an hour he sat in silence. Far below came the sullen roar of the surf pounding the rocky foundations of the island. A warm breeze rustled the green fronds of the palm trees on the terrace, and in the wonderful velvet sky the moon shone mistily white like a dew-drenched petal.

Blake stretched himself and fingered his bandaged head rather gingerly, then, knocking out the ashes of his pipe, entered the hotel, now in darkness.

The detective's room was on the first floor, and in a few minutes he had changed into his pyjamas and was soon between the sheets.

Not a sound disturbed the silence of the night, save the dull boom of the sea five hundred feet below, and the occasional shrill call of a seagull. Blake's head drooped wearily on the pillow, and almost immediately he sank into a dreamless slumber.

An hour later he awoke with a start – conscious of a vague scratching at his door. Immediately his hand crept towards his pillow, and as his fingers clutched the comforting butt of his automatic, he leapt out of bed and listened intently.

Silence – then a faint rattling of someone or something trying the bedroom door.

Blake had his hand on the electric-light switch, ready to snap the room into light, as he stood there keyed and tense.

Motionless as a statue he waited for the midnight intruder – and he smiled grimly as he heard the sudden swift intake of breath from behind the locked door.

Was it another member of the Mafia, or – ? Whoever it was that was trying to break in had evidently thought better of it, for a moment later the slight rustling sounds ceased, and Blake heard soft footsteps pad-padding on the thick pile carpet of the hotel corridor.

Swiftly he dashed to the door and cautiously opened it. A solitary figure in pyjamas was disappearing round the corner of the passage. The broad shoulders and erect bearing were familiar – and Blake started as he caught a fleeting glimpse of a strangely deathlike face – almost like a skull – the resemblance heightened by a pair of horn-rimmed spectacles.

It was that of Booster Bruce – publicity man!

Very thoughtfully Blake closed the door. What had the American been up to? Why was he prowling round the hotel, like a thief in the night. With that strange, uncanny expression on his face?

*   *   *

The next morning, Sexton Blake and Tinker were down early. Captain Briscoe had already breakfasted, and had gone over to his improvised landing ground to see to his beloved 'bus'.

Over their honey, rolls and coffee Blake told Tinker of Bruce's nocturnal prowl.

'Blessed if I heard a thing, guv'nor,' said the youngster, with a look of amazement. 'I slept like a log. What do you think his giddy game is?'

Blake shook his head and frowned moodily.

'I don't know, Tinker, but I believe we shall find out everything before the day is out.'

He pressed a warning finger to his lips as the dining-room door opened suddenly and the broad-shouldered figure of the American entered, with a cheerful smile on his countenance.

'Good-morning, Mr Blake! Morning, Mr Tinker! And how do the balmy breezes of Rosario go down?'

'Quite nicely, thanks,' said Blake non-committally. 'I did not sleep very well last night, however,' he added; and watched the American's face keenly.

If he had expected Bruce to betray anything he was disappointed, for the American clucked his tongue sympathetically.

'Wal now! That's pretty bad! Myself, I could sleep the whole durn clock round in Rosario. I told you I'm going to bill it as "The Island Where Time Stood Still"? Lord Lavendale and Mr Gunn were tickled to death with the place. They'd have stayed another month if it could have been managed.'

'Tell me, Mr Bruce – how long have you been Rosario's publicity agent?' broke in Blake suavely.

'Why, about two months, I guess. You'll sure see some humdinging publicity ideas when you get home. Say, bo', I'm plastering the whole of London with Rosario posters. Lord Lavendale's disappearance and reappearance will set Fleet Street buzzing around to rediscover Rosario. I hear you were in a bit of a scrap last night,' he added. 'More publicity. D'ye mind if I hit the cables with the story? It 'ud look well in print:

SEXTON BLAKE CAPTURES CROOK!
ROMANCE IN ROSARIO ISLAND PARADISE!'

Blake laughed

'You must not let your fertile imagination lead you too far astray, Mr Bruce. You'll excuse me now, won't you, I have some business letters to write.'

He shot a meaning glance at Tinker: who turned to the American.

'I wonder if you'd care to show me the sights of Rosario, Mr Bruce?' he asked eagerly. 'I'm quite new to the place, and I hear there's a marvellous mediaeval castle on the hill somewhere.'

'Why, sure, bo!' Booster Bruce said as he left the dining-room with them. 'After I've had my morning iron-water. Care to join me. It is imbued, as Dickens once said, with the flavour of warm flat-irons, but it surely keeps you fit!'

Tinker laughed.

Sexton Blake strolled out of earshot, and re-entered the hotel, while Tinker and the American sauntered over to the pump-room to taste the somewhat overrated charms of Rosarian iron-water.

The detective watched them as they passed through the crowded terrace, and then, with a grim little smile playing round his finely chiselled lips, he strode purposefully down the corridor of the second floor. There was no one about at that hour, and Blake nodded with some satisfaction as he halted outside the American's bedroom door. Very gently he inserted a slender wire instrument into the lock, and, after a few minutes of experimental joggling, the catch flew back.

His keen grey eyes scanned the room swiftly and scientifically, and a low cry escaped his lips as he noticed a wooden cupboard in the corner. It was locked, but that was no hindrance to the Baker Street sleuth. A little gentle teasing with the aid of his flexible wire skeleton-key soon opened the frail brass barrier. Inside the cupboard was a heap of carefully creased suits. Blake tossed them aside, and then whistled softly, for beneath the clothes reposed a wooden box, about a foot square, with handles of brass.

Sexton Blake smiled significantly. The strange tangled skein was now at last unravelled and the mystery of Professor Llewellyn's stolen bacilli was now solved.

Blake replaced the clothes over the brass-bound box, and relocked the cupboard door. It was with a very thoughtful mien that he re-entered the hotel lounge and crossed over to the bookcase. He lit his pipe, and took out a leather-bound volume, and for the space of half an hour read its closely-printed pages with eager interest.

It was nearly lunchtime when Tinker and Bruce returned. Sexton Blake rose to his feet as they entered the lounge, and stepped over purposefully to the American.

'Mr Bruce,' he said swiftly, and there was a steely glint in his grey eyes, 'What do you know of chronoperdia?'

The American flushed.

'Why, what d'ye mean, Mr Blake? I – '

'Don't you think we'd better talk this matter over?' broke in Blake icily. 'I think it's about time that you explained your somewhat oblique methods of publicity.'

The American blinked at him nervously through his horn-rimmed spectacles, and then shrugged his shoulders.

'You're some sleuth, Mr Blake! I am durned if I know how you got wise to this proposition, but I guess I'd better tell you everything before you judge too harshly. Will you come upstairs?'

Tinker looked at Blake in some surprise as they followed in the American's wake.

Blake's face was very grim and stern as he sat back in the luxurious armchair in Bruce's sitting-room.

'Well, Mr Blake you've called my bluff,' said Bruce. He was standing in a self-assured fashion, with his back to the fireplace. 'I guess I owe you an explanation.'

'What were you doing outside my bedroom in the middle of the night?' demanded Blake.

'Durned if I know, Mr Blake. I swear to you I never left my – ' He checked himself suddenly, and lowered his voice. 'To tell you the truth, Mr Blake. I have a confession to make. I have discovered recently that I am a somnambulist, and perhaps I was walking in my sleep. It isn't the first time that this has happened to me, and if you saw me in your room last night, believe me, I had no felonious intent.'

Blake looked at him sternly.

'That may be, Mr Bruce.' he said. 'But you have still to explain why you're in possession of stolen property!'

The American's mouth sagged opens and his eyes, oddly magnified by the horn-rimmed spectacles, goggled a little.

'Say, what in thunder do you mean, Mr Blake? I – '

Sexton Blake rose to his feet, and he glanced squarely at the publicity man.

'No bluff, please! Let's have the whole story,' he said.

Bruce laughed.

'Look here, Mr Blake, I'll put all my cards on the table. I am Bruce – Booster Bruce, as they call me over in the States. I guess, according to your remarks about chronoperdia, you've sized up my proposition. I am a publicity man. I boost things, but I don't boost things in an ordinary fashion. Professor Menkin is a stepbrother of mine. I admit what I did was not strictly legal, but it's up to him and Professor Llewellyn to prosecute if they want to.'

Tinker hunched his shoulders, and glanced despairingly at his governor. He hadn't the vaguest notion what chronoperdia meant.

Blake smiled.

'Ah, that clears up many things, Bruce,' he said suavely. 'Your methods are irregular, but I must confess they have a certain amount of originality and success.'

'Success!' repeated the American. 'Why, every durned newspaper in Europe is talking about Rosario. I guess I've an apology to make to you, Mr Blake. You see, you have an international reputation. I wanted to focus the public eye on Rosario; that's why I prevailed upon my partner, Mr Michael Malone, to come and see you. Sexton

Blake is always a name to conjure with, and I tried to get you linked up with that spoof monarch stunt, but it wouldn't work. Still, you're out here, and that's all I wanted.

'Now to revert to chronoperdia.' He glanced across at Tinker with an amused smile. 'You see, my stepbrother, Professor Menkin, has been, conducting researches in various obscure germs. Chronoperdia comes from the Latin; it means loss of time. You will remember, Mr Blake the case recently reported in the newspapers of a workman who lost all sense of time?'

Blake nodded.

'I see you study newspapers pretty closely,' he said. 'Well, Professor Menkin has discovered that very rare germ, the chronoperdia bacillus. If a man is infected with the germ he loses his time sense. That is the reason of Lord Lavendale and Mr Tom Gunn's very protracted, but very enjoyable stay.'

Blake nodded.

'A very pretty scheme, Mr Bruce! You infected the chalybeate spring here with the germs?'

The American nodded.

'As a matter of fact, Mr Blake, I did. I want Rosario to be known as The Island Where Time Stands Still. I guess my methods sound a bit mad to you, but, durn me, if a man is on holiday he don't need to be worried about time. Professor Menkin told me about his joint discovery with Professor Llewellyn. I called round to see that peppery old Welshman just before Menkin's departure for America, but you know what an absent-minded old ass he is!'

Blake nodded.

'If you think that I am committing a felony, Mr Blake, you are mistaken,' added Booster Bruce. 'My stepbrother gave me a letter to Llewellyn, asking him to let me take charge of the chronoperdia germs; but as the old bird was keen on a new and particularly virulent set of flu bacilli at the time, he probably forgot. Anyway, he let me have the box, and you can verify that by cable, if you like.'

Sexton Blake nodded.

'It's an extraordinary story, Bruce,' he said crisply. 'Time will show whether you're speaking the truth or not. You deliberately infected the drinking water of Rosario in order to advance your publicity schemes. You are a little devious in your methods, even though you are successful in publicity. It's not my business to prosecute; I can leave that to other people.'

Booster Bruce laughed.

'Gee, Mr Blake, it's the finest stunt I've ever put across. There's absolutely no harm in the chronoperdia germ: its effect on the system is only temporary.'

Sexton Blake laughed shortly.

'Publicity pays, Mr Bruce, and I hope publicity experts will do so. It has been an interesting little problem, but —'

'Say, Mr Blake, just name your fee for loss of time and your researches,' said the American. 'I've got my cheque-book here, and the whole funds of the Rosarian government are back of me.'

Sexton Blake smiled.

'Please make it out for one thousand guineas,' he said.

Booster Bruce sat down at his writing-desk and signed a cheque with a flourish.

'Cheap at the price, Mr Blake. The whole world is talking about Rosario. It's my job to boost. I guess I've succeeded!'

Tinker looked at the American with wide eyes. He was a new kind of fish, even to the lad who had, in the course of his adventurous life, met an extraordinarily miscellaneous collection of characters.

'You take the cake, Bruce,' he said. 'You surely do. Say, was it you who thought of that phantom hound stunt in the tube?'

The American stuck a cigar aggressively in the left-hand corner of his mouth. 'Sure,' he said. 'But that was only a sideline of mine. And now, what about a little lunch?'

The One Possessed

E. W. HORNUNG

Lieutenant-General Neville Dysone RE VC was the first really eminent person to consult the crime doctor by regular appointment in the proper hours. Quite apart from the feat of arms which had earned him the most coveted of all distinctions, the gigantic general, deep-chested and erect, virile in every silver-woven hair of his upright head, filled the tiny stage in Welbeck Street and dwarfed its antique properties as no being had done before. And yet his voice was tender and even tremulous with the pathetic presage of a heartbreak under all.

'Dr Dollar,' he began at once, 'I have come to see you about the most tragic secret that a man can have. I would shoot myself for saying what I have to say, did I not know that a patient's confidence is sacred to any member of your profession – perhaps especially to an alienist?'

'I hope we are all alike as to that,' returned Dollar, gently. He was used to these sad openings.

'I ought not to have said it; but it hardly is my secret, that's why I feel such a cur!' exclaimed the general, taking his handkerchief to a fine forehead and remarkably fresh complexion, as if to wipe away its noble flush. 'Your patient, I devoutly hope, will be my poor wife, who really seems to me to be almost losing her reason – ' But with that the husband quite lost his voice.

'Perhaps we can find it for her,' said Dollar, despising the pert professional optimism that told almost like a shot. 'It is a thing more often mislaid than really lost.'

And the last of the other's weakness was finally overcome. A few weighty questions, lightly asked and simply answered, and he was master of a robust address, in which an occasional impediment only did further credit to his delicacy.

'No. I should say it was entirely a development of the last few months,' declared the general, emphatically. 'There was nothing of the kind in our twenty-odd years of India, nor yet in the first year after I retired. All this – this trouble has come since I bought my house in the pine country. It's called Valsugana, as you see on my card, but it wasn't before we went there. We gave it the name because it struck us as extraordinarily like the Austrian Tyrol, where – well, of which we had happy memories, Dr Dollar.'

His blue eyes winced as they flew through the open French window, up the next precipice of bricks and mortar, to the beetling skyline of other roofs, all a little softened in the faint haze of approaching heat. It cost him a palpable effort to bring them back to the little dark consulting-room, with its cool slabs of aged oak and the summer fernery that hid the hearth.

'It's good of you to let me take my time, doctor, but yours is too valuable to waste. All I meant was to give you an idea of our surroundings, as I know they are held to count in such cases. We are embedded in pines and firs. Some people find trees depressing, but after India they were just what we wanted, and even now my wife won't let me cut down one of them. Yet depression is no name for her state of mind; it's nearer melancholy madness, and latterly she has become subject to – to delusions – which are influencing her whole character and actions in the most alarming way. We are finding it difficult, for the first time in our lives, to keep servants; even her own nephew, who has come to live with us, only stands it for my sake, poor boy! As for my nerves – well, thank God I used to think I hadn't got any when I was in the service; but it's a little hard to be – to be as we are, at our time of life!' His hot face flamed. 'What am I saying? It's a thousand times harder on *her*! She had been looking forward to these days for years.'

Dollar wanted to wring one of the great brown restless hands. Might he ask the nature of the delusions?

The general cried: 'I'd give ten years of my life if I could tell you!'

'You can tell me what form they take?'

'I must, of course; it is what I came for, after all,' the general muttered. He raised his head and his voice together. 'Well, for one thing she's got herself a ferocious bulldog and a revolver!'

Dollar did not move a doctor's muscle. 'I suppose there must be a dog in the country, especially where there are no children. And if you must have a dog, you can't do better than a bulldog. Is there any reason for the revolver? Some people think it another necessity of the country.'

'It isn't with us – much less as she carries it.'

'Ladies in India get in the habit, don't they?'

'She never did. And now –'

'Yes, general? Has she it always by her?'

'Night and day, on a curb bracelet locked to her wrist!'

This time there were no professional pretences. 'I don't wonder you have trouble with your servants,' said Dollar, with as much sympathy as he liked to show.

'You mayn't see it when you come down, doctor, as I am going to entreat you to do. She has her sleeves cut on purpose, and it is the smallest you can buy. But I know it's always there – and always loaded.'

Dollar played awhile with a queer plain steel ruler, out of keeping with his other possessions, though it too had its history. It stood on end before he let it alone and looked up.

'General Dysone, there must be some sort of reason or foundation for all this. Has anything alarming happened since you have been at – Valsugana?'

'Nothing that firearms could prevent.'

'Do you mind telling me what it is that has happened?'

'We had a tragedy in the winter – a suicide on the place.'

'Ah!'

'Her gardener hanged himself. Hers, I say, because the garden is my wife's affair. I only paid the poor fellow his wages.'

'Well, come, general, that was enough to depress anybody – '

'Yet she wouldn't have even that tree cut down – nor yet come away for a change – not for as much as a night in town!'

The interruption had come with another access of grim heat and further use of the general's handkerchief. Dollar took up his steel tube of a ruler and trained it like a spyglass on the ink, with one eye as carefully closed as if the truth lay at the bottom of the blue-black well.

'Was there any rhyme or reason for the suicide?'

'One was suggested that I would rather not repeat.'

The closed eye opened to find the blue pair fallen. 'I think it might help, general. Mrs Dysone is evidently a woman of strong character, and anything – '

'She is, God knows!' cried the miserable man. 'Everybody knows it now – her servants especially – though nobody used to treat them better. Why, in India – but we'll let it go at that, if you don't mind. I have provided for the widow.'

Dollar bowed over his bit of steel tubing, but this time put it down so hastily that it rolled off the table. General Dysone was towering over him with shaking hand outstretched.

'I can't say any more,' he croaked. 'You must come down and see her for yourself; then you could do the talking – and I shouldn't feel such a damned cur! By God, sir, it's awful, talking about one's own wife like this, even for her own good! It's worse than I thought it would be. I know it's different to a doctor – but – but you're an old soldier-man as well, aren't you? Didn't I hear you were in the war?'

'I was.'

'Well, then,' cried the general, and his blue eyes lit up with simple cunning, 'that's where we met! We've run up against each other again, and I've asked you down for this next weekend! Can you manage it? Are you free? I'll write you a cheque for your own fee this minute, if you like – there must be nothing of that kind down there. You don't mind being Captain Dollar again, if that was it, to my wife?'

His pathetic eagerness, his sensitive loyalty – even his sudden and solicitous zest in the pious fraud proposed – made between them an irresistible appeal. Dollar had to think; the rooms upstairs were not empty; but none enshrined a more interesting case than this sounded. On the other hand, he had to be on his guard against a weakness for mere human interest as apart from the esoteric principles of his practice. People might call him an empiric – empiric he was proud to be, but it was and must remain empiricism in one definite direction only. Psychical research was not for him – and the Dysone story had a psychic flavour.

In the end he said quite bluntly: 'I hope you don't suggest a ghost behind all this, general?'

'I? Lord, no! I don't believe in 'em,' cried the warrior, with a nervous laugh.

'Does any member of your household?'

'Not – now.'

'*Not* now?'

'No. I think I am right in saying that.' But something was worrying him. 'Perhaps it is also right,' he continued, with the engaging candour of an overthrown reserve, 'and only fair – since I take it you are coming – to tell you that there was a fellow with us who thought he saw things. But it was all the most utter moonshine. He saw brown devils in flowing robes, but what he'd taken before he saw them I can't tell you! He didn't stay with me long enough for us to get to know each other. But he wasn't just a servant, and it was before the poor gardener's affair. Like so many old soldiers on the shelf, Dr Dollar, I am writing a book, and I run a secretary of sorts; now it's Jim Paley, a nephew of ours; and thank God he has more sense.'

'Yet even he gets depressed?'

'He has had cause. If our own kith and kin behaved like one

possessed – ' He stopped himself yet again; this time his hand found
Dollar's with a vibrant grip. 'You will come, won't you? I can meet
any train on Saturday, or any other day that suits you better. I – for
her own sake, doctor – I sometimes feel it might be better if she
went away for a time. But you will come and see her for yourself?'

Before he left it was a promise; a harder heart than John Dollar's
would have ended by making it, and putting the new case before all
others when the Saturday came. But it was not only his prospective
patient whom the doctor was now really anxious to see; he felt
fascinated in advance by the scene and every person of an indubitable
drama, of which at least one tragic act was already over.

There was no question of meeting him at any station; the wealthy
mother of a still recent patient had insisted on presenting Dr Dollar
with a 15hp Talboys, which he had eventually accepted, and even
chosen for himself (with certain expert assistance), as an incalculable
contribution to the Cause. Already the car had vastly enlarged his
theatre of work; and on every errand his heart was lightened and his
faith fortified by the wonderful case of the young chauffeur who sat
so upright at the wheel beside him. In the beginning he had slouched
there like the worst of his kind; it was neither precept nor reprimand
which had straightened his back and his look and all about him. He
was what John Dollar had always wanted – the unconscious patient
whose history none knew – who himself little dreamt that it was all
known to the man who treated him almost like a brother.

The boy had been in prison for dishonesty; he was being
sedulously trusted, and taught to trust himself. He had come in
March, a sulky and suspicious clod; and now in June he could talk
cricket and sixpenny editions from the Hounslow tramlines to the
wide white gate opening into a drive through a Berkshire wood,
with a house lurking behind it in a mask of ivy, out of the sun.

But in the drive General Dysone stepped back into the doctor's
life, and, on being directed to the stables, he who had filled it for
the last hour drove out of it for the next twenty-four.

'I wanted you to hear something at once from me,' his host
whispered under the whispering trees, 'lest it should be mentioned
and take you aback before the others. We've had another little
tragedy – not a horror like the last – yet in one way almost worse.
My wife shot her own dog dead last night!'

Dollar put a curb upon his parting lips.

'*In* the night?' he stood still to ask.

'Well, between eleven and twelve.'

'In her own room, or where?'

'Out of doors. Don't ask me how it happened; nobody seems to know; and don't *you* know anything if she speaks of it herself.'

His fine face was streaming with perspiration; yet he seemed to have been waiting quietly under the trees; he was not short of breath, and he a big elderly man. Dollar asked no questions at all; they dropped the subject there in the drive. Though the sun was up somewhere out of sight, it was already late in the long June afternoon, and the guest was taken straight to his room.

It was a corner room with one ivy-darkened casement overlooking a shadowy lawn, the other facing a forest of firs and chestnuts on which it was harder to look without an instinctive qualm. But the general seemed to have forgotten his tragedies, and for the moment his blue eyes almost brightened the sombre scene on which they dwelt with involuntary pride.

'Now don't you see where the Tyrol comes in?' said he. 'Put a mountain behind those trees – and there *was* one the very first time we saw the house! It was only a thundercloud, but for all the world it might have been the Dolomites. And it took us back . . . we had no other clouds then!'

Dollar found himself alone; found his things laid out and his shirt studded, and a cosy on the brass hot-water can, with as much satisfaction as though he had never stayed in a country house before. Could there be so very much amiss in a household where they knew just what to do for one, and just what to leave undone?

And it was the same with all the other creature comforts; they meant good servants, however short their service; and good servants do not often mean the mistress or the hostess whom Dollar had come prepared to meet. He dressed in pleasurable doubt and enhanced excitement – and those were his happiest moments at Valsugana.

Mrs Dysone was a middle-aged woman who looked almost old, whereas the general was elderly with all the appearance of early middle age. The contrast was even more complete in more invidious particulars; but Dollar took little heed of the poor lady's face, as a lady's face. Her skin and eyes were enough for him; both were brown, with that almost ultra-Indian tinge of so many Anglo-Indians. He was sensible at once of an Oriental impenetrability.

With her conversation he could not quarrel; what there was of it was crisp, unstudied, understanding. And the little dinner did her the kind of credit for which he was now prepared; but she only once took charge of the talk, and that was rather sharply to change a subject into which she had been the first to enter.

How it had cropped up, Dollar could never think, especially as his former profession and rank duly obtained throughout his visit: he had even warned his chauffeur that he was not the doctor there. It could not have been he himself who started it, but somebody did, as somebody always does when there is one topic to avoid. It was probably the nice young nephew who made the first well-meaning remark upon the general want of originality, with reference to something or other under criticism at the moment; but it was neither he nor Dollar who laid it down that monkeys were the most arrant imitators in nature – except criminals; and it certainly was the general who said that nothing would surprise him less than if another fellow went and hanged himself in their wood. Then it was that Mrs Dysone put her foot down – and Dollar never forgot her look.

Almost for the first time it made him think of her revolver. It was out of sight; and full as her long sleeves were, it was difficult to believe that one of them could conceal the smallest firearm made; but a tiny gold padlock did dangle when she raised her glass of water; and at the end of dinner there was a second little scene, this time without words, which went far to dispel any doubt arising in his mind.

He was holding the door open for Mrs Dysone, and she stood a moment on the threshold, peering into the far corners of the room. He saw what it was she had forgotten – saw it come back to her as she turned away, with another look worth remembering.

Either the general missed that, or the anxieties of the husband were now deliberately sunk in the duties of the host. He had got up some Jubilee port in the doctor's honour; they sat over it together till it was nearly time for bed. Dollar took little, but the other grew a shade more rubicund, and it was good to hear him chat without restraint or an apparent care. Yet it was strange as well; again he drifted into criminology, and his own after-dinner defect of sensibility only made his hearer the more uncomfortable.

Of course, he felt, it was partly out of compliment to himself as crime doctor; but the ugly subject had evidently an unhealthy fascination of its own for the fine full-blooded man. Not that it seemed an inveterate foible; the expert observer thought it rather the reflex attraction of the strongest possible horror and repulsion, and took it the more seriously on that account. Of two evils it seemed to him the less to allow himself to be pumped on professional generalities. It was distinctly better than encouraging the general to ransack his long experience for memories of decent people who had done dreadful deeds. Best of all to assure him that even those unfortunates might have outlived their infamy under the scientific treatment of a more enlightened day.

If they must talk crime, let it be the cure of crime! So the doctor had his heartfelt say; and the general listened even more terribly than he had talked; asking questions in whispers, and waiting breathless for the considered reply. It was the last of these that took most answering.

'And which, doctor, for God's sake, which would you have most hope of curing: a man or a woman?'

But Dollar would only say: 'I shouldn't despair of *anybody*, who had done *anything*, if there was still an intelligence to work upon; but the more of that the better.'

And the general said hardly another word, except 'God bless you!' outside the spare-room door. His wife had been seen no more.

But Dollar saw her in every corner of his delightful quarters; and the acute contrast that might have unsettled an innocent mind had the opposite effect on his. There were electric lamps in all the right places; there were books and biscuits, a glass of milk, even a miniature decanter and a bottle of Schweppes. He sighed as he wound his watch and placed it in the little stand on the table beside the bed; but he was only wondering exactly what he was going to discover before he wound it up again.

Outside one open window the merry crickets were playing castanets in those dreadful trees. It was the other blind that he drew up; and on the lawn the dying and reviving glow of a cigarette gave glimpses of a white shirt-front, a black satin tie, the drooping brim of a Panama hat. It was the nice young nephew, who had retreated before the Jubilee port. And Dollar was still wondering on what pretext he could go down and join him, when his knock came to the door.

'Only to see if you'd everything you want,' explained young Paley, ingenuously disingenuous; and shut the door behind him before the invitation to enter was out of the doctor's mouth. But he shut it very softly, trod like a burglar, and excused himself with bated breath. 'You are the first person who has stayed with us since I've been here, Captain Dollar!' And his wry young smile was as sad as anything in the sad house.

'You amaze me!' cried Dollar. Indeed, it was the flank attack of a new kind of amazement. 'I should have thought – ' and his glance made a lightning tour of the luxurious room.

'I know,' said Paley, nodding. 'I think they must have laid themselves out for visitors at the start. But none come now. I wish they did! It's a house that wants them.'

'You are rather a small party, aren't you?'

'We are rather a grim party! And yet my old uncle is absolutely the finest man I ever struck.'

'I don't wonder that you admire him.'

'You don't know what he is, Captain Dollar. He got the vc when he was my age in Burmah, but he deserves one for almost every day of his ordinary home life.'

Dollar made no remark; the young fellow offered him a cigarette, and was encouraged to light another himself. He required no encouragement to talk.

'The funny thing is that he's not really my uncle. I'm *her* nephew; and she's a wonderful woman, too, in her way. She runs the whole place like a book; she's thrown away here. But – I can't help saying it – I should like her better if I didn't love him!'

'Talking of books,' said Dollar, 'the general told me he was writing one, and that you were helping him?'

'He didn't tell you what it was about?'

'No.'

'Then I mustn't. I wish I could. It's to be the last word on a certain subject, but he won't have it spoken about. That's one reason why it's getting on his nerves.'

'*Is* it his book?'

'It and everything. Doesn't he remind you of a man sitting on a powder-barrel? If he weren't what he is, there'd be an explosion every day. And there never is one – no matter what happens.'

Dollar watched the pale youth swallowing his smoke.

'Do they often talk about crime?'

'Always! They can't keep off it. And Aunt Essie always changes the subject as though she hadn't been every bit as bad as uncle. Of course they've had a good lot to make them morbid. I suppose you heard about poor Dingle, the last gardener?'

'Only just.'

'He was the last man you would ever have suspected of such a thing. It was those trees just outside.' The crickets made extra merry as he paused. 'They didn't find him for a day and a night!'

'Look here! I'm not going to let you talk about it,' said Dollar. But the good-humoured rebuff cost him an effort. He wanted to hear all about the suicide, but not from this worn lad with an old man's smile. He knew and liked the type too well.

'I'm sorry, Captain Dollar.' Jim Paley looked sorry. 'Yet, it's all very well! I don't suppose the general told you what happened last night?'

'Well, yes, he did, but without going into any particulars.'

And now the doctor made no secret of his curiosity; this was a matter on which he could not afford to forgo enlightenment. Nor was it like raking up an old horror; it would do the boy more good than harm to speak of this last affair.

'I can't tell you much about it myself,' said he. 'I was wondering if I could, just now on the lawn. That's where it happened, you know.'

'I didn't know.'

'Well, it was, and the funny thing is that I was there at the time. I used to go out with the dog for a cigarette when they turned in; last night I was foolish enough to fall asleep in a chair on the lawn. I had been playing tennis all the afternoon, and had a long bike-ride both ways. Well, all I know is that I woke up thinking I'd been shot; and there was my aunt with that revolver she insists on carrying – and poor Muggins as dead as a doornail.'

'Did she say it was an accident?'

'She behaved as if it had been; she was all over the poor dead brute.'

'Rather a savage dog, wasn't it?'

'I never thought so. But the general had no use for him – and no wonder! Did he tell you he had bitten him in the shoulder?'

'No.'

'Well, he did, only the other day. But that's the old general all over. He never told me till the dog was dead. I shouldn't be surprised if – '

'Yes?'

'If my aunt hadn't been in it somehow. Poor old Muggins was such a bone between them!'

'You don't suppose he'd ended by turning on her?'

'Hardly. He was like a kitten with her, poor brute!'

Another cigarette was lighted; more inhaling went on unchecked.

'Was Mrs Dysone by herself out there but for you?'

'Well – yes.'

'Does that mean she wasn't?'

'Upon my word, I don't know!' said young Paley, frankly. 'It sounds most awful rot, but just for a moment I thought I saw somebody in a sort of surplice affair. But I can only swear to Aunt Essie, and she was in her dressing-gown, and it wasn't white.'

Dollar did not go to bed at all. He sat first at one window, watching the black trees turn blue, and eventually a variety of sunny greens; then at the other staring down at the pretty scene of a deed ugly in itself, but uglier in the peculiar quality of its mystery.

A dog; only a dog, this time; but the woman's own dog! There were two new sods on the place where he supposed it had lain weltering . . .

But who or what was it that these young men had seen – the one the general had told him about, and this obviously truthful lad whom he himself had questioned? 'Brown devils in flowing robes' was perhaps only the old soldier's picturesque phrase; they might have turned brown in his Indian mind; but what of Jim Paley's 'somebody in a sort of surplice affair'? Was that 'body' brown as well?

In the wood of worse omen the gay little birds tuned up to deaf ears at the open window. And a cynical soloist went so far as to start saying, 'Pretty, pretty, pretty, pretty!' in a liquid contralto. But a little sharp shot, fired two nights and a day before, was the only sound to get across the spare-room windowsill. . .

The bathroom was next door; in that physically admirable house there was boiling hot water at six o'clock in the morning; the servants made tea when they heard it running; and the garden before breakfast was almost a delight. It might have been an Eden . . . it *was* . . . with the serpent still in the grass!

Blinds went up like eyelids under bushy brows of ivy. The grass remained grey with dew; there was not enough sun anywhere, though the whole sky beamed. Dollar wandered indoors the way the general had taken him the day before. It was the way through his library. Libraries are always interesting; a man's bookcase is sometimes more interesting than the man himself, sometimes the one existing portrait of his mind. Dollar spent the best part of an absorbing hour without taking a single volume from its place. But this was partly because those he would have dipped into were under glass and lock and key. And partly it was due to more accessible distractions crowning that very piece of ostensible antiquity which contained the books, and of which the top drawer drew out into the general's desk.

The distractions were a peculiarly repulsive gilded idol, squatting with its tongue out, as if at the amateur author, and a heathen sword on the wall behind it. Nothing more; but Dollar also had served in India in his day, and his natural interest was whetted by a certain smattering of lore. He was still standing on a newspaper and a chair when a voice hailed him in no hospitable tone.

'Really, Captain Dollar! I should have asked the servants for a ladder while I was about it!'

Of course it was Mrs Dysone, and she was not even pretending to look pleased. He jumped down with an apology which softened not a line of her sallow face and bony figure.

'It was an outrage,' he owned. 'But I did stand on a paper to save the chair. I say, though, I never noticed it was this week's *Field.*'

Really horrified at his own behaviour, he did his best to smooth and wipe away his footmarks on the wrapper of the paper. But those subtle eyes, like blots of ink on old parchment, were no longer trained on the offender, who missed yet another look that might have helped him.

'My husband's study is rather holy ground,' was the lady's last word. 'I only came in myself because I thought he was here.'

Mercifully, days do not always go on as badly as they begin; more strangely, this one developed into the dullest and most conventional of country-house Sundays.

General Dysone was himself not only dull, but even a little stiff, as became a good Briton who had said too much to too great a stranger overnight. His natural courtesy had become conspicuous; he played punctilious host all day; and Dollar was allowed to feel that, if he had come down as a doctor, he was staying on as an ordinary guest, and in a house where guests were expected to observe the Sabbath. So they all marched off together to the village church, where the general trumpeted the tune in his own octave, read the lessons, and kept waking up during the sermon. There were the regulation amenities with other devout gentry of the neighbourhood; there was the national Sunday sirloin at the midday meal, and no more untoward topics to make the host's forehead glisten or the hostess gleam and lower. In the afternoon the whole party inspected every animal and vegetable on the premises; and after tea the visitor's car came round.

Originally there had been much talk of his staying till the Monday; the general went through the form of pressing him once more, but was not backed up by his wife, who had shadowed them suspiciously all day. Nor did he comment on this by so much as a sidelong glance at Dollar, or contrive to get another word with him alone. And the crime doctor, instead of making any excuse to remain and penetrate these new mysteries, showed a sensitive alacrity to leave.

Of the nephew, who looked terribly depressed at his departure, he had seen something more, and had even asked two private favours. One, that he would keep out of that haunted garden for the next few nights, and try going to bed earlier; the other, an odd request for an almost middle-aged man about town, but rather flattering to the young fellow. It was for the loan of his Panama, so that Dollar's hatter might see if he could not get him as good a one. Paley's was the kind that might be carried up a sleeve, like a modern handkerchief; he explained that the old general had given it him.

Dollar tried it on almost as soon as the car was out of sight of Valsugana – while his young chauffeur was still wondering what he had done to make the governor sit behind. It was funny of him, just when a chap might have been telling him a thing or two that he had heard down there at the coachman's place. But it was all the more interesting when they got back to town at seven in the evening, and he was ordered to fill up with petrol and be back at nine, to make the same trip over again.

'I needn't ask you,' the doctor added, 'to hold your tongue about anything you may have heard at General Dysone's. I know you will, Albert.'

And almost by lighting-up time they were shoulder to shoulder on the road once more.

But at Valsugana it was another dark night, and none too easy to find one's way about the place on the strength of a midsummer day's acquaintance. And for the first time Dollar was glad the dog of the house was dead, as he finished a circuitous approach by stealing through the farther wood, towards the jagged lumps of light in the ivy-strangled bedroom windows; already everything was dark downstairs.

Here were the pale new sods; they could just be seen, though his feet first felt their inequalities. His cigarette was the one pin-prick of light in all the garden, though each draw brought the buff brim of Jim Paley's Panama within an inch of his eyes, its fine texture like coarse matting at that range. And the chair in which Jim Paley had sat smoking this time last night, and dozing the night before when the shot disturbed him, was just where he expected his shins to find it; the wickers squeaked as John Dollar took his place.

Less need now not to make a sound; but he made no more than he could help, for the night was still and sultry, without any of the garden noises of a night ago. It was as though Nature had stopped her orchestra in disgust at the plot and counterplot brewing on her darkened stage. The cigarette-end was thrown away; it might have been a stone that fell upon the grass, and Dollar could almost hear it sizzling in the dew. His aural nerves were tuned to the last pitch of sensitive acknowledgment; a fly on the drooping Panama-brim would not have failed to 'scratch the brain's coat of curd. . .' How much less the swift and furtive footfall that came kissing the wet lawn at last!

It was more than a footfall; there was a following swish of some long garment trailing through the wet. It all came near; it all stopped dead. Dollar had nodded heavily as if in sleep; had jerked his head up higher; seemed to be dropping off again in greater comfort.

The footfalls and the swish came on like thunder now. But now his eyelids were only drooping like the brim above them; in the broad light of their abnormal perceptivity, it was as though his own eyes threw a dreadful halo round the figure they beheld. It was a swaddled figure, creeping into monstrosity, crouching early for its spring. It had draped arms extended, with some cloth or band that looped and tightened at each stride; on the rounded shoulders bobbed the craning head and darkened face of General Dysone.

In his last stride he swerved, as if to get as much behind the chair as its position under the tree permitted. The cloth clapped as it came taut over Dollar's head, but was not actually round his neck when he ducked and turned, and hit out and up with all his might. He felt the rasp of a fifteen-hours' beard, heard the click of teeth; the lawn quaked; and white robes settled upon a senseless heap, as the plumage on a murdered pigeon.

Dollar knelt over him and felt his pulse, held an electric lamp to eyes that opened, and quickly something else to the dilated nostrils.

'Oh, Jim!' shuddered a voice close at hand. It was shrill yet broken, a cry of horror, but like no voice he knew.

He jumped up to face the general's wife.

'It's not Jim, Mrs Dysone. It's I – Dollar. He'll soon be all right!'

'Captain – Dollar?'

'No – Doctor, nowadays – he called me down as one himself. And now I've come back on my own responsibility, and – put him under chloroform; but I haven't given him much; for God's sake, let us speak plainly while we can!'

She was on her knees, proving his words without uttering one. Still kneeling speechless, she leant back while he continued: 'You know what he is as well as I do, Mrs Dysone; you may thank God a doctor has found him out before the police! Monomania is not their business – but neither are you the one to cope with it. You have shielded your husband as only a woman will shield a man; now you must let him come to me.'

His confidence was taking some effect; but she ignored the hands that would have helped her to her feet; and her own were locked in front of her, but not in supplication.

'And what can any of you do for him,' she cried fiercely – 'except take him away from me?'

'I will only answer for myself. I would control him as you cannot, and I would teach him to control himself, if man under God can do it. I am a criminal alienist, Mrs Dysone, as your husband knew before he came to consult me on elaborate pretences into which we needn't go. He trusted me enough to ask me down here; in my opinion he was feeling his way to greater trust, in the teeth of his terrible obsession; but last night he said more than he meant to say, so today he wouldn't say a word. I only guessed his secret this morning – when you guessed I had! It would be safe with me against the world. But how can I take the responsibility of keeping it if he remains at large as he is now?'

'You cannot,' said Mrs Dysone. 'I am the only one.'

Her tone was dreamy and yet hard and fatalistic; the arms in the wide dressing-gown sleeves were still tightly locked. Something brought Dollar down again beside the senseless man, bending over him in keen alarm.

'He'll be himself again directly – quite himself, I shouldn't wonder! He may have forgotten what has happened; he mustn't find me here to remind him. Something he will have to know, and you are the one to break it to him, and then to persuade him to come to me. But you won't find that so easy, Mrs Dysone, if he sees how I tricked him. He had much better think it *was* your nephew. My motor's in the lane behind these trees; let him think I never went away at all, that we connived and I am holding myself there at your disposal. It would be true wouldn't it – after this? I'll wait night and day until I know!'

'Dr Dollar,' said Mrs Dysone, when she had risen without aid and drawn him into the trees, 'you may or may not know the worst about my poor husband, but you shall know it now about me. I wish you to take this – and keep it! You have had two escapes tonight.'

She bared the wrist from which the smallest of revolvers dangled; he felt it in the darkness, and left it dangling.

'I heard you had one. He told me. And I thought you carried it for your own protection!' cried Dollar, seeing into the woman at last.

'No. It was not for that' – and he knew that she was smiling through her tears. 'I did save his life when my poor dog saved Jim's – but I carried this to save the secret I am going to trust to you!'

Dollar would only take her hand. 'You wouldn't have shot me, or anybody,' he assured her. 'But,' he added to himself among the trees, 'what a fool I was to forget that *they* never killed women!'

It turned almost cold beside the motor in the lane; the doctor gave his boy a little brandy, and together they tramped up and down, talking sport and fiction by the small hour together. The stars slipped out of the sky, the birds began, and the same cynic shouted 'Pretty, pretty, pretty!' at the top of its strong contralto. At long last there came that other sound for which Dollar had never ceased listening. And he turned back into the haunted wood with Jim Paley.

The poor nephew – still stunned calm – was as painfully articulate as a young bereaved husband. He spoke of General Dysone as of a man already dead, in the gentlest of past tenses. He was dead enough to the boy. There had been an appalling confession – made as coolly, it appeared, as Paley repeated it.

'He thought I knocked him down – and I had to let him think so! Aunt Essie insisted; she *is* a wonder, after all! It made him tell me things I simply can't believe. . . Yet he showed me a rope just like it – meant for me!'

'Do you mean just like the one that – hanged the gardener?'

'Yes. *He* did it, so he swears . . . *afterwards*! He'll tell you himself – he wants to tell you. He says he first . . . I can't put my tongue to it!' The lapse into the present tense had made him human.

'Like the Thugs?'

'Yes, like that sect of fiendish fanatics who went about strangling everybody they met! *They* were what his book was about. How did you know?'

'That's Bhowanee, their goddess, on top of his bureau, and he has Sleeman and all the other awful literature locked up underneath. As a study for a life of sudden idleness, in the depths of the country, it was enough to bring on temporary insanity. And the strong man gone wrong goes and does what the rest of us only get on our nerves!'

Dollar felt his biceps clutched and clawed; and the two stood still under more irony in a gay contralto.

'Temporary, did you say? Only *temporary*?' the boy was faltering.

'I hope so, honestly. You see, it was just on that one point . . . and even there . . . I believe he *did* want his wife out of the way, and for her own sake, too!' said Dollar, with a sympathetic tremor of his own.

'But do you know what he's saying? He means to tell the whole world now, and let them hang him, and serve him right – he says! And he's as sane as we are now – only he might have been through a Turkish bath!'

'More signs!' cried Dollar, looking up at the brightening sky. 'But we won't allow that. It would undo nothing, and he has made all the reparation . . . Come, Paley! I want to take him back with me in the car. It's broad daylight.'

The Great Pearl Mystery

BARONESS ORCZY

You are quite right there. Skin o' My Tooth did have everything to do with the unravelling of that complicated knot which the sensational press at the time called the Great Pearl Mystery, and my opinion – which is shared by many in authority – is that but for the activities and courage of my chief, a grave miscarriage of justice would have been perpetrated.

What happened was this. The Countess Zakrevski, an American lady married to a Russian of great wealth, had dined one evening with her husband at the Majestic, their host being the Honourable Morley Everitt, a son of the countess's first husband, who was Lord Everitt of Rode, and brother of the present peer.

Mr Morley Everitt was a very popular and smart young man about town, and a devoted attendant upon his stepmother, whom he helped in her entertainments and to whom he acted as a kind of secretary and factotum in her magnificent house in Belgrave Square. She, in return, kept him lavishly supplied with money, and the two were the best of friends.

The dinner party in question consisted, in addition to the Count and Countess Zakrevski and the host, of the Marquis and Marquise de San Felice of the Italian Embassy, Lady Dewin, who was a connection of the Everitts, Madame Hypnos, a Greek lady, and a certain Major Gilroy Straker, lately come over from Australia. He had brought letters of introduction from well-known people in Australia, to other equally well-known people in London.

The party stayed on till rather late and then went home in two motors, the one a large Rolls-Royce belonging to Count and Countess Zakrevski, and the other, a small Essex, belonging to Mr Morley Everitt.

On that occasion the Countess Zakrevski wore – as she often did – the famous Kazan pearls, an heirloom of great value and historical interest. They consisted of three ropes, magnificent in size and lustre and perfectly matched; their value was said to be incalculable. They were insured for £50,000.

The Countess only discovered the loss of her pearls when she arrived home, and her maid helped to divest her of her cloak. I won't, of course, recapitulate all the details of the search which was immediately instituted, inside and outside the house, in the garage and the car; there were telephone calls to the Majestic, to the police and to the chauffeur. Subsequently as much as £10,000 reward was offered. But all these efforts were of no avail. Day followed day and no news of the missing pearls.

The loss, or rather theft of the Kazan pearls was, however, only the first phase of an extraordinary tragedy. It was about a fortnight later when Madame Hypnos, who had many friends in London society, was found murdered in the service flat which she occupied in Curzon Street, Mayfair.

The flat consists of three rooms and bathroom opening on a narrow passage; two of the rooms, bedroom and sitting-room, communicate with one another, the third is just a small kitchenette. The unfortunate woman's body was found lying on the floor of the sitting-room. She had been stabbed in the back with a large curved knife of Eastern design which lay close beside her.

The discovery was made by a Mr and Mrs Mortimer who had a flat on the same floor. They had been at the theatre and on returning home had heard a fearful row going on in Madame Hypnos's flat. They paused for a moment or two on the landing in order to listen, and they heard Madame's voice shouting repeatedly: 'You shan't! You shan't!'

However, they felt that it was no business of theirs and after a while they went into their own flat. About five minutes later they heard an awful shriek. Mrs Mortimer was in the kitchenette heating up some cocoa. Suddenly she heard the front door of the flat across the landing open and close, and footsteps clambering downstairs. Then only did she put the saucepan down and run to her husband. He, too, had heard the shriek. Together they went out on the landing.

The well of the stairs was in total darkness, which was odd, because one light was always kept up on each landing all through the night. These lights were controlled by a single switch in the main entrance hall, and someone must have turned that off after the Mortimers had gone into their flat.

The man's first instinct was to run downstairs as fast as darkness would allow and turn the lights up again. When he came back to his own landing, he found his wife almost swooning with terror. She was speechless, and with trembling hand was pointing in the direction of Madame Hypnos's flat, whence could be heard at intervals heart-rending groans.

Without pausing to think, Mr Mortimer smashed the stained-glass panel of the door of Madame Hypnos' flat, put his hand through the hole and turned the handle of the door. The wretched woman, who was lying in a pool of blood, was even then drawing her last breath.

Mr Mortimer sent his wife back to her own rooms and ran down to rouse the hall-porter and send him for the police.

On the face of it, robbery appeared to have been the primary motive of the crime, because every article of furniture in the place had been ransacked. Drawers had been pulled open, and locks smashed: the mattress and pillows on the bed, as well as upholstery, had been ripped up with the same knife probably that had finally done the deed.

*   *   *

Inspector Richards, one of the most able men of the CID, was at once put in charge of the case. One thing was certain, the murderer had been on familiar terms with his victim: the flat had not been broken into. Whoever it was who had come to visit Madame Hypnos that evening had been let in by her. She kept no servant of her own. The visitor had been made welcome by Madame Hypnos: there was a half-bottle of whisky and a syphon on one of the tables, two tumblers which had contained whisky stood on the mantelpiece and there were a couple of ash-trays filled with dead matches and cigarette ends.

But the great disappointment that confronted Richards was the total absence of fingerprints other than those of the murdered woman herself. These, strangely enough, appeared on both the tumblers that stood upon the mantelpiece, and also, though here they were very much blurred, upon the handle of the knife with which the crime had been committed. But beyond that, nowhere.

What Richards soon discovered, however, was the actual motive of the crime. To begin with there was, lying close beside the fender, a torn and crumpled copy of *The Times*. Richards smoothed out the creases and looked at the date: it was a week old. The page that lay uppermost was the front one, and there in flaring letters in the personal column was the advertisement of the assessors, offering £10,000 reward for the recovery of the Kazan pearls.

This gave Richards the clue to what the thief or thieves had been after. He set to work to search the flat, and it was after three hours' minute search, when he had almost given up hope, that he chanced to turn over a gallipot that contained washing soda, and there, hidden underneath the soda, was a handful of pearls, some clinging to their string, others loose – one of the three ropes of the Kazan pearls.

Richards was now hot on the scent. Enquiries of the hall-porter of the flats, and also the other occupants of the block, brought to light the fact that Madame Hypnos received many visitors – mostly in the evenings, and mostly men. Asked to describe some of these visitors, the hall-porter hesitated.

Madame had not been in the flats very long, and he had not had time as yet, apparently, to take stock of her visitors. But there was one young gentleman who had recently come once or twice to the flat. Mr and Mrs Mortimer had seen him, too: he was young and tall, they said, with fair, curly hair and blue eyes. The first time this young man called was about three weeks ago. Mr and Mrs Mortimer volunteered the information that on the evening of the tragedy that same young man had called at the flat. They were just off to the theatre when he got out of a taxi outside their front door. They took that same taxi on to the theatre.

The taxi was easily enough traced. The chauffeur said that he had originally been taken up by a gentleman outside the Dominions Club in Hanover Square, and had driven him to a block of flats in Curzon Street, where a lady and gentleman had taken him to the Duke of York's Theatre. Enquiries at the Dominions Club elicited the fact that one of the members had been one of the party at the dinner when the Countess Zakrevski lost her pearls. This was Major Gilroy Straker. He always kept a room, it seems, at the Dominions Club.

The major was summoned to give evidence at the inquest; he was identified by the taxi-driver, the hall-porter of the flats and Mr and Mrs Mortimer, and even before he had begun to give evidence the police obtained a search-warrant against him, and amongst his effects in his room at the Dominions Club they found the Kazan ropes of pearls, with the one row broken and about fifty or sixty pearls missing.

At the close of his evidence Major Gilroy Straker was arrested, and the verdict of the coroner's jury was one of wilful murder against him. His arrest created a great sensation in London, more particularly in the little coterie that had taken him up. It was a very smart coterie, by the way, one chiefly made up of wealthy foreigners. Countess Zakrevski and her husband were among its leaders; no foreigner of distinction ever came to London without an introduction to the popular couple.

Major Straker had come to London with introductions to the countess from friends of hers in Sydney, and she had, as it were,

passed him on to Mr Morley Everitt, her stepson. The latter had
been more than kind in seeing to it that the young colonial had a
good time in London. This was an easy task, as the major was good-
looking and an excellent dancer.

With regard to Madame Hypnos, matters were not quite so
simple. It seems that Countess Zakrevski had only been kind to her
at the request of Major Straker: she had only had her once to tea at
her own house, and Mr Morley Everitt had, again at Major Straker's
request, very kindly asked her to be of the party that night at the
Majestic. It transpired that neither Mr Morley Everitt nor Count
and Countess Zakrevski, nor any of the party that night, knew
anything about Madame Hypnos beyond the fact that she was a
friend of Major Straker.

Skin o' My Tooth, I must tell you, was from the first very much
interested in this case: he always had a wonderful *flair* for intricacies
and problems long before they cropped up in evidence. He and I
went daily to Bow Street to hear the Australian major give an
account of how he came to be in possession of two ropes of pearls
belonging to the Countess Zakrevski, while the third rope, or a part
of it, was found in the flat of a lady whom he had visited the very
evening on which she came by a violent death.

His history appeared so curious as to be unbelievable. What
Major Straker had told the police, the coroner and the magistrate
was this. He had arrived in England, he said, about three months
ago from Australia, where he had been managing director of a firm
of wool merchants in Sydney. He had gone out to Australia when
quite a lad, but had – until quite recently – a mother and sister living
in Worcestershire, which was his original home. He had been to see
them after he landed at Southampton, and then came up to London
to have a good time. He was taking a long holiday and had brought
letters of introduction to Countess Zakrevski and one or two other
people in town from some friends in Sydney. During the war he had
helped to found the Dominions Club, for colonial officers, and a
room was from the first reserved for him there.

Count and Countess Zakrevski and Mr Morley Everitt were very
kind to him; he soon made friends, and went about a good deal. He
had met Madame Hypnos at one of the smart charity balls at the
Albert Hall. She was in the crowd at the buffet and he offered his
services to get her something to eat and drink. She accepted
gratefully; said she had been cut off from her friends in the crowd
and was afraid that they had left her in the lurch.

Major Straker had no cause for complaint: she was pretty and charming; he asked her to dance and she was an exquisite dancer; then he asked her to supper and she accepted. She suggested Eugène's and thither they went. Mr Morley Everitt happened to be there having supper with a friend; mutual introductions ensued, they all spent the rest of the evening very happily together, and finally the major saw Madame Hypnos home to her flat in Curzon Street. She asked him to call again, which he did the very next day, and once or twice after that he took her to a theatre or to a restaurant. She did not seem to have many friends in London and she did not tell him anything about herself. It appeared that Mr Morley Everitt had also been greatly taken by the pretty Greek widow – she did say that she was the widow of a Greek officer killed in the war; he had also called upon her and had even gone to the length of presenting her to his stepmother, and finally asked her to the dinner party on the night when the Kazan pearls were stolen.

'That night,' Major Straker went on with his statement, 'I was driven home from the Majestic by Count and Countess Zakrevski and took leave of them outside their house in Belgrave Square and started to walk home to the Dominions Club. It was long past midnight then, and I was walking along Maddox Street when out of the narrow passage immediately behind St George's Church two men fell upon me with the suddenness of lightning: one had me by the throat, while the other got hold of my legs and very nearly brought me to the ground.

'However I had been taught ju-jitsu by a famous Japanese exponent. We had a brief, but desperate struggle, and my assailants were already getting the worst of it, when fortunately a policeman's whistle sounded somewhere quite close and they took to their heels. Well! I didn't want to be bothered with any police, and I had suffered no damage from my adventure, so, before the police arrived, I, too, had vacated the scene of action and turned into the club.'

All this, of course, you will say, appeared reasonable enough. It was the remainder of the major's story which the coroner and the coroner's jury, as well as the police magistrate, absolutely refused to believe. Major Straker said that when he undressed that evening, he found the pearls in the outside pocket of his smoking suit. He had not the remotest idea how they got there. Just for a moment the thought darted through his brain that the assault upon him was in some way connected with those pearls.

'I had,' the major went on to say, 'the fullest intention to take the beastly things to the Lost Property Office at Scotland Yard the next day, but the first thing in the morning, before I had time to glance at any paper, a telegram was brought up to me. It was from my sister. My mother had had a seizure. Her life was only a question of hours. Would I come immediately? So without thought of anything else, I threw a few things into a suitcase and was off to Paddington, and down to Worcestershire by the first available train. I suppose that I did buy a paper at the station and that I glanced at it on the way, but I have no recollection of what I read.

'I was away a week or ten days, long enough to see my dear mother buried and to make arrangements about the letting of the house. My sister had a pal in London and she expressed a wish to go and stay with her for a few weeks, until she and I had time to think about the future.

'I suppose that when I left London I just stuffed those stupid pearls into a box; probably if they had been left lying loose in a drawer I should have seen them and taken them to the Lost Property Office as I had originally intended. But there it is! I thought no more about them.

'Amongst the letters which were waiting for me at the club on my return were two or three from Madame Hypnos, asking very kindly what had become of me, and desiring me to come and see her. It seems that she had also telephoned more than once to ask after me.

'Frankly, I was not in a mood to see anybody just then, but during the course of the day, the lady telephoned again. This time the hall-porter, unfortunately, told her I was in and put me through. She recognised my voice at once, and then entered into a voluble explanation about the loss of some beads the last time we had dined together at Eugène's. She described the beads to me.

' "Three long rows," she said, "of imitation pearls. They are of no value really, but I miss them rather, as they were good of their kind."

'Still on the telephone, she recalled the incident of her loss: "Don't you remember?" she asked me. "I told you that I had broken the clasp, so I took the beads off and stuffed them into the pocket of your coat. I forgot to ask you for them when we met again at Mr Everitt's dinner-party and I suppose you forgot about them too. You *must* remember!"

'Well! I didn't remember the incident at all and told her so. I had found some pearls in the pocket of my coat, and she described these so accurately, clamp and all, that I had no doubt whatever that the pearls were hers. I promised that next time I came to see her I would bring the beads along with me.

'She begged me to come at once. Well, I could not do so that day or the next, but on the Friday at about eight o'clock Madame telephoned again, and as I was sick of the whole thing, I got into a taxi and drove round to her flat with the pearls in my pocket. Madame, however, appeared quite indifferent when I gave them to her, which rather surprised me, considering all the fuss she had been making, and she left them lying on the mantelpiece.

'At one moment she got up to fetch something or other out of the next room, and while I was waiting for her I picked up *The Times* which was lying on a table close by. The first thing that caught my eye was the advertisement for lost pearls in the personal column. I must say that I had to read it through three times before its full significance entered into my brain. £10,000 reward! and three ropes of pearls lost at the Majestic on such and such a night – but even so I was only vaguely conscious of the connection between this advertisement and my adventures with Madame Hypnos and those pearls.

'I remember picking them up from the mantelpiece and weighing them in my hands, when Madame suddenly re-entered the room. She stood for one moment in the doorway looking at me, her eyes blazing with fury. The expression on her face confirmed my vague suspicions. I taxed her with trying to cheat me out of the reward which I should get for the recovery of the pearls, and I deliberately stuffed them back into my pocket. But she was upon me like a vixen, tearing and scratching and biting.

'There was a curiously shaped knife on the table, and at one moment she seized that and would have gone for me, only that I managed to wrench it out of her fist. What she did succeed in doing, however, was to get hold of a part of the pearl rope that was protruding from my pocket. We fought for that, and during the fight the rope broke, some of the pearls were scattered, and for an instant she slackened her hold on me in order to watch them rolling on the carpet. That was my opportunity. I had had enough of this fighting vixen and I made a bolt for it. I was out of the flat before you could say "knife".

'My intention was to restore the pearls to their rightful owner the very next morning, and claim the £10,000 reward. The trouble was that when I had glanced at the copy of *The Times* in Madame's flat, I had not the time to make a mental note of the name and address of the assessors who were advertising for the pearls; and when I bought a copy of *The Times* the following morning, the advertisement did not appear in the personal column.

'What I did see in the paper, however, was the murder of Madame Hypnos. Needless to say that I, at once, connected the tragedy with those wretched pearls. To be quite frank, I got a touch of cold feet after that, because I realised that my story of how I came to be in possession of those pearls might sound unbelievable. As I was going to see my lawyer next day, who is an old family friend, I made up my mind to tell him the whole story and get his advice. Anyway, I could do nothing till I had got an old copy of *The Times* that had the name and address of the assessors in it.

'I don't think I was alarmed or even very much astonished when the following morning I received a summons to attend the inquest on Madame Hypnos. You know the rest; while I was in attendance at the coroner's court, the police obtained a search-warrant and the pearls were found among my things, And,' the major concluded with a quaint little sigh, 'that's all there is to it.'

*   *   *

The arrest of Major Gilroy Straker on a charge of murder was one of the sensations of that memorable London season. The evidence against the unfortunate man appeared overwhelming, and his story of how he came by the pearls quite unbelievable. It seems that his youth had been rather wild, and that he had originally gone out to Australia in consequence of some trouble. In the end, the magistrate committed Gilroy Straker for trial on the capital charge. He pleaded 'not guilty' and reserved his defence.

A moving figure throughout the magistrate's enquiry, and also at the inquest, had been the sister of the accused, a pale-faced, youngish woman whose eyes rested with the most tender solicitude and unvarying trust upon her unfortunate brother. It was the day after the magistrate had committed Straker for trial, that she called upon Skin o' My Tooth. I saw her when she entered the office, dressed very quietly in black. She sent in her name, Mary Straker, and I told her that Mr Mulligan would see her immediately. As usual, I took my place 'behind the arras', notebook in hand. Unseen, I watched the play of the poor girl's features throughout her interview with my chief.

She began by explaining to him that the solicitor, a very old friend of the family, who was looking after her brother's interests, had himself advised her to call.

'My brother and I have a little bit of money, Mr Mulligan,' Mary Straker went on with a wan little smile. 'You only need to name your fee – '

But this part of the interview was soon got over. Skin o' My Tooth said very little – he never does say much – he just let her go on talking about her brother, his early youth, which had been rather wild, then his departure for Australia, his determination to make good, his love for his mother.

'She died in his arms, Mr Mulligan,' the girl concluded, with a catch in her throat, 'and he swore to her then that he would continue to make good and always lead a straight life for her sake. To imagine for a moment, after that, that he would commit such a hideous crime is impossible. He did not do it, Mr Mulligan. God knows he did not do it, but human justice does err at times, and – well! it's no use saying anything more – is it?'

I knew from the first that Skin o' My Tooth would take the case up. It was just the sort of intricate problem that would appeal to him. What he said to her at the close of the interview was characteristic of him and of his methods.

'Can you,' he asked the girl with that earnestness of conviction which has brought hope to so many despairing hearts, 'can you cast aside all sorrow and fear outwardly for a time? Have you sufficient confidence to act a part under my guidance and sufficient pluck to see it through?'

She looked him straight in the eyes and replied briefly: 'Any amount.'

'Then listen to me,' he concluded solemnly. 'If your brother is innocent he shall not hang, for I will bring the murderer of Adèle Hypnos to justice.'

Matters being satisfactorily settled thus far, Skin o' My Tooth started on what he called his preliminary tour of inspection. He had a long interview with Major Straker – which apparently put him in rare good humour – after which I was allowed to accompany him and his friend Mr Alverson, of the CID, to Madame Hypnos's flat, where we were met by Inspector Richards.

Richards had in his precise, self-satisfied way, reconstituted the crime for us, pointing to each and every object just as he had found it when first he arrived on the scene.

Nothing had been moved except the body of the murdered woman; there were the glasses with the dregs of whisky in them upon the mantelpiece, the curved knife lying on the floor, the gallipot with the washing soda, the open drawers, the torn furniture. Skin o' My Tooth, silent, with eyes downcast and a gentle smile upon his nice pink face, made no attempt to interrupt.

'How do you account for the absence of fingerprints?' he asked Richards, when the tour of inspection was ended.

The inspector shrugged his wide shoulders.

'Just my contention, Mr Mulligan,' he said. 'Straker is an

experienced criminal. He took the precaution to wear gloves. We found a glove button in this room, with a bit of the glove clinging to it, where it had been torn during the struggle with his victim.'

'But you didn't find the torn glove among my client's affects, I understand?'

'No, we did not,' Richards replied. 'He was clever enough to get rid of it before we came on the scene.'

'Though not clever enough to dispose of the pearls before he went to Worcestershire. But there's no accounting for criminal psychology, is there?' Skin o' My Tooth concluded with his imperturbable smile. 'May I see the glove-button when next I call at the Yard?'

'Of course,' the Inspector replied laconically. 'You can have a good look at it whenever you like.'

'An innocent man's only hope of safety hanging on a glove button, with a scrap of yellow washing kid still attached to it!' Skin o' My Tooth remarked to me when we were back at the office. 'Give me the evening paper, Muggins, and let's think of something else.'

And not only did he think casually of something else, but he appeared deeply absorbed in the account of the loss of a flexible diamond and emerald bracelet belonging to a certain Mrs Dunfie. She had dined three or four nights ago at the Diplomatic Club and on her return home had missed her bracelet. Advertisements and offers of reward had so far been of no avail.

Skin o' My Tooth became quite excited over a short paragraph relating to this matter and ordered me to bring him twenty or thirty of the latest back numbers of *The Times*. After Skin o' My Tooth had turned over fourteen or fifteen of the most recent numbers, he gave a sigh of satisfaction.

'You'll be interested to hear, Muggins, that Lady Orliffe lost a valuable diamond brooch the night she dined at Eugène's just three weeks ago.'

After that he let the matter drop.

My chief wasn't at the office the whole of the next day, but I went round in the evening to see him at his rooms. He was sitting in dressing-gown and slippers reading a French novel; his face was pink, his eyes downcast, and a smile curled round his lips.

'I've done a good day's work, Muggins,' he said to me.

'I'm sure you have, sir,' I replied. 'Any further clues?'

'Only the glove button, Muggins,' he rejoined with a sigh. 'Only the glove button and an Italian waiter.'

'Yes, sir?'

'We dine at the Majestic on Wednesday next, Muggins,' he went on with a chuckle. 'Swallow-tails, you know, and all that.'

'By ourselves, sir?'

'No, Muggins, no. I am the guest of the Count and Countess Zakrevski, and you will dine with Mr Alverson and Richards at the next table. You'll have some fun, Muggins, I promise you.'

'I'm sure of that, sir,' I retorted.

*   *   *

The following evening I was ordered by my chief to come round to his rooms at about ten o'clock. I found him in hat and coat, waiting for me.

'Come along, Muggins,' he said, 'we're going out.'

My chief's rooms are in the Adelphi. We took a taxi as far as the corner of Tottenham Court Road; then we walked up in the direction of Goodge Street. Presently we turned into a smart-looking little restaurant in Percy Street. The name of the licensee over the door was Italian – Pincetti, I think it was – and the restaurant, I saw at a glance, was run on foreign lines.

Some people – not many – sat about, some drinking coffee, others liqueurs, and so on. It all looked very clean and respectable. We sat down at a table in a corner of the room and ordered coffee; my chief asked for the evening papers. Nothing happened for a time.

It was getting late. Signor Pincetti's customers went out in groups of twos and threes until only two tables, besides our own, remained occupied. At one of these sat a man who looked like the manager of a successful catering establishment; he wore a top hat on the back of his head, and had on a frock coat, striped trousers, white spats and a white waistcoat. His eyes were small and his face red and clean-shaven.

He was in the company of two young women, who were smeared with paint up to their eyes and very showily dressed, and all the time that he talked with them, with great volubility, he was chewing the end of a fat cigar. The women said very little; they smoked cigarettes all the time and giggled in response to the man's jokes.

At another table sat a quiet-looking man who might have been a member of a theatre orchestra. He looked like a Scandinavian, but might have been a German. He had quantities of untidy, very fair hair, and a fair beard and moustache. His dress was very slouchy, and he wore his shirt in that horrible foreign fashion – open very low down at the neck, with a wide, soft kind of Eton collar and a huge butterfly bow of a tie.

Behind the desk sat a fat, foreign-looking woman of the usual type, and a pale-faced boy in a white coat and black trousers was in attendance behind the bar.

I had just finished taking stock of this mixed company, when a belated customer came in – obviously an Italian, who might have been a waiter. He was quite young and very neatly dressed. He sat down and ordered a vermouth. For the next quarter of an hour he appeared to be absorbed in an Italian newspaper, but it struck me that he cast more than one glance in our direction. Presently he got up and went to the bar, presumably to pay for his drink. Then he went out of the restaurant.

It was getting near closing time. The man in the frock coat and the top hat called to the waiter and paid for his drinks; the Scandinavian, on the other hand, did the same as the Italian and paid at the bar. We were the last to leave.

*　　*　　*

We walked for a bit and then took a taxi. As soon as we were inside, Skin o' My Tooth rubbed his hands together as if in complete satisfaction, and said: 'Now our little party will be quite complete.'

Then he told me what he had done. He had prevailed on Count Zakrevski to organise a dinner-party, at the Majestic, which would comprise all those who had been present on the night when the Kazan pearls were stolen.

'I wanted not only the same guests to be there, but the dinner served by the same staff of waiters. At first I approached the countess herself. Her decision was final; she would have nothing to do with any scheme that might defeat the ends of justice. In her view Major Straker had murdered his confederate, that odious Madame Hypnos, and the best thing that could happen would be that he should be hanged.

'I couldn't move her,' Skin o' My Tooth went on with a chuckle, 'until her husband unexpectedly appeared upon the scene. He was very stiff and pompous, but appeared sympathetic, and what's more, his magnificent wife seemed to stand somewhat in awe of him. Anyway, in spite of the lady's antagonism, I told him about my scheme and he fell in with it, and simply ignored his wife's opposition. She was furious with me, of course, and if looks could kill, I shouldn't be here now. The dinner-party was then fixed for Wednesday, and Count Zakrevski promised me that he would invite the same guests who had been present at the previous gathering, with, of course, the exception of two: the unfortunate Madame Hypnos and Major Straker.

'The next question was that of the staff of waiters. I went to the Majestic and interviewed the head-waiter. A substantial tip got me what I wanted, namely, the man's promise that all the waiters who had served dinner on the previous occasion would do so again this time. Then he hesitated a moment and said: "I was forgetting, Bocco is no longer here."

'Bocco was one of the waiters, it seems, and he had left some time ago, to go to Eugène's. I flew to Eugène's, only to be told that Bocco was now at the Diplomatic. Here I ran my elusive gentleman to earth. I got Richards to set one of his men to watch Bocco's movements, and heard this morning that Bocco went most nights to have a drink at the café in Percy Street, also that he was apparently out of work, having lost his job at the Diplomatic a few days ago.

'Back I went to the Majestic, and once more, by dint of a tip, prevailed on the head-waiter to offer Bocco a temporary job. Now that's done. Bocco accepted the job, and as Count Zakrevski has also fallen in with a pleasant little scheme of mine, I feel sure that our little party on Wednesday will be very successful.'

I was rather intrigued to know why Skin o' My Tooth had been so keen on running that one waiter to earth.

'It didn't strike you, Muggins,' he said with a smile, 'that Lady Orliffe lost her diamond brooch at Eugène's a fortnight after the Kazan pearls episode, and that Mrs Dunfie lost her bracelet at the Diplomatic a fortnight after that. Compare that with Bocco's odyssey and you will understand why I am so keen on his being a member of our pleasant little party on Wednesday.'

The evening came. Mr Alverson and Richards met me at my rooms and we went on to the Majestic, well supplied by Skin o' My Tooth with money for our dinner. Soon after we arrived, Count Zakrevski's party filed into the restaurant. I had understood from my chief that he would be with them, but he certainly was not there.

To my astonishment, however, a little later on Mary Straker came in. She looked excessively pretty, and not only was she beautifully dressed, but she wore a beautiful row of pearls round her neck. She was accompanied by a stout, florid man, of obviously foreign nationality, with thick black hair and heavy dark moustache. They sat at a table not far from Count Zakrevski's party.

It was towards the end of dinner that Count Zakrevski, turning casually in the direction of Mary Straker and her foreign companion, seemed to recognise the latter, and rising from his seat went to greet him most cordially. They talked as if they were old friends, and Mary Straker was then introduced to the count. The result of this little episode was that Count Zakrevski persuaded Mary Straker and her companion to join his friends for coffee and liqueurs in the lounge.

Mr Alverson, Richards and I also adjourned to the lounge, and the first thing I noticed was that it was the waiter Bocco who was serving coffee to Count Zakrevski's party. The next moment I had recognised my chief in Mary Straker's foreign companion.

Never had I seen such a marvellous disguise, and it said much for Count Zakrevski's powers of self-control that, though he was of course aware of the comedy, never for one instant did he betray nervousness or surprise.

The countess was gay and chatty. She certainly was a very handsome woman. Mary Straker had evidently been given the task of flirting with Mr Morley Everitt, and this she was doing to perfection. My chief had arranged to meet me, directly after the party broke up, at the Percy Street café, while Mr Alverson and Richards lingered a little while longer in order to give final instructions to the staff of detectives outside, some of whom were being told off to shadow every single member of the party, as well as every one of the waiters.

*   *   *

I was the first to arrive at Percy Street. Sitting at a corner table I noticed the florid man whom, on our previous visit, we had put down as a prosperous caterer. He was alone this time. Soon Skin o' My Tooth turned up. He was still in his marvellous disguise as the black-haired, foreign plutocrat. I noticed that, as he entered, the florid man gave him a quick, searching look and then glanced across to the pale-faced boy at the bar, who gave an almost imperceptible shrug. Presently the young, shock-haired Scandinavian came in. The florid man gave him a sign and he then went across and sat down at the other's table.

It was now close on eleven o'clock; all the other customers had left. There were only the four of us in the place. Presently Skin o' My Tooth rose and went across to the other table.

'You will forgive my saying this to you, my friends,' he said abruptly and with a marked foreign accent, 'but that ass Bocco will ruin us all if he goes on in this way'

Quick as lightning the whole aspect of the room had changed the moment Skin o' My Tooth began to speak. The boy at the bar ceased polishing his glasses and came out as it were into the open; the fat woman at the desk had put down her pen and sat like a veritable statue.

Instinctively I had jumped to my feet, because I had seen that the shock-haired Scandinavian had suddenly thrust his right hand inside his coat. But Skin o' My Tooth remained perfectly bland; he put up his podgy hand with a gesture intended to calm the agitation of all these persons so keenly on the alert, and sat down beside the young Scandinavian.

'It would be a mistake to try and shoot me, my young friend,' he said urbanely. 'Shooting makes so much noise, what? – and the police, you know – eh? – Would I know about Bocco if I was not your friend?' Then, as the other two made no reply, but sat there sullen but attentive, the Scandinavian still with his right hand inside his coat, Skin o' My Tooth continued: 'Bocco made a mistake the night when he pinched the Kazan pearls – not? He had instructions to put them into the pocket of the young gentleman who sat at the left hand of our late lamented sister, Madame – what was her name? – Hypnos? – but like a fool he slipped those bee–oo–tiful pearls into the pocket of the young gentleman who sat on her right. And see what a lot of trouble we have had since – and our poor sister, Madame – er – Hypnos – what? She had to be put out of the way because she would not part with the few bee-oo-tiful pearls our young friend the Australian major had unwillingly left in her lily-white hands – Pity, no? And now again this mistake – Tut-tut-tut – !'

'What do you mean, and who the devil are you?' the florid man blurted out in a rage, while the Scandinavian half drew his hand from under his coat so that from where I stood I caught sight of a small Colt which he was clutching.

'Luckily,' Skin o' My Tooth replied with a smile, 'I am the man in whose pocket that fool Bocco slipped the pearls which he pinched tonight, or we should have had more trouble – not?'

And still smiling amiably, he drew out of his pocket the row of pearls which Mary Straker had been wearing at dinner. He passed them once or twice through his podgy hands, and then slipped them back quietly into his pocket. The others made a menacing gesture, and the pale-faced boy came a step or two nearer.

'Easy, easy, my friends,' Skin o' My Tooth rejoined, 'I am not going to quarrel with you over this business. I can't get on without you, and you can't get on without me, eh? In my nice little shop in Amsterdam I sell the trinkets which you find for me in England – not? I did not even quarrel with you when I did not get the Kazan pearls which I should have had. So why quarrel now?'

Then he beamed at everyone around, including myself, and pointing to me he said: 'That is a young English friend of mine. He had a little misfortune a few years ago in connection with that forgery affair on the Colonial Bank, and so he is very devoted to me – very devoted to me. Now shall not our other young friend here put up the shutters and we will all have a bottle of the best champagne? What?'

Again he beamed on us all. At another sign from him the pale-faced boy went to put up the shutters and closed the door of the restaurant. Skin o' My Tooth was rubbing his podgy hands content-edly together. When the boy had closed the shutters he fetched a couple of bottles of champagne from the back of the bar, and placed them, in their ice-buckets, upon the table; he also brought four glasses.

'No! no!' Skin o' My Tooth rejoined cheerily. 'Are we not all friends? Are we not six of us here to rejoice that that fool Bocco's mistake did not bring more trouble on us all? Madame too, eh?' he concluded, making a polite gesture of invitation in the direction of the woman at the desk, who came forward obviously very pleased.

We now sat round the marble-topped table, I on one side of Skin o' My Tooth, who had the Scandinavian on his left. The florid man and the Scandinavian had exchanged a quick glance. I could see that suspicion still lurked in their minds. Then the Scandinavian shrugged his shoulders and both the men dived into their pockets and brought out a pair of gloves, which they proceeded to put on while Skin o' My Tooth continued to chatter pleasantly.

'Ah!' he said turning to the Scandinavian. 'A very wise precaution – very wise indeed. One never knows, eh? Fingerprints are tiresome things, not?'

The next moment he had grabbed the Scandinavian's right hand, and at the same time shouted to me, 'Shoot, Muggins!'

While Skin o' My Tooth gave the word of command, 'Hands up!' which was instantly obeyed, he kept his eyes fixed on the Scandinavian and his hand gripped the man's wrist.

My shot was a signal for Richards and his men, who had made their way into the house through the back entrance. They came into the restaurant with a rush. I was covering the florid man. The other two were obviously terrified and gave no trouble whatever.

'Take off that elegant fair wig from my friend here,' Skin o' My Tooth said to Richards, 'and the beard, of course. A charming disguise, my dear Mr Everitt,' he continued blandly. 'I myself was deceived the first time I saw you here.

'And now the glove, Richards,' Skin o' My Tooth went on calmly. Just for an instant Everitt made a desperate effort, not so much to free himself as to destroy the proof of his guilt in the murder of Madame Hypnos. But he was in the grasp of Richards and his men, who held his arms pinioned while Skin o' My Tooth quietly removed the glove. There was the tell-tale tear; the button with the piece of kid still hanging from it fitted the place exactly.

* * *

Once the police held the principal members of this gang of malefactors they quickly brought the whole lot to justice. All Skin o' My Tooth's deductions proved to be correct. The florid man – whose name was Pincetti and who was the proprietor of the Continental restaurant – was the head of the organisation. Bocco, the waiter, and Morley Everitt were his principal lieutenants, but there were about a dozen others, all of them young men about town, smart, impecunious, who had chosen this means of earning a livelihood.

Bocco was a marvellous sleight-of-hand trickster; it was his business to detach the piece of jewellery from a woman's arm or neck, and he had orders to drop 'the swag' into the pocket of any member of the gang who happened to be present. At the time of the theft of the Kazan pearls he had never seen Morley Everitt without disguise. As Skin o' My Tooth so cleverly guessed, he had been ordered to slip the pearls into the pocket of the young man who sat on the left of Madame Hypnos, and by some unexplainable error he thrust them into the pocket of Major Straker, on her right.

The case against the Australian soon collapsed. But the jury at the trial of Morley Everitt did not, I suppose, consider the evidence of the glove button sufficient on which to find him guilty of murder. It went to prove that Everitt had visited the flat that night, but not that he had murdered the woman. Anyway, the whole gang got several years' hard labour and are still doing time.

WORDSWORTH CLASSICS

General Editors: Marcus Clapham & Clive Reynard

JANE AUSTEN
Emma
Mansfield Park
Northanger Abbey
Persuasion
Pride and Prejudice
Sense and Sensibility

ARNOLD BENNETT
Anna of the Five Towns
The Old Wives' Tale

R. D. BLACKMORE
Lorna Doone

ANNE BRONTË
Agnes Grey
*The Tenant of
Wildfell Hall*

CHARLOTTE BRONTË
Jane Eyre
The Professor
Shirley
Villette

EMILY BRONTË
Wuthering Heights

JOHN BUCHAN
Greenmantle
The Island of Sheep
John Macnab
Mr Standfast
The Three Hostages
The Thirty-Nine Steps

SAMUEL BUTLER
Erewhon
The Way of All Flesh

LEWIS CARROLL
Alice in Wonderland

CERVANTES
Don Quixote

ANTON CHEKHOV
Selected Stories

G. K. CHESTERTON
*Father Brown:
Selected Stories*
*The Club of Queer
Trades*
*The Man who was
Thursday*
*The Napoleon of
Notting Hill*

ERSKINE CHILDERS
The Riddle of the Sands

JOHN CLELAND
*Memoirs of a Woman of
Pleasure: Fanny Hill*

SELECTED BY
REX COLLINGS
*Classic Victorian and
Edwardian Ghost Stories*

WILKIE COLLINS
The Moonstone
The Woman in White

JOSEPH CONRAD
Almayer's Folly
Heart of Darkness
Lord Jim
Nostromo
The Secret Agent
Selected Short Stories
Victory

J. FENIMORE COOPER
*The Last of the
Mohicans*

STEPHEN CRANE
*The Red Badge of
Courage*

THOMAS DE QUINCEY
*Confessions of an English
Opium Eater*

DANIEL DEFOE
Moll Flanders
Robinson Crusoe

CHARLES DICKENS
Bleak House
Christmas Books
David Copperfield
Dombey and Son
Great Expectations
Hard Times
Little Dorrit
Martin Chuzzlewit
Nicholas Nickleby
Old Curiosity Shop
Oliver Twist
Our Mutual Friend
Pickwick Papers
A Tale of Two Cities

BENJAMIN DISRAELI
Sybil

THEODOR DOSTOEVSKY
Crime and Punishment
The Idiot

**SIR ARTHUR CONAN
DOYLE**
*The Adventures of
Sherlock Holmes*
*The Case-Book of
Sherlock Holmes*
*The Lost World &
other stories*
*The Return of
Sherlock Holmes*
Sir Nigel
The White Company

GEORGE DU MAURIER
Trilby

ALEXANDRE DUMAS
The Three Musketeers

MARIA EDGEWORTH
Castle Rackrent

GEORGE ELIOT
Adam Bede
Daniel Deronda

WORDSWORTH CLASSICS

WORDSWORTH CLASSICS